Some of God's Children

By

Robert Dean

ISBN: 1-4033-2274-0 (e-book)
ISBN: 1-4033-2275-9 (Paperback)
ISBN: 1-4033-2276-7 (Hardcover)

This book is printed on acid free paper.

1stBooks - rev. 11/15/02

PREFACE

Let us assume that when any event begins, it will continue for an indefinite time, as opposed to a chance stroke of lightning. Some beginnings seem to have no conclusion, especially when they span more than one's lifetime. In looking at some deceased person's lifetime, there is a subjective end to those one's experiences. Whether or not this is truly the end of that person's experience has long been debated. No satisfactory answer has been reached that has universal appeal. To a person's conception of reality, a beginning has been implanted in the consciousness. It may be at the first realization of an identity, or tales handed down by ancestors, provided this person was not the first. A fact that will place a dilemma on the thought process. In this case, a hypothesis of origin must be developed in the mind, acceptable to the individual, to maintain a modicum of sanity. Whether this hypothesis is true or not is unimportant, since it cannot be refuted at this time. If one somehow finds a mate and the procreation urge had been implanted, soon there will be someone to share the idea. Then the hypothesis can be questioned. A schism will develop and this is good.

Other ideas will be argued. And better and more logical concepts can arise and will continue as the population increases until a leader with superior reasoning powers emerges and forces a workable doctrine upon the confused masses. At this point, freedom of thought is ruthlessly suppressed. Infinity cannot be discussed for it is beyond human dialog. Materialistic concepts are pursued for the betterment of society as a whole.

If mates were to expire when their first offspring reach puberty, the population explosion would be slowed and the ultimate end postponed. But this is not the case and it really makes small difference except in what era an individual is born. Lifestyles change for the worse as a saturation point nears. Something will probably happen before the situation gets untenable. Long before this happens, the intelligence pool will be so diluted that the majority of the population will be reduced to a lower form of life and drastic measures will be taken by the intelligentsia to insure their own survival, and these actions will be repulsive in democracies. The one man-one vote system will be scrapped. This will be necessary to prevent those in power from buying votes with funds taken from the working class.

There will be another beginning. History is filled with many beginnings. Pagan Rome was not the first. Hitler and Stalin will not be the last. Cyclical phenomena can approach infinity. If there really is a depository for departed souls as many claim, the same problems could manifest there, not because of a procreation urge existing, but because of the volume in transit.

Various solutions have been toyed with by beings not yet involved at this level.

CHAPTER ONE

As He sits beside the Great White throne, J.C. says, "Well, I'm not going to say 'I told you so', and I know I was a part of this crazy scheme, but We have to do something about this mess We have wrought."

"I know, J.C., and I have given this much thought. All master plans have many variables and measures must be taken to correct bad judgment. It is not of any great consequence, but I have compassion for the beings that have been created. Consider this idea. Go out among these masses of souls and find some with redeeming qualities. We will create a third plane of existence to which We can elevate them. Give these elevated ones instructions on the proper playing of stringed instruments sitting under graceful trees beside a placid pond of blue water to create beautiful music to keep frustrations to a minimum until We can figure out a permanent solution."

Having attended to this command, J.C. now asks the Father as to the disposition of the remainder.

"What criteria would apply to the sorting?"

"I pulled the dossiers from the data bank, I was looking for outstanding deeds acted on by a sense of worth and compassion unrelated to survival or self-aggrandizement. I must admit I was shocked by the small number."

"You should not have been. Remember there was no Divine inspiration. Things will get better in phase two."

"And pray tell, what in Our Name is 'Phase Two'?"

"Place a trap door, centrally located among the masses and let it be operated by the moment of conception by copulation on the lowest level. The jostling of the hordes on the Second Level will insure at least one soul of being recycled."

J.C. asks, "But how can we be sure they will improve the second time around?"

"The first experience will be implanted in the subconscious and influence their dreams and emotions. Of course there is no guarantee two trips will produce an Upper Level candidate, but being as we are, time has no meaning."

"As usual, this is Infinite Wisdom, of which You are so famous."

* * *

"Thank You, We shall see."

Reporting back before the Great White throne, J.C states "Things are picking up. Level Three is filling up. We must find better things to occupy their time. Time is something with which we are not acquainted."

"Let there be some sent back to Level Two to mingle and to show some of the second cycle's group ways to get bumped upstairs."

* * *

"I hate to keep bringing small problems to You, but some of the ejected second cycle group are showing back up at Level Two from below and, by their nature, need reprocessing down again."

"How are they entering Level Two?"

"From all directions. If there were points of a compass here, it could be said they are entering from North, South, East, West and all points between. I have seen a few coming back through the trap door while it was momentarily open. These could be the results of terminated pregnancies."

"Let there be placed around this multitude an impenetrable wall and, at one place, a pair of massive gates inlaid with pearl and adorned with gold. And above this gate let there be placed a beacon of pure white light shining on a Golden Staircase to guide souls in the proper ascension."

After installing the great wall and gates, J.C. notices a mass confusion at the gates. Inquiring as to the problem, He is told by many that the trip up the Golden Stairs was truly a blissful experience. But what happens now? And once again another problem is dumped on the Father. "It is understood that We are all knowing and possess Infinite Wisdom, so We must hasten to correct this lest Our credibility be damaged."

"Go into the Third Level and find One most enlightened in our Way. Place this One at the gate with a Golden Wand and a terminal connected directly to the universal data bank. In this way, candidates may be screened and some may be wanded straight to Upper Levels. Others, well, We might have to figure out other alternatives."

* * *

Sitting on throne number two, J.C. informs, "I have placed an exceptional one at the Gate and things are getting better. By the way, his name is Peter."

"Is he the one that had a little trouble in Rome?"

"Yes, but he will not discuss it, saying it is all in his past and he has forgiven them."

"Yes, I remember, a high quality soul."

"Of course, but he does have some idiosyncrasies."

"For instance?"

"You know he had some really traumatic experiences back down there, and even though he claims he has forgiven them, he has this nagging compulsion that some of this ilk may need different processing. He has been wanding some over to the left, on the outside of the wall to a place that he has designated as 'Limbo'."

"What does he intend to do with them?"

"He says that was not in his job description and he defers to Us."

"Hmm, is that troublemaker, Lucifer, still disrupting things up on the Third Level?"

Agonizing, J.C. complains, "Oh yes, he is a thorn in My temple and a sword in My side."

"I have never understood his rebellious nature. How did he get here in the first place?"

"He has always been here, as his kind will always be everywhere."

"Move him out to this so-called Limbo place and let him figure out what to do."

"I hope this will not be another of Our great mistakes."

"Time, of which we know nothing, will tell."

"How is Lucifer doing with this Limbo place?'

"You won't believe this, what am I saying? of course You will, I am your only begotten Son. Anyway, he is gone. Limbo is gone. And all the inhabitants are gone. All that is left is a big black hole. I went over to the edge and it was a bottomless pit. It was in the middle of a most beautiful cloud. But I sensed danger and backed away. Peter is now wanding some poor lost souls over to the black hole."

"Maybe this will be the last We hear of him. All things may not be recyclable."

"If this is the last We hear of him, it will be because We have lost Our hearing."

"Do You really think so?"

"You must be aware of the mischief he was causing up on the Third Level. I believe He was trying to usurp Our Omnipotent Power."

"I am aware of everything, and have been contemplating a solution. Possibly this has solved the problem."

"I certainly hope so. I enjoy Our position."

"It is my duty to report all that you seem to ignore, the activity around the black hole is growing with monstrous proportions. The dossiers of many are filling with foul deeds that cannot be attributed to the imaginations of virgin souls on their first trip down. They are being influenced by some external force coming from unknown places."

"This can only be the work of the trouble maker."

"I concur, but by what process?'

"We shall send a scout into the black hole."

"Ah, a spy!"

"That is not the proper term for a Messenger from Above."

"Very well. A scout he shall be."

"How deep is the black hole?"

"I did not see, but it seems as to be of infinite depth."

"Then our Messenger must be well equipped for the return journey. Find an incorruptible soul and fit him with a pair of sturdy wings."

* * *

"I have found the perfect one for the journey. His name is Icarus. He has had some experience with this sort of thing back at the lower level."

"Prepare him and send him on his way."

* * *

Much later, Icarus was seen by J.C. crawling out of the black hole. He fell down on the fluffy white cloud adjacent, exhausted, with his golden hair and beautiful wings singed by some intense heat."

"Oh, J.C. was it ever so hot down there! It was as hot as from where I have come."

"How can that be? There is no thermal activity except at the first level."

"I went far past the first level." Icarus exclaimed, "The region seems to be alien to all creation by the Magnificent Father and You."

"Please do give credit where it is not due. I came along much later."

"I do not understand."

"I have always been here, but not as long as The Father."

"I still do not understand, J.C."

"Nor shall you ever, Icarus."

"Well, back to the matter at hand. I had the weirdest feeling that this place was the work of Lucifer, the fallen one."

"Go and repair the damage to your person. You are really a mess. You shall be called after this has come to pass."

* * *

Please bear with this interruption for an explanation of the gender specific. With the exception of the lower level, there is no sex, as it is known at the lower level. A necessary requirement for the tranquil operation of these higher levels. Thank you for your patience.

* * *

"Icarus brought back revelations from below that may be disturbing to You."

"Really? I, disturbed? Surely you jest!"

"Well, perhaps I should have used a more appropriate term."

"Indeed. Summon the messenger and We shall hear these tidings."

"Very aptly phrased. Much better than 'disturbing revelations'."

"Naturally."

* * *

"Messenger Icarus, share with Us the information that has been gleaned from your somewhat hazardous journey."

"O Omnipotent One, Creator of all that is known and unknown, I have just returned from a strange place not of Your creation, be that strange as it seems. This place reeks of evil of the foulest imaginable kind. It is not of a nebulous character, but is hewn out of solid granite. Great power must been have employed to create the myriad tunnels and enclosures. And greater power is harnessed to maintain a thermal agitation necessary to prevent any soul from languishing in any comfort whatsoever. There is no hope for escape except through the will of their master. There is even a sign in many languages at the entrance portal that proclaims 'Abandon all hope, ye whosoever enters'."

"Under the prevailing conditions, how did you manage your escape?"

"I bore the insignia and icons, representing all that is good and pure."

"And how did you acquire these?"

"Through J.C."

"J.C., enlighten me."

"Oh, I had some of my accessories replicated and adorned Icarus' raiment."

"And what led you to believe this might assist Icarus on his journey?"

"I had noticed when I entered the Third Level while Lucifer was still there, he would cringe and turn away from Me when the Everlasting Pure Light was reflected from my neck-piece."

"This is well and good. We shall keep this in mind. Perhaps they will come in handy dealing with this evil one."

"Icarus, what seems to be the purpose of Lucifer's endeavor?"

"It is difficult to fathom, but I did notice that certain ones were separated from the doomed flock for further processing. They were the most depraved and sadistic to be found and enjoyed special privileges. Some were assigned to keep the furnaces running efficiently; others were like shepherds but used pitchforks rather than gentle hooks. I even saw a few electric cattle prods, probably from the technical revolution being experienced on the lower level."

"How gross! Please continue."

"The most cruel of these associates were recruited to return to the lower level to act as missionaries to spread his anti-gospel."

"This explains the increase of travelers through the black hole. Severe measures must be employed to combat this new development. J.C., get on this right away and report back to Me."

"Oh no, do not tell me to go down again!"

"Calm down, it can probably be handled from up here."

"I certainly hope so!"

* * *

J.C. then appoints Icarus as chairman of a select group to find answers. The select group creates a fact-finding committee to bring the select group up to date on the developments transpiring below in the hole. The fact finding committee, having an aversion for climates not experienced at the Second Level, recruits many late commando types recently in from the torrid deserts of the lower level. Their mission was to descend into the black hole and infiltrate the ranks of Lucifer's associates. After learning the mechanics and logistics pertinent to the motives of Lucifer, they are to return by whatever means possible. Icarus was little help in this area, because the commando group had not yet qualified for wings. Only the ones at the Third Level were considered for wings. A lieutenant was appointed to lead the infiltrating party. His name was Hannibal. After briefing his party, they mingled with the latest horde wanded to the hole by Peter.

Due to the ethereal quality of this group, and the compression caused by the decreasing diameter of the hole, various separate souls were merged, causing some contamination of the chosen ones. Fortunately, Lt. Hannibal did not suffer merging, as he was the leader and entered first. At the termination of downward migration, he attempted to assemble his squad. He noticed a distinct personality change in most and he was required to call upon his leadership to refuse the squad into a workable unit. The first duty was to discover some method of practical egress.

"Go ye all out to the far reaches of this evil domain and seek whatever there is to deliver us from this evil place when our work is done."

After an exhaustive search of all the labyrinthine corridors and catacombs, none was discovered.

Sgt. Olaf Thor rose and asked for the floor. "Sir, I may have discovered something that may help us out of this quandary."

"Please do enlighten this group."

"Copious amounts of energy and heat abound. And I have discovered the sources. It will be a simple matter to harness this abundant energy and use it to bore a lateral connector from the source to the wall of the hole. This will create a massive convection in the hole and due to our ethereal quality, we can ride the current to freedom."

"Thank you, Sgt. Thor. Let it be done."

Sgt. Thor set about this task with a zeal not seen before in this dismal place of doom. He was inspired by the thought of extricating his party from this place in short order.

"Sgt. Thor, since it was your genius that has brought this to pass, you have the honor to test your theory first."

"Thank you sir, please monitor my ascension and keep your hand on the damper. Away I go!"

One factor was not considered. Due to the increasing diameter of the hole as Sgt. Thor ascended, there was a point of equilibrium established where the convection velocity decreased in relation to the mass of our traveler. And he stopped ascending at a level approximately halfway home.

While enjoying this euphoric state of suspension, he happened to glance up to see a small group of Peter-wanded souls approaching on the way down. It was a slow approach, due to the convection, but descend they did. And he was in the path.

"Lt. Hannibal! Lt. Hannibal! Please close the damper, quick! I have no desire to be co-mingled. And get out of the way!"

* * *

Lt. Hannibal and his squad worked long and hard to extricate Sgt. Thor from the goo of melted lost souls. Melted, because they had yet to be sent through the conditioning ovens to prepare them for the intense heat. It worked like this: once the oven was loaded, the temperature was slowly increased to the ambient temperature of the main hall. This worked like cooking a live frog. A frog being a cold-blooded creature, can adjust to extremes of temperature with no apparent ill effects. Up to a point. But then it will lose consciousness before the damage is done. (Cooked).

A huddle is called. "Something has been gained. We now know how to block the hole. If we melt enough souls in the hole, it can be permanently blocked. Have any of you noticed how the goo solidified into a hard mass?" One private went over and kicked the hard goo. His steel tipped combat boots were dented.

"But if we seal the hole, how can we return?"

"It doesn't look like we can use it anyway, and maybe we can upset Lucifer"

"Let's go for it!"

"P.F.C. Yehudus, block the damper on the most open position to divert maximum thermal energy into the black hole and return quickly to our huddle."

* * *

"Sir, I have obeyed your instructions and the convection velocity has increased ten fold."

"Thank you, P.F.C. Yehudus. Since the influx has been curtailed, we now have free movement in this environment without experiencing gridlock. We must now disperse to all extremities of this domain to gain sufficient knowledge helpful in our return. So it has been said, so let it be done. Anyone that has discovered any beneficial information, report back promptly."

* * *

"Ho Peter how goes the wanding?"

"Hello J.C., if You will glance over to the left, You will notice that the black hole is no more and the area is getting congested as in olden times."

"This shall be discussed with the Higher Authority."

* * *

"It seems that Lt. Hannibal, in some way, has blocked the black hole and Peter can wand no more to eliminate the confusion that was prevalent outside the wall as in olden times."

"Instruct Peter to wand the rejects back down the Golden Stairs to be recycled immediately without the benefit of cleansing."

"This action might well reduce the quality of existence on the lower level, and our efforts to upgrade the character of beings dwelling there will suffer a great setback."

"Be that as it may, We cannot afford to corrupt the Second Level."

"But of course, it shall be done."

"Besides, due to the increased activity of mating on the lower level, We are depleting the supply of qualified candidates to be returned."

"I, too, have noticed this, the trap door has been rebuilt many times."

"Perhaps the problem will be alleviated as the populace is enlightened in the art of restraint."

"Optimism is a Divine Thought."

"Nevertheless, pessimism breeds hopelessness."

"True words of Wisdom."

* * *

Lt. Hannibal, while relaxing on a hot rock waiting for the return of his scouts, was seen by Lucifer who was cruising around in his Hotmobile inspecting the facilities.

"What, in the name of this place, is a soul like yours doing in a place like this? I thought you would have been exempt. What happened?"

"It was simply an administrative error. My team and I were caught in some friendly fire on the lower level and were entered into the Great Record Book as perpetrators of a great atrocity."

"And where may I ask is the rest of your team?"

"Oh, they were wanded with me into the black hole and, as we speak, they are running amok in your facility."

"This will never do, Hannibal! You and your team do not meet our stringent requirements to abide here. We must correct this error quickly."

"I whole heartily agree, Lucifer, but what can be done? You may have noticed that for some reason, the black hole is no more. And we cannot egress in that fashion."

"Yes, Hannibal, I see that the hole is sealed. That will explain the curtailment of the candidate influx, and I must look into this problem later. But now we have to deal with the problem at hand, which is untenable. Your group must leave at once before you upset the delicate balance in which I dwell. I have developed a system in which I send souls indoctrinated in my way back to the lower level to do my bidding. Even though you and your team do not qualify, I feel I can modify the ejection process to accommodate your group."

"But upon our arrival, what type of vessel shall we occupy?'

"Unfortunately, Hannibal, I have no control over this process. This part of the operation is truly random."

"How about our memory of this?"

"Also out of my control. There may be some residual in the subconscious, and manifest in some dreams or nightmares whichever may be the case. In rare instances, more than one soul ejected may occupy the same vessel and multiple personalities may emerge during the lifetime."

"How can this happen?"

"There is some controversy concerning this subject, but I feel that at the moment of conception of these vessels, if multiple souls are ejected simultaneously and an adequate number of vessels are not conceived at this moment, some doubling up may occur."

"But there are so many of us, what are the chances of all of our group occupying the same vessel?"

"I don't think you should worry about this. The mating frenzy is rising rapidly at this time and there is no end in sight. This fact should be to your advantage."

"I never dreamed that I would be happy because of this problem," comments Hannibal.

"Problem? What problem. This frenzy works to my advantage in perpetuating misery and sorrow that I endorse."

"Maybe you, but not I."

"But of course, you belong to a different school. It is not of your doing. I don't forgive you, as it is not my nature, but I do understand. You do not need to make a pact with me to extricate yourself; I want you out as much as you. Assemble your group and report to the ejection and you all will leave perdition post haste."

* * *

"Any word from Lt. Hannibal and his team, J.C.?"

"Not as such, but as I was casually viewing at a lower level monitor, I noticed one young man who seemed to possess some of Lt. Hannibal's traits. I feel that somehow he has managed to get himself and his group recycled."

"And his group? Explain."

"Well the vessel has been causing some confusion in the family he was born into, and at least two different personalities have emerged. So far."

"This is very interesting. Is this not unusual?"

"Not really, it has occurred in the past, but lately the odds of occurrence are increasing. Probably because of Peter's indiscriminate wanding, in conjunction with an increasing reproduction frenzy, and I might add that the urge was incorporated into the original model."

"But only to insure a stable and desirable growth."

"Maybe the pleasure quotient was overdone."

"This was necessary because the original intent of the urge could be subdued by the increase of the intelligence quotient."

"Then a happy balance should have been met, but there is no happy balance in sight."

"Blame Lucifer and his evil influence, not Me."

"We must give this problem more thought."

"Of course. But now back to Lt. Hannibal, et al."

"Oh, it will not be long before they are back with Us and then We can clear the confusion in their minds as they will remember all past and then be separated."

"Why leave them as co-joined and let him benefit by their many past experiences and get bumped up to a higher level sooner?"

"But all the other souls will be assimilated by the dominant personality, Hannibal, and will lose their individual identity."

"What difference does it make? All will merge ultimately at the most highest level and be as One with Me."

"We all look forward for this to happen, bur right now it seems in the far distant future."

"Future, past, present. What means this to Us? As you should know, time was created solely for the benefit of beings at the lower level, to prevent all things from happening at once as it does here."

"True, it is all the same, but impatience rules supreme on the lower level."

"Contemplation and pure thoughts will assist in their endurance."

"There are many down there that believe Our streets are paved with gold, a materialistic belief associated with their greed."

"A rude awakening awaits."

CHAPTER TWO

At Three Fifteen on the morning of October the Nineteenth in the year of our Lord, One Thousand and Forty Four, in the delivery room of The Grady Hospital in Atlanta, Georgia, there was born one male child. Exactly nine months and two days after P.F.C. Patrick Alfred Pitts and his bride, Mary Maloney McDonald checked into the Cloister Hotel at Sea Island, Georgia. They had just been married in Aiken, South Carolina, a town famous throughout the South for expediting marriages with or without parental blessing. A sense of urgency hovered over the couple by the fact that Patrick was to embark on a troop ship to Europe, heading for the great conflict two weeks after finishing basic training at Camp Wheeler, outside Macon, Georgia.

Patrick had met Mary on one of his weekend passes into Macon. She worked behind the counter of Cheeseman's Ice Cream Parlor on Third Street, a popular gathering place for infantry trainees. He had ordered a triple dip black walnut, vanilla and chocolate cone and their hands touched upon delivery of the cone. Whether it was static electricity, the mental state brought on by the abstinence required in transforming a high school graduate into a fighting machine or Divine intervention can be debated, but something happened to the toucher and touchee. Both heard heavenly music. Both saw rainbows and shooting stars. Both experienced giddiness and a floating sensation. This occurrence was of such a magnitude that it was impossible for either to ignore. Mary said that if he could, come back at closing time. This was Saturday night and he did not have to report back until Monday morning. He felt he had hit the big jackpot. And so did she.

They walked the streets and sat on park benches and they told each other about themselves and their aspirations. She had no steady boyfriend and went to a girl's high school. The local board of education had long ago segregated the sexes to curtail promiscuity and the schools were miles apart. Only boys lucky enough to belong to an affluent family with access to a second automobile could seek out girls after school. Everybody seemed to work during the war except the silver spoon group. Her father worked as a clerk at the Railway Express Agency. While this job provided for their simple wants, it did not furnish them with the luxuries enjoyed by the better-educated class.

When war was declared, Mrs. McDonald went to work at the Naval Ordinance Plant in South Macon, locally known as the "Fuse Plant." And Mary started dipping ice cream. They lived in a fairy decent rented house in Bellevue in West Macon on the bus line, so things were not too bad.

Patrick came from Pittsburgh. He was informed at an early age that the city was not named after his ancestors. Had this been true, his father would certainly not have been working in the steel mill. Such are the quirks of fate, if that is what it is.

Patrick said, "I thought I had a girlfriend back home, but now I know I did not. I knew not of rockets or rainbows. Now I have a girlfriend."

"And now I have a man for life. I will bear your children. I feel I now have a purpose. I will not now drift aimlessly through life heading toward oblivion."

"We must consecrate our union soon, for I must leave to fulfill a prior commitment not of my choosing. I cannot ask for special consideration from the powers that control my destiny for I feel no more important than any others who join me in this struggle. If I do not return, I leave part of me with you. Maybe this will be my purpose for existing here. I have had none before. Everyone needs to feel special. I did not. Maybe kings feel appointed by God to serve their subjects, but they seem to exploit them instead. Creation seems a farce. Or perhaps a big joke or wager among higher Beings as to the outcome of this colossal experiment. Maybe someday I will face Them and ask 'WHY?'."

"There is too much beauty in this world for all of it to be one great accident."

"Do not forget the ugly and evil that also exists."

"How could beauty and good be recognized if there was nothing with which to compare it?"

"I will remember your innocent thoughts to sustain me in my upcoming trials."

* * *

In June of that year, Mary's father was transferred to Atlanta with a small raise. They rented a larger house on Gordon Street in Southwest Atlanta. Mary was more comfortable here and wrote Patrick daily. Then his letters stopped. Her mother consoled her by saying that he was probably in a place where he couldn't write as often as he would like to. And he was.

It was the fiercest battle to date against the German infantry. The Germans had to call up second-string snipers for reinforcements. One of these was Hans Fricht. He had never hit a bulls-eye on the practice range. He was always a little off to the left. The instructor shifted him to the reserves and there he stayed until the great battle. Casualties were great among the Germans and Hans was assigned to a tree overlooking the American lines. Soon he had Patrick in his sights. If Patrick had known who had him in his sights, he would not have worried because the sniper always missed his mark six inches to the left. The moment after firing, a gust of wind moved the projectile six inches to the right. Now Patrick can go ask the question, "WHY?"

Mary received the telegram two weeks later. And she asked "WHY?" But now she had Hannibal, et al growing inside her.

The responsibility of a new life being developed prevented her from an irrational act in an effort to join Patrick. She remembered Patrick's words and they sustained her in dark moments.

"I will wait for a more opportune time to join him." Little did she know that the time would be five decades later.

After Hans Fricht shot Patrick, the wind picked up and the limb supporting him broke and he fell to the ground. He sustained a fracture of his right leg and lay immobilized as the Americans overran his position. The Germans were in full retreat, except Hans. He was captured and moved to the rear lines on a stretcher by the medics. After his leg was set, he was loaded on a returning troop ship and interned at Camp Wheeler, Ga.

He was one of hundreds that were transported through the streets of Macon to the outlying farms to work in the fields, the same streets that Mary and Patrick had walked just a few months before. No stones were hurled, no curses voiced. He was just another anonymous prisoner whose presence in this country was considered as one more who would kill no more.

Hans Fricht was heard of no more in this country. On the fiftieth anniversary of the invasion of Normandy, there appeared an obituary in an obscure newspaper in a small town in the Bavarian Alps notifying the local populace of his demise:

Hans Ludwig Fricht, Born 10-19-1920 Died 6-6-1994
Survived by his wife, Gerta Maria Fricht
One son, Hans, Jr.
Mr. Fricht was retired
from the German Railway.
He had served as a clerk for forty years.

Hans Jr. died as a bachelor some years later surviving his mother by only two weeks. There were no heirs. The new tenants in the apartment they had rented since 1947 when Hans and Gerta were married found his father's uniform. It was sold at a rummage sale for five marks.

A great ceremony was conducted at the Normandy beach that day of June 1994 honoring the fallen ones. There was no mention of Patrick Alfred Pitts or Hans Fricht then. They were only two of many thousands who given their lives fifty years before.

But there was in Seville, Florida an old woman who still remembered. She was waiting to join him.

And she remembers that cold early morning of October fifty years ago.

Patrick Alfred Pitts Junior arrived on this plane of existence kicking and screaming as if to reject the whole idea. He had an incredulous look on his tiny face; with eyes darting from side to side as if wondering where was he and how did he get here. Then in one short moment his countenance changed to one of peace and he smiled up at his mother. This was the first of many mood swings he would experience in his short lifetime.

* * *

"Welcome, Hans Fricht, I find no wrongdoing in the data bank. You may pass through."

"But I have many questions."

"It is not my place to answer. If I took the time to try to answer all the questions of all the souls that pass this way, I would never get my job done."

"What is your job?"

"To pass worthy ones."

"And I am worthy?"

"You were not in control down there."

"I do not understand."

"Farther along you will, all by and by."

* * *

"Mother, I shall call him Junior."

"Why, Mary? His name is Patrick."

"He is not Patrick. I will not call him as the same as his father. I do not want to confuse the two."

"How could there be any confusion? There is no resemblance."

"Perhaps I should rename him."

"This is insanity Mary, He has been christened."

"Besides, he needs his own identity."

"Well, if you insist. I will ask Father Louis of the possibility."

* * *

Thus saith the keeper of records, "Greetings and salutations, J.C., what prompts your visit to the monitoring department?"

"Oh, I was only curious if anything out of the ordinary is happening down on the lower level."

"Not really, just the routine wars, starvation, pestilence and general misery. But wait, I remember a very unusual request for a name change. Unusual, because of all the other problems facing mankind, this seems insignificant. And this is a newly produced vessel."

"Names mean nothing here. It is only an earthly connotation for identification purposes only. Why is this request made?"

"It seems that the female producer does not wish to confuse the product vessel with the co-producer. And in retrospect, realizes an error was committed initially induced by convention."

"What does the co-producer think of this?"

"He is out of the scene. He came up a short time ago."

"And he cares not?"

"He is still in debriefing."

After mulling it over, J.C. says, "I see. Well, if possible pass down a dispensation."

"It shall be done."

* * *

The child was re-christened "Harold Gilmore Pitts." Mary's mother wondered how Mary chose this name.

Mary explains, "I know of no one with this name and feel that it has a uniqueness that might represent his character."

"But character takes years to develop."

"I do not know why, but I feel he already has one. I have studied him more than you have and he manifests an eerie quality."

"Don't be silly, this is just your imagination.'

"I don't think so, Mother, we shall see."

* * *

Harold started walking when he was four months old. At least some of the time. In fact, he was running at this age. At least some of the time. When he collided with some object, such as the coffee table or door, he would be laid out flat on the floor. After he regained consciousness, he would resume crawling like a normal baby and would continue for weeks as if he had never learned of otherwise. Other times he would wave his arms as if in an attempt to fly. And finding himself unable, he would frown up and start crying, and continue until Mary would pick him up by one arm and leg and swing him around in a circle. He would then laugh with glee and flap his free arm.

When Harold was in his more ambulatory states he also possessed the gift of speech. Not "Goo-Goos and Maa-Mass" as expected, but precisely formed words with perfect diction. But not of a language his mother could understand. These new developments that Mary considered abnormal to say the least, upset her to a point that she and her mother considered it necessary for them to consult a specialist.

Harold was taken to one such person at Emory Hospital and an ambulatory state could not be induced. The specialist hinted that the mother and grandmother might instead be in need of his service. Indignation and a hasty exit came forthwith. After this embarrassing incident, Mary determined that this behavior was exhibited only in her or her mother's presence. In other words, "we have a closet genius."

Joe, Mary's father, was deeply involved in his new position and had little time to spend with his family. He was in management now and it was not a nine to five job. And it required the use of the family car, a 1934 Ford four-door sedan, the same one that was loaned to Patrick and Mary for their honeymoon. Grocery shopping was primarily done on Saturday, when the car was available. At other times, the Atlanta Transit System was called upon. This was not too inconvenient as a streetcar ran down Gordon Street. Incidentally, Joe was not aware of Harold's peculiarities. This fact alone was instrumental in maintaining some semblance of peace at home. Joe was not of a character that could tolerate anything out of the ordinary, or things not explainable by the proper authorities. So it was prudent to keep Joe in the dark about the antics of Harold.

As soon as she was able, Mary found a job as sales clerk at Richs' department store, leaving the care and feeding of Harold to Grandmother Dolly. The appointed baby sitter had developed a small circle of friends in the surrounding neighborhood. This pleased Dolly well, as she had very little to do now, since she had not worked after leaving Macon. When various friends called at the McDonald home, they all remarked about how sweet the baby was. Except one. Harold would exhibit his peculiarities in her presence. She remarked that she had heard this strange language before but could not place where. Her husband was a retired professor from the University of Georgia in Athens and had taught ancient language. She said she would ask him about this. After quoting a few phrases she remembered, Doctor Whittle said it sounded like Sumerian; an ancient language spoken in Babylon thousands of years ago. And he said he must witness this speech in person.

"Mary, Otto wants to see Harold in his altered state, he feels he may shed some light on the problem."

"Irma, I am sure Harold won't convert with Otto here. He is male, and he has never done it with any men around."

"Perhaps some subterfuge is in order." and Irma suggests, "Let's hide Otto in the living room closet and see what happens. At least he can listen and maybe be able to crack the door and watch."

"Very well, I will take Harold upstairs to mother and you get Otto. Once Otto is in position, I will instruct mother to bring Harold down and we will see what happens."

When Dolly brought her charge down, he greeted them in his strange tongue.

"Harold, I know you understand what we are saying, so why do you persist in this foolishness? Is it because you cannot form the words that we use?"

Harold nods his head and utters "ayunka."

"Is this an affirmative response?"

Another ayunka and a nod.

"Oh, this is great! How would you like mommy to get someone that can help you speak our language? But I must warn you he is a man."

"Nubke, nubke!" cries Harold and bolts for the kitchen door to hide.

"What did I tell you? He will have nothing to do with a man."

Otto pokes his head out of the closet. "I have a suggestion. Let me go to the kitchen door and speak to him in his language. Granted, this is the first time I have heard this language in what I believe is its true form, but I know the written word and I understand the basics."

* * *

(The following conversation has been translated for the reader's understanding.)

"Harold, this is your good neighbor, Dr. Otto Whittle, Ph.D. I only seek to help you."

"Dr.Otto Whittle, Ph.D. what manner of strange talk is this? I am not acquainted with this title. Please be more specific."

"Doctor is a title bestowed upon persons of great learning in certain fields. The term means that I have mastered an art."

"Well, you must have great learning to be able to converse with me, considering that your vocal cords are not accustomed to my spoken word. I am sure it will improve in time."

"Thank you, Harold, I am honored, and if we pursue this dialog with me occasionally throwing in a few words of my language, we can help each other."

"I am not opposed to this pursuit, sir. Let us continue."

"This is good, Harold, may we now go back to the living room and include ones that love you, in our endeavor?"

"I have no objection."

"Harold please be seated facing the ladies, and we will begin with me speaking my language and you responding in yours. I will translate your responses for their understanding."

"This should work until I have mastered your speech and then we can use this new language exclusively for it seems mine is an obscure and obsolete medium which I believe is no use to me at the present time."

"Do you feel that you might need it sometimes in the future?"

"One never knows."

"I feel that you might know more about that than you care to reveal."

"One never knows."

"Harrumph, for the time being, I will let that pass."

"Thank you for not being pushy."

"Now back to our pursuit. The lady seated directly in front of you is the one that helped bring you into this world. Her name is Mary, but most children choose to call their mother either mother, mommy or mama. Attempt to speak these words."

"Moree, momwa, momo."

"Oh Harold! You may call me whatever you like, I am thrilled and I love you!"

"Momo, Momo, Momo! I trust my pronunciation will improve with practice."

"And on her left is Momo's mother. She helped to bring Momo into this world. Her name is Dolly."

"Mo-Dolla, Mo-Dolla, Mo-Dolla."

"Harold, that is a little weird, but I accept it."

"Seated to the right of Momo is my wife, Irma."

"Is there any fruit from your union?"

"I regret to say that it was impossible."

"Then I designate her as Unma."

"Graphic, but acceptable."

"Irma, do not be sarcastic."

"I am sorry, Otto, but I still love him."

"Thank you, I may also love you. When I find out what is meant by your conception of love."

"It may take a lifetime to find the true meaning."

"Or even longer, Doctor, this is not the time to discuss that."

"Might you be inferring some knowledge that has escaped us?"

"Not escaped, just not experienced."

"By that, do you mean not experienced in this life, but beyond?"

"Possibly."

"Incredible."

"Does not my existence affirm that fact?"

"There could be many explanations for this."

"Really Doctor, do you believe any of them?"

"Frankly, even though I was indoctrinated in conventional ways, I have secretly questioned them."

"An open mind is indeed in your favor."

"Harold, you do not seem to be with us at all times."

"I share and sometimes will be displaced."

"And to where are you displaced?"

"I know not the place. I have no recollection."

"How can that be?"

"Perhaps I suffer amnesia in transit, such as I did upon initially entering this plane."

"You speak as if other planes exist."

"Planes, dimensions, whatever."

"And you remember nothing of these places?"

"Nothing."

"How can you say for sure they exist?"

"Where could I go? And my sharers?"

"Good point."

Mary asks, "Could my beloved, Patrick be there somewhere?"

"Everybody has to be somewhere."

"Why do you think you have come to me?"

"Momo, I am only a babe, only recently arrived. I have few answers, but I feel an error has been made. Who knows? An accident, mistake, a necessity or planned? I am not the one to answer your question. Let's try to make the best of the circumstance, since at the present time, we have few other choices."

"Oh Harold, please do not be offended. I meant no harm. It is only that I have so many questions."

"No more than I, dear Momo."

"We shall exist together and learn as time goes by."

"Do not forget my sharers."

Otto asks, "You keep mentioning sharers. Would they be separate entities or only various facets of your personality?"

"I feel they are diverse entities, who unfortunately for some do not possess a vessel of their own."

"I have discussed this occurrence, which is known to exist in our society, with a friend who practices psychiatry. He has treated persons that manifest similar effects. And through hypnosis, merged the lesser personalities into the dominant one. For all practical purposes they seem to be 'cured'."

"This would be a disservice to the others, I believe. They have the same right to exist and demonstrate their personalities as I have."

"This is not always possible in our accepted society."

"And just what sets the standard of performance in your society?"

"Consternation, embarrassment, ostracism and the fear of ridicule of others. And possibly a paternal or maternal urge to mold their progeny to their expectations, selfish as it seems."

"And this system works?"

"Not very well, I confess."

Dolly adds, "There are exceptions. Joe and I never forced our beliefs upon Mary, except to instill moral values."

"You may be a minority. The economics of your lifestyle may have influenced you."

"Harold, this continuing dialog is becoming nonproductive to our original purpose. We must find a method to help you to gain proficiency in the spoken word. I cannot be here at all times to translate."

"I assume you mean your spoken words. I am already adept in my language."

"Amazingly true."

"How to proceed?"

"You must have a tutor."

"Possibly yourself?"

"No, no, maybe a kindergarten teacher, who could teach the rudiments as to a normal child."

"But the teacher would not understand my language."

"You must be silent except to repeat words and phrases taught."

"What if I slip and utter some of my strange talk?"

"Muddle through and make it sound like baby talk. Some of it sounds like that anyway."

"Baby talk, indeed! This language served the Babylonian Empire for centuries."

"Please forgive me, Harold, I meant no offense."

"Apology accepted."

"You can do it. After all, you reside in a baby's body. Dolly, would you know someone that might qualify and be willing to take on the task?"

"There is a kindergarten class held in this friend's living room for the neighborhood tots. But I feel that Harold might be out of place among the larger kids."

"You are quite right. See if she can devote a few hours a day on a one on one basis."

"Her charges are picked up at three in the afternoon, I will approach her tomorrow afternoon."

"Just tell her that you think Harold is an exceptional child and you feel his talent will be wasted if he has to wait a few more years. Do not tell her what we know, which we cannot explain in any case."

* * *

"See Jack, see Jack run."

"Oh Harold! I am so proud of you! Just think, after only two days."

To himself (This is a piece of cake. I am way ahead of you. I just have to drag it out so as not to arouse suspicion. While the teacher was out of the room, I read the first ten pages of her dictionary and can pronounce all the words.)

"Maybe tomorrow you will learn about Jill."

(How boring.)

"See Jack. See Jack run. See Jack. See Jack run. See Jack. See Jack run. See Jack. See Jack run. See Jack. See Jack run. See Jack. See Jack run. See Jack. See Jack run."

Mary exclaims, "Wonderful, but now that is enough for today. Shut up and go to sleep. I will see if we can squeeze in a few more hours tomorrow."

(Hopefully.) "Good night Mother dear".

The next afternoon when Dolly took Harold over to Sara for the next session, Sara remarked, "Dolly, this child is amazing. When I talk to him he so attentive. I honestly believe he understands every word I speak. It is so uncanny. It seems he needs only to master the function of speech. He is bored by the repetition of my simple words. I think I will to teach him by asking him to watch my mouth, lips and tongue while forming sounds. And place his small hand on my throat while doing this. He may pick up the vibrations of my vocal cords."

Within two weeks Harold had mastered all the words spoken by a normal child leaving the first grade of school. (And he had finished reading the teacher's dictionary.) His tutor explained she was not qualified to take Harold any further and suggested finding a more capable person to carry him on to greater accomplishments. Then he ran into another obstacle, a coffee table in the McDonald's living room. He who was known as Harold went to the unknown place and another emerged.

"Mary, Mary! I am so heartbroken! Has all this work been for naught?"

"Mother dear, please do not be distraught. We knew this possibility might occur. We still have Harold, perhaps not as the one we have learned to love, but still one that needs our nurturing and care."

"This is true, but I have grown accustomed to having someone around to whom I can converse with intelligently. Why, this one cannot even walk!"

"What other recourse do we have? Hit him in the head?"

"Never! We will just have to start over and act like normal parents."

Sara called to inquire of Harold's progress with his new teacher.

"Thank you for your interest, Sara. We have decided to give him a rest for a while and let his small body catch up with his mind."

"What brought this on? He was doing so well."

"He seems to be sort of 'out of it' right now and needs a rest."

"Well, you probably know best. Please keep me informed."

* * *

"Mother, we cannot call this baby 'Harold'. This is not Harold. And we do not need to be confused anymore than we already are. So Gilmore he shall be."

"And Gilmore he is."

* * *

"What ho, Hannibal. When did you get back and what are you doing hanging around the monitors?"

"Hi J.C. Just a while ago. And I am checking on my vessel. I might have to go back."

"In the hole?"

"No, the lower level."

"I had a feeling that you might be down there. Why there and not here? How did you accomplish this?"

"We had no means to return here after the hole was sealed and Lucifer discovered us and wanted us out. He has a highly sophisticated ejector he uses to send some souls back to the lower level to do his bidding, and he packed all of us in it and turned a lot of dials and pushed a lot of buttons."

"That sounds interesting. We might be able to use one of those. You will not be under his control?"

"Oh no. He was only too glad to be rid of us and no pact was made."

"Why might you have to go back?"

"I am involved in an interesting situation down there and seem to be bonded to some souls there. When I might go back is beyond my control. I must wait till something happens down there."

"You must be referring to the multiple occupancy reported to Me."

"I believe so. This was a first for me. Lucifer mentioned that this might happen."

"Well, do what you have to do and I will see you later."

"What I have to do right now is hang around and wait until other developments transpire."

"Carry on."

Hannibal pulled up a fluffy white cloud and made himself comfortable for he was to stay two earth orbits around that sun. During this time his earthbound contemporaries led what seemed to Hannibal to be a mundane boring existence. Things must be altered to improve their lifestyle. And he spent the last two years considering options. He had come up with some interesting ones. But he must wait for something to happen to Gilmore.

* * *

Gilmore stayed around and entered Sara's kindergarten when he was four years old.

"Sara, this is Gilmore and we want to enter him into your regular class."

"And this is not Harold?"

"No, Harold is away. And please do not ask any more questions. I am not at liberty to discuss our situation concerning the boys now. Maybe later on."

"Boys? You mean as in more than one? How many?"

"I cannot say."

"This will cause me many sleepless nights."

"Not as many as I."

* * *

Gilmore progressed as any normal child and entered the first grade at the usual time. He did not exhibit any outstanding qualities; he was just a regular average child like the other thirty children in his class.

About this time Joe got another promotion that required his traveling around the state to inspect branch offices. For this he needed a more reliable car and he purchased a 1946 Buick

Roadmaster. He gave the old Ford to Mary and Dolly. Mary would use it to drop Gilmore off at school and then drive to work in it. The school was only three blocks from their house and Dolly would walk over and meet him when school let out. This procedure attracted the attention of the larger children and Gilmore was branded as a "Mamma's Boy." The derision that was laid upon him did not seem to bother him at all. If he was indeed a Mamma's boy, he was happy in that capacity.

His ignoring of these taunts was upsetting to one bully in particular. Naturally his name was "Butch." He was ten years old and oversize for his age. His father was a self-employed backyard shade tree automobile mechanic and his mother worked in an all night diner on Highway Forty One near Jonesboro. Butch had all the qualifications necessary to assume his role in life. Restraint was not a virtue in the circles to which Butch gravitated. If taunts did not produce the desired results, more appropriate actions must be employed. The first of which was occasional bumping into Gilmore in the hallways. Even this was not the catalyst needed to ferment rage in the victim. The next step was to be a direct confrontation. After classes, with plenty of pre-event publicity. Between the front door and the street. Preferably on the steps.

Now Gilmore was no wimp, but he had no chance to meet Butch on equal terms. Butch had twenty pounds in weight and six inches in height to his advantage. Even with this in his favor, being the coward he was, he required back up from one of his fellow hoodlums.

One cohort knelt down behind Gilmore during this confrontation to assist Butch in pushing him over. The result of this altercation was the victim striking his head on the lower step. Exit Gilmore. Enter Harold. Much to Butch's sorrow, as he will soon learn.

From his vantage point at the monitor, Hannibal was completely familiar with the goings on of his roommate. He did not consider himself a caped crusader, as do many youths in their fantasies about justice, fair play and equality. He was plain damned angry about the treatment to which Gilmore had been subjected. Being on the adversary's turf and not restricted by the ethics of the upper level, he felt that some small exhibition of violence was in order. Upon arriving at the scene, he called upon some of the supernatural expertise that he had acquired during his sojourns to the various levels.

His first act after removing himself from the sidewalk was to suspend Butch approximately five feet off the ground to render him inoperable temporarily until he could gather himself for the task that lay ahead. Butch was squirming and squalling reminding one of a fish out of water. Harold then inverted Butch and placed him at eye level. He then pulled hard on his ears and tweaked his nose. He then pulled Butch by the ear and lowered him head first into a trashcan with only his legs visible. The can being the receptacle of lunch remnants discarded by the students three hours prior. This time lapse was sufficient to attract hordes of flies and ants, which considered this new addition to their feast manna from heaven. In one indirect sense this could be construed as the truth.

Before too much damage was inflicted to Butch's countenance, his bewildered classmates extricated him. Harold admonished him about considering the consequences of rash acts before administering any.

"You were lucky this time. Some go on for years doing wrong and get set in a pattern which is practically impossible to change before disaster strikes."

It is doubtful that Butch heard one word spoken by Harold. He was in a state of shock over the circumstances in which he was involved. His mind was occupied with thoughts of removing his body to safer places. The sanctuary he considered safest was his home, located about a mile distant. The time elapsed in making this travel would have qualified him for the track team. Sliding in the dirt to a halt beside an old car his daddy was working under and spraying dirt into his daddy's shoes diverted his attention to his son. Crawling from under the car and looking at Butch as if this was the first time he had seen him since birth, he asked "why did you kick dirt in my shoes?"

"I didn't mean to, please don't hit me. I'm scared. A mean boy did some bad things to me after school. He picked me up and threw me head first into a trashcan and the flies and ants starting eating my face. And I was stuck and couldn't get out until some other kids helped me. Then I ran home."

"Wow! He must have been a big strong boy to be able to do that."

"Oh, he was! He must have been at least twelve years old and very big. I didn't have a chance."

"Well we will have to do something about him. Do you know where he lives?"

"Yeah, over on Gordon street with his mother and grandfolks."

"When I get through here, we'll go over there and do something about this. Nobody can push us around."

"Let's just forget about it, he really didn't hurt me. I was just scared."

"No, we need satisfaction and I gonna get some. Now shut up."

Meanwhile Dolly arrived at the school to walk Gilmore home. Harold was sitting on the steps waiting. When Dolly saw him, she knew that this was not Gilmore. "Is this you, Harold? Where's Gilmore?"

"He is with me now. I am dominating. This is best. He will benefit from my experience. I am more qualified to deal with the problems he is facing in life."

"Oh Harold, if this is true, we now have you both. We have really missed you. Do you know where you have been?"

"It is no place, rather a state of being. It is hard for a soul occupying a vessel to understand. I do not fully understand why I am here. Let's just enjoy."

"Oh, I do, I do. In time I may understand."

"Not while you are here."

"Are you ready to go home? Do you know the way?"

"Of course, I am also Gilmore, remember?"

"This is hard for me."

Arriving sometime later, they saw Butch and his daddy sitting on the front steps.

"I understand you have an overgrown kid who bullied my Butch."

"Sir, surely you are mistaken or have the wrong house. This is my only grandson and the only child that lives here. How can you believe this small child bullied this larger boy sitting there with you?"

"I don't. Butch, is this the boy you are accusing of hurting you?"

"Er, yeah, but he is a lot littler now."

"Butch, if you ever again come crying to me with a bunch of lies, you won't be able to sit for a week. Now git home. Lady, I'm sorry about this. Please accept my apologies."

Harold spoke up. "Sir, you need not apologize. What your son told you is partly true. He was indeed inverted into a garbage receptacle for acts not conducive to peaceful co-existence among students in an attempt to show him the error of his ways."

"And you did all this by yourself?"

"Yes, but do not consider your son a weakling, I enjoyed a distinct advantage during the altercation."

"Well, I don't know about that, but I do know you have the advantage when it comes to talking. Could you help my son learn to talk like you?"

"Probably not, it may be genetically impossible along with other factors which are not under our control. It is best to accept the life that fate has bestowed upon you and make the best of it. This can eliminate a lot of frustrations in an effort to elevate yourself beyond the station you are destined for."

"You said a mouthful. I know it is true. I am a good mechanic and make a living at it, but I know my limitations. I will never have a big shop and hire a lot of mechanics. I wouldn't know how to start. But I would like something better for my kid."

"He will have something better if he learns how to control his jealousy concerning other people. Do not envy others, but find out how they achieved what they enjoy. The methods they employed might not be acceptable to your moral standards. You may even be shocked and outraged."

"You scare me. You are too young to know what you know, but I don't think I want to know how you did it."

"Trust me, you don't."

After Butch's father left, Dolly asks Harold what that was all about. "Oh, Gilmore was having a small amount of trouble with Butch and when he fell and hit his head, I stepped in and corrected the problem."

"How long had Gilmore has this trouble with Butch?"

"Ever since school started."

"And you never told me about it?"

"It was no big deal with me. He had not caused me any discomfort until today and then Harold came in and took care of it. By the way, I am glad Harold showed up and I welcome him."

"Thank you, Gilmore."

"Now you two stop this. It is more than I can handle."

"I will accede to Harold, the dominator. Just call me if I am needed."

Mary was delighted now that she had both Harold and Gilmore under her wing. She eventually stopped calling on Gilmore when she found that he was always there in Harold's presence.

Harold was getting increasingly bored with the schooling that was normal for a child like Gilmore. He decided to relinquish the floor to Gilmore during school hours, finding it possible to wander around detached from the immediate environment, but always on call if needed. When he developed this function, he was able to expand his horizons and gather more knowledge that was beneficial to both Gilmore and himself. Because of this, Gilmore excelled in geography. His teacher repeatedly asked him if he was sure he had not visited a certain country they were studying. His response was that if he had, he was not aware of it.

"Are you inferring it means that you acquire this knowledge unconsciously?"

Harold steps in. "I am inferring nothing. You seem unaware that there are other ways to gain knowledge besides sitting in a classroom."

"Such as?"

"Books, libraries, travel brochures and other means."

"What other means?"

"I am not at liberty to divulge this information to you. Perhaps you might discuss this with my mother."

"I just might do that. You are acting very strange."

That night Miss Brooks called Mary about Gilmore's strange behavior that day. "Could you possibly drop by my room in the morning before you go to work? I think it is important that we talk."

"May I come a little early, you know I work?"

"Yes, I think thirty minutes will be enough to clear this up."

A greater understatement was never made.

"Good morning, Mrs. Pitts, please sit down. Gilmore, please wait in the hall while we speak."

"Yes'um, call if you need me."

"Now Mrs. Brooks, what has Gilmore done to upset you?"

"He has not exactly upset me. It's just he seems to know a lot about things he couldn't have possibly learned in class. Especially things concerning geography. He acts like a sophisticated world traveler. He seems to know more about Mexico City and London than Atlanta. And what is stranger, the cities he describes may not be as they are today."

"I don't understand. How are they?"

"Well, we were discussing Mexico City the other day and he was describing it as it was during Maximillian's rule, close to one hundred years ago."

"Oh dear, this must be Harold's doing."

"I beg your pardon, Harold, who is Harold? I am not familiar with this person"

"Mrs. Brooks, we do not have enough time to go into this right now. Let's just say that Harold helps Gilmore with his studies."

"We will pursue this at a later time. Please tell Harold to confine his tutoring to the present century. Send Gilmore in as you leave."

"Now Gilmore, I am not opposed to Harold helping you in your studies but try to convince him to stay in the area we are studying."

"Did mother tell you about Harold?"

"She mentioned he helps you with your studies."

"Is that all she said about him?"

"I believe so, is he your neighbor or what?"

"You are confusing me with your questions and my head is beginning to hurt. Please let me rest until classes start."

"You may be seated, but I have many more questions."

"Please take them to my mother."

"I shall call her tonight."

* * *

When Dolly came that afternoon, Harold was waiting for her. "Mrs. Brooks is going to give us some trouble if we don't figure out what to do about her snooping. She is asking questions that Gilmore can't answer and I shouldn't, that is, without discussing this with you and mother."

Mary was really upset with this new turn of events. "I can see in my mind's eye, Mrs. Brooks getting the principal involved. Then probably a bunch of scientists from Georgia Tech and Emory putting Gilmore in a cage to study him. I will not allow it!"

Harold agrees. "At this time you are probably right. I think that we are living about forty years too soon to exercise our rights. We would have no recourse if our rights were violated. It might be best for me to back off on influencing Gilmore for a while."

"Harold, please don't leave, we want both of you to stay around."

"Don't worry, mother, I will stay close. This might be an opportune time to visit upstairs."

"I don't understand. I am sure you are not talking about the attic."

"It was only a figure of speech, mother. Do not take it literally."

"You are so strange. But we still love you."

"Gilmore, tell Mrs. Brooks that I have decided that Harold will not help you for a while and we will see how you do."

"Yes'um."

CHAPTER THREE

Things settled down for Gilmore as in the pre-Butch days. Butch was no longer a problem. In fact, since his enlightenment he became a good friend of Gilmore's. Perhaps he was adhering to the trite adage, "If you can't beat 'em, join 'em". He was Gilmore's self-appointed protector and bodyguard. He was no match for Harold/Gilmore's intellect and was easily manipulated to Gilmore's advantage. This is not to say that this was not to Butch's advantage also. Like all equitable reciprocal arrangements, both parties share benefits.

Butch's association with Gilmore improved his grades tremendously and his teacher was amazed with his improvement, she wrote a note to his parents praising his progress. When Butch took the note home, his parents were at a loss to understand what had come over him. When questioned, Butch stated, "that he had seen other lifestyles and found that there are other things to do besides working on cars and waiting tables for peanuts. I have got a friend that will help me to a better life, one that he takes for granted. The secret is learning all I can. Then maybe I will be able to take advantage of any opportunities I may stumble upon."

"Son, where did you pick up all that fancy talk? I bet that Pitts boy has something to do with it."

"Would you object if he had?"

"Oh hell no! If he can make a difference in your life for the better, I'll not complain. I wish I had had somebody to help me when I was your age. Then maybe I could have done better by you and your mother."

"Perhaps he can help us all."

"Gilmore, your family seems well off. You live in a nice house and you all have two nice cars and nice clothes. How did it happen?"

"Grandma and grandpa worked hard during the war and my daddy got killed in it. Momma must have got some insurance money or a pension. But she still has to work for us to live like we do. I wish she didn't so we could be together more. And we hardly ever see grandpa. He is always gone off to some other city. I think I would be better off with a father figure around. Mama and grandma are OK, but sometimes I need to ask man type questions."

"I think I know something that will help."

"Like what?"

"Well, you know where I live. It ain't exactly like the Northside, but it's the best my folks can do. My Pa thinks it's because he didn't get enough education when he was little and he thinks that if you can help me, you can help him."

"That's silly, what did I do?"

"You didn't have to do anything, some of your culture has rubbed off on me just by our association."

"Really? I didn't know that."

"Well it did, and maybe you could rub some on Pa if we hung around my house some after school."

"Maybe, I'll talk to my folks about it."

"Yeah, and we might learn something about cars so we can keep one running when we get old enough to have one."

"I thought you said you didn't want to be a mechanic."

"I don't, but if you know how a car works, then people like my Pa can't gyp you."

"You don't think your Pa cheats people, do you?

Not really, but sometimes when somebody comes in to pick up their car, they accuse him of putting on parts that they really didn't need."

"Do you think he does?"

"I don't know. He sometimes uses a lot of parts trying to find out what's wrong. Maybe he can't take the parts back to the store and he can't afford to keep them and not charge somebody for them."

"Maybe ignorance can be confused with dishonesty."

"I guess so. If he knew more about what he was doing, he could fix a car cheaper and faster and make more money."

"You're right, and then he would have so much business he would have to hire some people and just tell them what was wrong and he wouldn't have to work so hard."

* * *

"Greetings, Hannibal. I haven't seen you around much lately. What have you been doing since you escaped?"

"It's nice to see you, Henry. I've been around, just not over here in Tycoonville. I never amassed great wealth and don't seem to be able to relate to anyone who has,"

"We are no different from any other. It was only that what we enjoyed doing reaped many material benefits. Personally my ambition was to give every family some economical means of locomotion."

"No one can deny that you did that, big time."

"I am sure you did not come over here to talk about the past. What have you on your mind?"

"I find myself in a position to render a great service to a person that can also help one of mine, but I will need knowledge of the internal combustion engine and all the peripherals necessary to make a modern vehicle."

"Modern has no meaning here. You know that. In fact, neither has vehicle in the term used by you."

"You are still a stickler for detail, aren't you?"

"Habits are hard to break."

"Has your personal knowledge been entered into the archives?"

Henry ruminates, "Yes, but bear in mind that to attain the success I reached, one must delegate. And in this delegation you lose some control in the operation. There were many problems that were solved without ever being brought to my attention. To grasp a comprehensive overlook of the great scheme, one must delve into the myriads of lives and personal experiences involved in a great endeavor. No one entity has ever been exposed to the whole truth."

"To give a mortal access to the whole truth would be giving this individual powers equal to those at the highest plane. This is not allowed and I understand this, I only want to impart enough knowledge to this one for him to improve his station in life."

"Would this not be interference?"

"Can you honestly say you had no Divine impetus?"

"No, if you think I know enough to help your friend, I will indulge you."

"Your modesty overwhelms me!"

"You may be surprised at how little I know."

"Look, all this man wants to know is how to repairs cars efficiently. And I might add the majority are Fords."

"In that case, let's have a go at it."

"We shall go to the 'need to know' room and don the transference helmets. It will be easier this way."

"You spend too much time downstairs, Hannibal, you forget there is no urgency here."

"I am sorry, but as you said, 'old habits are hard to break'."

"Touché'."

* * *

"Mother, I will be taking over for Gilmore after school every day for a while. And I need your permission to visit Butch's house in the afternoons."

"Harold, what in the world are you up to? I hope you are not planning to do harm to Butch. He has gotten to be good friends with Gilmore. And what I have seen of him, he has really turned over a new leaf and is trying to make something out of his life."

"And to this end I am pursuing. Just bear with me. I have on good authority this will come to pass."

"Whatever you say, you always know best. I feel like your daughter rather than your mother."

"Believe me, you are a real mother in every sense of the word."

"Thank you, Harold."

The next afternoon Dolly picked up Harold and Butch and walked with him over to Butch's house. She told Harold Mary would pick him up after she returned from work. This was to become an every day occurrence.

As usual, Mr. Jones was under an old Ford. He had a rusty old chain hoist tied to a limb of a giant oak tree which he used to lift the front end high enough for him to crawl under. This was behind the house and the yard had no grass, only sand. He used a piece of plywood to lie on under the car. For safety he placed cement blocks under the frame in the case the limb broke. With this arrangement, he was forced to make many trips from under the car for the proper tools. After watching for a few minutes, Harold volunteered to hand him tools, as he needed them.

"What do you know about tools? I'll be wasting my time trying to describe them to you."

"The first thing I'm going to say to you on your road to enlightenment is not to assume anything about anybody with which you are not familiar. Now tell me what you need."

"All right smart ass, give me a twelve point 11/16 offset box end."

Within seconds one was laying in the man's hand. Respect was instant.

"Mr. Jones, for the sake of eliminating confusion, I would like for you to address me as Harold."

"This might eliminate confusion in your mind, but it does not help me at all. I thought you were Gilmore. But when I think about it, Gilmore knows nothing about tools or cars."

"I think it will be best if we leave this where it lies."

"Whatever you say, 'Harold'."

"My sole purpose in spending my afternoons here is to help you elevate your station in life which will consequently enhance the quality of Butch's also. I am not the mild mannered boy you saw in Gilmore. In my pursuit of this goal, I am of one mind and will relentlessly see it to the desired end. Therefore do not toy with my emotions."

"As I said before, 'whatever you say, Harold'."

"Thank you."

"Let's see if you can help me get this old Ford running. I have put three new fuel pumps on it in the last two months and now it needs another one. They just stop pumping."

"Mr. Jones, you know the pump is operated by a lobe on the camshaft, but not directly. There is a push rod between the pump lever and the cam lobe. Where this rod comes in contact with the camshaft, wear occurs. Henry designed this rod to be made of a softer material than the cam lobe because the rod is easier to replace than the camshaft. An after market cup was made which could be placed over the upper end of the rod to compensate for the wear. Your parts house should have these. They are much cheaper than a new rod. You have been replacing good pumps."

"I have never heard of this before. I wonder why the parts house didn't tell me about this?"

"I imagine they would rather sell pumps than cups or rods."

"Maybe that is why he drives a new Cadillac and I drive this old pickup truck."

"Do not envy another for what he knows, but try to learn more yourself. Knowledge has its own rewards."

"Could I have found this out the way you did?"

"I am afraid not. At least not in time to use it to your advantage."

"Then what hope can I have?"

"You must learn to cleanse your mind of mundane problems at some time during the day or night. You must use your blank and open mind as a receptacle for knowledge and inspiration that will come to you in the pursuit of all good things. Avarice and greed are negative forces that will work against you. You cannot have the wrong motives to want to succeed. Do not attempt to be the envy of anyone. Do not want anything just because you know someone that has one. If you do not understand this, think about one's wheelchair or wooden leg."

"I think I'm getting it. I must understand my needs first."

"Bravo!"

"Do you think I need a better place to work on cars?"

"Let me put it this way. A better working environment is conducive to more quality workmanship and the proper frame of mind to perform efficiently."

"This sounds like a chicken or egg situation. Which comes first?"

"There are two different paths to follow. One is to improve your lot a small amount daily or to be impatient and want it all at once. The former can be successful with dedication and perseverance. Provided there is no one in your immediate family without the same patience. The other route involves more risk and more rewards. Failure in this pursuit sometimes results in self destruction and eternal damnation to some, depending on the religious persuasion of the individual."

"Are you telling me there is no great rule book which applies to everyone?"

"I am. How could this book be available to everyone that has existed or ever will?"

"This contradicts a lot of instruction I was exposed to as a kid, but I remember having a lot of questions that I was not allowed to express."

"False words are sometimes necessary to control unbridled desires of ignorant masses. This works well for all but a few free minds that cannot accept classical dogma. Once the consequences of this kind of deviation were dealt with by thermal conflagration. Happily this practice has been discontinued, but social ostracism is still practiced. This leads to closet philosophy and hypocritical lifestyles."

"I think I will take the slow road. I don't even know how to get on the other. What do you think of first paving an area so I won't have to work in the dirt and mud?"

"This will be the first step of a long journey."

"Then maybe a roof so I can work when it's raining?"

"Do you have charge accounts at the parts houses?"

"Yeah, but I don't use them much. I usually pay cash."

"Why?"

"I'm afraid I'll spend the money on something foolish and then won't be able to pay the bills at the first of the month."

"Making practical purchases is not foolish. What is foolish is spending your profit on things you don't need."

"It seems that Effie Lou or Butch are always needing something."

"Tell them that some small sacrifices now will reap great rewards in the near future. Put priorities in the proper perspective."

"We will pour the floor this weekend. And put a roof up next week."

"And with the better working conditions, by the end of the month, you will still be able to pay your bills."

"Great! And by the way, Harold, with your superior intellect, I feel uncomfortable with your calling me 'Mr. Jones'. Please call me 'Carl'."

"Now I shall be uncomfortable. Perhaps in private, I will."

"I will be honored if you will, in public or in private."

CHAPTER FOUR

The seemingly unnatural alliance between Carl and Harold in the ensuing months produced results beyond anyone's wildest expectations. Carl, heeding Harold's suggestion, entered into an agreement with a local contractor to trade work on the contractor's trucks for work on the garage. The contractor, Mr. Antonio Garibaldi, knew nothing about the care and maintenance of his trucks and up until this agreement, was at the mercy of anyone that knew even a small amount more than he. Carl knew even less about the construction of safe structures suitable to conduct service on vehicles. The care of trucks used by persons in business proved more profitable than working on the family auto. The majority of owners were of the opinion that 'if it ain't broke doesn't fix it'. Preventive maintenance was hardly ever practiced. On the other hand, Tony Garibaldi was of the school that prescribed an ounce of prevention was worth a pound of cure. And Carl could provide that ounce. This arrangement proved beneficial to both parties.

Business got so good that Butch's mom, Effie Lou, quit her job to help in the office they had built on to the house. She answered the phone and kept books, such as they were. They were not concerned with the accuracy, only the fact that the input exceeded the output. The fact that the bank did not call about any overdrafts was enough to satisfy any anxious moments.

Harold liked Effie Lou because she didn't smoke and always had a mouth full of bubble gum. It was not unusual to see them sitting in the office with gum spread from their nose to chin after some really big ones burst. It was in this office where Harold learned to drink Coca Cola with peanuts floating in the bottle.

Soon after Carl got Tony's truck business, he had to hire two mechanics. He was not satisfied with their abilities and he did not want them to learn about Harold. So he had to act as a middleman to implant Harold's knowledge in them. Then he got concerned that when they learned too much about trucks, they might quit and start a shop of their own. After some thought, he devised a scheme to confuse. Various ploys were used. Sometimes when Harold told him an ignition wire was broken under the insulation, he would tell the mechanic the distributor was defective. When the mechanic went to the stockroom to get another one, Carl would fix the broken wire. Then he would return the replaced distributor to stock. Effie Lou would only bill the customer for labor as no new parts were used. The mechanic would feel good about learning a distributor fixed the problem. Once he even told one of the men to turn the front tag over as it was upside down. While he was doing this, Carl went to the rear and fixed a pinched gas line. In those days a lot of turnip trucks came through Atlanta going north to the markets.

Harold did not approve of some of Carl's antics. He felt there should be better ways to insure loyalty. Of course, Carl should always be looked up to as some kind of Guru who had access to knowledge not readily available to the common man. And in his benevolence, he should be considered as a protector of his underlings. He must get out if the shop and his coveralls and don the white shirt and tie to command the proper respect.

Harold also suggested Carl should start taking the deposits to the bank rather than Effie Lou. In this way he might be exposed to some culture in the high finance circles. This worked too well. Carl soon joined the Businessmen's Club and started the classic three Martini lunch. This would consume two to three hours of good productive time needed at the garage. Were it not for Effie Lou, Butch And Harold's efforts, the business would have floundered. This is not to say that Carl's mingling did not have its advantages. New business was acquired, but the workload was overcoming the hired help. The only solution was to hire a shop manager. One was pirated away from a local Ford dealership by financial inducements.

His name was Jonas Perkins and there might have been other inducements. Jonas had worked at a Southside dealership on Stewart Avenue up the street from Hapeville. But he lived in Jonesboro and every day he went by Effie Lou's former place of employment and naturally after working in a hot shop for eight hours, he needed a few cool ones. The diner was very convenient for this purpose. An innocent relationship developed between Jonas and Carl's wife. This halted abruptly when she quit and went to greater things. When Jonas heard of this, he felt he had lost a good friend forever because there was absolutely no reason for him to go sniffing around the now famous Jones's Service Shop. Then one day, he bumped into Carl at the bank. Jonas had met Carl when he would frequent the dealership for parts. Jonas inquired as to how the business was doing and Carl told him all his troubles about not being able to handle it. This was the crack in the door where Jonas needed to place his foot. After more conversation the door was wide open welcoming him into the organization.

Jonas' employment was all that was needed to get the company into high gear. Everything was going fine. Carl had more time pursuing the grape and golf ball. Skirts would come later. Jonas was again close to Effie Lou. They put another desk in the small office. Neither thought it too cramped, instead it was more to their liking. Effie Lou welcomed someone to keep her company while Butch and Harold were at school. As this association grew, she began to resent the time that the boys showed up after school. She was being deprived of an intimacy she had become to enjoy.

The boys sensed the change of atmosphere of the office. Harold felt his work was done as far as Carl was concerned, even though things had not turned out as he planned. He told Butch that it was time to apply some pressure on his parents to make his life a bit more comfortable now that they could afford it.

"Start wearing your worst clothes to school so they may see how neglected you are. Ask for more lunch money because you're not getting enough to eat at home."

Effie Lou was the first to notice the change in Butch. She confided in Jonas about the situation. "What in the world am I to do? I don't have time to fix decent meals anymore or keep the house as I should."

"Hire a combination cook and maid. You can afford one now."

"I don't know anyone who would work for me."

"How about that young colored girl who cooked on the late shift at the diner?"

"You mean Marybelle Griswold?"

"Yeah, that's the one. She's real nice and clean and has her own car. I bet she would welcome a good daytime job. And it would be easier work."

She went out to the diner the next afternoon and asked Marybelle if she would entertain the idea she had in mind.

"Consider the idea entertained and accepted! When do I start?"

Effie Lou squealed and jumped up and hugged her. "Oh. I'm so glad! You can start anytime you want!"

"Maybe I better give a notice. They have been good to me, even though they don't pay much. I know. I'll give them one day. That's more than they gave the last person they let go."

The next afternoon when the boys got there from school, Effie Lou took both into the house and introduced them to Marybelle.

"Butch, this is Marybelle Griswold. She is going to help us keep the house clean and cook some good meals."

Butch thought she was the prettiest thing he had ever laid his eyes on. She had long straight black hair and beautiful blue eyes. She just had to be an Indian princess. It was love at first sight. Even though he was not old enough to know about carnal lust, he was aware something wonderful had just happened to him. When their hands touched in a handshake, the sparks flew again as they had with Gilmore's mother and father. Marybelle knew this could not be, he was just a kid and besides, he was white. And this was Atlanta, Georgia, in the early fifties. These obstacles did not concern Butch. He just knew things would have to work out for him. Somehow.

The condition of the house kept other problems out of Marybelle's mind for the next few weeks. The only problem she had with Butch was to try to keep him from underfoot. He was with her constantly except during school hours. This was when Marybelle was able to do the most work. She started helping him with his homework. When she read to him, he would sit in her lap and lean his head against her small breasts. And she was the best cook on the Southside of this city, according to Butch. He thought she smelled like the magnolia tree in the front yard when it was in bloom. Or maybe the honeysuckle vines on the fence. She was a great influence on him, greater than Harold but in a different way. She was of this world and closer to nature, not some abstract place that resides in one's mind only. She taught him to appreciate all living things and the beauty in the trees and the clouds and a gentle summer rain. She was poetry in motion. She did not question her purpose in life, but accepted it with gratitude.

This new situation did not escape Harold's notice. While he appreciated her earthly beauty, he could not relate to the feelings Butch was experiencing. Maybe he had gained too much universal knowledge and it had destroyed the innocence he might have once had. While contemplating this, a dark feeling of melancholy descended over him. He felt he was not of this world and its pleasures. Then he subconsciously felt the feeling of ecstasy he experienced upon arriving at the upper level and realized there is a time and place for all feelings.

These feelings are fleeting and must be savored while one can before moving on to other experiences. Do not mourn your losses, but instead look forward to what is in store for you.

With these thoughts in mind, he felt it might not be right to interfere too much into circumstances of others. Would things have been different for Carl, Effie Lou or Jonas or did I only speed up what was going to happen anyway? How about Butch and Marybelle? I think I will back off and let whatever is going to happen, happen.

* * *

"Well, Harold, welcome back home. What happened over at the Joneses to send you back home?"

"Mother, I feel I have meddled where I should not have. I feel like some missionaries that have converted a bunch of Hindus."

"That's a strange thing to say. Why shouldn't they?"

"In a land full of fanatical Hindus, what chance do a handful of fanatical Christians have? They will probably be torn limb from limb."

"Don't talk like that. It's not nice."

"Sometimes this is not a nice world."

"I felt that way when your father was killed in the war."

"Would you rather he had not went and felt the shame of a deserter?"

"At the time, yes. Now I don't know."

"No one knows where optional paths will lead."

"I guess the important thing is not to do anything you might regret."

"I will be leaving you for a while, but Gilmore will be here to keep you company."

"Oh dear, must you?"

"I think it is best at the present."

"We will all miss you."

"And I, you."

* * *

"Hannibal you are becoming a frequent flyer. What are you doing back? Your time is not up just yet."

"I know, J.C., I just had to get away for a while."

"Messed things up down there?"

"Possibly, I was just trying to alter some things that did not seem right."

"Right by whose standards?"

"I get your point. I am not qualified to judge?"

"I can't believe that you would even consider you were. Perhaps you need further processing."

"Maybe I had better get back down there."

"Maybe you had better."

"It must be hard to be perfect."

"You better believe it."

CHAPTER FIVE

"Hello mother, how did things go while I was on sabbatical?"

"Welcome back, Harold. You have been missed. Let me bring you up date while I fix supper. A lot has happened since you departed."

"What are you preparing?"

"It's a dish Marybelle taught me years ago."

"Years ago? I don't understand. How long have I been gone?"

"You mean you don't know? Why, it's been over ten years!"

"Wow! No wonder I feel different. Gilmore has really taken good care of our body! I must say that you don't look much different."

"Well, I'm not working as hard as I used to."

"You must have got a promotion at Richs'."

"No. I haven't worked there in a long time. I work for Carl Jones now."

"I can't believe all this. You hardly knew him. What happened?"

"This is going to take some time. Do you remember the two old houses between Carl's property and the corner?"

"Yes I remember that they were about to fall down from neglect. I couldn't understand how those people lived in them."

"Well, for one thing they were renting and the slumlord wouldn't spend any money on them. Anyway, the Christmas after you left, a Christmas tree in one of the houses caught fire and destroyed the house and due to the proximity of the other, it naturally went also. All the people escaped with their lives only. The people next to Carl's got in their old car and went back to Blairsville where their relatives lived. The other family went to Hendersonville, North Carolina. They all had enough of the big city life. They probably resumed making moonshine."

"This is very interesting, but what has it got to do with you?"

"The owner of the property decided not to rebuild because the district was going commercial and he felt he could realize more out of a sale. He was right. Carl paid him more for the vacant lots than he could have made in twenty years of renting. To say nothing of what it would cost to rebuild. Carl got Tony to clear off the lots, pave them, build a small two room office in the middle of the lots and put an eight-foot chain link fence around all of it."

"Sounds like a good place for a used car lot."

"You guessed right, but it was like no other one I've even seen before. He found an old ramp type grease rack and put it in front of the office with a fairly nice car on it. In front of the rack he put a fifty-foot telephone pole and stretched chains of different colored lights to each corner of the fence. And he made them blink in sequence, it was really some show."

"I imagine, but it doesn't sound too original."

"True, but that was not all. He put another string of lights up the pole about six inches apart down the top thirty feet of the pole. Adjacent to each lamp there was a small sign with a price on each. These prices varied from the average retail for the car down to ten dollars. All day long the lamps would chase up and down the pole, randomly stopping at one spot at six o'clock each afternoon."

"I can guess the rest. This determined the price the car would sell for."

"That's right."

"This must have attracted a lot of people every day."

"It did. In fact, it caused traffic jams and the police had to be there every afternoon to keep order."

"How did everybody find out about it?"

"Well, the first day there were only about fifty people there who stopped during the day to see what was going on. When the light stopped on thirty dollars and a clean 1947 Buick Special was on the ramp, everybody stormed the office to buy the car. Many people were taken to the hospital for treatment. The news reporters that hung around the emergency room naturally wanted to know what had happened. That was all it took. Carl got a hundred thousand dollars of free publicity the next morning in the Atlanta Constitution newspaper and on the Channel Two six o'clock news."

"Go on."

"The next day was when the police had to be there. The four houses across the street with the nice front yards were not so nice anymore. There was no way to keep the crowds off the lawns and bushes. And the owners threatened to sue. Carl calmed them down by buying all the houses for about three times market value. This cured that problem but the crowd wrecked his fine fence when a clean Fifty Chevy went for one hundred dollars. Jonas suggested that numbered tickets be distributed to the crowd and the winner be drawn from a hat. Effie Lou had a better idea. Instead of just passing out the tickets. Give one to everyone that made a purchase."

Carl and Jonas wanted to know exactly what everyone was expected to buy. Effie Lou said "We could use one of the empty houses as a diner and sell hot dogs, hamburgers and soft drinks. We could give a ticket away for every dollar spent."

Carl said, "This is great, but we want to sell cars not hot dogs."

"Well, give tickets also to those that buy a car."

Effie Lou said "I'm outta here. I've handed y'all the ball so now run with it."

"Jonas you know this can get out of hand if we don't rig the lights."

"Yeah, and the tickets should be good for one day only to keep them from piling up."

"I think we could keep them valid for one week."

"That's right, if the lights stop on a high price, every body will come back for a better deal."

"If we keep the average price above wholesale and below retail, we should sell at least five or six cars a week."

They worked out all the details with a mathematical expert from Ga. Tech who knew all about probabilities and permutations.

Jonas was moved up to general manager and others were hired as managers of service, sales and personnel.

People from all over would drive by every day to see what model was on the ramp. This gave his lot exposure to ones thinking of trading and a lot would stop and look at all the cars on the lot.

Something else evolved from this scheme. If a winning ticket was for a car that was substantially below retail and the winner didn't want it because it was too much money for him to spend at the time, he would offer it for sale among the other ticket holders for the highest bid. Most of the ticket winners were not too adept at the fine art of auctioning. A lot of confusion resulted. Carl noticed this and saw another opportunity here. He had Tony build a small podium and he hired an auctioneer he knew to work an hour every afternoon. They charged a ten percent consignment fee and a ten percent buyer's premium. One afternoon the auctioneer whose name was Phillip said asked the crowd if anyone had a ticket to sell. When there was none, a person yelled out "Phillip you need to auction off something."

Carl jumped up on the podium and made an announcement.

"I have a box here with about five hundred tickets good for the rest of this week. Let's see what they are worth to you."

They brought one hundred dollars. Later Phillip told Carl in private that he didn't think that was a very good idea. "You are treading on dangerous ground. I think this could be construed as a lottery, which I think you know is illegal."

"Tell the crowd that if they have won a bargain, they might want to sell their old one at the auction here. If they can somehow nurse it down here, we will sell it to the highest bidder. But the purchaser must move it that day."

The next day four cars showed up to be disposed of. This was really turning into a circus. Phillip wondered why did they have to limit it to automobiles.

Carl announced, "This is so much fun, let's try other things of value. Bring any thing you think will sell."

"Anything?"

"Anything within reason and not too large."

The next afternoon, when Carl walked over to the auction lot, he saw a mule, three goats and six piglets. Over to the side but close to this menagerie was an assortment of household items. Among these were baby carriages, an old icebox, some space heaters and miscellaneous floor and table lamps.

Again Carl jumped to the podium. "I see some more ground rules are in order. In order to keep this fair and so that no one person can monopolize or take advantage, I will limit items to one per ticket held by anyone."

At six o'clock the next day there appeared an old two-ton stake body truck loaded to the gunwales with assorted "merchandise", the purchaser of the five hundred tickets drove it. Never underestimate the imagination of entrepreneurs. The people loved it.

Carl thought, who am I to question the wisdom of the masses? I can't beat them, therefore I shall join them.

People then started buying more snacks at the diner just to get tickets to enable them to bring more "merchandise" to foist off to their fellow participants.

"This is about the time I appear on the scene. Carl sent Butch over to ask if I could help out at the auction every afternoon after I got off from work. He said I would enjoy it, it was more fun than a three-ring circus."

"And?"

"So I said I would try it. And try it I did. I told Carl that it was so much fun that I would work for nothing if he couldn't pay me. He said 'That was against the law so I would have to accept his modest stipend'."

"What did he have you doing?"

"A full-blown auction requires a lot of help. The consignees have to register and are given a seller's number. The buyers also have a number. This is written on a paper plate for them to wave at the auctioneer or on a wooden paddle if they are regulars and are assigned a permanent number. As the items are sold, the price and the bidder's number must be recorded on a tally sheet so the funds can be collected at the end of the auction. This was my job. Others helped bring the items to the auction table and helped the auctioneer keep up with who was bidding. And you must have a security force to prevent anyone from removing any merchandise without a proper paid receipt."

"This doesn't sound like fun to me. It sounds like a lot of hard work."

"It would be if the auctioneer were not a natural born comedian. He can either make or break the whole operation. And it can be the most economical entertainment a person can buy."

"I shall reserve my opinion until I have participated in one. Why do people want this junk?"

"Sometimes a person will be hired to clean out an attic or perhaps a whole house after it has been vacated and before it is put up for sale. There can be truly treasures to be found. Somebody will appreciate all of these items. The trick is to expose them to the right people. An auction is one of the best places for this."

"While I have been spending my time studying philosophy and the workings of earthly things, I have missed the greatest experiences one can have, the participation with the human race."

"This is indeed hard for you to do, what with your constantly jumping in and out."

"Maybe this time I can stay. I have so much to look forward to."

"Living has many rewards. I have enjoyed the past few years more than any since your dear father died. I am into the pulse of humanity now. I am prepared to leave the hereafter to the time I arrive there and will concern myself with it no more, until then."

"This is truly a human thought. Probably because you are. Tell me about Marybelle and Butch. They were becoming an item before I left."

"Butch has matured a lot since then. He becomes sad when thinking about what might have been, if they had been closer to the same age and in a time and place when prejudice and hate were not known."

"There has never been such a place or time. And I don't believe there will ever will be on this earth."

"True, but that is what dreams are made of, and Butch is a dreamer."

"This doesn't sound like it interfered with your job at Richs'.

"It didn't at first but let me explain. The auction grew so much that Carl had the four houses moved down the street to some vacant property he had purchased and fixed them up and rented them out. I was also to be the rental agent. He cleaned off the auction lot and got Tony to put up a long metal building with bleachers down one wall and an office and snack bar on the other. In the middle was a drive through with large doors at each end. This was a permanent indoor all weather auction. With these changes the auction started at five P.M. and lasted until after eleven. I was making more money in less than six hours than I made in three days at Richs'."

"And this was now interfering with your job."

"By all means. Mother and Gilmore would come after they had supper and finished with the dishes. Gilmore helped by bringing in items to the table and carrying some back to the buyer's automobiles. He made a lot of tips this way, which he saved in a bank account we opened for him. Mother caught the buying fever and if you look around the house you can see the results."

"Yes, I noticed this place is looking like a museum or antique shop."

"Would you believe an antique shop is exactly what it is turning into? Mother has built up a good clientele of antique lovers who come by regularly and make some very large dollar purchases."

"Do you mean the stuff she picks up at the auction? Why don't those fine ladies go to the auction themselves?"

"Ha! These types wouldn't be caught dead in a place like that. It would be completely beneath their station and dignity."

"I understand. Maybe they just can't afford to be seen there. Like a bank president's wife."

"Yes, they are not necessarily hypocrites, sometimes there are practical reasons why people act as they do."

"It is nice that you understand this and can take advantage of the situation."

"This is what makes the world turn."

"Tell me more about Butch and Marybelle."

"I think Marybelle was the more level headed one and convinced Butch he was suffering from a bad case of puppy love. She told him there was a time for everything and now was the time for him to enjoy growing up and going to college. Now they are only great friends. At least that's how Marybelle feels. I still wonder about Butch. Together they run the snack bar and share the profits. The profit motive probably keeps their minds off romantic endeavors. Butch is now going to Ga. Tech. We don't know what will happen when he graduates, and by the way, with honors."

"You don't mean it!"

"Yep, in the top five. Out of over four hundred. And he says he owes it all to you. He has missed you terribly."

"I bet that was after Marybelle turned the hose on him."

"That's not a very nice thing to say, even though it is probably true."

"You know it is. You are not so old that you do not remember about you and dad in Cheeseman's Ice Cream Parlor."

"Harold! You frighten me. You can't possibly know anything about that! That was before you were even born."

"Don't you think I know how I came to be born?"

"I'm sure you do, but that doesn't explain about Cheeseman's."

"Er, I must have heard you and grandmother talking about it."

"I never discussed that with mother. You have to come up with something better than that."

"What can I say? I guess I'm just plain weird."

"You are a lot of fun, but you still frighten me. Call your grandmother and let's eat."

"Mother, did you notice that Harold is back with us?"

"Mary, I knew that the moment he opened his mouth to call me to supper. Harold, don't you interfere with my relationship with Gilmore. You have been gone so long that I have developed a good rapport with him and I don't want your messing it up."

"Why, grandmother, do I detect a note of hostility in your speech? Do you not love me anymore?"

"Of course she does, it's only because she's upset that you stayed gone so long and never once contacted us."

"This was not of my choosing. Other factors beyond my control were involved."

"There must have been. Did you know someone else showed up in your absence?"

"I don't understand."

"Gilmore was displaced by some wild one who called himself Oliver Thornton. He said he was a counterpart of Olaf Thor, whatever that meant."

"The name sounds vaguely familiar, but right now I can't place it. Maybe it will come to me. What happened with this Oliver person?"

"He disrupted the whole household. Thank goodness it was before mother and I got so involved with the auction. He left before too much damage was done."

"Where was Gilmore when this was going on?"

"Mercy, I don't know. He just left and didn't return until this Oliver vamoosed."

"What did he say when he got back?"

"Nothing much. He acted as if nothing had happened. He was a little confused about the time lost, but he thought you had taken over for some reason."

"Tell me about this Olaf or Oliver, whichever."

"He had a heavy Scandinavian accent and had a great fascination for high temperatures. I even caught him once sitting in the kitchen in front of the stove with the oven door open and the thermostat set on maximum. If I hadn't happened upon him, I believe he would have melted down."

"Are any of your ancestors from that part of the world?"

"Not to my knowledge. The McDonalds came originally from Scotland and the Smiths came from England."

"The Vikings were known to raid the Scotch and English Coasts. Maybe some fraternization took place. For the sake of our sanity, let's assume this."

"Yes, we are not blessed with a normal existence."

"Are you complaining?"

"Absolutely not. It is very interesting and I love it!"

"Did Oliver ever go over to Carl's with you?"

"When he first got here, I was still working at Richs'. In fact I remember when he heard the fire engines going by to the shack fires, he followed them and really enjoyed the show. He came back later red faced and with soot all over him. His eyebrows were even singed. He told me he had a great time."

"You don't think he had anything to do with the setting of the fires, do you?"

"No way. We all had been at home for hours before the fire engines came by. Why do you ask?"

"He sounds like a firebug to me."

"Well, he did like matches and cigarette lighters but he seemed to have enough sense not to play with them."

"How did he happen to leave?"

"One day he was caught down the street when a sudden downpour came up and he started running home. When I looked out the window, I saw a large steam cloud surrounding him and lightning flashing around him. It was like some terrible reaction was taking place because of the cold rain. When he reached the front door, he was gone and Gilmore was back. He never showed up again, thank goodness."

"My vessel seems to be like a bus full of strange characters. I must exert better control."

"No real harm has been done. Yet."

"You still have a lot to tell to bring me up to date. Please resume the narration."

"Gosh, so much has happened, I don't really know where to begin."

"Start with more about Marybelle and Butch."

"Do I detect a note of erotic curiosity in your voice?"

"No, just concern about two good friends."

"We found out more about Marybelle one day when Butch was pouring hot water into the coffee maker and spilled some on his hand. It looked like a boiled lobster. Marybelle grabbed his hand with both of hers and held it close to her mouth and mumbled some strange words over it. His hand immediately returned to its natural color and all the pain disappeared. I had heard of some persons possessing this gift, but this was the first time I saw and believed it."

"How did she acquire this ability?"

"She told me her mother passed it on to her. It had been passed down for five generations from one ancestor who was a full-blown Cherokee Indian that had married a red headed blue eyed Scot."

"That explains her blue eyes, but what about her African blood?"

"The daughter of this first union was stolen in a raid by the Creeks and sold to an English slave trader who sold a group on the slave market in Louisville, Georgia. This child was brought up in a plantation owner's home as a companion of the owner's wife. The proximity of this situation produced a line of hybrids which eventually resulted in Marybelle."

"This combination indeed produced a fine specimen."

"Word of her abilities spread around the neighborhood and her services became in demand. She limited her help to the ones which patronized the snack bar that has since become a fine diner with a small consulting room in which she practiced."

"You mean she's a witch doctor?"

"Not really. You might say she applies primitive mountain psychology in helping the superstitious with imagined ailments."

"The mind is surely a powerful instrument."

"Yes, modern physicians are only now discovering the value of nature's treatments."

"What happened to Carl, Effie Lou and Jonas?"

"As the business grew, more and more of rooms were needed as office space. Carl and Effie Lou finally had to buy a nicer house in a nicer neighborhood and turn the whole old one into offices. Naturally more help was needed and Effie Lou hired an office manager to keep the office running smoothly. He did such a good job that her services were no longer needed and she retired to her new home on West Paces Road in fine splendor. This spelled the end of Jonas' attraction for her."

"Why? It seemed they had something special going."

"When she moved, she got addicted to television soap operas and chocolate covered cherries. The result was a net gain of two hundred pounds. It was not that Jonas did not appreciate her fine mind, but he felt that an illicit relation should offer rewards other than dialog only. This was not a slow drifting apart. Jonas had to go on a buying trip that along with other duties, kept them apart for six months. When he finally returned, he casually dropped in one day to see Effie Lou. He casually dropped out and has never been back since. This leads me to assume the liaison was based solely on physical attraction."

"An astute observation. What about Carl?"

"He checks in from time to time to see if she is comfortable and in want of anything. He is hardly noticed anymore. He is very close mouthed about his actions and whereabouts. I guess he is happy and has finally got what he has always wanted."

"It takes a lot to satisfy some."

"He has never lost a loved one but at the same time, I don't believe he has ever really loved anyone. A person like this must rely on material rewards. This is sad, but the world is filled with these types."

"Tell me about your place in the romance department. Surely after all these years of being alone you have entertained some thoughts along this line?"

"To tell the truth, with Dad on the road most of the time, Mom involved with her antiques and Gilmore becoming more self sufficient, I must admit that my thoughts have been leaning toward a more fuller relationship."

"That was a really fancy way of saying 'the fire ain't out yet'. Go on and admit that you get lonely."

"This is not to say I don't still love your father, but as I have found out, you should let the hereafter take care of itself and get on with the world at hand. There is really nothing anyone can do about that aspect anyway. What will be will be."

"The social intercourse that you have been involved in at the auction has really changed your outlook on life. I am glad. I was afraid you would turn into a recluse."

"I might still, if somebody doesn't come along. I don't believe the clientele at the auction gives me a selection that appeals to me. I try not to be a snob, but I can't see myself running around in a beat-up pick up truck looking for people's discards. And I am afraid that would be how I might wind up."

You could get more involved in the church."

"That's exactly what mom has trying to get me to do, but the church has not been much help with my dealing with the loss of your father."

"Maybe you were expecting too much. A church does not have all the answers, maybe not any. Everyone goes to church for his or her own reasons. It gives some peace of mind. It gives others a means for social or financial advancement. Others use it only for funerals and weddings. All these different people are welcome. You would be also even if you were only looking for a stud."

"Harold, you are the most outrageous lovable person I have ever encountered."

"Speaking the truth can brand one as such."

"I'll make a deal with you. I'll go if you go with me."

"Ha! I'm not looking for a bedfellow, you are!"

"The way you carry on, I'm sure a few trips to church will help civilize you. You certainly need civilizing sometimes. I don't know where you spent the last ten years but it seems like it was in a poolroom!"

"Dear mother, I assure you there were no poolrooms there. Perhaps someday when they gain some respectability, some might be added."

"Please go to church with me a few times. I am desperate!"

"Only for you, dear mother."

CHAPTER SIX

"Harold, you are very pensive. Did the sermon upset you?"

"Not really, mother, I was just thinking how Christians can distort the truth to fit desired circumstances."

"How do you mean?"

"Take when Father O'Malley was talking about the Stigmata. As you know the wounds always appear in the palms."

"What's wrong with that?"

"Any self respecting historian, whether he was there or not, knows what the Romans knew. That the palms, with a spike driven through, will not hold the weight of a body suspended on a cross. The spikes were driven through the wrists. Even the famous shroud of Turin shows this. Ignore that last statement, you probably don't know about that yet."

"Then why do the wounds always appear in the hands?"

"The myth surrounding crucifixions originated centuries after the practice was no longer used as a means of punishment. The powers had now taken up the burning alive of persons that offended the Church. It was at this time the details of a crucifixion were forced upon the true believers. It was believe this or else. The power of suggestion was so great among the truly pious, that some developed the false Stigmata and it became the norm."

"What difference does it make?"

"To female logic, none."

"And exactly do you mean by that?"

"It is a question if reality viewed from different perspectives, male as opposed to female."

"Real is real regardless of the eyes that view it."

"Are you sure? To an optimist, a cup could be half full and to the pessimist the same cup will be half empty. The closer to the ground you fly, the faster you seem to be going. A female bookkeeper has to balance the books to the nearest penny. A male might balance to the nearest dollar, or maybe the nearest ten or hundred. Either system will work if practiced long enough."

"If you are so precise about history, why do you treat another's financial accounting so loosely?"

"The keeping of books are for personal benefit only. The keeping of history is for all mankind. Mistakes should not be tolerated. If lies are told long enough, they shall become the truth to many. And all mankind suffers. An example of this will manifest itself in the distant future when dialectical materialism fails and the masses find out the truth about it."

"Do you think that this will happen to the Church's Dogma?"

"We will have to wait and see. Maybe humans are getting smarter, but I doubt it."

"Are you saying an enlightened society has no need for faith?"

"Of course not! I only contend that true faith comes from within, not from some antiquated doctrine that technology has rendered obsolete."

"You confuse me. First you tell me to go to church and then you say not to listen to what is said."

"Not really, just practice selective deafness. Eat only what you can stomach!"

"I do not believe I have the wisdom to differentiate."

"To thine own self be true."

"I have read that before."

"It is true, I am not the originator of the phrase."

Grandpa Joe, in the front seat with Dolly driving the family home from church, had kept his mouth shut as long as he could. But now he had to get involved. "Harold Gilmore! (He was called this by his grandfather) your brain needs re-aligning. I don't know where you get all these radical ideas from, but I think you are wrong sometimes and now is one of those times. You seem to have no idea why any religion was established."

"Ah! A dormant tongue awakens! I have finally spoken the magic words to elicit a response from a recluse!"

"I will tolerate no disrespect from you. Either you keep your mouth shut and listen to what I am going to tell you or I will stop the car and bodily remove you and you will have to walk home!"

"I'm sorry, grandpa, but it was so much of a shock for you to involve yourself in our conversation. I just got carried away. Do enlighten me. Tell me what I need to know."

"That's better. The survival of any living creature is dependent on many factors. Humans are not unique in this respect, but we differ from lower life forms in our ability to think and anticipate the immediate future. With this in mind, the most intelligent of a group would take control of the group for the benefit of all. Certain rules are needed to be impressed upon the others to keep order. The best way to accomplish this is through mystical rites and rituals, which appealed to the superstitious masses. In this way the truth was distorted, but only for reasons beneficial to the group. This worked generally, but there were always some agnostic that would question the wisdom of the rules. Anyone doing so only showed their ignorance to the purpose of the rules. If he couldn't be shown the error, he would have to be banished before he spread his contagion through the populace and wreaked havoc."

"Somewhat like being ejected from this vehicle."

"Son, only disrespect can endanger your position among us. Your beliefs can be altered, I hope."

"I always forget that this reality is subjective."

"What do you mean by that?"

"A person that has not been subjected to any historical data has only his observations from which to draw conclusions. This inhibits one from seeing reality from someone else's view."

"You are saying there is no universal truth that can be attained by enlightened ones."

"The enlightenment required is not available to anyone confined to this plane of existence and is of no consequence to beings elsewhere."

Mary said, "Changing the subject, I think we should go to a nice cafeteria and eat the normal after-church lunch."

Harold agreed. "That would be the Christian thing to do."

Grandpa said, "You are playing with an ejection."

"Ignore that last stupid statement."

While waiting in the line, they ran into Effie Lou, Carl and Butch. They introduced Joe to Carl and Effie Lou. He knew Butch. He had met him one evening at home when he came by to see Gilmore. They found a table large enough to accommodate the seven and Carl started eating before Joe got through the blessing. And Effie Lou was right behind him. Joe didn't realize this because he had his eyes closed. But Butch and Harold saw it all. They winked at each other and did a unified amen when Joe finished. Carl turned his head away just in time for Joe to miss seeing the food he had stuffed into his mouth.

"Harold, what are you doing to that fork?"

"Mother, I am in the process of straightening the tines. I do not consider myself paranoid, but I seem to always get the one that has been distorted by the dishwasher."

"Don't be silly' I get one sometimes."

"And it does not bother you?"

"Not at all, why does it upset you"?

"It feels uncomfortable to my teeth when I am pulling a piece of meat off the fork."

"You all must excuse Harold, I am blessed with a weird son."

Trying to be sociable, Joe asked Carl how was business. Having a mouthful, all he could do was grunt. Joe, mistaking this for a groan, and thinking business was terrible, tried to sympathize by saying, "I'm sorry to hear this, but this is the chance you take when you choose not to have a steady and secure job. I do hope that Gilmore chooses to find a profession with a firm that has a future."

"Mr. McDonald, you have misunderstood my response to your question. When you asked it, I had too much roast beef in my mouth to give a proper answer. Business could not be better. And I chose not to have a steady job because I did not have the book learning that you must have had. Everyone is not fortunate in having means to get a good education. And as far as a secure job is concerned, I hear that R.E.A. is in trouble because the trucks are taking the bulk of small freight away from the railroads and your future might not be so secure after all."

"I think they will last long enough for me to retire and then I'll let other people worry. And if I don't, I think I can get a good position with U.P.S. They are growing by leaps and bounds."

All this talk has upset Dolly. "Joe, I didn't know anything about any of this. You never tell me anything."

"I didn't want to upset you. Don't worry, we are pretty well set for our golden years."

Carl jumps back in. "No one is ever well set because nobody can know what is going to happen. If you don't keep climbing, you will fall back. I think y'all ought to open a fine antique shop, with Dolly running it and you coming in after you retire. I'll finance the whole thing for a small interest in it."

"What do you call a small interest?"

"Say ten percent and considerations."

"The percent sounds fair, but what kind of considerations?"

"I was thinking about my furnishing the building and leasing it to our new business at a nominal fee."

"What do you call a nominal fee?"

"Joe, you don't need a lawyer. You do very well without one. We should get along famously. I was thinking about a ten year lease at a figure that would amortize the total construction cost and six percent simple interest."

"How about a lease purchase agreement to be executed at the termination of the lease? You would still own ten percent of the property and without the company paying rent, your portion of the profits would increase."

"Joe, I'm liking you better every time you open your mouth. Toss this around. I don't believe in a company owning real property. It can become a tax liability. It might be better if we form a holding company as a separate entity to own rental property. We can write off the rent as a business expense and set up a depreciation schedule that along with the upkeep will keep our tax liability to a ridiculous minimum. And when the program terminates, we sell the property and take a capital gain."

"But if we sell, we lose control."

"Not if we sell it to Butch and Gilmore."

"Knowing them, we still lose control."

"No, we will lend them the money to buy it and have them so tied up they will have to think twice about any wild ideas."

"Slow up. Let me get this in my head. You build the building. We as a corporation lease it from you until the building is paid for, then we form another corporation to buy the building. This corporation rents the property to the first corporation until it has been depreciated off the books. Then we sell it to Butch and Gilmore on time and they rent it back to the original corporation, which are we. We pay them rent which they in turn use the proceeds to make payments back to us and we still wind up with all the money plus interest. What will the I.R.S. think about this?"

"They will be more confused about the deal than we are."

Butch injects, "If they will be more confused than I, we will have nothing to worry about. I say let's go for it."

Joe says, "Wait a few, Dolly hasn't had a chance to say anything yet, we have monopolized the conversation. Speak, wife."

"Inventory. I have gobs scattered around the house in all rooms. I will require the company to take it off my hands at a reasonable figure so I will realize something for my efforts and the company can still make a profit."

"Your efforts! That's a joke. I have watched you at the auction and you were having the time of your life and picked up all that junk for peanuts."

"Carl, are you saying that one should not enjoy their occupation?"

"Aw Dolly, you know better than that, you know I love my work. I just meant that one should not make too much money off their friends."

"Well, I'll set a reasonable price and submit it to the group for approval. And I, as a member of the group hereby give my approval."

Joe explodes. "I protest! That definitely a conflict of interest and furthermore you have not examined the list, so how can you give your approval on something you have not yet seen?"

"Joe, you forget I am a woman and as a woman enjoy certain privileges that men cannot understand."

"Is this based on your child bearing faculties, which I might add, was performed admirably once and only once and then you abdicated the duty?"

"That is a terrible thing for you to say to me. You know very well what the circumstances were. The late twenties and early thirties were not the best times to start a family."

"Oh mother, are you saying my birth was a mistake?"

"Mary, Mary, please forgive me. You were not an accident. But we decided to wait until later to add to our responsibilities. But then there was the depression and then the Great War. And then we were grandparents and Gilmore filled the void quite nicely. Now back to answer Joe's question. No, my statement was based on female prerogatives which defy male logic."

"Excuse me! For a minute I had a lapse of memory about the workings of the female brain. But please remember some adjustment may be necessary if you are to succeed doing business in a man's world. This is a lot different than selling quaint items to a bunch of old ladies sipping tea in your living room. They understand your style of logic because they also use it. The rule is 'if it is not in your favor, do not attempt to understand the problem'."

"Humph! I shall compile an inventory list and prices for the committee's approval. Just exactly who is the committee?"

"If this is to be a closed corporation, we must decide now who wants in. Who wants in?"

Mary, "Me."

Dolly, "Me."

Butch, "Me."

Carl, "Me."

Gilmore, "Me."

Effie Lou, "Not me."

Carl, "I expected that."

Harold, "How about me?"

Unison, "You voted."

"That was Gilmore."

Unison except Joe, "Only one vote per body."

Harold, "Oh, all right."

Joe, "What was that all about?"

Unison except Joe, "Just a private joke."

"It must not be very private if everybody except me is in on it. What's going on?"

"Joe, this is not the time or place to go into this. I will try to explain after we go to bed tonight."

'Very well, I am willing to let the snoozing canine recline temporarily. Now back to the discussion at hand. After we agree on a price for Dolly's inventory, funds must be raised for the purchase of it and other necessary items to start a business. Now Carl has committed for ten percent by furnishing the building. He should have a choice of upping his interest by participating in the inventory purchase. Carl, what are your thoughts on this?"

"I am in a position to underwrite the whole ball of wax, but that would cut most of you out. You all have indicated you want in. To what extent has yet to be determined. I am willing to sit back and let all of you contribute what you can afford and I will pick up the remainder at the prorated percentage. In other words, ninety percent is up for grabs, and if you come up with eighty percent, then I will contribute the other ten percent and will end up with twenty percent of the company. You probably will find the purchase of the inventory to be a small portion of what is needed."

Gilmore; "Why do you say that?"

"To name some, license fees, utility deposits, printing costs, office fixtures, office supplies, a substantial bank account to tide you over until the money starts rolling in and incorporation costs and attorney fees. And don't forget insurance. You will need all sorts of protection. And unless you are as blessed as I was, advertising will be a great expense and once you start advertising you can't stop."

Dolly; "Why can't you?"

"You will be afraid to. If you are successful, you might not know why and the advertising might be the cause. The only way you can find out is to stop. And if it was, you could lose a lot of business."

Butch; "Let's don't start. Harold and I will work on this. Maybe we can come up with some gimmick to get some free publicity like Carl lucked up on."

Carl; "I take exception to that last remark. Luck indeed! It was pure calculated genius and you know it."

"If I remember correctly, I believe Harold participated."

"My memory fails me."

Joe, "That sounds like female logic."

Carl; "Whatever."

Mary; "It looks like everyone has finished eating and we cannot resolve this until mother prepares her list, and my feet hurt. I hereby make a motion that we adjourn until we have more to discuss and my feet feel better."

Harold; "We cannot adjourn a meeting that has not been called to order. I suggest we just pay the cheek and go home."

Unison except Harold; "Good thinking."

CHAPTER SEVEN

The next month saw a new building being built on a very desirable lot a few miles north of Jonesboro. It was on heavily traveled U.S. 41. Although this was one of the main routes to Florida for the Yankees of the Midwest, this was not the main reason for this location. The specter of the impending Interstate highways was looming throughout the country at this time and was threatening all tourist businesses along the old U.S. highways. Only a fool would invest heavily in a business catering to tourists on one of these routes knowing what was going to happen in the near future. And these were not fools investing in this enterprise, although the logic behind it escaped most average persons, especially ones with shortsighted vision.

It was realized the local auction would not be able to supply adequate inventory to stock an endeavor of this magnitude. So other sources would have to be called upon. It was discovered that regions south of this location was an ideal place to purchase primitive items because until only a few years ago, this area was indeed very primitive, and the worth of such items were not yet appreciated by the inhabitants. This is not to infer they were stupid, only uninformed. The participants in this scheme were not above taking advantage of other's ignorance. This seems to be the American way.

These sellers, when coming to the great city of Atlanta will be taking advantage of the great interstate system and will have very small chance of ever seeing the items they foolishly practically gave away, sitting in a store with an astronomically ridiculous price tag attached. Anyway, all they will be interested in will be the new factory made furniture that the stores haul down from North Carolina.

Another area to be used for purchases will be the small towns of Yankee land off the beaten path. Towns that will be all but forgotten when affluent northern masses clog the new highways headed for the Sunshine State when the first snowflake is seen.

As the urban blight spreads across the length and breadth of Fulton County, a mass exodus takes place headed to adjacent counties to the north and east of Atlanta. There is a building boom in these once Kudzu covered acres. These new mansions will have to be furnished with fine antiques. Not wanting to purchase their needs in their own neighborhood, they gravitate to the south side where they think bargains are to be found. They will take advantage of the ignorance of the population that has shops there. They do not realize they have been second-guessed and blind-sided.

One spring Monday morning, there appeared a startling item on the front page of The Atlanta Constitution. The finer details of this episode have yet to be explained by authorities. It might be noted that the participants were acquaintances of Butch and Harold. This is not an indictment, only a statement of fact.

JETS DOWN UFO OVER JONESBORO

Marietta. Officials at Dobbins A.F.B. stated Sunday morning that two fighter aircraft were scrambled Saturday night to investigate reports of an unidentified object reported by many citizens of Jonesboro. It seems that on approach, the object made menacing movements toward the two aircraft and action was taken. The result of this encounter was a huge fireball that illuminated a greater part of Clayton County. In the de-briefing, the pilots explained that the object was spherical and glowed with increasing intensity toward the lower part. It was the glowing lower part was what prompted the pilots to take defensive action. At intervals, the sphere seemed to lean over and the low glowing intensified which was interpreted to be a hostile act. The area was scouted after the encounter but due to darkness, the search was called off after nothing was seen. The aircraft then returned to Dobbins.

This paper sent investigators to the vicinity Sunday morning to interview possible witnesses. Persons interviewed said the occurrence seemed to happen in the sky over the new antique shop that had opened just north of town. Going to this location, our reporters were stopped at a roadblock and detour one half mile from the Old Dixie Antique Shop. Parking on one of the side streets and walking through backyards towards the site, it was noticed that the area was strewn with sheets of thin plastic and shards of what remained of some kind of high-pressure container. The following is a description of the scene by our reporter: "The items scattered over the scene were exceeded in number only by the presence of many federal agents equipped with automatic weapons, metal detectors and Geiger Counters. There was a distinct odor of combustion permeating the atmosphere even hours after the explosion. The greatest concentration of agents was in and around the antique shop. We were not allowed any closer than three hundred feet to the shop and any further reporting would be only speculation as to what happened."

Our newsroom will keep close contact with the authorities and will keep our readers informed as more information is released.

* * *

In The Old Dixie Antique Shop, Dolly, Butch and Harold sit surrounded by numerous agents, Federal, FBI, Army Intelligence, Air Force investigators, representatives from the Clayton County Sheriff's department, the mayor of Jonesboro, some civil defense officials and other self appointed protectors of the civilian population. At this particular time none are speaking. Several technicians are setting up various cameras, microphones and tape recorders.

Special Agent in Charge (S.A.I.C.) Adams, Joseph A. was the first to speak. "If we have to, we all will stay here for as long as it takes until I have a satisfactory explanation of what happened here and your part in it. Flying saucer, my ass! I know damn well what it was. It was a hot air balloon and it was tethered to that post in your parking lot. And you can't tell me that a bunch of little green men put it there."

Harold responds; "I have no intention of telling you that. If you were not so paranoid, you could have figured out what happened. There is a simple explanation and everything that we had a part in was perfectly legal."

"This had better be good. Your ass is on the line and if I can, I'm going to barbecue it."

"To be a representative of our government, you certainly have a foul mouth and I am a respectable lady in good standing in the community and if you can't act civil, you shall be reported to your superiors and you might wind up as latrine cleaner at the Justice Department."

"Grandmother, let me handle this. If, sir, you are an example of the caliber of men employed by our government, may Heaven help us. I have in my hand a document stamped with the approval of the FAA, the Clayton Bureau of licenses and fees and the fire department. This paper gives us permission to loft one hot-air balloon for advertising purposes for one month starting yesterday. The hot air to be furnished by a propane burner from a special container made to withstand extremely high pressures necessary to keep the device aloft for a reasonable length of time."

"Let me see that. Hmm. Why was our department not informed of this?"

"You may have jurisdiction over flying saucers, but I do not believe it extends to simple balloons that carry no passengers. Green or not."

"Well, this could present a hazard to incoming flights and we certainly have something to say about that."

"Man get real, you are grabbing at straws. Didn't I tell you that we had FFA. approval? And besides the flight paths are well to the north of this location. It is not our fault that our trigger happy guardians filled our propane storage tank with fifty caliber tracers and started this panic."

"Gentlemen, let us retire to the parking lot and discuss this situation while these people compose themselves."

Harold retorts; "What you mean is that the composing will be on your part of some likely tale to cover embarrassing over-reaction to a simple advertising project."

"Whatever, we will notify you of our decision."

* * *

The Air Intelligence officer is speaking. "Agent Adams, initials J.A., just what in the hell does the J A stand for? Possibly jackass? You certainly acted like one in there. Did you get hold of some bad coffee this morning? I believe that nice lady in there has some clout in high places and I think you should apologize to her before this gets out of hand."

"I'm sorry, but you know I don't believe in flying saucers and get bent out of shape every time some Tom, Dick or Harry calls in and reports something. And this looked like some practical joke to cause more confusion."

"Let's get on with the matter at hand. The news media is breathing down our neck for an explanation of what occurred. If we tell them what really happened, we will all be laughed out of our jobs as a bunch of bumbling idiots, which I suspect some of us are."

"Don't lay the blame in my lap. It was not my department's pilots who blew this innocent balloon out of the sky. I will go in and apologize to the people and leave the problem in the Air Force's capable hands. Where it should be."

"Begone, I will take care of that problem."

* * *

"Mrs. McDonald, Harold, Butch, I trust that agent Adams has extended his apologies to all of you for his disgraceful behavior. He is not usually this hostile. He had just this morning learned his teenage son had totaled the new family car he purchased only a week ago. And the circumstances surrounding this unusual incident only compounded his anxiety. He will bother you no more."

"I can understand the problems Harold and Butch have innocently caused in trying to help make this enterprise a success. We have invested our life savings in this endeavor and have depleted our capital before making arrangements for any advertising. And if we do not get any publicity, we will be forced to close."

"Madam, I think their efforts were a resounding success. Boys you have accomplished with minimum resources what would have cost a fortune through regular channels. I must commend you on your ingenuity. Also I must condemn your actions as very foolhardy and dangerous. It was only through dumb luck that this fiasco did not result in a major disaster. Do you realize how explosive high-pressure propane is? I admit the interference by our aircraft was a factor that no one could foresee. Their involvement will be investigated further. Under wraps of course. The credibility of our Air Force is at stake. What we must do now is come up with some satisfactory explanation to the media and we will require your full cooperation in this matter. You must be sworn to secrecy. I have in my briefcase the standard forms for you to sign swearing you to secrecy under the pain of prosecution. This is standard procedure in cases like this."

Harold; "Sir, am I to understand that this is a common problem that happens so frequently that you must carry these forms with you to any investigation of unusual incidents?"

"I am not at liberty to comment on that question."

"I understand perfectly."

"I cannot speculate on your speculation."

"Even if my suspicions are incorrect?"

"You must keep your conclusions to yourself or you will be in violation of the secrecy agreement."

"How about the thousands of others that witnessed this event?"

"You will find we are experts in denying the obvious."

"Just what kind of cock and bull story will you come up with?"

"Just keep your eyes on the newspaper."

* * *

"Grandmother, Butch and I went up to inspect the roof and found that the concussion warped some of the metal panels and split the seams. We fear that if we have a torrential downpour, we will need hip boots to wear in the showroom."

"Mercy! Did you find any other damage?"

"Not on our property, but the pine trees on the land surrounding us are leaning at a forty-five degree angle away from the point of impact. And most of the needles have turned brown. I believe they all will die."

"Oh dear, we must make restitution to the owners."

"We cannot without admitting complicity and then we would be in violation of the security agreement."

"The least we can do is to notify the owners so they can clear cut before they die."

"Yes, we can say that we were all home in bed whenever whatever happened."

* * *

EXPLOSION KILLS 20 ACRES OF PINES

Jonesboro. Remember the mysterious object fired upon by the A.N.G. fighters last weekend? It seems that the ensuing explosion damaged all the pine trees surrounding The Old Dixie Antique Shop on three sides and will have to be harvested because it looks as if they will die. The owner said this was of no great consequence because he was planning to cut them later on this year anyway. Were it not for the survival of the antique shop, we would think that a giant meteor impacted that area.

The Air Force has yet to issue a statement about this incident. If anyone has any information that may shed light on this mystery, please call our newsroom.

* * *

The remainder of that week and many weeks thereafter, old U.S.41 was jammed for miles in both directions in the vicinity of The Old Dixie Antique Shop. The results of this free publicity far exceeded the results of Carl's efforts back in the early fifties.

On weekends Harold and Butch set up a shed in the parking lot and hawked souvenirs. These were the remnants of the now famous explosion that took place in the heavens above the antique shop. These items were bits of plastic and metal that the boys wisely gleaned from the surrounding area. A lot of residents of the area actually paid them to clean up the mess in their yards. They collected money to replace the whole roof. They could not wait for an insurance settlement because the rainy season was approaching and the insurance company was balking about the claim. They contended that the Air Force was responsible and besides, it was an act of war that was not covered in the policy. Even Harold's gifted tongue was no match for the all-powerful insurance company and it seemed they could be tied up in litigation for years. God's rain could not be tabled.

All this activity was starting to interfere with Butch and Harold's educational pursuits and Dolly was faced with the problem of hiring more help. This did not escape Joe's attention since he was getting worried about his job. He decided to take an early retirement, which suited his employers fine.

* * *

The Air Intelligence Officer reports to the General in command of Dobbins A.F.B. "It seems that our pilots were somewhat hasty in their judgment of the situation. When they got no response to the I.F.F. query, they assumed the object was hostile and took action."

"They should have done a fly by first to confirm what it was."

"When they first spotted it, it was too low for a safe inspection. And then it ascended vertically a great distance very rapidly. They were concerned about losing it."

"How was it able to make this rapid ascent?"

"The tether broke."

"I see. But what caused the tremendous explosion?"

"Three hundred gallons of propane. Under extremely high pressure."

"I would have liked to have seen that."

"If you happened to be anywhere on the Southside of Atlanta that night you would have."

"I think everybody else down there saw it. Our switchboard was flooded with calls, even before the explosion."

"We must come up with some plausible explanation for the media."

"So far, we've been stonewalling it, but we can't get by with this very long. I think we should turn it over to Project Bluebook at Wright Patterson."

"If we do, we can't tell them what we know. They wouldn't touch it."

"We won't tell them. They form their own conclusions about strange happenings anyway, regardless of the facts. The media won't believe them but that is nothing new. They have told so many lies that they have lost all credibility. At least the monkey will be off our back."

"Good thinking. We will refer all questions to them."

"I really would have liked to have been there. Too bad I am tied to this desk now. I miss the combat."

* * *

Nothing else was ever reported to the media and in time the incident was forgotten. Of course the crowds dwindled to a small trickle that could be handled by Dolly and Joe. Everybody was happy except the media.

The first year's operation generated a fifty-cent dividend on five hundred thousand shares of common stock. The issue never went public.

CHAPTER EIGHT

Carl would take off from his duties on the golf course frequently to go on buying trips to New England and South Georgia and Northern Florida. A large van would follow to pick up the purchases. By Carl's eagerness to make these trips, some ulterior motive was suspected by all but Effie Lou, always the last to find out.

Sometimes on short trips, Phillip Morse would accompany Carl, since he was an auctioneer and familiar with the primitive artifacts found in the South. On these trips, Carl would behave himself. That is, until he found out Phillip was also of like mind, with roving eyes and hands. They made quite a pair, trying to outrun the following van to certain cities. Since this activity interfered with Philip's duties as auctioneer, a fill-in was hired to work when the scoundrels were spreading joy along the trails in search of merchandise and other things not of a business nature.

About this time interest was picking up in old advertising signs and other related paraphernalia. Naturally this would take them to out of the way places with abandoned stores that did not survive the last depression. After lengthy inquiries to determine the legal owners of these structures and finding they had years ago moved to Atlanta and other large population centers to seek new fortunes, they would proceed to enter and clean the premises. On one such occasion, they discovered an old vintage slot machine. They considered this a prize well worth the risk in taking, knowing full well there was a possession law in Georgia which prohibited even owning any gambling device for any reason whatsoever.

When they were on these kinds of trips, the van did not follow. Their gleanings were put in the back of the station wagon in which they traveled. Due to the panoramic exposure the wagon's windows offered to all viewers, they considered it prudent to allow the slot machine to accompany them into the motel room where they were spending the night. Well, rather shall we say adjoining rooms because of the other activities they enjoyed required a certain amount of privacy? The preparations for the evening's activities required a bucket of ice, glasses and chasers. And sometimes a few goodies to munch while waiting for the mood. With the addition of the slot machine as a participant, the primary mood was deferred to the age-old urge of the majority to hazard the coin of the realm. On the insistence of the ladies, Carl was required to go to the motel office and buy a few rolls of quarters. The device seemed to be in fine working order and the jackpot was full of old liberty head quarters, a prize in itself, with great collector value. There were no keys found and so the only way to get the coins short of any physical damage was to play them out. What did the greedy ones not know was the fact that the former owner of the device had installed a gimmick on one of the wheels that made it impossible to hit the jackpot. The result of this was many trips to the office for more quarters. The fifth trip gained the attention of the clerk and he assumed the role of Peeping Tom to satisfy his curiosity. Looking through the half closed blinds, he sees four persons, half female and half male and all half naked. They were drinking whiskey and playing a slot machine! Now being a deacon in the New Elim Primitive Baptist Church at the Hooterville Crossroads, he could allow this kind of carryings on to happen where he had some say. He calls the local sheriff. "Lordy, Lordy, Gamblers! Fornicators! Drunkards!"

"What in the world! Calm down! Compose yourself! Try to tell me what's going on! I won't be able to help if you don't get control. First tell me your name."

"I am Ephriam Jebediah Tompkins. I am the night clerk at the Lonesome Pines Motel out on US 84 West. I have rented two rooms to the Devil's own spawn from Fulton County."

"What terrible sin have they committed?"

"They are running around one of the rooms half naked and drinking whiskey!"

"And how do you know this?"

"Er, I peeked in the window."

"I can arrest you as a Peeping Tom. What they do in the privacy of their own rented room is nobody's business but their own, if they are not disturbing anyone else. Why did you get so nosy?"

"One of them kept coming to the office wanting rolls of quarters and I got curious."

"Now you've got me curious. What else did you find while you were snooping?"

"Sheriff, they've got an old slot machine in there and are playing the fool out of it. Whooping and hollering every time it spits out a few coins!"

"Now by God! That's serious! Ain't nobody going to have any slot machines in my county! I'll be out there in ten minutes! Stay away from them. They sound desperate and dangerous. Ain't no telling what kind of weapons they have."

The sheriff calls all his off-duty deputies and tells them to meet him at The Lonesome Pines Motel out on US 84 West and bring the drug sniffing dog and all the heavy artillery they have.

Before twenty minutes had elapsed, The Lonesome Pines Motel out on US 84 West was surrounded by the county's finest armed to the teeth. The sheriff parked behind the station wagon in front of room number six and got out his bullhorn.

"Attention you people in room six. This is the sheriff of this here county and I have you surrounded. Come out with your hands in the air. Do not bring your weapons. Come out one at a time. Do not make any sudden moves. You will be shot if you do. You have one minute to obey. If you do not come out in one minute we will start shooting!"

"Oh my God! Carl, did you hear that? What's going on?"

"There's got to be a mix-up. I'll go out and see what's happening."

"Don't shoot! Don't shoot! We have no weapons! A mistake has been made! You've got the wrong room, I guess."

"Keep your hands in the air! Are you the only one in there?"

"No, I have a friend traveling with me and there are two local ladies with us."

"Tell them to come right now!"

"Phillip, you and the ladies come on out. Everything's all right, but put your hands up."

Phillip comes clad in his drawers only. The sheriff asks, "Where are the ladies?"

"They are putting on their clothes. Please give them a few more minutes. They are locals and would be really embarrassed being seen the way they are."

"I understand, we'll give them a few minutes more. In the meantime, you two keep your hands up!"

"Sheriff, I don't know what brought this on. We are successful businessmen from Atlanta on a buying trip and stopped in your town for a little fun and games. This is not a dry county and our whiskey is store bought. The ladies are single and over twenty-one. Now what's the problem?"

"Mister, you are in a mess of trouble. I hear you have a slot machine in that there motel room and you all were playing the hell out of it."

"We were only trying to get the old coins out of it without tearing it up. Maybe we might have got a little carried away in our enthusiasm, but we are the only ones checked in here so we couldn't be disturbing anyone."

"All right, all you deputies go home. I can handle this myself from here on out. Ephriam, you get back in your office and don't come back out until we all leave."

"Sheriff, how about us going back into the room so we can discuss this in more pleasing surroundings?"

"That sounds like a good idea. You got any of that booze left? All this excitement has left me dry."

"We got plenty. And I need more than one after the scare you gave me."

"Don't get too relaxed. You ain't out of the woods yet."

"I am confident we as intelligent adults can come to some mutually beneficial agreement."

"Is that some fancy way of offering me a bribe?"

"Heavens no! That would be illegal."

"What do you think that slot machine is?"

"If an item does not legally exist, how can anyone possess it?"

"In the eyes of the law, you can't."

"Are you not the law?"

"What are you getting at?"

"Well, if it don't exist and I can't possess it and it has no protection under the law, it is at the mercy of whomever comes upon it. And you have just come upon it."

"I think I understand. It must have been in this room when you rented it."

"It could have been. I have no control over something I can't legally own."

"Of course you understand I must confiscate it. I could be accused with malfeasance of office if I did not."

"What about my quarters?"

"Don't push your luck."

"Sheriff, you need a refill."

"You ladies stop hiding in the bathroom. I want to see you."

"Oh sheriff, we're so mortified. These kind gentlemen were only trying to help us escape boredom for a short while."

"Don't I know you two?"

"Not personally, but if you ever did crossing guard duty at the grammar school, you probably saw us. We both teach there."

"Well, I do declare! A couple of pretty school marms."

"Oh sheriff, how carry on!"

"Well it's a fact. You are a couple of the prettiest things I popped my eyes on in a month of Sundays."

"You're not so bad yourself, to be such a fierce lawman. Do we really have to stop playing the slot machine now? We need to try to get our money back."

"I reckon you can play as long as the whiskey holds out."

"Phillip! Run over to the liquor store before it closes and stock up. Hurry!"

"Carl, remember I've got to get back to run the auction Monday."

"We'll make it. These girls have to teach school Monday also. We got all day tomorrow and Sunday to get those quarters."

"They wanted us to teach Sunday school before church Sunday, but if we call in, they can get substitutes. Sheriff, I'm glad you didn't let Ephriam see us. We go to his church."

"That old fossil is a dried up old prune. I bet he never smiled once in his whole life. If he is working for the Lord, he should be fired."

"I will mention him in my prayers."

"You are a good woman, Nellie. The church could use more like you."

"Let's not go overboard. We must think of the children."

"Now back to the business at hand. We've got to get those quarters out."

"Lilly, now don't you get carried away. We might not ever hit the jackpot. In my dealings with all kind of characters I run across in my job, I have seen some so low that they would rig machines so they could never hit."

"Do you mean to tell me that we might have been wasting our time, not to mention the money we dumped in?"

"Don't look at it that way. Think of all the fun you all had."

"Tee hee, we did, didn't we?"

"We could smash into it and get the quarters. Sheriff, do you have a hammer or an ax in your car?"

"Oh no! This device is the property of the county and it is my duty to see it remains intact until the judge makes final disposition of it."

"What difference does it make? It will probably be destroyed anyway."

"Maybe and maybe not. The judge totes a lot of keys. And he might to be able to open it."

"What in the world would he be doing with a lot of slot machine keys?"

"A judge's powers are broad and it is not healthy to question them."

"Ignore that last stupid question and let's take another drink."

All in unison; "AMEN"

"Phillip, I heard you mention something about running an auction. Tell me about it while I dig out some ice."

"Sure sheriff, I work for Carl at an auction he owns on the southwest side of Atlanta."

"So Carl, you own an auction. You must do well at it."

"It does pretty good. I have other interests too."

"Oh? Like what?"

"Well I run a truck repair garage specializing in big heavy rigs. I've got my finger in a diner at the auction and now have an interest in an antique shop in Jonesboro."

I reckon that town was named after you."

No, that's a coincidence. The town was there long before I was born."

Hmm, Jonesboro, I recall something on the news a year or so back about a UFO over an antique shop outside Jonesboro. Any connection?"

"Yes, it was a shock to all of us. It damaged the shop's roof when it exploded."

"Was it really a UFO?"

"We can't really say. The authorities have kept pretty quiet about the whole thing."

"Yeah, I know how that can be. I received reports of one over Hooterville some years back and when I investigated, I saw something strange. When I reported it to Moody at Valdosta, they said they would look into it. I never heard anymore about it."

Nellie says; "I was taken to ride in one once."

"Why Nellie! You never told me anything about that."

"Would you have believed me, Lilly?"

"No and I don't now. I think you have had too much of that joy juice."

"Well, it's true I don't think about it until I've had a few. But that doesn't mean that it didn't happen."

"Where did they take your pretty body?"

"I guess it was to Heaven, sheriff. I have never had such an uplifting experience in my life. Even when we have an all day singing and dinner on the grounds at The New Elim Primitive Baptist Church at the Hooterville Crossroads. And I am here to tell you that if you ain't never been there, you sure need to go to one of them one time. You ain't never heard such beeutyful music or et such great vittles in all yore borned days!"

"Lilly! Take that drink away from her! She's reevertin'."

"Aw, sheriff, I'm all right. It's just when I start thinking about some things, I get goose pimples just about all over my pretty body."

"I know the feeling, but it's been a while. I ain't no spring chicken anymore. Just a tough old rooster with a lot of memories."

Lilly says; "Nellie, you wouldn't know the difference in an uplifting experience and a good orgasm."

"Tee, hee, is there any difference?"

"If you don't know, then you haven't had either one or the other.

"Girls! Girls! Y'all quit it y'hear. We ain't gonna have no contest tonight. Besides we don't have enough people to have a good singing much less enough to eat. And we're short one lady for anything else."

"Phillip, you look a little green around the gills. Why don't you go into the other room and rest your eyes a bit?"

"It has been a long day, but I'm afraid I'll miss out on something."

"Miss out on what? All we gonna do is drink a little and play the slot machine. All good clean fun."

"Sugar, we'll wake you up if anything happens."

"OK Nellie, you come and wake me up for anything. And I mean just anything at all."

"Trust me, I certainly will."

"I think we all know each other well enough now to be on a first name basis and skip the formalities. My name is Joe Billy Buford The Third, but y'all can just call me Joe Billy like all my friends do."

"Why thank you Joe Billy, it is a distinct pleasure to make your acquaintance. I have always held our protectors of the peace in the highest esteem."

"Well, we get misjudged by a lot of people. Especially when we try to enforce unpopular laws. I try to tell them I don't make them and they should try not to break them. A lot of times they plead ignorance. This usually works the first time with me because it's probably true, but not the second time."

"Joe Billy, you are truly a fine southern gentleman and I respect your fine opinion. Now what do you think we really ought to do about this slot machine?"

"Carl, I wouldn't mind if you took it back to Atlanta with you, but that nosy Ephriam knows I seen it and he is as big a gossip as he is a religious fanatic. Before Monday morning the whole damn county will know about it and I sho' better have it in my jail come the first of the week or I will be in big trouble."

"Do you think there is any way we can shut him up?"

"Just let me go over to the office and spend a few hours with him and I'll guarantee he'll never open his mouth to anyone about this. He might even resign as deacon."

"Lilly, I can't allow you to do this. You will not compromise yourself for me to have this slot machine, Joe Billy, let's put it in your trunk right now and forget about it."

"Not yet. I'm gonna go across the street and see if the liquor store has any quarters. You have got me wanting to get at those old quarters as bad as you. I'd hate to see the judge wind up with them."

“Wouldn’t he turn them in to the county treasury?”

“He ain’t no fool!”

“Let’s not throw away any more money trying to hit the jackpot. We have got all the old money out of the tube and all that’s left is in the jackpot and like you say, it is probably rigged so it won’t hit.”

“Yeah, you’re right. Hey, I know what we can do. Let me get a hammer out of the car and we can smash the glass!”

Joe Billy brings the hammer in and starts to beat on the glass. He manages to put a few cracks in it, but it still holds together. It is the kind that has chicken wire imbedded in it.

“Lemme see if I can find some wire cutters. Be back in a few”

“Joe Billy, this is not working. Let’s give up.”

“The hell I will! This thing has got me all riled up and I ain’t gonna let some stupid machine get the best of me! I’m gonna get those quarters out of there if I have to rip it to pieces!”

“What about the judge?”

“To hell with the judge! To hell with Ephriam! I ain’t gonna let some mealy mouthed, bible totin’ fool intimidate me. And as far as the judge is concerned, I’ll tell him it fell out of my trunk when I hit that bumpy railroad crossing between here and town while traveling seventy miles an hour. He will probably be too drunk to tell if I’m lying.”

“You know more about that than I do. Will you want any of the quarters?”

“Naw, I’m having too much fun to worry about that. Besides I wouldn’t know what to do with them. Are they worth a lot of money?”

“It will take an expert to determine that.”

“Do you know one that you can trust?”

“I think so.”

“All I ask is if they are worth a lot of money, think about your old buddy.”

“Rest assured, I shall.”

Three trips were necessary to carry all the pieces to the patrol car. They were now reduced to drinking only to entertain each other. Well, not entirely, but we will not get into that.

“Nellie, we got sidetracked. I want to hear more about your trip.”

“What trip, honey?”

"The one in the UFO."

"Oh, that one. What do you want to know?"

"Everything."

"Well, I was born in Albany back in 1932."

"No Nellie, I mean everything about your trip and events leading up to it."

"What trip?"

"The one in the UFO."

"Oh, that one. I had just left the school and was driving out to check on granny out at the farm. She lives on the old home place fifteen miles out of town. You know the dirt road that turns off the highway and goes by the springs? I used to have a lot of fun down at that old spring when I was a teenager and me and my date would go there to park and talk. But I wasn't born out there; my mother went to Albany to have me. That was in 1932. I have noticed lately that nobody keeps up the spring anymore and it's all growed up and filled with cattails now. I hate that. I loved that old spring."

"Yes, yes, go on."

"Don't be so pushy, I have to recollect. Oh yes, I remember I was in my Volkswagen. That's because it is my only mode of transportation."

"We know that, Nellie."

"I really want a larger car, but I'm afraid I can't afford the extra gas. Do you know how many small cars you see in the scrap yards nowadays? It's because the drivers of the larger cars don't respect them. I get scared sometimes driving mine. But I'm afraid I can't afford the extra gas. I have to help my granny out financially. My mother died back in '52 and I'm the only one left in the family. Anyway I guess it was lucky that I was in a little car when it happened. Because I don't think I could have pushed a larger one."

"Why did you have to push it? Did it break down?"

"You can't say it broke down. It sort of stopped running. It was like you turned off the switch. I had plenty of gas. I had just filled up after I left the school. You know that station Jim Bob runs out on 84? That's where I filled up. I don't like to stop there because he always tries to seduce me, but it was on the way to granny's and I was in a hurry. It happened where the railroad crosses right before you get to the springs. The radio stopped working too. I was listening to that country station out of Thomasville. It stopped right in the middle of one of Hank Williams' songs. Just right after he went to the wedding. I always wondered what his girl's name was. Do any of you know?"

"No Nellie, please continue."

"When the radio stopped playing, I heard the train. I always play the radio real loud because it sounds better that way. Don't y'all think so?"

"I like it loud when they play fast songs like 'Down Yonder' and 'Rocky Top', but not on slow belly-rubbing music."

"Lilly please let her talk."

"I was only stating my preferences. Then what happened?"

"When?"

"When you heard the train."

"Oh. I always thought springs were found in a depression of the land, but here it must be on a rise because there is a long grade in the tracks coming up to the crossing. That old steam engine was really huffing and puffing. It must have been pulling two miles of loaded cars. It was coming slow enough for me to push my car off the track before we were both squashed. It was so close; it blew hot steam up my dress and the back of my legs looked like I had been standing before a hot fireplace warming my backside. Lilly, I know you have done this when you lived in that old drafty farmhouse when you were a kid."

"Many times."

"It took a half hour for the train to clear the crossing. It's a good thing that some rabbit farmer was not taking a load to the market. His truck might have been overloaded by the time the train passed. You know how prolific those little critters are."

"Nellie, you are cursed with female deviation."

"I am only trying to relate the experience."

"Continue relating."

"I think that whatever was going to happen was waiting for the train to pass because as soon as it passed, I started to feel giddy. You know sort of light headed. Sort like I feel now. But I wasn't drinking then."

"It might behoove us to curtail it now to maintain an intelligent narrative."

"Curtail what?"

"Ignore that last suggestion and continue."

"I'm trying to cooperate, don't get nasty."

"I apologize. Go on."

"As I was saying, after the train passed by, I guess I passed out or something. I don't remember what happened next. The next thing I remember I was in a small circular room that looked like its walls were made of something like mother of pearl. It glowed in iridescent pastel colors. It reminded me of the inside of a seashell I once found on a deserted beach on an abandoned island off the coast near Brunswick. We joy riding in a speedboat and happened upon this island across the channel from St. Simons. It was a strange place with a lot of deserted summer mansions scattered around. We saw no one so we decided to camp out on the beach. This was when I found the shell."

"What did this have to do with the UFO?"

"Nothing really. I was just describing the color of the interior."

"Did you notice anything else on the walls?"

"If you will stop interrupting I will try to remember, Joe Billy."

"I'm sorry, but you have really got me interested."

"Oh yes, there were bench seats against the wall on about half of the circumference of the room. On the other half was located a counter about waist high. It was sort of like the new kitchen I had installed in the farmhouse when I had the kitchen rebuilt about eight years ago. Or maybe it was seven years ago. Let's see it's now 1964. I remember it was before I bought the little Volkswagen. It's a 1958 model and I think I bought it about a year after we did the kitchen. Or maybe it was more like two years."

"Carl, pour me another drink and make it stiff. I think I need it."

"OK Joe Billy, I know damn well I do."

"Do what?"

"Loan me your pistol, Joe Billy."

"Carl, can't you take a joke? I was only kidding. Go ahead, Nellie."

"Anyway, they didn't look exactly like granny's counter but you get the idea, I hope. Granny's back splashboard was only about five inches high and here is where the difference was. The backboard in this room was I know, at least two feet high. And it was loaded with all kind of pretty flashing lights and levers and switches and dials.

You remember how the old theater marquees had all those pretty lights chasing each other around? Well, this was not like that. There was no chasing pattern. It was more random. But it was just as pretty."

"Where were you when you were noticing all this?"

"All what?"

Moans and groans were heard clear across the parking lot.

"Let's take a break and go down to the barbecue shack across from the jail and fill up on some ribs. They got the best in South Georgia."

"The best what?"

"Shut up and go get in the station wagon."

While Nellie waited in the wagon, Carl asks; "Joe Billy, is this story worth the agony we are being put through? Besides, her story has got some holes in it."

"Like what?"

"You know she said her car stopped like from some electrical interference? Why didn't the train stop also? It uses electricity too."

"She's got you there, Carl. That old freight train she was talking about is the last steam train running in the whole yew ess of ay!"

"Well, I'll be damned! Maybe it's the truth after all. But how in the hell are we going to listen to her and still keep our sanity?"

"I'll think of something. Maybe if we fill her up on ribs and some coffee, it might plug some of those holes in her head."

"Sounds you're calling this girl an airhead."

"No, she has got a bad case of attentus nondirectus."

"What in the hell is that?"

"Not being capable of controlling the direction of her attention."

"And coffee and ribs might help the problem?"

"It sho' as hell can't hurt. The worst it can do is put her to sleep and that won't be bad at all."

"Yeah, at least then her mouth will be shut."

"Lilly, go wake up Phillip and tell him let's go eat."

Fifteen minutes passes with Nellie sitting in the station wagon and Lilly still in Phillip's room.

"Lilly! What in the hell are y'all doing in there? We are getting mo' hungry by the minute and Lawd only knows what Nellie is doing sittin' all by herself out in the wagon. Y'all git yore cans out here and let's go!"

"Oh, I'm so sorry, Joe Billy, but I just plum got forgot what I went in there for and decided to entertain Phillip while I tried to remember. Then I got so involved that I plum forgot that I was trying to remember something."

"Oh Lordy! We are in the midst of an epidemic!"

"If we can't fight it, maybe we can join it if we take another drink."

"Fight what?"

"Joe Billy, get hold of yourself and try to fight this evil thing off."

"Everybody get in the wagon right now! We don't have a minute to lose! Hurry!"

"What in the world kept you so long? I been sitting out here all by myself for what seemed like hours. I thought I started seeing strange lights in the sky, but then I realized that was reflections in the windshield of cars passing by out on US Highway 84 West. I don't why there is so much traffic out there tonight. Joe Billy, is there something going on somewhere down the road from here?"

"Not that I know of, maybe somebody saw another one of them flying saucer things."

"I went for a ride in one once."

"We know, we know, Nellie. Carl, hurry up and get us to that Rib Shack. Things are getting worse."

"I wish you would look at all the cars! There's not a place to park. Joe Billy, is there some other place we can go?"

"Just drive around to the back past that deliveries only sign. We can go in the back door. Which might be better. I ought not be seen here. I'm s'posed to be on duty. Just park over there by that dumpster. Watch out for them cats. And kick 'em out of the way when you open the doors. They'll try to get in the car. I parked back here one night and due to my condition, my reflexes weren't too good and before I knew it, I bet twenty jumped in. The county had to pay for a complete upholstery job. Even a new headliner. These cats are wild and have the sharpest claws you ever seen. Lemme out first. I see a big stick over there and maybe I can fight 'em off."

"I like cats. We used to have a bunch out in the barn to keep the mice out of the dried corn. On a farm you store dried corn in the barn and the rats love it. I remember before granny got the cats, I went out to the barn for something, I can't remember what I went out there for, but I saw a million rats. I ran back to the house screaming. Granny got out her old double-barreled shotgun and ran out there blasting away at those varmints. She killed maybe four rats but she destroyed that year's seed corn. The next spring we had to go in to feed store to buy more seed corn."

"Joe Billy, hurry up with that stick! It's getting bad in here again!"

"I think it's safe to come out now, but high tail it to the back door."

"Oh Lordy! They got the damn door locked!"

"Beat on it!"

The cook opens the door. "What in the hell are y'all doing out there? Don't you know we got a front door? I have to keep this one locked since I found out some of the help was stealing meat and hiding it in the dumpster. That's when all them damn cats showed up and we can't get rid of them. Why, hello sheriff, I didn't see you out there. Y'all come on in. I just took a bunch of racks off the pit and made a new pot of coffee. And y'all look like you need some."

"That's a gross understatement."

"What is?"

"Oh no! It's done spread over here!"

"I don't know what your problem is but these ribs and coffee might help."

"I think that maybe you might need to eat some too."

"I never eat my own cooking. I go down to the City Cafe when I get hungry."

"From what I hear, I think that's a mistake."

CHAPTER NINE

The group takes a large table in the back of the room where some people just got up. Lilly says, "This is the messiest table I have ever seen! Just look at this tablecloth. It'll never come clean. If I was the manager, I'd make them pay for it. And look at those kid's clothes. And look at their trousers. They've wiped their hands all over them. And the daddy's not much better. Just look at his beard! It's completely red with sauce. It's even on his nose! If I wasn't so hungry, I'd just walk right out of here! That busboy had better come over here and clean up this mess so we can sit down. I'm scared to get close to this mess."

Joe Billy is as hungry as the rest so he takes matters in his own hands. He grabs all four corners of the tablecloth and gathers it up in a bundle.

"Carl, open thet damn window back there. I'll show you people how to bus a table!"

Carl opens the window just in time before the contents of the cloth crashes into it. Within seconds after it hits the ground, the sounds of a most horrible catfight fills the room. Before Carl has a chance to close the window, three large cats clear it and start jumping from table to table creating chaos in their wake. Before they are chased out the front door, all the customers looked like the ones that had vacated our group's table.

Nellie grins and asks; "Are we having fun yet?"

The manager comes out of his office when he hears the commotion. "Hey Joe Billy! I didn't realize we were honored with your presence this fine evening. Did you see what happened out here?"

"Not really, I believe those cats came in the front door when that last group left that was sitting at this table we took."

"I must commend the busboy for cleaning this table so promptly for our distinguished guests. He's certainly going to have his hands full with the rest of the room. It looks like everybody left at the same time."

Carl volunteers; "There must be some late night function going on down the road. We saw a lot of cars heading out when we drove in."

"Which way did you come from?"

"From out at The Lonesome Pines Motel out on US Highway 84 West. Let me introduce myself. I'm Carl Jones and this is Phillip Morse and we're from Atlanta down on a business trip. And these ladies are Nellie and Lilly, local schoolteachers helping us in our research. We are trying to put together a book on South Georgia primitive artifacts and we felt that the ladies might be of some help."

"And have they?"

"In more ways than you can imagine."

"Phillip Morse, hmm, do I know you? Your name sounds awful familiar. Are you some kind of celebrity?"

"I wish I were. It sure is funny though; you are not the first to think they know me. Just about everybody I meet asks the same questions."

"I know damn well I heard that name just the other day. I think it was when I was filling in for the cashier."

"I'm sorry, but I can't help you."

"Maybe it'll come to me later."

"If it does, please let me know. I would like to meet the gentleman. Here's my card, call me collect."

"I certainly will. Now I've got to get back. It was nice meeting all of you."

"He sure is a nice man."

"Nellie, every man you meet is a 'nice man'."

"Now Lilly, that's not true. I've met some bad ones."

"Name one."

"One of them in the flying saucer."

"How many was in there?"

"How many what?"

"Hurry up with those ribs!"

"Here you go sheriff, I hope y'all enjoy them. Just holler if you need any more. Theys plenty more where they came from."

"Thank you, kind sir. Rest assured we'll let you know if the need arises."

"Lilly, you're drooling all down the front of your blouse."

"Lawdy, I jest can't hep it! These are just about the bestest things I ever popped a lip on."

"Bring on more coffee! We got another reevertin'. Lilly you are a fine one to talk about how messy those other people was."

"Carl, I have seen the light! Now I understand how they got so carried away and lost all their ettyket."

"Jedge no one lest ye be jedged."

"AMEN" In unison.

"We seem to have fought off the attack of the epidemic, but now we suffer from reevertin'."

"Better this than that."

"Maybe when we finish off these fine vittles, we can resume our questionin' uv Nellie. That is if one of us can translate."

"Me being the High Sheriff, and full to the brim of pig, I feel quite capable and qualified to have the honor."

"What honor?"

"Phillip, now you need another rack of ribs."

"No, I don't think so. I was just thinking about those poor cats. Don't y'all have a local chapter of the S.P.C.A.?"

"Naw, the closest one is over in Albany and I don't think they would come way out here just for a few wild cats. They probably have their hands full with the problem over there."

"You mean they have a Rib Shack there too?"

"Not like this one, but they do have plenty of restaurants and diners."

"I have an idea. How about dragging an old ham behind the station wagon and lead them out to the farm? Y'all need to meet granny anyway."

"Yes. we feel that we already know her, Nellie."

"It will take more than one ham to survive the trip way out there down a dirt road. A whole hog might. I bet that nice manager would spring for one if he thought it would rid him of those cats. Ain't no telling how much money he lost when all those people stampeded outta here awhile ago."

"Nellie, I think you are cured! That's a great idea."

"Cured of what? I ain't been sick."

"And then again, maybe not. Forget it, Nellie."

The manager was more than willing to go along with the idea. He was glad to donate the pig that had been on the spit for the past ten hours. Everybody fought his or her way into the station wagon and the cook and the manager tied the pig to the rear bumper with a thirty-foot rope. Carl maneuvered the wagon around and pointed it up the driveway. He then waited until the aroma had attracted all the cats to the pig and they had started fighting among themselves. Then he slowly started up the driveway.

Lilly screamed; "It's working, it's working! They're following. Some are even riding the pig. This is a sight to see. Now we are having fun!"

The station wagon's air conditioning didn't work too good with this many people in it so all the windows were rolled down. The radio was blaring out some country music for all to hear. Both inside and outside the wagon. This was a spectacle, which this sleepy town had never in all its existence experienced. The vehicle was creeping down the road so as not to lose any of the felines and do too much damage to the pig. Before they got to the turn off on to the dirt road, traffic was backed up for miles because this was a two lane road with plenty of yellow lines due to the curves. The impatient drivers raised a cacophony of discordant music with their horns. This attracted more attention, if possible, and others standing on their porches thought it was a great parade to somewhere and they didn't want to miss out. So they joined in. When the entourage got to the turn off, the impatient drivers kept going straight to their various destinations. But not the newly added ones. Some effectiveness was lost, but the enthusiasm of the newcomers made up for it. They kept blowing their horns and all rolled down the windows and blasted away with the same radio station. The ones with emergency blinkers had them blinking. When the lead car passed the springs and kept going, the cats nor any of the vehicles followed it.

Now it was Nellie who screamed; "Something has happened to our cats! They're not back there. Not even the ones that were riding the pig. Carl, turn around and let's see what happened."

"I've got to find a place to turn around."

"There's a small track leading into a watermelon field about a quarter mile up on the left."

Joe Billy says to Carl. "Just drive into the field and make a circle. Don't try backing up. It's too dark and the side ditches are pretty deep."

Quite a few watermelons were trashed and the pig was lost during the circumnavigation of the field. The rope could stand no more. We might never know what the farmer thought the next morning when he came out to inspect his crop.

They could go no farther than the springs. The road was blocked with vacant cars and pickup trucks. The larger of the springs was close to two hundred feet in diameter. And sitting on the bank of about half of its circumference were the multitude of cats, with their attention riveted on a point somewhere around the center of the spring. And behind all these cats were all the people with their attention riveted on the cats. And behind this group were our five friends with their attention riveted on both the cats and the people.

"Have all these cats and people lost their sanity or have we?"

"Maybe it was all that pork us and them cats et."

"Joe Billy, all these people didn't eat the pork. I think I'll go ask some of them what's going on."

"Be careful Carl, they might be dangerous. They ain't no tellin' what's come over 'em."

"Hey, Bro. What's happening?"

"Hey Dude! Gimme five! Where yo' comin' from?"

"We were in the lead car and when we saw that our group got sidetracked, we came back to check the scene."

"Well Dude, you see what we see. And we don't know from nothin'."

"We were trying to relocate these cats out to a farm up the road that has a rat problem. It seems that something around that spring is more interesting that a whole barbecued pig."

"Where do that pig stay now?"

"It's about a quarter mile up the road in a field full of ripe watermelons."

"Hey men! You understand what this white dude is sayin'? We done found our ticket to heaven. That is if we can eat up that pig and our share of watermelons before the man comes. Let's shag outta here!"

The world's record for the quarter mile was then broken by ten happy souls.

"All you did was create a big dust cloud. Lemme try."

"Excuse me sir, I'm the sheriff of this fine county and I am trying to determine exactly what is going on here. Is this some kind of convention of cats and fools?"

"Hi Sheriff, I have absolutely no idea. You know how a bunch of sheep will follow a goat? Well, I ain't the goat so I must be one of the sheep. Find the goat and you will find the answer."

"I personally know the goat and he don't know anymore than us sheep."

"I'm sorry I can't help you. Sir, how am I to going to get back to the main road? There's ten cars in front of me and at least one hundred behind me."

"Did you see that bunch of black dudes take off up the road a few minutes ago?"

"Yeah, why?"

"Were they parked in front of you?"

"Yeah, why?"

"Do you know about what time the farmers get into their fields every morning?"

"Yeah, about six thirty. Why?"

"Then you might get out around seven if you and the dudes are lucky."

"I'll be in deep shit if I don't get home before my wife. She says she plays bridge with a bunch of ladies and they play until midnight. She won't tell me where they play."

"Maybe you ought to go with her one time."

"I tried, but she will have no part of it."

"I know a lot of good lawyers."

"I won't need one if you can give me a ride. Your station wagon is not blocked."

"We can't get out either. That old bridge across the creek on past the farmhouse fell in last week and the only way out is back the way we came in. And we will probably be staying at the farmhouse. The grandmother of one of the ladies with us owns it. And we can't go inviting any strangers into somebody else's house."

"Write down some of those lawyer's names."

"Nellie, we're not going to find out anymore here tonight. Let's go on up to the farm and see if your granny can put us up for the night."

"What are you going to do, back all the way to the watermelon field?"

"I don't know what else we can do."

"I know a nice clearing over behind the spring where we can rest. I used to do it all the time over there."

"Do what? Oh hell, now I'm doing it. Ignore that last question."

"All I was talking about was resting a little."

"I realize that. Please forgive me. This has been a trying day. And it looks like it's not over yet. Show us that place and let's try to get a little rest. And whatever."

The crack of dawn awoke our little group and when they untangled their bodies and looked around, all the cars were gone. All the people were gone. And all the cats were gone.

"Carl, last night you wanted to know what got into those cats. I did too. But now I'm more curious about what happened after we went to sleep."

"I'm sure there's a rational explanation. Maybe all the people got together and found who was blocking who and they all backed out to the main highway. I know that sounds far fetched for that many to get together to do anything right, but it might be possible. Look what we did during the last Great War."

"OK, but what happened to the cats?"

"It'll take me a little longer to explain that."

"A little longer, my ass! I bet you can't do it in six months!"

"You're on."

"Now that the road is cleared and we can turn around in the drive into the springs, let's go out and see granny."

"That's a great idea, Nellie. Maybe if we hurry we might get there in time for breakfast."

"Joe Billy, do you ever think of anything except something to put in your stomach?"

"You know I do. I put up with hours of your rambling before I got the pig urge."

"You better behave yourself or I'll tell granny not to fix you anything."

"Aw Nellie, I was just foolin'."

"Carl, don't you back off into that spring or we'll never get outta here."

"Phillip, you stay outside and watch my rear. I think I can do it, but we better be safe. This is not the watermelon field. Speaking of that, I wonder how our track team made out last night?"

"We can stop there and see what happened."

When turning into the watermelon field, Carl says, "Isn't that the pickup they were riding in out there where we lost the pig?"

"It sure is! And look the bed is full of watermelons. But where is all our track team? They must have took off on foot and took the pig with them."

"No, I see a pile of bones over there where the rope broke."

"Well, I'll be damned! And look how shiny they are! They look like they've been polished."

"That's what ten good sets of teeth can do."

They turned around and headed towards the road when they saw the gate blocked by a farmer sitting on his 1938 Case Model R tractor with a shotgun across his lap.

"If y'all think you can sneak back out here and get your truck loaded with my prize watermelons, you got another think comin'. Now all of you climb out of that car slowly with your hands up. I done called the sheriff's office and they're trying to find him right now. We'll all just wait here for him."

"Well Zeke, yore wait is over! Here I is."

"Joe Billy! I see you done caught this bunch of thieves."

"No Zeke, you got it all wrong. We was on the way to Nellie's granny's farm when we saw this here truck out here in the middle of your watermelon patch and thought you had bought yourself a new pickup truck to haul some of your crop to the market up in Cordele."

"Well, I didn't buy me no new truck, but I shore got me one now!"

"If it ain't yours, who do it belong to?"

"By the time honored laws of forfeiture and possession it is now mine. Whose it was before now, I don't know or care."

"Before what?"

"You too, huh?"

"Shut up Joe Billy and let Zeke finish."

"I came out here at the crack of dawn to see if they were ready for the market and I seed this bunch of coons loadin' that there truck with my fine watermelons and I fired a couple of rounds amongst them.

Man! You shoulda seen 'em scatter. They took off runnin' in all directions 'cept towards me. They all cleared that back hog wire fence in a single leap. They could qualify for the Olympics."

"I bet that was a sight to behold."

"Not near as big a one as I seed about three o'clock this morning."

"What did you see then?"

"I just woke with the urge to relieve myself. My old prostate is acting up and I have to go about three times every night after I go to bed."

"There's a doctor over in Albany I think can help you. My uncle had that trouble and he went over there and that doctor did something to him. He walked around bowlegged for a week cussin' a blue streak but he finally got better and had no more trouble. Now he can piss over his tractor. Granny told me about it. Uncle was too embarrassed to say anything about it. I can find out the doctor's name if you want me to."

"Never mind. Sounds like the cure is worse than the ailment. Besides, I just step out the kitchen door. It's not like having to go all the way to the outhouse. I don't have the dysentery."

"For God's sake tell us what you saw!"

"I was gettin' to that. As I said, I was at the back door relievin' myself and you know like when you're doin' that, you look up at the stars. That seems to help. My house faces away from the direction of the springs, so my back door looks right at it. Well, that's a figure of speech cause my back door can't see anything. And if it could, it couldn't see all the way to the springs. They're a good two miles down the road."

"Nellie, is Zeke any kin to you?"

"I don't think so, why?"

"Never mind. Zeke, please continue."

"I will, if you are through talking for a while. You know some stars are bigger than others. And some planets seem bigger than the stars. But they don't get too big. This thing was bigger than any planet I ever seen. Relatively speaking, that is. Any fool knows that the closer something is to you, the bigger it seems to be. Like the moon looks bigger than Venus. But we know it's not."

"How close did it look like it was?"

"Judging by the clarity of the night sky, the sky was really clear. It was like I had read about how it is out in the desert out west. They say it looks like you can reach up and touch the stars. Taking that into consideration and observing the details of the construction, I would surmise that the distance from me did not exceed the approximate distance of the springs to my dwelling."

"Talk about reevertin'."

Lilly breaks in; "Excuse me, Zeke, but I must ask the boys something."Y'all have mentioned 'reevertin' a number of times in the last sixteen hours and I have absolutely no idea just what in the hell you are talking about. I want to know!"

Carl explains, "The way I understand it is when you have a lot of book learning mixed up with a lot of local dialect, you need to keep them separated according to what type of company you are in. Take one of them high-class new television announcers on a national network. He has to get years of schooling to talk like that. You would think he had did it all his life. But get him with his hair down and having a good time and drinking among some of his old buddies and he will reevert."

"Seems like Zeke was doin' a little reeverse reevertin'. Zeke, where did you get yore book larnin'?"

"Joe Billy, I hold a doctorate in physics from the Massachusetts Institute of Technology. It was my desire to go into nuclear research."

"Oh dear! What in the world happened?"

"Nellie, things never work out like you plan them."

"How well I know it. I myself had theatrical aspirations. But that's another story. Let's try to finish at least one before starting any more."

"AMEN." (Unison.)

"After receiving my degree, I came home for a vacation before pursuing my career. While I was lying up in the bed sleeping, my poor old paw was out in the field stump pulling. It was on this very tractor I am now sitting upon that did him in. He had it down in the granny gear and had it hooked to a particularly stubborn stump and when he let out the clutch it reared up like a wild horse and came all the way over on top of him. He didn't have a chance. I have since installed a mercury switch in the ignition circuit so when the tractor exceeds a forty-five degree angle, it will cut off."

"That's sheer genius!"

"Not exactly. There was a bug. When the switch cut the ignition, the front wheels headed back for the ground and in its descent, the engine ran backward. When the switch closed again, all hell broke loose. Engines are not designed to run backwards. On the normal exhaust stroke the piston is supposed to be going up to force the burnt gases out. It is now going down, sucking unburned fuel from the exhaust manifold, which now has become a temporary intake manifold, and into the cylinder to be compressed by the power stroke which has also reversed. The firing of the spark plug now ignites this mixture. After ignition, the piston is forced down on a temporary power stroke. Somewhere around bottom dead center, the intake valve opens which now has become an exhaust valve and the burnt mixture is forced into the intake manifold which now becomes a temporary exhaust manifold, but instead of leading to a muffler, it now heads to the fuel rich carburetor that promptly ignites with a spectacular display. This explosion is now diverted to the oil bath air filter that also ignites. The net result of this episode is a melted carburetor and a destroyed air filter. Needless to say you only try this once. After I repaired the tractor and still liking the idea of the mercury switch I rewired the circuit. I fed the ignition through a fuse that was shorted to ground by the tilt switch. This would blow the fuse and the engine then could not start while it was running backward."

"When this happened, did you suffer any injuries?"

"Nothing that a bar of lye soap did not repair. Anyway, due to the untimely death of my father, I was forced to forego my plans to keep maw from losing the farm to the bank. It might have been for the best. I am quite content now after being here in the twilight of my years. And I always have my watermelons and pigs and cows for solace."

"Er, I believe you were describing a bright light you saw early this morning?"

"Oh yes, I am sorry I strayed, but it was not my fault. Somebody asked a question that required an answer in detail."

"But this is so interesting."

"Nellie, everything in life is interesting, but we don't live long enough to get exposed to everything that happens. There's a lot going on we are going to miss."

"I know, I know, and it's a shame. Do go on, Zeke."

"When I first saw it, it wasn't that big or that low. It seemed to come in at a forty-five degree angle from the south. At first sight, I would compare it to Venus at full quarter and it progressively got larger as it descended until it stopped at what I think was the vicinity of the springs. It hovered there for about ten minutes beaming a light like a spotlight on a police car. You know, Joe Billy, like the one on yours. This beam came right of the center of the underside and traveled back and forth in a close semi-circle arc over the spring. Then it went back as it came. The last I saw of it, it looked like any other star."

"Carl, the bet's off about the cats."

"What cats?"

"Joe Billy, take Zeke off to the side and tell him about the cats. I don't want to hear anymore about anything else today. I'm tempted to check out of the motel and high tail it back to Atlanta where normal people live."

"You sayin' we ain't normal?"

"Well, maybe just different."

"We don't go flyin' around in high powered jets blowin' UFOs out of the sky."

"I'll tell you what the Air Force thinks about you people down here. They think y'all are so backward, they don't pay any attention when you call in and report something strange."

"I bet they do when I tell them about the cats!"

"You do and they'll take you away to the funny farm!"

"You're probably right. I wouldn't believe it me if you told me. Maybe we better keep our mouth shut. Let some of the fools that followed us last night report it."

"You think they saw something?"

"If they saw anything at all, that was more than we saw. We were all asleep."

Nellie says; "I wasn't"

"Oh no! I know damn well I'm going back to Atlanta now. I'm not going to live long enough to question you anymore."

"I know what we can do. I'll get together with Zeke and we will put what we saw on paper and maybe publish it. Maybe we can interview some of the people that followed us last night too."

"Let me know when you finish it. I might want to publish it. If I live long enough to see y'all finish writing it."

"Let's go see granny."

CHAPTER TEN

By the time they got to the farm, granny was already out in the back yard slopping the hogs. When she saw this strange station wagon from way up in Atlanta, Georgia, pulling up in her front yard, she ran back in the house and came out the front door with her rat killin' shotgun.

"Now y'all hold it right there! Stay in that new fangled awtymobeel! I knowed where y'all come from 'cause I seen that Fulton County tag. And I know how to read. I don't know nobody from that far up north and you ain't got no business out here botherin' a pore old woman who don't ask nothin' from any crooked politicians from up at the state capytul! Who sent you down here that fool governor, Eugene Talmadge? And what in the hell do you want? You better have a good excuse 'cause if you don't, I'm gonna start blastin' with this here home deefender!"

"Granny, this is Nellie. Put that damn shotgun down before you hurt somebody. These here people are all friends of mine I brought out to visit a spell. We thought we might have a little breakfast with you."

"Nellie! I do declare, this ain't Sunday. You ain't been out here 'cept on Sunday in years. Is anything wrong? Is the world comin' to an end?"

"No, the world is not ending, we were just out this way and thought you might want to meet these fine people."

"Ha! I ain't never met anybody thet came from north of Fote Valley, Ga. thet I considered fine people. They has all got those evil ways. Drinkin', gamblin', dancin', and Lord knows what else. You ain't done took up with the likes of thet kind, has you?"

Joe Billy, whispering to Carl. "I believe this old gal is kin to that nut, Ephriam."

"Whuts thet you say mister?"

"Nothing, mamn, I just saw a bug tryin' to git in Mr. Jones' ear an' I was tryin' to blow it away."

"Yew don't sound like no Northerner. Git out of thet car and let me git a better look at yew."

"Yessum."

"I know yew. Yew be the sheriff of this here county. How come yew done took up with these scallywags?"

Carl steps in, "Lady, we came out here on a sociable call with good intentions. Not to start another war between North and South Georgia. We don't even consider ourselves from the north. Atlanta is still in the Deep South, even if some people up there don't act like it. And by the way, Old Gene has been in the ground for many years now, and he came from down around McRae that I think is south of Fort Valley. And a finer true redneck Southerner has never been born. If we are not welcome here, we'll just go back into town to get some breakfast. We're not freeloaders. We fully intend to more than compensate you for your trouble."

"Like how?"

"Say about ten dollars a head."

"Welcome, friends! I always knew thet there wuz good people from up there but I never expected to lay my eyes on enny. Y'all git outta thet fine awtymobeel an' come into the parlor whilst I rustle up some vittles."

"My God! This place is practically crawling with valuable antiques! Nellie, there's enough merchandise right here in this parlor to keep your granny in high style for as long as she might live."

"I don't know Carl, she is a tough old biddy and she has already seen more than eighty birthdays. And as mean as she is, I wouldn't doubt she will see half that many more. Everybody in this family has been blessed with a long life, of course except mama."

"What happened to her?"

"An ornery old cow kicked her in the head when she was trying to milk her. Threw her clean across the barn and split her head wide open. I was in college up in Americus when it happened. We put the insurance money in a savings account to help me finish school."

"Where wuz yore paw?"

"Oh, he took off with a barmaid shortly after I was born. I guess he couldn't stand my crying at night. Mama said I cried a lot until I was about two years old. She said I acted like I was lost or homesick for some place. I never figured that out because I was already home."

"That's funny, I know a young man that acts like that sometimes."

"Who's that, Carl?"

"Aw Phillip, you know how Harold acts sometimes."

"Yeah, I hadn't thought about it before now, but he does act homesick sometimes."

"Where is he from?"

"About three blocks from where I have my truck garage."

"Most babies raise hell when they are first dropped, like they have been sentenced to a long jail term."

"Well, isn't that true, Joe Billy?"

"I guess so, life shore ain't no picnic."

"Harold has some funny thoughts about life at times. We were talking about all the pain and suffering going on and he said that you have to have a little pain every once in a while so you can fell real good when it stops."

"That's a hell of a thing to say. I can feel good without having to go through some pain to get there."

"Now Joe Billy, you know that if you felt good all the time, pretty soon you'd get used to it and forget you felt good. Then when you got hurt, you couldn't handle it."

"That's what makes spoiled brats. I sure see a lot in the classes I teach."

"I do too, Lilly. But I don't think that's why I cried so much."

"I'll ask Harold the next time I see him. He seems to know a lot of answers."

"I'd like to meet Harold, he sounds like he could help me with my book. How old is he?"

"He will be twenty this coming October. He's going to Ga. Tech. now but he might be willing to come see you this summer."

"That's a mite young for me, but we might get along on a platonic level."

"What else did you have in mind?"

"Joe Billy, you know how lonesome it can get down here in this Bible belt. Choice male companionship is at a premium."

"Carl, something's buggin' me. Did you leave yore keys in the wagon last night?"

"I believe so, why?"

"If you didn't, we got another mystery on our hands. I was wonderin' how the Olympic team got their truck past the wagon. There wasn't enough room for them to get by it. They must've pulled it up into the spring lot and then put it back after they passed."

"But that doesn't explain why they came back and got the truck to load up the watermelons. They knew they couldn't get back the way they came."

"They probably didn't know the bridge was out."

"That'll make Zeke a nice truck if he takes all the foxtails off and rips that continental kit off the tailgate. The way they got it fixed, you can't even let the gate down to load anything big."

"It's a shame the way some people can mess up a good pickup truck."

"Walk a mile in their shoes."

"Most of 'em don't wear shoes. Least wise during the week. They got one pair they wear to church on Sunday, each, that is."

"I bet we've seen the last of them. They're probably crossing the Florida line by now. Hey, Granny! You need any help in the kitchen?"

"Naw' Nellie. But you can git out the good chinaware and set the table. All I lak is cookin' the aigs. An' the biskits is 'bout done in the oven."

"That ham and coffee shore smells good. I'm 'bout ready to knaw a leg off this here dinin' table."

"Joe Billy, now you know that would ruin your teeth."

"They be garnteed. Awtuh be forever for whut they costed."

"There's a place up in Florence, South Carolina that they say can make a set in six hours and they don't cost but fifty dollars."

"I heered 'bout that but I never could find the time to go way up there. With all the crime they is around here."

"Now sheriff, you know that we haven't had a major felony in this county since that old Lizzie Bowen caught her old man in bed with that hussy and blew them both away with her double barrelled squirrel gun. They say that was really a bloody mess."

"You ain't just whistlin' Dixie 'bout that! When I got out to their house, they wus alreddy a big crowd gathered and the ones that had looked in through the bedroom window wus out there in the side yard pukin' their guts out. Man, it was a mess. I had to get the volunteer fire department out there to wash the room down befo' I could carry on my investygashun. Granny, I shore hope yew fixed some red eye gravy to go with them biskits."

"If I hang around here much longer, I might get the urge to write a book myself."

"Carl, nobody up around Atlanta would believe a word of it."

"Those hillbillies in North Georgia would."

"Do they still make thet good 'shine lak they usta?"

"Some do, but they are more into chicken plucking and rug making now."

"Now that's a goldarn shame! Some of the finest apple brandy I ever drank came from up around Blairsville. They even have a statue of the apple in Cornelia honoring the brandy."

"Nellie, that just isn't so. That statue honors the apple not the brandy."

"Whatever. I still like to think it's for the brandy."

"Nellie, you an' Lilly come help tote these here vittles to the table."

"Granny, you ever think of selling any of your fine furnishings? Please pass the ham."

"Hell no! Some of these pieces belonged to ma granddaddy. Please pass the aigs."

"No offense was intended. I only thought that selling off a few pieces might give you some extra funds to make life more comfortable. Please pass the biscuits."

"He was with Lee at Gettysburg. Please pass the coffee pot."

"Who was? Please pass the jelly."

"Lordy, Lordy, it's startin' agin. I need some more aigs."

"Ma old granddaddy. Lilly, swat thet fly off the biskits."

"Yessum. He must've mighty young. I want some grits."

"Frum what's been tole me, he wus borned in ateteen ninteen so he warn't no spring chicken when bluebellies attaked us. Pass the ham."

"Granny you got it all wrong. We fired the first shot on Fort Sumter off Charleston. Please pass the butter."

"Thet ain't the way granpa tole me it happened. Pass the molasses."

"What did he say about what happened? Please pass the ham. Damn! It sure is good."

"It come off my favo-rite hawg. I sho do miss him. He was so sweet. Please pass the gravy."

"He still is sweet."

"He said thet they waited till the sun went down an' under the kivver uf darkniss, they snuk inta town an' set fire to the old slave market."

"He must've been a very valuable pig indeed if he said all that. It seems a shame that he was butchered. Please pass the eggs."

"Fool! I wus talkin' 'bout granpa, not Horatio! All he could do wus grunt when he wus eatin' an' oink when he wus hongry. I need another biskit."

"So Horatio wasn't your granpa. Why was he butchered?"

"Fool! We didn't butcher granpa. He died in bed when he wus atey one. Now I'm outta gravy."

"It's real hard to make everything come out right. Please pass the grits."

"Carl, I gotta go out to the wagon fer a minit. Is that medicine still under the front seat?"

"What are you trying to do, build up some immunity to the epidemic?"

"Yeah, an' I shore hope it works."

"What works?"

"Bring it back in here. We're all going to need some."

"Some what?"

"Hurry! Hurry! Please pass the butter."

"Why are you in such an all fired hurry for the butter? Did you burn yourself on the coffee pot?"

"Ooo, I didn't burn myself. (Sob) I'm not in a hurry for the butter. (Sob) I need some butter for my biscuit. (Sob) The coffee pot has a wooden handle and won't burn anybody. (Sob) All I was trying to do was to get Joe Billy to hurry back with the medicine. (Sob) Please pass some ham."

"Carl, I don't know what it is, but I think something we said has upset you. Please stop crying and pass the gravy."

"Thanks Lilly, I don't know what come over me. I guess I was thinking about Horatio. He must have been a great pig. I believe just one more slice and I will be set until lunch time."

"If you think you're hangin' around this here place till lunch, yo're crazy as hell. I ain't never seen such a bunch of gluttons as the likes of you. I made a hell of a mistake sayin' I'd feed y'all fer ten dollars a head. I might have to sell something now to make it till my ole folks check comes on the furst uf next munth. Now pass me thet last piece of ham."

"Glory be! Here comes Joe Billy with the medicine! Nellie, go git those pint Mason jars outta the cupperd an' let's finish with a sip to settle our innards."

Phillip was the first to speak after finishing his large sip. "All those biscuits and that molasses reminds me of my childhood days. I grew up on a farm much like this one but it was during the great depression. We didn't have any fine China like this. We had to eat out of tin plates. Have you ever tried to sop molasses out of a tin plate? The bottom of the plate is slick from all that washing and the tabletop is just as slick from all that polishing. All this slickness is not conducive to efficient sopping. I, in my great wisdom, came up with an idea to remedy this situation. You know them bigheaded roofing nails? You know the ones about three quarters of an inch long? Well' I took one of those nails and got me a hammer and nailed my plate to the table right in front of my usual place. Mama raised hell because then she couldn't take it out back to the pump to wash it off. So I told her I would clean it where it lay after each sopping. This worked real well for a while. But you know what happened? Within six months I had completely sopped the head right off that nail. I then gained the name of The Syrup Sopping Son of A Bitch of Lower Alabama. (L.A.)"

Nellie says, "We all had to make do back then. I was real little back then but I remember things were tight. How did you manage to clean your plate while it was nailed down?"

"Ha! That was the easy part. We had an old hound dog named Bruce and after mama went out the back with the other plates, I would call Bruce in. He would jump up on the table looking for scraps and find the plate. No other instructions were necessary."

"Then it's possible that you gained your fame under false pretenses."

"Why do you say that? Please pass the medicine."

"Isn't it possible you gained your fame through a dog's tongue?"

"I guarantee you that I sopped a hell of a lot more than he licked."

"I think he should have got a little credit anyway."

"Hound dogs don't need credit. All they want is a little food, chase rabbits and then sleep in the dirt under the front porch. Now I admit if I had a pretty filly like you around to clean my plate, I would have given you all the credit."

"Oh Phillip, how you carry on!"

"Well we ain't got no hound dogs around here to wash dishes fer us, so y'all girls git to the kitchen sink an' lick these plates clean."

"That's not in our job description. Please pass the medicine."

"Granny, they're right. The only time the customers have to wash dishes is when they can't pay. And you have been more than amply rewarded for your efforts."

"Well, I guess I did git carried away with all this praise yew laid on me an' my cookin'. I'll do 'em later. Please pass the medicine."

"Granny, we sure did enjoy your hospitality, but we got to be leaving now, since all the medicine is gone and we might suffer an attack before we can get back to town and restock. If you ever decide to sell off any of these things, let the sheriff know. He knows how to reach me.

"What things?"

"Goodbye, Granny."

CHAPTER ELEVEN

"What are we going to do now?" Asks Phillip.

Carl suggests, "Let's go back to the motel and talk about it."

"We need to stop at the pharmacy first."

"By all means. How can we talk intelligently if we don't?"

"I hope that fool Ephriam is off duty."

"Oh, he will be. He's the night clerk, Nellie."

"That means we'll be safe until eight tonight."

"And we got this strong handsome sheriff to protect little old us."

"No way, Lilly. I got to put in some quality time down at the jail with the prisoners. I plum forgot to git their breakfast. Oh well, jail time ain't 'sposed to be easy time."

"We'll all miss you."

"And I, y'all."

"There goes a fine man. I have discovered a new respect for our local protectors."

"Carl, I have always felt that way about law enforcement at a local level. It's the state and federal agencies I feel animosity toward."

"You're right, Nellie, the higher levels of government bureaucrats seem to give the impression that they enjoy a certain immunity from the opinion of the little man. A result of such attitudes in France was the Revolution in the late Eighteenth Century. Of course that was against the aristocrats rather than the bureaucrats."

Lilly asks Carl, "What's the difference?"

"The aristocrats were the landed gentry who ruled by the misconception of divine right as opposed to political appointments of the bureaucrats. Inheritances do seem to give some semblance of respect to ones fortunate in enjoying them. They have the advantage of being able to gain a good education and if they use it wisely, they can earn the respect of the masses."

"What does that do to your spoiled brat theory?"

"Of course there will always be bad apples, Nellie, but they are apparent. You will find them among the jet setters and polo players. The ones of conscience will take up causes or create charitable foundations. Don't you and Lilly consider yourselves part of the establishment?"

"Carl, you be kidding! Grammar school teachers occupy the lowest rung of a very tall ladder and the rungs immediately above us are rotten. If we did try to pull ourselves up, the rungs would break and we would lose that precious position on the low rung. There are too many politics involved in the advancement. The most that we have to look forward to is to finally find a good man to marry and raise a lot of kids that might take care of us in our old age. Lord knows our small pensions won't."

"That wouldn't be too bad if you raise your kids right."

"Maybe, but nowadays there are too many outside influences that molds the minds of the young. At our school there is a group of children who consider themselves the 'elite' and above the law. Their parents are the political appointees of this county. They work in the tax offices. They work for the zoning board. They work for the board of education and every other job that is a political plum. These children form a peer pressure group that influences all the others in their mode of dress, popular music and attitudes relating to the freedom of the individual. This pressure overrides the parental influence. It helps perpetuate a system that violates the Golden Rule and basic decency."

"Nellie, you have a gift of great insight and are very fluent in your expressions. We as citizens of Georgia are suffering by the loss of persons of your caliber guiding us in the State Legislature. You must run in the next election. I shall personally sponsor you and contribute to your campaign."

"That's real sweet of you, Carl, but I think you have been carried away. Maybe it was the vittles or the medicine, I don't know which. And don't forget Zeke and I are going to collaborate on writing a book. Between that and school teaching, I won't have any time for politicking. But I'll keep your offer in mind for future reference."

"It sure would have been nice to have you close by up there in Atlanta, but I reckon the book ought to have priority right now. There will always be a mess up there for someone to help straighten out."

"You sound like there might be other reasons why you would like to have me around."

"My wife doesn't understand me."

"Most women do not understand the nature of polygamy. Except maybe Mormon wives."

"Most of us have tried monogamy and it has failed us."

"There must be some pain associated with pleasure."

"That's true, but only a small amount can be tolerated."

"You men are slaves of your passion."

"The urge to reproduce is God given. Look at all the animals."

"That's not true. In humans, the urge is for pleasure not reproduction. Do you really believe a dog is thinking of being proud papa when he is banging away on a bitch? That's the last thing he would think about, if indeed he can think at all. Men are no better than the rest of the animal kingdom."

"Ah ha! I've got you there! Men have known to fornicate for the express purpose of reproducing an offspring. I will admit that the primary motive is to produce a male heir to perpetuate his name."

"That's strictly an exercise of the male ego in an attempt at immortality."

"Not necessarily. Sometimes, more in centuries past than now, male heirs were needed to prevent the break up of large estates. Because of the dowries the fathers of the brides had to come up with, it was more economical for one to have male children. In China they used to drown the female babies. This was their contribution towards population control and maintaining a status quo."

Lilly jumps in, "Carl, that was a perfectly awful thing to say! How could anyone do such a terrible thing? To a perfectly innocent baby."

"Lilly, the poverty you saw during the depression can't even compare to poverty in countries which practice no birth control at all. The majority of the children will never see their tenth birthday. And the girls that do are pregnant before their twelfth. The Church that allows no artificial means of birth control dominates most of these countries' population. The sin is to bring children into a world that cannot give them an even break of surviving."

"I shall quit my teaching job and do my best to right this wrong with a good sharp straight razor!"

"Don't go off tilting windmills, Nellie, this would be a futile undertaking."

"Aw, I know, Phillip. I just got a little carried away thinking about it. Anyway, you don't have anything to worry about. I would never harm the likes of you."

"Thank you, Lilly. That takes a load off my mind. I was wondering how I could get my required eight hours of sleep with those thoughts on my mind."

"Do you think that the world's population will reach a saturation point?"

"What do you mean?"

"Will it get to a point where the land cannot support the population and everybody will starve?"

"It's at that point now in some countries and the starving people still have babies. You probably have heard the expression, 'I would rather screw than eat'. A lot of people take this literally."

Nellie re-enters; "Intelligent human beings are taught to weigh the consequences of their actions."

Carl gets back in; "You cannot judge everyone by your standards. A great many of the people of the world has little else to look forward to but a small amount of lovemaking."

"Then they should be sterilized."

"And how would you accomplish this?"

"Put something in their drinking water."

"But that would affect everyone regardless of their ability to care for their children."

"Develop a pill that would temporarily cancel the water's effect."

"How would you distribute these pills the worthy ones?"

"Have them fill out an application along with a financial statement and education resume."

"Nellie, as I said before, I like your ideas. But this one tampers with the Creators intentions."

"And I assume the informed Carl knows His intentions?"

"I would never presume such, but I am sure your ideas don't fit in the grand scheme, if there is one."

"Now are you inferring that this whole mess might be an accident?"

"Not necessarily, things might have just got out of hand."

"I can't believe that. I would rather believe that we do not have the wisdom to understand some things."

"I see. If this attitude were shared by everyone, there would be no inquiry into things not yet understood and the human mind would stagnate."

"You are not going to let me get in the last word, are you?"

"Sure, all you have to say is, 'you're right and I'm wrong'."

Lilly jumps up and looks out the window. "Phillip, what time is it? I don't want that Ephriam to see me here."

"It's just five. We still have plenty of time. Is anybody getting hungry?"

Carl says, "Maybe some junk food or some snacks. Is there a beer joint close by?"

"There's one about a block up the road towards town. Why?"

"Well, I'll tell you, Nellie. If it is anything like the other ones I've been in, they'll have a card on the counter full of smoked herring in little plastic bags and they are fine eating. Of course they are better if you drink beer with them. The last time I stopped and got me a few and started to eat them while I was driving, I had eaten all of them about ten miles down the road and had to go back and get me some more. That time I bought him out."

"Phillip, you seem to be the gofer."

"OK, I need to get some beer too."

"Hurry back."

* * *

"Carl, they didn't have but three cards of those smoked fish so I subsidized them with a few packs of Slim Jims."

"Well, they do pretty good too. I have had to make do with some of them at times. Of course I prefer the fish."

"Because this is your treat, you start on the fish and we start on the meat sticks."

"Phillip, that won't be fair. Because there are three of you and only one of me, I'll eat three fish to y'all's one. That way we will all get a fair share."

"Whatever you say, 'boss'."

"Do I detect a note of sarcasm in your voice?"

"Not really, boss, I was just wondering who was your math teacher."

"If I'm not mistaken, she also taught you. But I remember one other thing she taught me."

"And what was that?"

"Rank carries certain privileges."

"I repeat, 'whatever you say, boss'."

"You split that one fish while I eat my three."

"We need Jesus and a loaf of bread."

"Nellie, don't you go religious on us. We can work this out on our own."

"It don't hurt to call upon Him when we are in the middle of a crisis and we are going to have one when the fish gives out."

"Maybe I should re-figure the division ratio."

"I think it would behoove you to, if you want to keep this at a secular level."

"Peace and tranquility above all."

Lilly has a suggestion; "Let's lay all the fish on the table and everybody eat all as fast as they can and when they give out, then start on the Slim Jims."

Nellie says; "I will not participate in a feeding frenzy like a pack of hungry wolves. Lilly, that was a terrible suggestion. There must be some way we can sit down and enjoy a small snack without an act of congress. Try to modify your suggestion to conform with civilized consumption."

"All right, how about this? I've got a pair of dice in my purse. Let's roll high dice for each fish."

"What in the world are you doing with dice in your purse? You are not known famously for gambling."

"I took them off a kid running a crap game at school during recess. He wasn't but nine years old and was cutting the pot on every throw. I bet he had twenty dollars worth of quarters in his pocket when I caught him."

"Did you confiscate the quarters?"

"No, he claimed it was his lunch money."

"What is this world coming to? Let's roll for a fish."

Phillip and Nell rolled boxcars. Carl got snake eyes and Lilly rolled a seven.

"Phillip and I are both high so we each get a fish."

Carl says; "Oh no, the only fair way is to have a sudden death tie breaker. Nell, you and Phillip re-roll."

"Lilly, you thought up this mess. What do you think is fair?"

"If I am to be on the rule committee and I make the rules, will all of you abide by them?"

Everybody agrees.

"OK, my first rule; in case of ties the round is over and the fish goes to the rule maker. That's sort of like 'push pays the dealer' somewhat. There will be no discussion. You have all agreed to abide by my rules. Gimme that fish."

"What is this world coming to? Even the schoolteachers are corrupt! Roll the dice."

Luckily the fish were consumed before Ephriam came on duty. Nellie and Lilly left because they had to get up early Sunday morning to teach Sunday school.

They made Carl and Phillip promise to call them when they came back to town, telling them about the wonderful time they had. Carl told them he would see Harold before he saw them again because he was really interested in UFO phenomena and would come right down when he hears about the cats. "Nellie, you keep me posted on your conversations with Zeke. I think it will make a good book. And I believe that Harold can contribute something to it. He will surprise you. He is wise beyond his years. And I will tell him about your ideas on birth control"

"Phillip, let's finish that beer and hit the sack. It's been a long two days and we need one good night's sleep before we hit the road in the morning. I want to get out of here around five in the morning."

"Why so early?"

"I want to go up 19 and stop in Thomaston and Griffin to see some antique shops. We will be lucky if we get home before dark, and I'd like to talk to Harold tonight if possible."

CHAPTER TWELVE

Harold sleepily opens his door to Carl's insistent knocking, "Why hello, Carl, when did you get back and what are you doing here at this time of night?"

"We just got back a while ago and I came over here just as soon as I dropped Phillip off. I need to talk to you tonight."

"This must be important. What's up?"

"What do you know about cats?"

"Cats! This is weird. We have been studying about the cats of ancient Egypt in our archeology class all last week. What's going on?"

"You probably won't believe what I'm going to tell you. Give me about a half hour without interrupting. You are going to have a million questions."

After forty-five minutes of blah, blah, blah, Harold starts asking questions. "How many cats were there?"

"I dunno, maybe over one hundred."

"Could there have been as many as one hundred forty four?"

"I think there might have been."

"Did you see any with short tails?"

"I don't remember any."

"What was the spacing when they were in a semi-circle?"

"I didn't measure the distance, but it might have been about twelve inches."

"Could it have been thirteen inches?"

"Like I said, I didn't have a tape measure. Why couldn't it have been twelve inches?"

"It seems inconceivable that the spacing would be the square root of the quantity."

"Huh?"

"If there had been only sixteen cats the spacing would have to be four inches. A normal cat when it sits displaces more than that figure. Especially if some were pregnant. And the laws of probability determines that fifty percent are females and taking into consideration the gestation period, there were probably fifty percent of the females displacing at least six to eight inches. Therefore the cats would be uncomfortable in a space of less than thirteen inches. Especially if every other one was not a male. The probability of randomly placing a gross of cats in this alternate order is something like two to the one hundred and forty third power, if the sexes were equally divided, which is not guaranteed."

"Why not one hundred forty four?"

"We care not the sex of the first cat."

"I see, this is so much taurine feces."

"Dealing in matters such as this is not an exact science."

"So it would seem."

"A gross of hungry cats would not voluntarily abandon a feast such as you describe. Was the food supply depleted before the abandonment?"

"No, we drug the pig to the watermelon patch and no cat followed."

"Then there was a force involved that had more power than barbecued pig. This must have been truly a powerful force. Was any strange music heard?"

"I don't think so, the radios were blaring so loud, no one could have heard any if there were."

"And none of the radios went dead on their own?"

"Not while we were awake. We had one hell of a time getting to sleep with all that racket going on."

"Did the cacophony of mixed sounds seem to affect the cats?"

"When they were fighting over the pig, they were making more noise than all the radios combined."

"What happened when they abandoned the pig?"

"I don't really know. Nellie was the one that told me that the cats were not following. But I do know that all the radios were still on."

"When you got back to the spring, were the radios still on?"

"Not all of them. Some of the die hards were still partying but most of them had left their cars and were standing behind the cats."

"Were the cats paying any attention to the music or the people?"

"Not a bit. It was like they were in a trance. Some of the kids were poking at the cats with sticks and they paid no attention to the molestation."

"Then you don't know if the people left before the cats or not?"

"We were all asleep except maybe Nellie, when it happened."

"When what happened?"

"Oh no! Not you too! When whatever happened first."

"Me too what?"

"Forget it."

"Sometimes I don't understand you."

"And I, you."

"I think you have given me enough input to come up with a workable theory. Let me sleep on it and I will get back to you. One more thing. Did you see any Egyptians in the crowd?"

"I don't think so. Just some watermelon loving Ethiopians."

* * *

"Welcome back, Hannibal. Are here to stay or is this just a visit?"

"Just a quick trip, Peter. I need to find out something. In fact, you might be able to answer my questions."

"I shall certainly try, but answering questions is not in my job description."

"I trust you will bend the rules for me."

"For you, yes. You have performed a great service for us. What do you need to know?"

"Have you ever passed any cats?"

"Cats? Never! This realm was not created for them. It was created by Christians for Christians."

"I don't understand. Was not the creator involved?"

"No, this place only exists in the minds of the true believers."

"I had no Christian beliefs when I arrived here."

"Let me explain. Before J.C. came back up, there was great confusion. A gathering of a great multitude of souls believing many diverse earthly teachings. When He got back and saw the chaos, He remodeled the place according to His teachings. The ones residing here prior to this remodeling were allowed to stay unless they chose to be elsewhere."

"Then before that time, there might have been some cats here?"

"It is indeed possible, all I know is I have never seen any since I came up. That was shortly after J.C. came back. In fact, I followed Him here."

"It seems like you are trying to tell me that I don't really belong here."

"You are tolerated, but the paths of knowledge you are pursuing at the lower level might eventually lead you to another place that will develop in your mind."

"Then the answers I seek are not to be found here."

"Alas, no. We are too indoctrinated in the Way. We seek no more answers. We have found peace. Other Mansions do not interest us."

"Then there are other places?"

"More than the stars in the firmament."

"Then I may eventually forget all of you and this place?"

"In your conscious moments as Harold, do you remember us?"

"No. Only something deep in my mind that nags me."

"This too will pass, in time."

"I shall always need to call on the knowledge that exists here."

"You now so believe, but there will come a time when your knowledge will surpass ours. This path is open to all thinking beings. We that dwell here chose an easier path, and do not regret it."

"Thank you, Peter."

* * *

The next day Harold met with Carl.

"Carl, why are you interested in this occurrence that you witnessed?"

"When you see something you don't understand, the human curiosity in all of us demands answers."

"Of course. I understand, but aren't you curious about the size of the universe and if it has a size, what exists beyond its limits?"

"The mind cannot fathom such a question."

"This may be the case with the cats. I'm not trying to say it is, but pursuing an answer could become an obsession and wreck your life."

"That's why I called on you. I know my limitations and would be a fool to seek answers on my own."

"And I am not certain that I am the fool for the job either."

"Why don't you talk to Marybelle? She seems to know about the uncanny. She does some weird things over at the diner."

"Come to think about it, she does love cats. Maybe she can get into their heads."

* * *

"Let's talk some about cats, Marybelle."

"I love cats, they're cool."

"And don't forget mysterious also."

"I don't know about that. I will admit they are different from any other animal."

"Will they let you in?"

"Not very deep. Maybe if I tried harder. I never had the occasion to plunge."

"This might be the time. After I tell you what I know."

"I'm not a cat, but I'm curious. Tell me more."

"I wouldn't tell this to just anyone. Carl told me about it and I thought he was pulling my leg. Just remember I am just repeating what he told me. He seemed sincere when he was telling it, so consider me sincere when I tell you."

"Oh Harold, you know I feel like you are a brother to me and you have never lied to me. I will believe everything you tell me."

"Thanks, Marybelle. I wish we were more the same age so I could be more than just a brother to you."

"Not you too! You know I went through this with Butch once and we had to settle on a Platonic relationship. Please try to keep your hormones in check."

"Reluctantly. Just don't get too close to me. I have a weakness for honeysuckle and magnolias."

"Back to the cats."

* * *

After Harold's narration of Carl's experience, Marybelle exclaims, "Wow! That was an earful. You know, I have a few cats at home and sometimes one or two of them sit out on the backyard fence at night when there is no moon and stare up at the sky. Their tails are swishing like they do right before pouncing on a squirrel or rabbit.

They don't stay out long. When they come back in the house, they all lie down and go to sleep. Like they are waiting for the next time."

"Carl said that the cats he saw were not moving their heads or tails or anything else. Maybe they were getting ready."

"Ready for what?"

"I don't know. Perhaps waiting for something."

"There's a difference in those cats and mine."

"How so?"

"Mine are third generation house cats as far as I am concerned. These cats you describe probably have ancestors that go back farther than when they came in off the streets. My folks had cats as far back as I can remember. Those cats at the barbecue place were wild alley cats unaffected by human love. It is possible that our cats hang around us only because we show some affection towards them. If we didn't they might also call a taxi."

"I have heard of cats leaving one household and adopting another family down the street. If this was a voluntary exodus, they must indeed have great power to summon a vehicle large to accommodate a gross of cats."

"Harold, remember that this gross of cats might have been acting in concert. We have no idea the strength of this many minds working in unison. I believe they might have picked up some kind of vibrations emanating from an extraterrestrial vehicle cruising in the vicinity and considered this as a means of transport to a better environment. Humans are always dreaming of this. Why not cats?"

"Most humans are willing to wait until they die before entering paradise."

"That depends on their lot on earth. Some don't want to wait. They may be considered the movers and shakers in our society."

"Like us, Marybelle?"

"Don't put me in that category. The only moving and shaking I do is at the dance hall I go to on Saturday night."

"I bet that is a sight to behold. I'd like to go sometimes. Could I go with you?"

"No way. Unless you are ready for a quick trip to that paradise you been talkin' 'bout. I'm sorry I seem to be reevertin'. Just thinkin' 'bout last Satitidy night sends shivers up my spine."

"Why can't I go?"

"You must be forgetting that this is the Deep South in the mid-sixties. We have our sanctuaries the same as your kind have yours."

"Why Marybelle! I thought you were above this racial hatred."

"At times I think I am, then I get a taste of cold reality when I stumble in the wrong place by accident. And I don't want to see you get a taste of it by going where I go on Saturday night."

"Maybe we could summon that UFO and get the hell out of here."

"If only we could. I would settle just to be froze and come back in a hundred years from now when all this will be behind us."

"I'm afraid even if you wait a thousand years, you will find the same problem."

"Why can't people learn to live together in harmony?"

"Marybelle, do you have racial pride?"

"Of course I do! I am proud of my heritage."

"Then you are a racist also. Some of our ancestors tried in their own way to correct the problem. A lot of slaveholders in the South cohabited with the females in order to produce a group with no racial identity. You are an example that their efforts were in vain."

"All the races are equally guilty of this false pride."

"Of course, and thus will it continue to be until laws are enacted to eliminate this problem."

"And what do you suggest?"

"Anti or reverse miscegenation laws."

"You will have to explain that."

"The miscegenation laws were passed to prevent interracial marriage. Something about the purity of the races, meaning Caucasians. Hypocrisy in all its glory. What I propose is legislation that prohibits one from marrying into one's own race. We would not see the final results, but after a few generations there would be a new race of people with all the fine qualities of all existing races. The intelligence of some blended with the natural instincts of others."

"You mean like geniuses that can boogie?"

"Not only that. Maybe we could get closer to nature and work for a better and cleaner world."

"There are too many deep seated prejudices among us to tolerate such a scheme."

"Does that include you?"

"The occasion may have been proposed to me, but the ramifications of such a liaison has prevented me from indulging."

"Then you personally do not reject the idea?"

"No."

"Good."

"Why? Are proposing a frolic under the sheets?"

"Not against your will."

"It will take more than just us to correct the ills of our times."

"Suppose we started a new religion based on this concept?"

"We would suffer more persecution than Joseph Smith and his followers. And all they did was practice polygamy."

"You sound that like you might be an advocate."

"Not really. I can just appreciate some male urges. It's a hormonal thing. Let's get back to the cats. It's safer."

"As you wish, but I reserve the right to pursue this at a later date. Where were we?"

"Cat power."

"Oh yes. I don't think I go along with that. Cats seem too independent to band together for a common cause."

"It was just a thought. How about the vehicle sending out a specific signal to attract the cats?"

"In that case, they would want the cats for some reason."

"We can only speculate as to the motives. I don't think it is in the same category as the cattle mutilations we hear of happening in the West."

"Maybe the cattle mutilations are to feed the cats. A flying saucer full of hungry cats is a place I would rather not be."

"Could the cats be used as food?"

"I think these beings are vegetarians. If they were carnivores, they wouldn't have to worry about feeding the cats. They would simply eat them."

"Then why would they go to the trouble of catnapping?"

"What's catnapping got to do with it? We don't even know if they need sleep."

"I'm talking about kidnapping cats. Not catnapping."

"Oh."

"Well, if they don't eat them and I don't think they are experimenting with them, wherever they are taking them must have a deficiency of cats or a surplus of rats."

"With the advanced technology these beings exhibit, they should have no trouble with a rat problem. I would rather believe this has some religious significance."

"From what has been discovered in the tombs of ancient Egypt, cats held an honored place in their society. Maybe these aliens are descendants of the Egyptians."

"I think when they came down to help build the pyramids, a lot of their cats escaped and could not be rounded up before they had to leave."

"If that be the case, why do they have the power to round them up now?"

"I would say that their technology has advanced to that point since they left, and they came back to get them as soon as they could."

"They didn't take but a gross."

"That's all we know about and they might not be through yet either."

"After the cats, who will be next?"

"Some people have been reported missing mysteriously. Could be they have enough cats now and we are next."

"I believe that I won't pursue this any further. I'll tell Carl it will be best to forget about this. It's over our heads. Thanks for your help, Marybelle. I will see you soon about the other matter."

"I'll start looking for a vacant church tomorrow!"

"Praise the Lord, Marybelle!"

CHAPTER THIRTEEN

Harold asks Butch, "Are you over Marybelle?"

"When I am old and decrepit and my memory fails, and I no longer appreciate the beautiful things that this earth offers, you might say I will be. Not a moment before."

"Heavy."

"Facing harsh reality does not mean 'over', just resignation."

"I fear that this condition which possesses you has entered my thoughts also."

"I was beginning to doubt your humanity. Hell, ain't it?"

"It is the curse of mankind. Also its salvation."

"The thoughts which entered my mind concerning her did not include perpetuating the human race."

"These are not the motives I entertain. Yours are shallow thoughts, not ones to which to base an everlasting relationship upon."

"My motto is 'let the future take care of itself'. And the future has a bad habit of creeping up on one. I am reluctant to lay a course which I may eventually regret."

"Then I assume that my pursuit of this matter will not affect our relationship?"

"Just don't come around sharing the intimate details with me."

"You have my word."

* * *

After telling Carl his thoughts about pursuing the problem with the cats, Harold asked him to be on the lookout for an unused church that might be for sale.

"Don't tell me you have been 'called'. I did not think hypocrisy suited your character."

"My mission will not be to save souls, but rather to save humanity. We have no control over the hereafter."

"This may well be a worthwhile pursuit. The path we are now traveling seems to lead to mass destruction."

"No one has all the answers, but I feel that I may have something to contribute."

"Please give me a short synopsis. I am a busy man."

After explaining his thoughts to Carl, they were in agreement that a church must be found.

* * *

"Marybelle, I have Carl working on the church detail. He is very enthusiastic about our idea."

"That seems out of character for him, Harold, isn't he happily married?"

"On the surface, yes, but I think it is only for business reasons or maybe political. He is leaning in that direction and the image he needs to project is one of mom, apple pie and family. He wishes to remain anonymous in his role to help us."

"That is understandable. We need to keep a low profile until we get a movement started that is accepted as politically correct."

"Do you know anyone of mixed blood that we may approach?"

"I have heard of a night club over on the west side that will admit only light skinned coloreds as members. I am sure I could qualify for membership."

"Good, infiltrate this den of prejudice and try to recruit some disciples."

"There is one more thing we must discuss. To insure credibility, I believe we should present ourselves as husband and wife."

"I thought you would never ask!"

"Your family must be informed."

* * *

"Harold, this is sheer insanity! Have you taken leave of your senses?"

"Grandfather, times are changing. The underprivileged and downtrodden minorities in this country are gaining political voice and if the pattern of birth rate continues, they will soon become the majority and their voting power will be awesome."

"This cannot happen in our lifetime."

"Not in your generation, no, but I am afraid I shall live to see it. I can see it in the streets now. Before you die you will see a black mayor in Atlanta."

"That's absurd. There are too many white people in the city."

"You are not keeping in touch. There is a mass exodus happening as we speak. The ones who are able are moving to the suburbs. The whole city will soon be one huge ghetto."

"You may be right, but I cannot condone this alliance you propose. Besides, she is much older than you."

"She was once twice as old, but when she is eighty she will only be ten percent older."

"You are trying to confuse me."

"Grandmother and mother have not objected."

"They are incurable romantics."

Dolly dives in; "Joe, you are acting like you are ninety instead of sixty. Get with the program. Besides, what Harold chooses to do with his life should not concern you. I remember you did what you wanted to do when you were his age."

"Things were different then."

"That's exactly what he has been trying to tell you, stupid!"

"Do what you will, then. I'm going out and sit on the porch."

"You haven't said anything yet, mother. Have we your blessing?"

'Marybelle is a wonderful woman and I think the world of her. I am only concerned for your safety. This is a dangerous step to take considering the temper of the times."

"All pioneers have taken chances. Usually the rewards are worth the risk."

"Please be careful. A classic maternal admonition."

"Thank you mother. We shall keep all of you informed as we progress."

* * *

"Harold, my banker told me of a church over in East Point that is vacant and the deacons are looking for a buyer. They built a new church and they need the money. It has a small parsonage with it. If you get a charter you won't have any property taxes to pay. The bank will take a thirty-year mortgage and the payments will be very low. I can co-sign with you and if you screw up, I can get the building."

"Sounds good. I'll take Marybelle over to see it when she closes up."

"There's no hurry. It has been empty for three years."

"I bet the roof has fallen in by now. It will probably take a fortune to fix it up."

"Maybe not. Go look at it anyway."

"If we get it, we should insure it for as much as we can. If word gets out too soon about our intentions, we will need plenty of coverage."

"You might also consider an enormous life policy on Marybelle and yourself."

"Are you trying to frighten me?"

"No. All couples starting out should have good insurance."

"Of course, but especially us?"

"Especially you two."

"And who would be the beneficiary?"

"Joint survivorship."

"And if we go out together?"

"Me, naturally."

"Why you, naturally?"

"I am the co-signer."

* * *

Monday morning Harold asks, "Marybelle, how did your recruitment efforts go over at that club?"

"I don't think 'rednecks' is the proper term for them, but there should be an equivalent description for those people. They are more prejudiced than any low class white trash I have ever been exposed to."

"What happened?"

"They seemed to match your description of our intended descendants with a few exceptions. They exhibited great intelligence and had the rhythm and grace of movement of natural dancers but they lacked the humility which is necessary to become a whole people."

"Is there some reason for this?"

"They are too proud. I got the feeling that they believe they are God's chosen ones."

"I thought that honor was reserved for ones of the Jewish persuasion."

"Could both be right?" asks Marybelle.

"I would rather believe both are wrong."

"If we are successful in our efforts, Marybelle, we must formulate doctrines to prevent this from happening to our people."

"If we get anyone to join us, they will already have the proper attitude. I don't believe we have anything to worry about in that respect."

"Unless they have ulterior motives."

"Such as?"

"Maybe sampling forbidden fruit."

"Are you speaking from experience or maybe dark thoughts?"

"Only in my fantasies."

"Am I there?"

"I would be lying if I denied that."

"What will happen if I do not live up to your expectations?"

"It would be easier for elephants to fly than that to happen."

"I believe that the prudent thing to do is to test the waters."

"I am all in favor of sampling the merchandise."

"Let us retire to the fitting room."

* * *

"Marybelle, have you heard of Kirlian photography?"

"Yes, a person's aura can be seen using this method."

"Do you believe that a person's aura must be compatible with another's for good mating?"

"Oh yes, definitely, and I believe ours are."

"I know full well they are. I have the most fantastic feelings when I touch you. It is like we are pulsing into each other's space and when I give, you take and vice versa."

"I consider the test ride a smashing success and am willing to commit ourselves further. And you?"

"Onward and upward!"

"Praise the lord!"

* * *

By the first month of 1965, the church had recruited four hundred members. Most were young singles. There were a few mixed couples that sought refuge in an atmosphere of tolerance. They were welcomed with open arms by the congregation.

A diploma mill on the West Coast had ordained Harold. His credentials satisfied all the powers that be to gain a tax-free status for his ministry. It was so easy that Carl was contemplating converting his enterprises to enjoy the same shelter. Only his legal counsel, whom he retained for a small fortune, convinced him that it would not be the wisest thing to do. Disappointed at the failure of ploy, he then became the church's main sponsor with massive deductible donations. And with Harold's involvement, he was able to recover about half the amount as tax-free mad money. This arrangement suited all parties concerned and freed up large sums for clandestine projects.

The action was justified in their minds for as they saw it. No moral law was broken, only a most repressive political one. Carl's philosophy was "The politicians have their pork barrel and so shall we!"

In this day, white collars carried an aura of respect and the punitive action was minimal. Even many of the elected officials were enjoying the plums of political office while serving time at some of the government's finest country club institutions.

Good places to hide such funds were in tax-free municipal bearer bonds. These instruments were not registered in anyone's name and had coupons attached that could be pulled and cashed in at maturity. The bonds could be used as collateral for legitimate bank loans with no questions asked.

Being a devout person, Harold chose not to burden the church with a salary. All collections were used for the upkeep of the physical premises and the spreading of the word. Flyers were printed calling all persons who had suffered from prejudices to come and hear about a final solution, one that was definitely not a Nazi type. This attracted the curious, most whom rejected the theory. But the number that did not, grew by leaps and bounds.

Standing behind the pulpit Harold expounds, “Welcome, brothers and sisters…You are, you know…Under this thin veneer of diverse colors lie bodies molded from like clay…

“We intend to strip awaaayyy this veneer and with it the prejudices which dwellll within! Some will shout, ‘But this is our identity, without it we are nothing!’

“They are wrong! So wrong. Ask a man ‘Who are you?’ He will perhaps say “I am Jebediah Hawkins.’ This is not his identity!

“His parents bestowed this unlikely name upon him. He had no voice in the matter. Ask a man ‘What are you?’ He might say ‘I am a mechanic.’ Maybe a doctor. Maybe an electrician. This is closer…But not close enough!…

“If he tells you that he is the husband of a faithful wife and supports her and his three children working as an electrician, then you will know his identity!…This is what he is proud of…And rightfully so…No false pride here!…

“He did not say ‘I am a black man’…He did not say ‘I am a Jew’…He did not say ‘I am Chinese’…How can any man be proud of something he had no control over? Humans gravitate toward their like kind for many reasons…Maybe this is where they feel accepted…But isn’t there even unrest and dissension in that sanctuary?…Maybe this it is for greater political clout…

“But aren’t there too many cases where groups are exploited for all the wrong reasons?…If only we could shed this curse of our skin!….Could we not all live in peace and brotherhood?…This is our mission!

“You few who are gathered here today have started on this lonesome and tortuous path toward a future time where your descendants may enjoy this bliss. We are not here to save your souls…There are other ones far better equipped in that endeavor…We are here to try to save humanity…If we are successful, the hereafter will take care of itself! “Please do not forsake your religion because of us. We hold our services on Monday night so that it will not interfere with any other church. If your present church is intolerant of divided loyalty, then you must make a decision. Or maybe your church will make it for you.

"God bless you all...Go in peace...While you are going, please notice the shiny buckets located at each side of the doors. The more you give, the more can be reached."

"Rev. Pitts, might I have a few minutes of your time? Strangely, I answer to the name Jebediah Hawkins. How you came to call my name is indeed a mystery to my simple mind. I accept it as a calling nevertheless. I am at your disposal for any tasks you might see fit to honor me with."

"Brother Hawkins, how kind of you. Honestly, I had no idea that anyone in this world was so named. Possibly like you say, this might be divine intervention. What are you? In an occupational sense."

"I work with concrete, pipes, bricks and lumber."

"The church can always use men handy at such things. Do you think you could build a wooden cross that could be easily set afire?"

"Of course, but the reason eludes me."

"Brother Hawkins, do you not think that our church could use more members?"

"I have never seen a church that was satisfied with the size of the membership. And I don't think I ever will."

"You are so right. The problem is exposure. And proper exposure is very expensive. The Lord has sent you to our church to correct this problem."

"Oh, if only I could be an instrument of His will!"

"And Brother Hawkins, so you shall! You will build and erect an enormous wooden cross and place it on our front lawn to be ignited for all Atlanta to see! This will insure the necessary publicity to give our mission great impetus. Naturally, the igniter shall remain anonymous."

The following week the television and newspaper media was monopolized with the news of the dastardly burning of a cross in the yard of a small struggling church in East Point. The local hate groups disclaimed any responsibility for this action. (Naturally) The pastor had the following to say;

"We forgive the poor misguided souls that did this terrible thing. We understand our beliefs causes controversy among all races, but our mission is a noble one. The effects of our efforts may not be manifest in our lifetime, but in the face of eternity what is a few hundred years?

"We welcome all that who have not heard of us to come and let us explain our cause. If only a handful join our effort, then the perpetrators of this act will have furthered our cause. Thank you kindly.

"And as a constant reminder of the bigotry that exists in our midst, I am tomorrow going to petition city council for a permit to erect a permanent flaming cross in front of our humble church as a beacon to all that has lost hope."

"Jebediah, you have truly nobly served. I hereby appoint you as first deacon and custodian of the physical assets. Among your duties will be to keep the eternal flame lit."

"Oh thank you, sir. Thanks to my expertise with pipes, I can safely say that the cross, made of heavy black pipe and drilled with the proper size jets should produce a beautiful blue flame for years to come. As long as the gas bill is paid."

"That is covered by your responsibility as custodian. Just pull enough out of the buckets for that purpose. Did you notice the increase in attendance last Monday after your help?"

"Indeed I did and I am so proud. Not falsely, I hope."

"This type accomplishment is exactly what one should be proud of. By the way, we need to clean up the church for Saturday. We have two mixed marriages scheduled."

"I hope we don't have any trouble."

"I don't think we will. Very few are willing to be called bigots right now."

"Yes, thanks to you. But I have some doubts about our cause. You seem to think that this is a panacea. I can think of many other ills that beset us as humans. Economics and survival plays just as important role in world problems as prejudices and bigotry."

"Ah! I have entertained thoughts along these lines also. But this is not yet the time to spring them on our growing congregation."

"May I be taken into your confidence?"

"But of course. After all, you are number one deacon. Birth control!"

"You are right, this is not the time."

CHAPTER FOURTEEN

In addition of attracting new members, the flaming cross had other advantages. The neighborhood was cleared of annoying night flying insects. This did not go unnoticed by persons still plagued by this nuisance.

Jebediah built up a thriving business manufacturing and installing such fixtures in other neighborhoods. Of course he did not use the cross design as Harold held a design patent on the fixture. Instead circles were made. Flaming wings were made. One affluent section commissioned Jebediah to construct a gigantic replica of the Confederate battle flag in all its flaming glory in living color.

This caused Harold concern because some thought that this was a symbol endorsing slavery. Only the great monetary contribution the church gleaned from the sale of the device forced Harold to turn the other way. "The ways of The Lord are mysterious indeed."

A Star of David was constructed for another group. Only the insects suffered. The enterprise grew to such proportions; Jebediah was forced to move his operation from the church basement to a more practical location. Needless to say Carl furnished the building. Antonio Garabaldi even got involved by installing the larger icons. (He knew people in the Bureau of Licenses and Fees.) The building inspector forced the owners to install safety pilots in case the eternal flame went out for some reason. This would shut off the gas before the whole neighborhood went into orbit. Because of the size of some installations, new technology was developed to handle the volume of natural gas to be controlled. Harold's short stay on this plane was having its effect.

Carl told Harold of Nellie's concerns about the world's population. Harold wrote her explaining his church and his plans about pushing birth control later.

"I do declare! Mixing the races! The man is crazy! Can't you see me taking a black boyfriend to the Saturday night square dance at the D.A.V. Club at The Hooterville Crossroads?"

"Things must be different above the Fall Line", commented Lilly.

"They are not that different even above the Mason-Dixon Line. I am not going to have any part of it. That fool is going to get his ass and his church blown off the map!"

"Carl told me Harold went and married a high yaller."

"He must have no respect for human life. At least his or his wife's."

"I hope Carl stays away from that place. I like him. In one piece, that is. I don't think Phillip has anything to do with it."

"He's the smart one."

"Nellie, have you ever thought of other races? Romantically I mean."

"Once, when I was walking home with the setting sun in my face, I beheld a figure outlined in the sun's rays. I could only see the fantastic form offered to my vision. My heart skipped many beats until he came close enough for me to determine his color. Midnight on a night with no moon comes close to describing the color of this Adonis. I was mortified."

Lilly asks, "Why? Was this not a natural urge?

"That was what mortified me. I then realized that these urges are universal. Once you overcome the ingrained prejudice which is inherent in all of us."

"What do you guess was going through his mind, Nellie?"

"Probably like thoughts suppressed by fear."

"Indeed a tragedy."

"Maybe not, Lilly, a union based solely on physical attraction is one that cannot endure. A couple must have more in common. I cannot think of another single thought that we could have shared."

"How about the love of a good cold watermelon on a hot summer day?"

"That's an unfair question! I share that love with every living soul in Georgia! Regardless of race creed or color."

"You are so right, Nellie!"

"The next time I meet one, I hope he has a cold watermelon. Maybe fears and prejudices will be overcome."

"Is that what they sing about in that song?"

"I don't think so Lilly, it's probably more about riding buses and going to good schools."

"Nellie, don't you dare repeat this to a living soul, but I saw our esteemed sheriff messing around with some forbidden fruit one day."

"You don't mean Joe Billy Buffered the Third?"

"In the flesh! And a lot of that was showing. He was parked in that patrol car of his behind that big billboard out on US Highway 84 East where he likes to watch for speeders coming from Valdosta. He and this filly were going at it hot and heavy. He damn well was not trying to catch any speeders that afternoon.

"When I passed by I saw his car and nobody in the driver's seat where he always sits. I passed on by without thinking much about it. But the farther I drove the more I worried that something might have happened to him. So I turned around the first chance I had. It was in the driveway going to the Wilcox house. I parked on the shoulder; do you know they call it a 'verge' in England?

"I got out and walked over behind the billboard, and there they were, both in the back seat and the car was rocking like it was running down a washboard road."

"I do declare! Joe Billy Buford the Third! What did you do then?"

"I did the only thing any self respecting white woman would do! I snuck back to my car and got my Polaroid camera and used up two rolls of film. I probably have some prize-winning photos. If I can find a good contest."

"You don't need a contest, Lilly, you have the best prize imaginable"

"What do you mean?"

"Insurance! You don't have to ever worry again about his giving you another speeding ticket."

"That's blackmail"

"No, this is not extortion, only a small equalizer against the powers that control our lives."

"Viva le equalizer!"

"You know, Lilly, maybe Joe Billy isn't as intolerant as we thought."

"Why, he might even be a closet liberal!"

Nellie comments, "Well, he better keep it in the closet if he wants to keep on being sheriff. If word got out about this he wouldn't stand a chance."

"I don't know about that. Most men would think it funny as hell. And there's not enough independent white women that could swing an election."

"If the truth were known, I bet more than half the men in this county participates in this form of pleasure", Nellie giggles.

"Yeah! They're a bunch of hard tailed hypocrites!"

"Yeah! But don't we love 'em!"

Dreaming, Lilly says, "Perhaps if Harold is successful, we can love them all."

"Lilly, how you carry on!"

"Us females have equal rights. We should have equal time also."

"What, Lilly, sack time?"

"There's an old saying. How did it go? Something about gooses and ganders."

Getting up and stretching, Nellie Says, "Yeah, I have heard wives using it to justify cheating on their cheating husbands. I remember that Sarah Sue catching her husband checking out of the Lonesome Pines Motel out on U.S. 84 West when she was checking in.

"Old Ephriam shore had a job washing away all that blood that was spilled in the parking lot."

"That was really a shame, Nellie, everybody thought that was a marriage made in heaven. No one knows what evil thoughts lurk in the minds of men."

"Don't exclude women."

"It might be that the institution of marriage should be altered."

"In what way?"

"Well, monogamy seems to be dying out and marriages of convenience are getting more popular. Maybe the marriage vows need to be re-written. Modify 'honor and obey' to be limited to household chores only. 'To death do us part' is OK.

"Divorcing is too expensive and messy. And it's hell on the kids. And make 'love and cherish' optional, subject to re- negotiation at a later date."

"Remember that couple we saw get married in the Catholic Church, Nellie, and the ceremony lasted longer than the union."

"Lilly, marriages should be moved out of the churches into the lawyer's offices."

"Convenient marriages in a convenient place. I like that."

"What a great new world you and I, Lilly, are contemplating! Mixed marriages, birth control, more liberal marriages and what else?"

"How about complete female emancipation, economic independence, equal employment opportunities?" Lilly asks.

"I for one choose not to operate bulldozers or climb telephone poles or the like. I would prefer the men share labor pains. And delivery problems."

"Yeah! And breast feed the little varmints."

"That'll be the day!"

"It's possible because of our occupation, we are prejudiced against wedlock."

"I know I'm against the lock part."

"Nellie, how are you and Zeke coming on the great manuscript?"

"If I could keep him off that tractor for about a week, we might accomplish something. Every time I go out there it seems that he is down on the back forty either plowing, harrowing or planting."

"I guess it's in his blood. He certainly doesn't need the money."

"What money? You don't make money farming these days. You just don't starve to death."

"He probably needs very little. He doesn't have many responsibilities. He ain't married is he?"

"Not that I know about. When I go out there, the only person I see besides Zeke is an old black mammy that was washing clothes and cooking supper."

"Maybe she performs other duties also."

"I can't believe that. She is old enough to be his mama and I bet she weighs half as much as that old tractor he uses."

"You know, he's not a bad looking man and he's not too old. It's a shame he stays out on that farm all the time and does not participate in the social activities of the community."

"Lilly, you don't fool me. I saw the way you looked at him that morning in the watermelon patch. The only social activities you would like to see him perform would be only. And in private."

"I feel it is my duty to alleviate the suffering of unfortunate men."

"Well, don't start anything with Zeke until we finish the book. It's hard enough to keep him off that tractor."

"I couldn't buck like that tractor even if you tied me to a stump."

"Let's not get graphic."

"Oh, I was only generalizing."

"I did get to talk to him for a short while. He did some computing assuming the craft was around two hundred feet in diameter. Using that figure and guessing the time it took to disappear in the sky by diminishing at a constant rate, he estimated it reached fifty thousand miles per hour before it cleared our atmosphere."

"That's impossible! It would've burned to a cinder! And the G-forces would have killed any human inside."

"If they were human."

"How about humanoid? Or felinoid?"

"It seems you have discovered a new word. Anyway, Zeke has a theory about the absences of stress. He feels the whole craft and its environment is somehow isolated from outside forces. If the craft can create its own force field that the occupants and the craft are subject to, outside forces will be neutralized. Such as we are unaware of the earth's rotation and centrifugal forces."

"This sounds great on paper, but how about the effect of the craft on our atmosphere?"

"He has an explanation for that also. This self-generated force field would attract a cloud of molecules of air around its surface, which will travel along with the craft. And this envelope would ionize at the speeds involved and create plasma, which offer very small amounts of friction to the atmosphere it passes through. This would explain the phase shift of the corona associated with such objects which the Doppler does not explain."

"I hope you had on hip boots when he told you all this."

"Why?"

"Because you were knee deep in bullshit. All technical types will try to lay that on you. I call it 'scientific double speak'."

"At the time it sounded perfectly logical. At least he had an explanation, which is more than you will get from the Air Force. This approach will appeal to the ordinary reader and if we maintain the style, we will have a best seller."

"I impatiently await the publication of this masterpiece. It will clear up some questions many have."

"Sometimes a satisfactory explanation serves much better than the truth. If it were known."

"Indeed a profound statement."

"I might also delve into the problems that treating the speed of light as a constant creates."

"I have no problem with that."

"Oh, yeah? How viewing a universe with your naked eye that might not exist?"

"Undoubtedly I had no problem with this because I have never given it any thought. I see what you mean. If you assign a finite velocity to the propagation of light waves, you admit that anything viewed from great distances involving light years might not exist by the time the light reaches your eye. Ask Zeke about that!"

"I fear he has the disadvantage of a formal education and is not qualified to discuss this. The wrong questions can make great minds retreat into a silent shell."

"This is to preserve sanity in lower forms but should not be allowed among the intelligentsia. They should be models we aspire to."

"Do not forget, they are human also."

"This is getting us nowhere. Let's go on the prowl."

"Where? We have used up all the resources around here."

"Tallahassee appeals to me and it isn't too far."

"Lilly, I know us! We would never make it back in time for school in the morning."

"Well, I've got to do something. I think I could jump right out of my skin!"

"How about consuming a quantity of ribs? It seemed to help before."

"That was different. We were under the influence of those Atlanta people. What were their names? I forget."

"Lilly you do beat all! You know damn well it was Carl and Phillip."

"Mercy! How could I forget them? I know I need some ribs now. Let's go!"

CHAPTER FIFTEEN

The Rib Shack manager, Don, walks over to the table where Nellie and Lilly had just sat. "Hello girls, I haven't seen you two since the night of the cats. I hated to lose that pig, but it was worth it. All we have now is an occasional possum and they run when they see anyone coming. They eat more garbage than the cats and we don't have to haul it off as often."

"That's great! Maybe we could train some of them and put them out at the landfill and the bulldozer will last longer."

"I dunno, Lilly, the rats do a good job out there now. And they give the kids something to shoot at for target practice. I'd hate to see all those possums get killed."

"They are kind of cute, Don, at least what little I have seen of them. They are nocturnal animals, you know."

Nellie adds. "You talk like you're not."

"Lilly can't be completely nocturnal. Look at that great tan on her legs. She didn't get that running around in the moonlight." The manager comments eyeing Lilly's shapely legs.

"Don, you're making me blush, I wish I could sleep more in the daytime so I could run around more after the sun goes down. It's cooler then but I can't teach school at night."

"What can I get you ladies tonight?"

"Give us some slaw, some baked beans, some ribs and a pitcher of draft beer. And bring a couple of bed sheets to wipe our mouths. We are gonna make one hell of a mess."

"Ah! Two girls after my heart! Don't give me any women that eat ribs with a knife and fork, and need a finger bowl with lemon juice in it. And some are just as bad eating chicken."

"Oh, and Don, bring some vinegar. I understand it suppresses flatulence."

"You don't need that with my beans. I cook the farts out of them."

"Really? I'd like to have the recipe for granny. She cooks the gassiest beans in the county."

"I'm sorry, Nellie, but that's an old family secret handed down from father to son dating back to the days before the War Between the

States. If more people knew it back then, there might not have been a war."

"How do you figure that?"

"What do you think blew up Fort Sumter? It wasn't us. It was those entire damn Yankees eating all those baked beans. And smoking all them cigars. We just got blamed for it. And that's all the excuse they needed to attack us."

Nellie says, "Then the history books are wrong?"

"Victors modify history. Embarrassments are for the losers."

"If you gave me the recipe, we might prevent another war."

"Why? Does your granny feed a lot of soldiers?"

"No, but I'd hate to see the west side of the county turn into no mans-land."

"Nellie, you're over-reacting. Those men at Sumter were on a steady diet of dried beans for six months before they left us. And all of them were congregated in the small confines of the fort. If there had been any breeze at all, it probably would not have happened. You don't get my recipe."

Lilly says; "Enough of this! Bring on the vittles. My navel is playing with my backbone."

"As fast as I can get to the kitchen, I'll fill your order."

"I wish I could clean bones like those brothers in the watermelon patch."

"There's no way you can, Lilly. It took generations of practice to acquire that ability. Anyhow we can take the bones home and put them in a pot of soup. They'll be clean when they get through cooking."

"Nellie, that will take all the romance out of it. Maybe if we didn't order all you can eat, we might do a better job."

"We are a couple of decadent white women."

"Sinners all. Maybe the fact that we teach Sunday school at the New Elim Baptist church at the Hooterville Crossroads out on US 84 West will redeem us, Nellie."

"Don't bet on it, just clean your bones and sin no more."

Lilly asks, "How do you think he took the farts out of those beans?"

"How do you know he did?"

"I'm sure he did. Remember how many we ate on cat night? If he hadn't, we sure could not have spent the night in close proximity of the boys. And they were smoking cigarettes also."

"Yeah, Lilly, if they hadn't been de-farted we might have joined the cats in orbit."

"I just had a thought. Maybe the cats were special because they had been eating those beans. If the recipe is a closely guarded secret, those might be the only cats in the world with no gas. And maybe those aliens have very sensitive noses and need that kind of cats."

"I bet he puts a lot of apple cider vinegar in the beans while they're cooking."

"He did act a mite strange when I mentioned the vinegar."

"That can't be all he uses. That's too simple. I did notice something else. I don't think he uses sugar. It tastes more like honey. Come to think of it, Zeke has a lot of hives out at his place and I think I saw that manager coming back from out that way the other day. I bet he was coming back from Zeke's after buying some honey."

"You can find out that easy enough. This can't be a very sophisticated formula because it's over one hundred years old. At least to our knowledge."

"Don't forget there were a lot of smart people around back then."

"I think he puts banana peppers in it. It's not bell."

"Who gives a damn what that old fool puts in his beans? We should just enjoy them. I am certainly not going to open a restaurant and if I want fartless beans, I'll come here and pig out."

"We can't just sit here and eat without talking about somebody. That would not be ladylike."

"Let's talk about Joe Billy. I want to see those pictures. Do you have them with you?"

"I haven't hid them yet. Lemme see. Here they are, next to my driver's license. I felt that was a good place for them in case Joe Billy needed to see my license. Hee, hee, I am sure looking forward to that! If his neck is red now, I wonder what color it will turn then?"

"Lilly, it might be dangerous to toy with a man like him. You know he totes that big .357 Magnum and he has a short fuse."

"Hee, hee, that ain't all that's short. Maybe that was why that black gal was squirming so, trying to get more 'fuse'. On second thought, I don't want to see those pictures. You make it sound so disgusting. This is supposed to be a beautiful natural act and your description degrades it to an animal level."

"How would you know anything about Joe Billy's 'fuse'?"

"Oh, I heard some women talking in a rest room while I was taking a piss in a stall with the door closed. You'd be surprised if you be quiet and keep the door closed."

"Don't they look for feet before they start gossiping?"

"Lilly, I always stand on the seat in strange rest rooms, don't you?"

"Some of the time, if I'm not wearing high heels."

"You need to take off your shoes, Lilly, for hygienic reasons."

"Back to the pictures, if you look at them, there's no doubt who the animals are."

"I guess I must endure the view. Hand them here."

As Nellie was reaching for the pictures, the air conditioner blower came on. The vent over the table let out a cold blast of cold air that blew the pictures out of Nellie's hand and scattered them all over the dining room. Lilly screamed and jumped up and in diving for the pictures, overturned her chair and slid across the adjacent table that was full of ribs, beans, beer and people. Her slide ended at the head of the table in some fat man's lap. Along with ribs, beans and beer. While everyone in the dining room had their attention riveted on this hilarious scene, Nellie went crawling around the floor gathering pictures. She finally found fourteen. Lilly had taken sixteen. All Lilly said when they got back to their table was; "Oh shit!"

All they could hope for was that the finder of the two missing pictures would not connect them to these two women. He would probably be so overjoyed; he would not question this manna from Heaven.

The finder of this windfall considered his luck akin to hitting the Irish Sweepstakes. For he was the principal underworld figure of the county. If it was illegal, he had a finger in it. He was shrewd and lucky. He had managed to always keep one step ahead of Joe Billy, but it was hard work. Too hard for a successful criminal. This might be the way to an easier life. He must think about the ramifications of this stroke of luck. In the meantime he will retire the evidence to his lock box at the Planters and Farmers Bank.

Due to come rare coincidence, and to add more credibility to this story, it seems this nefarious character had attended high school with Antonio Garabaldi. This was in Atlanta before Lucius Popejoy (that's the underworld figure's name) was apprehended for selling joints in class and expelled from school. This was all the impetus needed to head him down the road to hell. They say this road is paved with good intentions and his intentions were to ease through life with as little work as possible. They also say the road of the righteous is straight and narrow and hard. Lucius was a firm believer in this and opted for a less arduous route.

Lucius remembered Antonio as a smart young man and figured he would go far. His figuring was correct as he learned of the successes Antonio had wrought since graduating. He became aware of this information when he saw Antonio's name mentioned in connection with the annual watermelon-eating contest held in Cordele. This did not surprise him as he remembered Antonio as a great watermelon connoisseur with a ravenous appetite. He also could do justice to mountains of spaghetti and lasagna.

He called Atlanta and talked to the famous watermelon trasher. After refreshing Antonio's memory about what good buddies they used to be, he asked him if he would avail himself of a small service. For old times' sake. "I have a couple of Polaroid shots that I would like to get enlarged and printed as posters. Since there is no facility anywhere near here, I thought you might help me. Also, the subject matter of these shots does not meet the usual moral criteria of most photo labs. In other words, this must be treated as a backdoor operation. I am willing to generously compensate any persons involved." He finally got Antonio's interest aroused.

"Anything can be accomplished provided the right incentive is applied. In this regard, Lucius, what did you have in mind?"

"About twenty posters measuring somewhere around sixteen by twenty four inches would be worth five large to me."

"I am not familiar with the term 'five large'. Would that be five hundred?"

"No, that would be five grand."

"Send me one of the shots and let me see what I can do."

* * *

Antonio goes to see Carl, "Carl, I have been approached to render a service which is slightly alien to my expertise and I thought of you as a collaborator in this venture. The rewards will be great."

"What is your definition of great?"

"How about half of five large?"

"Tony, where in the hell did you pick up that term? I haven't heard that expression since that night the cops threw me in the drunk tank to sober up after that wild party at the Biltmore Hotel. Two thugs were in the next cell and they were talking about what their mouthpiece was going to charge to spring them. I think they were drug dealers."

"This party that contacted me mentioned 'five large'."

"Does it mean what I think it means?"

"In my circles, it would be considered 'extra large'."

"You now have my extra large attention, Antonio, I assume this is something you would not share with your priest."

"Absolutely not! In fact I myself am somewhat reluctant to pursue this proposition."

"Please enlighten me and then we shall make a decision."

Antonio showed Carl the Polaroid and told him what was expected of them. "Good grief! I know this man! This is Joe Billy Buford the Third! He is the illustrious sheriff of Hoots County down in South Georgia. Phillip and I got real close to him on our last trip down that way. He's really a great man. I can't believe he's got himself in such a compromising situation."

"Are you saying he is above such an act?"

"Of course not! Getting caught is what I can't understand. I think we should call him and tell him what's going down."

"Then we can give an extra large kiss to that five large. And Lucius told me he had two pictures. If we blew the whistle on him, he still could contact somebody else to do his dirty work."

"Not necessarily. Call him and tell him the photo got destroyed in the attempt to enlarge it. See if he can send you the other one. Maybe we can get the cash up front and then Joe Billy can take care of him in his own delicate way."

"We might live to regret this, but what the hell, I never liked that scumbag anyway."

* * *

"Joe Billy, you have been caught with your pants down. And I mean literally. I sure hope that black gal was worth the embarrassment a good Polaroid can cause."

"Oh shit! Which one are you talking about?"

"Ha! Then this must not be a unique happening. You old devil, you!"

"Carl, I'll have you know I'm the soul of discretion in my liaisons with the opposite sex and color."

"I'm sure you try to be, but I have in my hand positive proof."

"What in the hell are you trying to pull? If you think you got my balls in a vise and are turning the handle, you ought to know I do my best work under pressure. I'm not above coming to the big 'A' town and emasculating you right downtown on Peachtree Street before a large crowd with my trusty .357."

"Hold your horses, Joe Billy. I called you to try to do a favor. I think someone down there is going to try to blackmail you. He sent a picture up here to one of my friends and offered him five thousand dollars to have it enlarged and some posters made from it."

"Holy shit! Who was that son of a bitch?"

"Lucius Popejoy. Do you know him?"

"Do I know him? Do I know him! You bet your sweet ass I know him! I been trying to put him in Reidsville for the last ten years! This is serious!"

"Calm down Joe Billy. I have a plan to handle this. If we can get him to send the other picture along with the five grand. Then you can take care of him in your delicate way."

"I can do that. I been looking for an excuse to get rid of him. This is one job I'm gonna enjoy."

"You've got to promise me you will. If you don't, my life won't be worth two cents."

"Don't you worry about a thing. You get the other picture and he'll never leave this county again."

* * *

Lucius answers his phone. "Lucius, this is Antonio. I've got some bad news. The man that agreed to do the work screwed up and the shot got messed up in the process. I need you to send the other one."

"You must be out of your skull! If he screwed up once he'll do it again."

"No, he's not going to have the chance. I found another man that knows what he's doing. That first one fed me a line of bullshit. He tried to do the job in his bathroom at home. This new one works at a professional lab and works at night some. It will be easy to sneak the job in one night."

"That sounds better. You should have gone to him to start with."

"The reason I didn't was this one wants the money up front and you need to send it along with the picture."

"You must think I'm a damn fool. Why should I trust you?"

"Remember our lifelong friendship. Would I shaft an old school buddy?"

"Well, I should know better, but I'll send all of it tomorrow."

"Good, but send cash. I don't want to pay sales tax on this."

"That's illegal."

"Big joke, coming from you."

* * *

Three weeks passes and Lucius has not heard a word from Antonio. "I should know not to trust that bastard. His answering service says he is out of the country. Probably spending my five large. He's not going to get away with this. I'll show him Lucius Popejoy is not one to trifle with. Tomorrow will see me on the high road to the big 'A'. When I find him he'll curse his mama for birthing him."

Before dawn cracked the next morning he was high tailing north. Before he cleared the county line, he heard a funny noise in the floor between his feet. "Sounds like my valves are rattlin'. It's got to be low on oil. I'll stop at the county line liquor store and have a look see." Something was rattlin' but it was not his valves. What it was, was a forty-eight inch diamond back coiled to strike. And strike it did. Halfway between has ankle and knee. He yelled bloody murder and lost control of the car. It swerved across the centerline and plowed head on into a venerable old oak tree festooned with Spanish moss. His head went into the windshield and the steering wheel penetrated his rib cage.

One of his ribs punctured his left ventricle and the lights went out permanently for both him and his car. One week later Carl received a clipping from Joe Billy. It was cut out of the Tallahassee newspaper. From the back page.

HOOTS COUNTY CRIME FIGURE EVADES JUSTICE THE HARD WAY

Lucius Popejoy, notorious for his talent of staying arm's length away from the clutches of local law enforcement met his match Monday in an encounter with a rattlesnake. His car was found crashed into a tree just south of the Hoots county line. It seems he lost control after being bitten by a four-foot rattler that was found in his car. When Sheriff Joe Billy Buford the Third was investigating the accident, he discovered the snake and efficiently dispatched the reptile with his .357 magnum that is famed for its accuracy in many a shoot-out. The sheriff speculated that the snake probably crawled into the car while Mr. Popejoy had stopped somewhere along the highway to relieve himself. This type snake is common to Hoots County and can be easily caught by professionals. One herpetologist when contacted stated there was no reason to kill the snake if one knew what he was doing.

* * *

What was not mentioned was the sheriff always won the annual Hoots County Rattlesnake Roundup. This is by no means an accusation. Just the facts.

CHAPTER SIXTEEN

"Lilly, I wonder what ever became of those two pictures we couldn't find?"

"Well, Nellie, I've been thinking about that. They probably got swept up with all the other trash and went to the incinerator, or maybe someone's saving them for using them later."

"I hope they got burned, Lilly, I'd hate to see Joe Billy upset. There's no telling what he's capable of doing."

"He sure as hell didn't see them. You notice how happy he's been lately?"

"He's probably been out behind that billboard again."

"I don't think he goes out there anymore. At least I haven't seen him and I have been looking."

Nellie asks, "Why? You want some more pictures?"

"Hell no, I think I am going to find that incinerator for the ones I have."

"Good thinking, Lilly."

"Now who will we talk about?"

"I'm sure we will find someone. Have you heard from Carl or Phillip lately?"

"No, I guess they're kind of busy this time of year. I miss them both", Lilly laments.

* * *

"Tony, look at this clipping Joe Billy sent me."

"Hey, this is great! Carl. I haven't had a decent night's sleep since this started."

"Was your conscience bothering you?"

"No, I just think I am too young to give up this earthly vehicle."

"Everyone thinks that. Even my ninety-year-old uncle. He wants to hang around for the second coming. He knows so many evil people that he wants to see get their just desserts."

"I don't think I want to be around when all those rotting corpses crawl out of the ground to stand before the throne of judgment."

"Do you think that's how it will happen?"

"Don't you believe what your mama told you, Carl?"

"Someone had to tell her, and they might have been wrong." Carl speculates. "I have heard that a dead person's hair keeps on growing after they are buried. Can't you just imagine a walking skeleton with hair down to his ass-bone?"

Still speculating, Carl says, "Some say you resurrect with your body in its prime."

"Some die before their prime. How about that?"

"A thinking person has to draw their own conclusions, Tony, of course, to exist efficiently in a society, one should keep these thoughts to themselves. The essence of hypocrisy is to avoid controversy."

"And that justifies it?"

"In some political arenas, survival may well depend on it."

"Carl, what's your opinion on Mary belle's and Butch's crusade?"

"All crusades are multi-purpose. The purpose of the middle age crusades were to rape and pillage under the cloak of Christian respectability."

"My Pope would condemn your thought as heresy."

"Your Pope is not my Pope, as your God might not be my God."

"There was a time when your beliefs would make you a prime candidate for a community barbecue."

"Thankfully, I live in a more enlightened time." Carl replies.

"We all benefit from the revelations of free thinkers."

"There are some that still reject the art of reason. They seem to be of the majority in the Bible belt in which we reside."

"As all of us, atheists, heathens and agnostics are protected by the Constitution."

"The Constitution only protects the affluent. Those whom can defy prejudice."

"Carl, the cynic. Thurgood Marshall is going to make a difference."

"In time, maybe, Tony, Clarence Darrow had no success in the Scopes trial back in the twenties."

"Ha! What was expected? It was held smack-ka dab in the middle of the Bible Belt."

"Why not say in Fundamentalist Red Neck Country?"

"What a wonderful choice of words, Carl. I cannot describe it better."

"Your religion avoids this dilemma by ignoring the Old Testament."

"I often wondered why this was. You might be right."

"We stray from the topic in question. Namely Marybelle and Butch. Where were we?"

"I was soliciting your opinion on their purpose."

"I really haven't given much thought to it. I am too wrapped up in the income it generates."

"Your motives are obvious, but what of theirs?"

"I am not privy to their innermost thoughts. I seriously doubt we will ever know. We would have to be a mind reader."

Carl and Antonio neither possess the ability of the author. Because the author is the creator of all the characters involved here in print, the dark recesses of the minds of the characters are not held sacred. First we shall probe into the mind of Marybelle; (The following text is not in quotes because she is not speaking, only thinking).

I feel so lucky. I have a good man who loves me. I wonder if it is for my mind or only my body. If I live long enough to become wrinkled and infirm, I shall know. I do not dwell on this. I am not one to examine the teeth of an equine gift. I do not share what I believe is his dedication to this cause he expounds. This is not repulsive to me. It seems worthy if not practical. Some of the followers may be sincere, but I suspect most are the victims of animal lust. As well as I might be. Things are working out between us. He makes few intellectual demands because of my limited education. We are great in bed. I want for nothing. Perhaps because my desires are simple due to my background. I have few peers with whom to compete. If I had attended an expensive university and associated with the daughters of affluent families and had been exposed to their lifestyles, I might have expected the same for myself. In this respect I consider myself fortunate. Their existence seems so shallow to me. I am not a spoiled brat. No demands were made of my parents that they could not afford. In turn I was loved not just tolerated, as I suspect of some. Harold has been my savior and I look no further for peace and consolation.

(All males should be blessed with such a companion. Now let's see how Harold feels about all this.)

I wonder what drives me. There is a difference in my character when I compare my actions to others. There is no urgency associated with my goals even though I give this impression on the surface to others. It would seem that if I fail in a certain endeavor, it would make no difference in the great scheme of things. Whatever that may be. Sometimes I feel like a visitor. Like a vacationer in Paris for a holiday. Observation without real participation. The effects of my involvement will not alter anything. If the truth were known about why I started my church, many would be shocked. My existence here I feel is purely accidental and I should take advantage of this happening for my own pleasure. Developing radical departures from the prevailing ideologies that surround me is done primarily to view the consternation caused by my actions. And possibly to stir thought in dormant minds. My one joy is Marybelle and I fear this is a fleeting thing. Our union was not 'made in heaven' as some love struck teen-agers believe of theirs. Such a thing would be rare indeed, if possible. One would have to believe in reincarnation to believe this and if you ask some of these star struck lovers if they do, they will reply in the negative. For a couple to stay together for one lifetime on this earth with so many factors against them is about all one can expect.

If when we are both old and wrinkled and are still together, I will consider our union a success.

I did not know my father. I often wonder if I had, what kind of attachment would I feel towards him? Just the fruit of his loins in a moment of passion or some deeper-seated connection? Why was he my father? Why was she my mother? Who am I? Just a product of a moment of passion or more? I feel no real bond to my mother. This is not her fault. She has been loyal and caring. Should I expect more? Would the bond be greater had my father lived? There is a hollow place in my soul like I have lost something. What could it be? My mother tells me strange things about my childhood. This might be a clue to my longing. She feels that I am not completely her son. Not like an empty vessel to be filled with love and understanding as I suspect normal offspring are. I probably will have to wait for my departure to know the answers. If even then.

LATER

The crater was over three hundred feet wide and forty feet deep in the center. Marybelle and Harold had driven home from Birmingham that night after attempting to organize a new church there. They were locked in a sleeping embrace when it happened. In that fleeting moment of consciousness before oblivion, they discovered the reality of the creator. And all were one. And one was all. This was their eternity.

The authorities said an accumulation of gas in the basement caused the catastrophe. They felt the carelessness of Jebediah Hawkins in making his icons was at fault.

We know better. Brother Hawkins had not used the basement for that purpose in many months. The happenings in Texas City shortly after the war gave inspiration to the evildoers.

* * *

There will be no resurrection of these bodies on the big day because no bodies were found. In fact, no church was found. A dark cloud hovered over the area for days. Somewhat reminiscent of Nagasaki or Hiroshima, but not on such a scale. A memorial service was held in lieu of a funeral. Because of the controversial mixed marriage, no church would allow such an unholy alliance to be honored with their sanction. It was held in the only place which all the mourners were familiar, Carl's auction barn. Butch was more than devastated. He had lost his best friend and the girl he idolized. The gaiety that usually permeated this happy place was absent and it would be many months before things returned to normal. In the diner there was placed a sculpture of magnolia blossoms festooned with a garland of honeysuckle. This was a permanent tribute to a wonderful lady who had brought joy to so many with her beauty and wit. No one who had known her could view this thing of remembrance with a dry eye.

CARL JONES SPEAKS AT THE MEMORIAL SERVICE

"I came to know Harold and Marybelle many years ago. I think it was in nineteen fifty-one when he was only seven years old. He was a strange child with knowledge that far exceeded his age. For me, he was a gift from Heaven for he delivered me from the depths of poverty and showed me the way to be successful in this life. He never once asked for any kind of reward. He often told me that the smile on my face was reward enough. I owe a lot to Harold; in fact I owe my life to him for the road I was traveling went straight to hell. I firmly believe he was an Angel incarnated to perform good deeds here on earth. Regardless of others opinion of him. He will remain in my heart as this forever.

Marybelle came along about two years later. She was hired by my wife as a menial to share some of the housework. It wasn't long until we found that her talent was being wasted. She was destined for greater things. Her natural beauty and her wonderful personality enabled her to assume a position of importance in my enterprises. Harold knew a jewel when he saw one and pursued her to that end. A brighter light will never shine in God's great Heaven. She will be missed by all that her golden hands touched.

I intend to fill the crater with a lake and dedicate it to their memory as a shrine and recreation center for children of all races. This may bring a better understanding to all who participate in its pleasures. An irrevocable perpetual trust will insure the survival of this moment long after we all have joined them in their Heavenly Home.

Mary, Harold's mother, Dolly and Joe, his grandparents have instructed me to convey their appreciation for your outpouring of sympathy at this sad time. They apologize for not speaking at this time because they feel they cannot. They might be able to see each of you individually later. There will be no refreshments at their home. This is not a proper occasion for this kind of revelry as has been seen at others. If any of you wish to participate in the construction of the monument, please contact me at my office later in the week. I now step down and invite others to speak if they so desire."

BUTCH JONES SPEAKS

"Most of you knew this person as Harold. I knew him at times when he was not Harold. He had many personalities. I did not know all of them. I was first aware of him when he was Gilmore. Once when I was only ten, Harold manifested himself after I was harassing Gilmore and proceeded to show me the error of my ways. This was the best thing to happen to me up to that time. Even though Gilmore was about four years my junior, Harold seemed ages older. If it were not for Harold, I might well have been a candidate for prison or at least reform school. I feel that I owe my life to him and I hope he and Marybelle are now enjoying their rightful place in paradise."

EFFIE LOU JONES

"I feel it appropriate to say a few words. I hope I can. I am devastated. They were so young and had so much to live for. They will never enjoy the fruits of their labors. They will never look forward to see the new model automobiles every year or the completion of the Interstate. Marybelle was a lot of help to me. She was faithful and made no absurd demands while she was in my employ. She will be hard to replace. I am so sorry to cut this short, but I have an important bridge appointment."

On that sour note the memorial Piano Red terminated service with some soul stirring music. Out of respect, no auction was held this night.

SOME PRIVATE THOUGHTS OF MARY PITTS

Poor Marybelle, she did not know what she was getting into with Harold. I hope the short time they had together was worth the consequences. They shared more time together than my beloved Patrick and I had. I have never regretted one moment. Of course I would have preferred more time for us to enjoy, but what will be, will be. We do not have control over our destiny. I shall grieve for them both. Perhaps I shall grieve for them as long as I have for my beloved. But as they say, life must go on. They were an inspiration for me to carry on in my sorrow. I must think of the future now. And I cannot endure in this sorrow alone. Mother and dad are in the twilight of their union and do not need me as much now. I must find reason to carry on in my solitude. I am not ready yet to join my beloved. My work will have less meaning now. Perhaps now is the time for me to find new distractions. I am only thirty-eight and might have at least another thirty years to spend here. Carl has agreed to share the insurance with me. He must have a conscience after all. Caution must be used to prevent some shallow infatuation from depriving me of a comfortable existence while I await the inevitable. I do not want to be a burden on my parents or cause them any anxiety. Perhaps the wisest thing for me to do is leave this town where I am so well known and start over. If I am discreet as to my windfall, I might find a companion with which to share some good few years. Who knows? It might develop into a fine relationship. No one knows whether or not loved ones meet again in an afterlife. I have heard of persons having a near death experience and being so overwhelmed by the experience that no thought was given to the ones left behind. It would be folly indeed to base a life on the expectation of a blissful reunion in the hereafter. Twenty-one years might be long enough for one to grieve. I worry about Marybelle, but maybe Harold has taken her to that place where he would disappear at times. If he could, I am sure they are not worrying about me or the racial turmoil here he was dedicated to abolish. And I know he is not worrying about where the cats went.

I shall give my situation more thought and talk to mother and dad.

EXCERPT FROM THE JOURNAL OF JOE McDONALD

I could not bring myself to speak at the memorial for fear of making a spectacle of my grief. I know I should have. My remaining loved one now will probably think I am callous and uncaring. Someday someone may read this and my true thoughts might be revealed.

Compulsive urgencies compel idiotic expression sometimes. This is one of those sometimes. Insomnia attacks. I grasp this opportunity to express some thoughts and commit them to record for posterity. Maybe it is not insomnia attacking. It might be insanity. I cannot judge. Perhaps the viewer of these words may. But be careful. You may be judging yourself. A lifetime of discipline takes its toll. Weighing selfishness against duty to family deprives one of the most precious experiences that should be one's God given birthright. A lifetime is short in the great scheme of things and if one thinks this is all that is allotted to an individual, certain thoughts will manifest that may be detrimental, if this may not really be the case. I am now in that time of life that I question the motives, which have driven me for the past sixty years of my life. Well, maybe not quite that long. The first few years were genetically influenced. I don't know exactly when an individual awareness was realized, but I imagine it was about the same time puberty attacked me. Speaking of puberty, this seems to be God's curse on mankind to perpetuate His great experiment. Namely the human race. Unless one can live in perfect freedom with wild abandon, thinking only of self gratification with complete disregard of fellow creatures who, through no fault of their own have been placed in this maelstrom of life, you will be cursed with a conscience. And this can be a great disadvantage. I am not a vegetarian, but I would starve if I had to kill to eat. I am a wimp. I am a parasite on the tree of life, like mistletoe or Spanish moss on a giant oak. This is not an apology, only a statement. A person should have only the mental faculties necessary to survive in a world of chaos, like an animal of a lower form. Any further development of the mind can only serve to drive one to the brink of insanity. The only explanation I can think of about this dilemma is that we are sentenced to this prison of life for some minor infraction on another plane of existence. On second thought, it must not have been very minor. I wish I could glide through life with no cares as I suspect that some do. It seems these have now become a majority. And they say the majorities are right. Heaven help us.

Harold, please forgive me for being so intolerant of other's feelings and so self centered about my own. God willing. I hope you and Marybelle are now embraced in the loving arms of our Creator.

CHAPTER SEVENTEEN

Effie Lou's performance at the memorial service prompted Carl to declare, "enough is enough". He would be the first to admit he was the primary contributor to her self-centered attitude, but what's a man to do? He had been too engrossed in his enterprises to hover over her and try to correct her misguided directions. Hell, he probably was not qualified anyway. Harold was the only one who could have made a difference and he had been busy keeping Carl straight. Heaven only knows what will happen now that his guidance is not available. But Carl knew one thing for sure. Effie Lou was not going to drag him back down to the level where he was before Harold came into his life. The only thing that kept him from soliciting Joe Billy's aid was the fact that she was the mother of his son. Maybe Jonas Perkins could rekindle his interest in her if she lost about two hundred pounds. The interest Jonas showed in her did not escape his attention back when she was a trim one hundred and twenty. The more Carl thought this, the more he was opposed to the idea. Hell, if she lost those extra pounds, Carl was afraid he would want her back for himself. She used to be great in the hay. Suddenly he had an inspiration. A sheer stroke of genius! His business had once taken him to Palm Beach and he was exposed to the richest, most pampered and decadent people he had ever met. Surely his wife could find that kind to her liking. Granted, it would cost a fortune to set her up in that society, but it would be damn well worth it.

"Oh Carl, That's a wonderful idea, but how could you manage your business from so far off?"

"Haven't you heard of airplanes? I will commute. I can catch the red eye Friday night and come back on the early bird Monday. You probably will see more of me than you do now."

"I don't think you need to come down every weekend. It will be too expensive."

"You might be right, but there's nothing wrong with you staying down there and enjoying yourself."

"Darling, you sacrifice so much for me. You must truly love me."

"Why else would I do these things?"

It took the better part of the year to get her moved or shall we say removed and set up. The bank account was nearly depleted and he would have to sell the West Paces Ferry house. He might have a small amount left after he bought her a Rolls. She called him up one day, crying about she being properly accepted because she only drove a Cadillac Fleetwood. And all her neighbors have Mercedes, Rolls and Daimlers. And she did not have enough domestic help. He must increase her allowance. He was definitely out of his league and in over his head.

Other avenues must be explored. He must do this alone. Harold could not be reached now. "Oh God, how I miss that boy."

* * *

"Effie Lou darling, I'm sending a group of my friends down to spend a week in our house. I'll be down later. Please welcome them and be a good hostess. They are very important and it will mean a lot for our business."

"Carl, this is such an imposition! It will interfere with my social activities."

"Effie Lou, now you shut up and listen closely! I'm sick and tired of you sitting on your broad ass and always complaining like a spoiled brat. Our business is in trouble and I need some cooperation out of you. This shit about you taking and taking and never giving has come to an end. If you can't help a little when I need you, you might wind up in the street sleeping in that damned Rolls. Now these people will be down there on Monday and I expect you to act like some decent lady. I know this will be an 'imposition' but you had better damn well do it!"

"Oh Carl! How can you treat me this way? We have been married so long and there has never been a cross word spoken between us. What has happened?"

"You showed your true colors at the memorial service. It broke my heart to hear you say what you did. I should have known there was no hope for you."

"I don't understand, what did I do that was so wrong?"

"If you don't know, I know damn well there's no hope for you. We will discuss this further after my friends leave."

Early Monday morning an airport limousine pulled up under the porte-cochere in front of the Jones mansion. After much unloading of luggage, there stood ten curious persons wondering where their host was and what should they do next. One enterprising individual proceeded to the front doors and began manipulating a gigantic brass doorknocker. After five minutes of continuous operating this device, there appeared a slovenly woman in curlers and housecoat. The knocker exclaimed. "My God! I feel that I'm still at home. All I need is a cup of coffee and you sitting across the table from me bitching! Are we at the right house? Is this the Jones' mansion? Where's Carl? We expected him to meet us."

"Don't get your feathers ruffled. Carl called and said he would be coming down later, and I didn't expect you people until the noon flight. Bring your luggage into the foyer and I'll see if I can round up the servants to see you to your rooms. The cook is preparing lunch, but I'll see if she can round up some coffee and Danish. Lunch will be served at eleven. I cannot let you interfere with my soaps."

"By no means let us disturb your routine. We are here only to inspect the premises and to determine if it is suitable for our purpose."

"What in the hell are you talking about? Carl told me to entertain you as his friends down on a holiday."

"Carl speaks with a forked tongue. We represent The Seminole Indian Nation, Oklahoma branch, and we are considering purchasing this property if we can annex it into our Florida branch."

"This is the craziest thing I ever heard. Sounds just like something a bunch of wild Indians would cook up. This is Palm Beach and you don't have a snowball's chance in hell of annexing this place!"

"Madam, I beg to differ. We represent an oppressed people that have for too long suffered the injustices imposed upon us by you invaders of our sovereign land. We shall take no more punishment. It is well past time for ancient wrongs to be righted. This very land you and your neighbors stand on was once ours, to roam freely and hunt game without pillage. Too long those who have no concept of natural beauty have defiled for this once pristine land. Your decadent monuments to mammon will in time turn back to dust and nature will again reign supreme as the Gods intended."

‘My, how you prattle! In what way will the purchase of this property enable you to gain your ambitions?”

“We aim to petition Congress for the right to carry on economic enterprises on our land without any local interference.”

“What type of ‘economic enterprise’ did you have in mind for my property?”

“First I need to remind you that ‘this property of yours’ belonged first to us and now Carl Jones has false claim upon it. We intend to open a large Bingo parlor here.”

“I love to play Bingo! Wait, what do you mean? I have no claim?”

“The title of this place is in Carl’s name only. He can dispose of it in any manner he so chooses.”

“I see now that we must terminate this discussion and let our respective attorneys thrash it out. Gentlemen, you are no longer welcome here. I suggest you check into a hotel and wait for Carl there. I shall summon transportation to convey your luggage and asses away.”

* * *

“Good morning, Jones Enterprises, how may I help you?”

“You may connect me with the head asshole in charge. (H.A.I.C.)

“You must mean Mr. Carl Jones. He is the only asshole in our fine organization.”

“You got that right, put him on the phone.”

“Whom may I say is calling?”

“This is his head bitch.”

“Oh, Mrs. Jones, I didn’t catch your voice. Hold on.”

Carl complains, “Dammit, I don’t want to talk to her. Tell her I’m out of town”

“I’m sorry, Mrs. Jones, he is on a trip out of town.”

“I see. And where did he just tell you he was going?”

“He said to tell you he is on the way down to Palm Beach to see you.”

“You tell him that if he is not down here by morning, his head bitch is going to torch his future Bingo parlor.”

“Before you do anything, wait until he gets there.”

"Who in the hell do you think you are? Telling me to wait."
"He just told me that on the way out the door."
"I bet you are a bubble gum chewing, peroxide bleached blonde."
"How did you know?"
"Intelligence has a way of oozing out. Didn't you know?"
"Know what?"

* * *

"Jonas I need your help. You once had a lot of influence over Effie Lou and maybe you can talk her out of doing something foolish."

"Carl, you know that was a long time ago and I have since learned the error of my ways. I cannot interfere in your domestic problems."

"You don't fool me one minute. If she was still a nice slim young filly, you'd be on the next plane to Palm Beach with me."

"Maybe, but she ain't is she?"

"Much to my sorrow."

"Ours. What's the problem?"

"Some damn fool rich Indians I sent down there to look at the house couldn't keep their mouths shut and got my ass in a crack."

"I've never seen a rich Indian."

"Well, for once some of them got the best of a bunch of us palefaces. They rounded up a lot of Creeks, Cherokees and Seminoles and dumped them out in a God forsaken place in Oklahoma to starve to death. And they almost did until oil was discovered on the reservation and those redskins laughed their asses off. The joke was on the palefaces."

"I haven't ever been to Oklahoma. Maybe that's why I never saw a rich Indian."

"You must not have been to Cherokee, North Carolina either."

"Come to think of it, I ain't."

"Will you go to Palm Beach with me? Your job may depend on it."

"Are you threatening me?"

"Hell no, It's just that if I don't get this shit straightened out, the business might go down the tubes. Then everybody's job will be gone."

"I see that I must rise above my petty disgust and do my duty as a loyal employee of so many moons."

"If you succeed in helping save the company, much wampum will be in your grasp."

"Let us mount the great white bird and journey to the pow-wow."

"We shall smoke the pipe of peace with our red brothers and all will be well."

"I must retire early to prepare myself for the ordeal with your once pretty wife."

"God willing, she may once again be."

"Why don't we take Butch along? He hasn't seen the place and he might have some influence on his mother."

"That's a great idea. I'll talk to him tonight. Be packed and ready to leave early in the morning."

"How long do you think we'll be down there? I don't want to run out of clean clothes."

"We're gonna stay as long as it takes to get her head straight. We can buy some more clothes. And Butch can find a Laundromat if Effie Lou high priced domestic help runs off when they see me coming. Heads will roll!"

CHAPTER EIGHTEEN

Butch has listened to Carl's plan and comments, "Dad, the closest I ever came to flying was the time we sent up that hot air balloon. Ha, Ha, that was a gas wasn't it?"

"Yeah, it really put The Old Dixie Antique Shop on the map. Why? Are you afraid of flying?"

"Not really, I was just thinking about my ears. Remember when you took mama and me up to the top of Brasstown Bald and I couldn't hear for a week? I'm afraid if that happens again, I won't be much help calming her down."

"You don't have to worry about that now, Son. The planes' cabins nowadays are pressurized and it doesn't affect your ears like it did back in 1948 when I flew in a DC3 down to Jacksonville and I was deaf as a post during my stay down there. I learned a lot of sign language on that trip. Most everybody gave me the finger when I kept asking him or her what he or she was saying. Even a cork popped out of a bottle I had on my hip. I was taken for a deaf drunk."

"You're not bull shitting me are you?"

"So help me, that's the truth. Now pack a bag. We gonna leave early in the morning."

After a short while into the flight, Butch asks, "Dad, when I agreed to come along, I didn't know this was a trans-Atlantic trip. What's all that water doing down there?"

"Just making waves."

"Let me rephrase that, what are we doing over all that water down there? I thought Palm Beach was in the United States."

"A lot of people don't think it is. I must have failed to mention that this flight makes its approach from the east. Don't concern yourself. We will be landing shortly."

"I suspect we are dangerously close to the Bermuda Triangle, Dad. And I don't want to wind up like the cats."

"What's this got to do with the cats, Butch?"

"Probably nothing, but I would hate for our disappearance to also be a mystery."

"All things are mysteries until new discoveries are made," Carl comments sagely.

"That would be small comfort to our loved ones."

"Do not exclude cat lovers."

"From what you told me, Dad, the cats were not loved."

"We were not familiar with their acquaintances."

"Who could love a bunch of wild pig eating alley cats?"

"Love takes on many forms."

"Do you still love mama?"

Carl squirms, "That's an unfair question. As I say, love takes on many forms."

"You are evading the question."

"If you love her and I love you, then I guess I do too. In my own way."

"And what way is that?"

"Long distance love."

"You certainly have a way with words. No wonder you are such a good salesman."

"Butch, A person does what he has to for survival."

"Are you inferring your survival depends on separation?"

"At least my sanity does. And it keeps me in a better mood."

The plane bounces on the runway, and Butch yells, "Damn! That landing nearly jarred my teeth out. What was that pilot doing, looking out the bottom of his bifocals?"

"He must have misjudged where the ground was."

"Yeah, by about twenty feet!"

"It's a wonder the tires didn't blow. I remember back when I was about your age, I went over a steep bridge going too fast and got airborne. When I landed, both front tires blew and the front spring broke. It was one of those Studebakers that the front end was held together by that damned spring and that car then looked like a cow that did a front leg split on an iced over pond."

"It sounds like you were pretty wild back then."

"Yeah, my pore old Paw stayed drunk most of the time to keep me from driving him crazy. I'm glad you are such a level headed boy."

"I owe it to Harold's guidance. God rest his soul."

"Amen. Butch, go over and rent us a car while Jonas and I find our baggage, if it's not in New York or some other place. Put it on my credit card. That way, we won't have to buy extra insurance."

"Do you think we need it?"

"I don't know how good a job Harold did on you."

"Aw, Dad."

"Git."

When Carl and Jonas carried the luggage out the front door, Butch was sitting behind the wheel of a practically new Chrysler Three Hundred. The engine was putting out a guttural purr like a four thousand pound kitten.

"Butch, what in the hell have you rented here? It sounds like a diesel truck. What's under the hood?"

"Oh, it's only a little 440 with three deuces on it. Don't worry. They told me the first tank of gas was free."

"Small consolation that is. That won't even get us out of the parking lot!"

"It's not that bad. It didn't take but a quarter tank to get here from the motor pool."

Any rubber left on the rear tires?"

As Butch heads out the parking lot like the green light just came on at a drag race, he yells, "Wow! This is a fun car to drive."

"Have you gone crazy?"

"Not really, you know all I get to drive around Atlanta is that Volkswagen and it won't pull a sick whore off a pisspot. I felt the need to feel the brute power of a dinosaur before they become extinct."

"There's not much danger of that happening. There will always be a bunch of fools around who have beasts like this."

"I don't know, there is not too many fools around that own gas stations. I won't ever be able to afford one of these, I don't think."

"I hope you never will. I'd hate to see you get killed and these things are killers."

"Not if you don't drink."

"How about those midnight drag races on the interstate?"

"That sport is reserved for fools only."

Due to the speed limits, Butch was afraid to find the top end in second or high gear, but they saw seventy in first and when he popped it into second, he left more rubber on the asphalt.

Carl sates, "Wow! If I had one of these when I was your age, we wouldn't be enjoying this now."

"Why not, Dad?"

"I would have got my ass killed. There wasn't a road in North Georgia that would handle it. Them moonshiners I knew sure could have used something like this. All they had were souped up flat head Fords. They did pretty well for themselves, but they were nothing like this."

"God bless modern technology!"

"God has nothing to do with this. This is the result of the Detroit horsepower race. Chrome and guts. You have impressed us with your ability. Now cool it. We need to get to the house in one piece."

The rumble of the car coming around the circular driveway attracted Effie Lou's attention.

"That sounds like one of those big boats coming up the channel, but it's coming from the front of the house. If some damn fool is trying to upset me, he's doing a good job. Carmella, go to the door and send whoever it is on their way. I'm trying to watch my soap."

"Si, si."

Before Effie Lou had time to pop another chocolate covered cherry, Carmella was back.

"Madam, I do not weesh to annoy you but there are three senors weeth suitcases at the door. They weel not vamoose unteel they see you."

"Dammit, don't tell me it's some of those Indians."

"I do not theenk so, they are gringos."

"Tell them to wait until there is a commercial break."

"Si, Si."

"Senors, you are to wait unteel the madam can find sometheeng that is no importante upon the eedyot box."

"Jonas, do you know what she is trying to tell us?"

"I believe Effie Lou is involved in a soap opera on the television and is waiting for a commercial break."

"Ha! All right you fugitive from a Cuban cane patch, you go tell this product of too much money and not enough sweat that if she is not at this door in ten seconds I will invade her sanctum sanctorum and personally with my bare hands smash her precious 'eedyot box' to smithereens and then she won't have to wait for a commercial break."

"I do not understand all thees words, but I do understand your tone. I weel tell the madam."

Faster than a jet plane and with more power than a locomotive, Effie Lou came crashing through the front door. She managed to come to a sliding halt before damaging the rental car.

"Oh Carl, I knew it had to be you when Carmella interpreted your message. Why didn't you tell me it was you?"

"How could I? That wetback clone of yours was blocking the door and there was not enough room for a midget to squeeze by. Have you completely lost all your marbles? What's this shit about torching some Bingo parlor? Do you need professional help? There are plenty of head shrinkers around here by the looks of all these mansions. Surely some are on your social register."

"The only professional help I need is a high priced ambulance chaser to clean your clock. If you think you can put me out in the street without a what-for, you are the one that needs a shrink!"

Jonas steps into the fray. "Carl, there seems to be some misunderstanding here. Please take our luggage up to our rooms while Butch and I talk to Effie Lou."

"If you think you can apply logic on this bitch, maybe you are the one needing a shrink."

"Excuse me, boss, I do not mean any disrespect, but shut up and git!"

Carl gets the message and leaves the field of battle to more level heads.

"Effie Lou, please understand, Carl has been under a lot of pressure lately. He has had some business reverses and what he needs most of all right now is help and cooperation. God, it's been such a long time since I last saw you. I wish you would come back to Atlanta so you could help us all."

"That's right, mama. Things seemed to fall apart when you moved to that big house on West Paces. Weren't you happy when we all lived in that small house beside the garage?"

"Oh Butch, I don't know what happened to me. I had worked all my life and thought that I deserved more. I felt a life of leisure was for me. Little did I realize how lonely life could be without true friends. I had none of either in that big house up there or down here. I have made mistakes, but what I don't understand is Carl. He, I know has also made some and I could forgive him if he would only forgive me. I have been thinking about what he said to me about my little speech at the memorial service. Now I know how wrong I was and if it was in my power, I would go back and correct my actions. I am so ashamed. And Jonas, you are a lying sack of shit! I know I am as big as the side of a house and don't think I'm proud of it. People take up bad habits when they are lonely."

"Effie Lou, I wasn't lying. I was always attracted to the inner you, but the package was better then. I don't know what exactly Carl has in his mind concerning you, but I do know what's in mine. You are worth salvaging and if he won't, I will."

"Oh Jonas, that's the sweetest thing I've heard in many years. I swear here and now that you shall soon see me as I once was. So help me, God!"

"Will you two please stop this syrupy blather! I am getting nauseous. Did not these elapsed years cool the fire any at all? This is reminiscent of my youthful ravings over Marybelle, God rest her soul."

"Now Butch, You know Jonas and I were only good friends. I believe your relationship with Marybelle went further than that."

"If only it had, then she wouldn't have got involved in that hair-brained scheme with Harold and they would both be alive today."

Jonas says, "You can't know that for sure. Every action we take diverts us down different paths."

"Jonas, I didn't realize you were such a philosopher. You didn't hang around Harold enough for his ideas to influence you very much."

"My old daddy had a lot to do with shaping my mind."

"Is that a fact? What did he do for a living?"

"He was the Grand Dragon of The knights of The Ku Klux Klan back in the twenties."

"I don't understand. I always thought that all of them was a bunch of intolerant bigots."

"No Butch, they got the bad name by some of the irresponsible members taking matters into their own hands over isolated racial problems. This was usually done without the blessing of the organization as a whole."

"Then what was blessed?"

"As now, there was always a small group of no account lazy white men that held their wife and children in virtual slavery through neglect and abuse. They were gamblers and drunkards and would throw their money away every payday and then go home broke and take it out on their family."

"Didn't the law take care of the problem?"

'No, Effie Lou. Unless he wound up killing one of his family, the sheriff's hands were tied. One Klan trip to the man's house was all it usually took to show the bastard the error of his ways."

"Maybe we could use some of that kind of justice today."

"They weren't completely lily white. They were also obsessed with racial purity. This was what I believe contributed to their downfall. A lot of bad things happened in the name of racial purity."

"Do you think that was what happened to Harold and Marybelle?"

"Butch, whether it's true or not, some hate group will be blamed. That's the way things are and will ever be thus."

"For a young person's dreams to be shattered by reality are very traumatic. What's a person to do?"

"Some people are able to acquire immunity through the acquisition of the almighty dollar."

"Isn't that the greatest contributor to the corruption of our society?"

"To our shame, Butch, I believe so."

Effie Lou says; "I remember back during the depression, we had black families in our neighborhood. Come to think of it, the family unit seemed closer knit than their white counterparts."

"Yes, that was their only hope of survival, considering the odds that were against them. But things have changed."

"What happened?"

"We got involved in a great war and all races had to contribute for the survival of the country."

"But Jonas that should have brought us all closer together."

"On the surface, it did, Effie Lou, but there were gross acts of discrimination which were not publicized."

"Like what?"

"Complete segregation in all the armed services. Capable men were delegated to the most menial tasks. Mostly behind the fronts. This was a terrible blow to one's pride. They were not considered fit to fight for their freedom because they would not gain freedom even if they were the victors. Of course there were some isolated exceptions like a squadron of fighter pilots that proved to be one of the best combat units of the war."

"If they knew what they would come back to, why did they participate?"

"Maybe they thought things would finally change. But things didn't change. I think this was about the time a new philosophy was conceived."

"I think I know what that was."

"Strength in numbers. Become a majority. Register to vote, make many babies, and get on welfare. Have more babies. Upset the economy of this country in our favor. Make Whitey pay. I doubt they used those exact words."

Butch comments, "I bet it comes close to what they discussed among themselves."

"Of course there were exceptions. There were those among them who had achieved some degree of immunity through success in financial and professional circles. They would not be privy to such an effort. It would not be to their best advantage. The situation suited them fine. A social revolution of this order would not be beneficial to their small group. They could not afford to be stereotyped with the masses."

Butch asks, "What did the masses think of them?"

"They were called 'Uncle Toms' and branded traitors to their race."

"What's an 'Uncle Tom', Jonas?"

"One that enjoys the benefits of a ruling class at the expense of his own race."

"Something like collaborating with the enemy."

"Yes, Butch, and they would have much to lose in a social upheaval."

"How could Harold been such a visionary at his early age?"

Effie Lou says; "I think he was an alien dropped off by a UFO"

"I don't think so, mama, he was too confused about the cats."

Carl descends the stairs just in time to hear something about somebody being confused about the cats.

"I am not confused about the cats. I have put that problem out of my mind. It now dwells on more earthly matters. Like the one at hand. Jonas, I hope you and Butch have talked some sense into this woman."

"Carl, there is nothing wrong with Effie Lou that a lot of hard work won't cure."

"Mentally and physically?"

"Idle minds and idle hands need activity."

"What do you propose, Jonas?"

"Let me take her back to Atlanta and take her under my wing."

"You will need the wings of a Giant Condor to accomplish that."

"Carl!"

"That was not to be taken literally. Where will she live? The house went down the tubes to maintain her life style down here."

"She could stay with you."

"No way! I don't have but one bed and I can't sleep on a hillside."

"She could stay with me."

"Can you sleep on a hillside?"

"I won't have to. I have two beds."

"In the same room?"

"No Carl, I have a three bedroom house."

"What's in the third bedroom?"

"That's my playroom."

"Without a bed?"

"Let me correct my description, call it my game room. I play a lot of poker."

"I guess we can try that. Temporarily, of course. If she loses some weight and behaves herself, she might be allowed to move back in with me."

"Oh Carl, could I?'

"Nothing would please Butch and me more. I believe in a strong family unit."

Effie Lou thinks to herself, (*I love the way you lie, baby*.).

"Jonas, you and Butch help Effie Lou pack all we can take on the plane. I'll go see those Indians and close the deal."

"What about all my fine furnishings?"

Jonas nudges Effie Lou. "Gal you best quit while you're ahead."

Carl comes up with a brilliant idea. "We can stay a few more days and have one helluva yard sale. It will probably be a first for this high class place."

"The mayor has become a good friend of mine since I moved down here. I bet he will allow it."

"When can you see him?"

"He lives behind me on the canal. I can call over there and he can meet me at the back hedge."

"I can't believe he lives in your backyard."

"He doesn't, I live in his."

"Call him. Maybe he can come over here. I'd like to meet the mayor of Palm Beach."

It took about ten minutes for the mayor to walk the five hundred feet to Effie Lou's back door. He was heavier than his backyard neighbor. Deep imprints of size twelve sandals marked his trail across the back lawn. It was concluded by everyone the route was not frequently used. He probably used the heavy-duty special built golf cart that was parked in his side yard.

"Hi Effie Lou, puff, puff, you sure live a long way from me. I would've been here sooner but my golf cart had two blowouts. I don't understand it. That's the third set of tires I've put on it in the last six months."

"You should get some of those six-ply tires like I use on mine. What I called you about is I'm moving back to Atlanta and I can't take all my fine furnishings with me. If it's not against any rules, I was thinking about a yard sale."

"You mean here in Palm Beach? We would be the laughing stock of the South Florida coast! A yard sale indeed! Do you know the element those things attract? Why, we don't even allow that type in Palm Beach period."

"But Abe, I can't move all this back to Atlanta. And I don't want to put it in storage. What shall I do?"

"Don't worry Honey, with my connections we can have a real high class auction. One that will interest only the affluent."

"How can you manage that?"

"By charging an exorbitant admission fee. Like say five hundred dollars."

"But won't that keep everyone away? I know damn well I won't come."

"The fee will be applied to any purchases."

"This is sounding better. Let's make a party of it."

"Yeah, like mixed drinks, champagne and heavy hors d' oeuvres. And maybe a steel drum band. Everybody down here likes them."

"Yeah, and after the auction, serve prime rib and lobster."

Carl says, "I'd pay five for all that even without an auction. This is a great idea. I can get Phillip down here to catalog everything."

"Who's Phillip?"

"Phillip Morse. He is an auctioneer on my payroll."

Abe says, "Hmn, That name sounds familiar. Do I know him?"

"I don't think so. I doubt if he has ever been this for south."

"Does he have a Florida license?"

"No, we would have to get somebody local, but he could work the pit. And we can bring Mary down to do the bookwork."

Effie Lou asks, "What do you mean 'work the pit'? We ain't having a cock fight."

"The 'pit' is the area between the auctioneer and the bidders. And Phillip will be taking bids from the floor."

"That sounds more in keeping with the clientele we are hoping to attract. Abe, you probably know a good auctioneer we can get."

"I sure do. I have a lot of favors out I can call in."

"Being mayor, I'm sure you do. Just don't use them all up, I might need some more before we leave."

"Carl, why do you say that?"

"Abe, look out front at the car Butch rented."

"Jeez! I might not have enough for that!"

"You are all misjudging me." Butch replies.

"We are not misjudging you. I think you are misjudging that hot rod. I wouldn't even trust myself in that and I'm hizzoner, the Mayor."

"It's a matter of self control and a healthy respect for the laws that govern our society, Your Honor."

"I would rather believe it is a matter of fear of incarceration and the cost of gasoline consumption."

"I reiterate, I am being misjudged."

"Whatever, now back to the matter at hand, we seem to have a peculiar habit of straying from the primary conversation. Carl, how else can I be of assistance with in this endeavor?"

"We will need exposure to the right people, so as not to attract any riffraff. I am sure you are acquainted with all the right people. Do you have a suggestion as to how to reach them and no one else?"

"I sure do. Every week everybody who's anybody at all gets together to talk about tight money and other things that affect us. Like the domestic labor rate and the price of imported champagne and caviar. I am a charter member of this group and I will mention the auction. Which by the way, the meeting is tomorrow night. Would you all like to be my guests?"

"We might not be considered anybody at all."

"We have been known to make exceptions in matters of great importance."

"Well, Abe, I for one consider this is a matter of great importance."

"And I too, Effie Lou. Fine furnishings need to be kept in the community."

"Is this a BYOB function?"

"No, only yourselves. We rotate hosts and he that is does."

"Is what and does what?"

"Is host and does furnish."

"A fair arrangement. Now where?"

"Where what?"

"Where he that is and does, resides, and who izze?"

"Let me think, Oh yes, he that is and does will be for tomorrow night one Guilanio Generoso who lives over on Pelican Way in that wild pink villa with the terra cotta roof."

"I've seen that house. His front yard looks like two football fields and the back looks like a yacht basin."

"That's Gullie's place for sure. Effie Lou, just wait till you see the inside. It looks like a small Smithsonian. He considers that to make anything collectable, all you have to do is collect it. Of course, this approach should be tempered with good judgment and taste."

"By whose standards?"

"His of course. What good is money without privilege?"

"Where does his money come from?"

"This is not discussed in better circles. This is one of the privileges that goes with money."

"Does the IRS share this sentiment?"

"The gathering of great wealth is accompanied with caution and prudence."

"I can understand how your position can be coveted."

"All high positions of authority carry these rewards. Otherwise we would live over in West Palm. We are straying again."

"What time will we be expected?"

"I usually get there about seven. Give me about thirty minutes to brief everyone of my purpose of inviting you. Don't worry, you all will be portrayed as the elite of Fulton County."

"Lawd, I hope I will live up to their expectations."

"Effie Lou, your previous performances qualifies you, and those that accompany you can bask in your limelight."

"Will Butch qualify?"

"I take exception to that remark."

"I'm sorry dear, I am just nervous about this."

"Especially Butch. These people like all young innocent people. It will be a refreshing change from the regular crowd."

"You are right about that, Abe, from what I've seen there's not a young one in that crowd, not to mention innocent."

"Innocent people do not qualify to purchase ostentatious mansions here."

"How did I get accepted?"

"I think you forget your husband owns this property."

"And he is not innocent?"

"Ask Carl."

"Well, Carl?"

"We are straying again. Acquisition of wealth is not discussed here. Isn't that right, Abe?"

"Effie Lou, there will always be things husbands do not share with their wives. This can be for their own benefit. What they do not know can't be discussed with the 'wrong people'."

"I don't associate with the 'wrong people'."

"One never knows. The world is filled with stoolies, snitches, professional informers who live on bounty commissions and assorted wimps, pimps and etc."

"Are you sure you're not paranoid?"

"If I am, it does not alter the truth."

"Then you might be."

"Possibly, I am not the one to judge."

Effie Lou remarks, "I am beginning to believe a discourse between intelligent persons is not possible without straying."

"Straying is a natural prerequisite to dialog among informed individuals."

"Abe, I think you are trying to justify a basic personality flaw."

"Carl, it is basic and universal."

"Probably a genetic problem." Jonas injects.

"I'm not as bad as Mother or Dad."

"Wait until you reach our age, Butch."

"Then it is a acquired fault rather than inbred?"

"As I said, probably genetic with cultivation."

"Yeah, like fine wine."

"If that be the case, we can bottle Mom and Dad and get ten thousand dollars a gallon."

"Honor thy Father and Mother. Proper respect is necessary to prevent bodily harm to offspring."

"Message received."

"Is this a black tie affair?"

"Oh, hell no! It's not exactly a come as you are because you might have just stepped out of the shower, but that's close."

"Sounds like a fun function. Is straying allowed?"

"It is a necessity. How could we discuss anything without it?"

"We shall look forward to tomorrow night with great expectations."

"Oh dear, I haven't a thing to wear."

"You'll need more than that, but not much more."

"Do any gropers attend?"

"Effie Lou, I don't think you quite understand what happens. All the women go out to the pool and sit around while the men stay in the study and discuss current events."

"Good. Now I'll find out if the women are as bad as the men about straying."

"This affliction does not discriminate. Even famous authors practice it."

"I guess it's natural when one loses direction. Some think a book's thickness determines its worth."

Carl says; "Just imagine some fool trying to document all the things we have experienced. It would be worse than a soap opera."

"Perish the thought. Dialogue by the best is terribly hard. Sanity is hazarded."

"He in all likelihood would give up."

We now pause for a commercial break brought to you by The Palm Beach Chamber of Commerce:

HAVE NOT IN OUR HARBOR A GREAT STATUE WELCOMING ALL.
THE HUDDLED MASSES AND THE DESTITUTE ARE NOT WELCOMED.
THEY MAY GAIN SUCCOR IN THE MELTING POTS ELSEWHERE.
WHEN YOU HAVE WON THE BATTLE FOR ECONOMIC SURVIVAL,
AND HAVE BEEN ADDED TO THE ROLLS OF THE FORTUNE 500,
WE WILL CONSIDER YOUR APPLICATION INTO OUR SMALL CIRCLE.
A BROCHURE EXTOLLING OUR MANY AMENITIES IS AVAILABLE
TO ALL INTERESTED PARTIES WHO REQUEST ONE. JUST SEND A
CASHIER'S CHECK FOR ONE THOUSAND DOLLARS TO;
PALM BEACH CHAMBER OF COMMERCE
PALM BEACH, FLORIDA. 33480
THANK YOU FOR YOUR INDULGENCE.

* * *

The next night the estate of Gulianio Generoso was lit by hundreds of citronella candles on sticks placed at strategic locations around the lawns in an effort to discourage the millions of mosquitoes blown in by a westerly wind from the Everglades. Having little or no effect on the hordes, Gullie called a friend who had a bunch of high-powered blowers used for frost dispersion in the orange groves. These things were placed around the perimeter of the property in a fashion to blow in a counter-clockwise direction. The purpose of these blowers was to create a vortex that would rise because of the convection associated with the heat generated by the blowers. This vortex created a low pressure in the area surrounded by the blowers. This low-pressure area ascended upwards at a high velocity carrying the obnoxious insects with it.

Outside this column of super heated air was a mass of cooler air that descended around the perimeter of the property. Others joined the mosquitoes trapped within this circulating system outside the system by attraction. The density of the insects trapped was increasing exponentially until the appearance was likened to a full-fledged tornado. The sound of the engines operating the blowers confirmed the existence of a tornado by all who viewed and heard it.

With the exception of those privy to the true facts, panic ensued among the population of the surrounding area. The civil defense alarms were howling giving more impetus to the fleeing masses in their autos. Horns were blowing, fenders were being smashed and the bridges over to West Palm were jammed. No emergency vehicles were able to get in. All lanes were filled with cars headed west.

The airport control tower was monitoring all this on radar and they noticed something peculiar about this tornado. It was not moving across the land, as all respectable tornadoes should do, destroying everything in its wake. An investigation was in order. Because it was stationary and posed no immediate threat to close observation, a pilot with a small plane volunteered to do a fly-by and report back with what he discovered. He flew too close and his engine sucked in enough mosquitoes to make it puke. He made a dead stick landing in four feet of water right outside Gullies estate. He extricated himself from his destroyed aircraft and walked out of the water fully clothed and headed straight for the group of ladies sitting around the pool. His clothes being soaking wet and festooned with seaweed and froth from the churning surf, he was mistook for some kind of monster from the deep whose sole purpose was to overcome and devour these delicate women.

Effie Lou was the first to see him as she was sitting facing the sea. "Lawdy, Lawdy, look at what's coming out of the ocean! Run for your lives! Help! Help! Carl! Butch! Jonas! Gullie! Abe! Hell anybody, come quick save us from this demon!"

Before she had finished her frantic call for help, the other ladies joined in screaming for their mates. Because the house was air-conditioned and all the doors and windows were closed, the cries fell on deaf ears in the study. But the cries were not in vain, for they fell on the ears of numerous persons in Gullie's employ as security for the premises, many who were situated on the upper rear balcony. They detected a movement in the shrubbery between the pool and the ocean. This was all it took to start a fusillade from their automatic weapons. The net result of their efforts was a clear view of the ocean and two dead pelicans. The dreaded creature from the deep was nowhere to be found. He had joined the exodus on foot and in his haste was completely dry and devoid of undersea vegetation. It might be said he was blow-dried.

He was not unaware that mosquitoes caused his engine trouble, but he explained that the engine failure was caused by some strange electrical interference that accompanies tornadoes. This explanation was more acceptable to the FAA and his insurance carrier.

When the men inside Gullie's house heard the firing and assumed that world war three had begun, they ran outside only to find the women running to the safety of indoors and the security people inserting fresh clips in anticipation of another attack.

Gullie cried; "What in the hell is going on? Who were you fools firing at? Look at my beautiful shrubbery! And my two pet pelicans! Who's gonna eat my fish scraps now?"

"We were shooting at a sea monster that had the women all upset. We didn't get a good look at it, but the women did. You need to ask them."

They all went back inside and Gullie started questioning his wife. "Are you sure that wasn't one of my couriers coming in from Freeport?"

"No dear, I'm certain of that. Besides your men never come on Wednesday. They know you might be having friends over."

"You're right about that. Do you think it was the Feds?"

"It looked more like a sea monster to me."

"There ain't no such thing. Are you crazy?"

"We all saw it. Just ask them. Effie Lou saw it first. Tell him, Effie Lou."

"I saw it first 'cause I was sitting facing the water. He came crawling out of the sea just like monsters do. Then he stood up! He had to be ten or twelve feet tall. He was covered with brown and green slime and had a smooth head and big dark eyes. He was staggering like he wasn't used to walking on land. He might have had a tail. I couldn't really tell."

Gullie's wife suggested; "It could be the mosquitoes attracted it. I have heard some sea monsters consider them a delicacy."

"If that be true, we might capture one and tie it out on the lawn. It sure as hell would be cheaper than all those infernal blowers making all that noise. It's a wonder that some of the neighbors haven't complained."

"You fool, all the neighbors are here with us. And they don't like insects any better than you."

"You're right about that and since I can afford it, what harm can it cause?"

Within the hour the wind shifted and blew the black cloud down toward Fort Lauderdale. The blowers were shut down and no one was the wiser but the pilot and he was keeping his mouth shut.

The chief of police called Gullie to see if the mayor was at his house. He knew it was Gullie's time to be who is and does. Abe got on the phone. "What's up chief?"

"You must be in an isolation chamber. Haven't you heard? A devastating tornado touched down where you are about thirty minutes ago. The whole damned city panicked and caused more damage than the tornado trying to leave. You might have to declare an emergency. Somebody just called in to report a plane down out there close to you. Is there someone there that can be sent down to the water to see if anyone is hurt? We can't get out there because of the traffic."

"Gullie, I think you heard most of that. Can you send some of your goons down to the water and check on a reported plane down?"

"I can send some of my men down. I don't have any 'goons'."

"Whatever."

"I can't understand how we could sit through all that without a clue of what was going down."

"Well, those blowers were making a goodly amount of noise."

"They don't bother me much. I guess I have got used to them."

"Either that, or they have damaged your ears."

"What's that you say?"

One of the goons, er, men comes in and reports to Gullie.

"We found a wrecked plane, but there was nobody around. Only about ten million dead mosquitoes. There were some human tracks leading from the water up towards the pool."

"I think we have discovered who the sea monster was. The pilot. I wonder what he was doing snooping around my place? Abe, I want you to check into this. My rights might have been violated."

"Tomorrow at the latest."

Effie Lou asks; "Is paranoia contagious? This town seems full of it."

"Everybody over here has big closets."

"What's that 'sposed to mean, Abe."

"Plenty of room for skeletons to hide, Effie Lou."

"I thought graveyards were for them."

"It seems some won't die."

Carl mutters, "Where we come from, we bury them deep."

Gullie says, "Some have a bad habit of scratching out no matter how deep they are buried."

"I thought the statute of limitations were something like seven years."

"Limitations do not apply to tax fraud or murder."

"I do declare! Ain't nobody around here done any of that, have they?"

"Some questions are best left unanswered, Effie Lou."

"I see. That's against proper etiquette."

"And it's a health hazard."

"Message received. And well taken."

Carl says; "Effie Lou, this is why wives should not pry too deep into their husbands' affairs. Be satisfied with being kept in comfort."

"That's exactly what got me into the pickle I'm in right now. Jonas, you wouldn't treat me that way, would you?"

"I am just a hired hand. I do not know the subtle workings of high finance."

"Maybe all you told me was just a lot of hot air."

"No, I believe that two people can survive by going to church and keeping their nose clean. Just don't get involved in things you have no control over."

"Yes Mom, I have some buddies at Ga. Tech. That believe everything is fine. They shut out all the undesirable things in life like it just don't happen. They seem to get along fine. Even if you told them of some injustice like a man wrongfully accused and sent to prison, they simply say if they were innocent, they would not be in prison. They believe justice is pure and simple. They only see black and white. Pity the person that appears before a jury of this opinion."

"Butch, it would be rare indeed to find twelve men on a jury with that opinion."

"It only takes one to cause a mistrial, Dad."

"Of course you are right. I caused one once."

"What happened?"

"I ignored the judge's charge that no matter what we thought about a certain law, it was our duty to weigh the case on evidence only, not the merit of the law. Then I told the foreman the law was antiquated and did not apply today in our enlightened society and soon the law would be repealed.

"Therefore I was prepared to stay in that deliberation room until hell froze over or an acquittal was decided upon."

"Then what happened?"

"I didn't have to wait for hell to freeze. Most of them needed to get back to their jobs. Economy over principles."

* * *

"Welcome, ladies and gentlemen to the Carl Jones estate auction. My name is Simon Legume and I will be the auctioneer. Do not confuse this with an estate sale where in all likelihood, the principal is deceased. This is not the case here; witness the fact Mr. Jones is standing beside me and full of life. He has decided to close his house here and sell off the contents rather than moving them back to Atlanta. This is a rare opportunity for you to purchase many valuable items at your own price. You probably noticed the gorgeous bikini clad young ladies standing in the aisles. Consider then as your personal waitresses. They are here to serve your every whim, whether it is a martini, old fashioned or caviar. Please do not be timid either for your wants or your bids. Let me remind you the ladies are to act as waitresses only, so limit your whims to food and drinks."

"This hunk standing before my podium will be acting as an extra set of eyes for me, if I miss your bid raise, hopefully he will catch it and scream it at me. Do not be alarmed by his antics. I assure you he is not mentally incompetent. His name is Phillip Morse and no, I don't think you have met him before. He does practice in Georgia only and if you have not attended the famous Jones weekly auction in Atlanta, chances are you only think you know Phillip."

"The nice lady sitting at the desk to my left is the charming Mary Pitts down from Atlanta to help with the bookkeeping. Please see Mary after the auction to settle up for any purchases you might have made. Please do not engage in too much small talk while settling. There will be plenty of time for that when the post auction festivities hold forth."

"Butch, Carl's son will assist Phillip in his duties. I understand he screams fairly loud himself."

The first item offered was a Chippendale occasional table.

"AllrightIneedonethousandforthisfinepiecewho'sgonnabethelucky onetotakeithome? Do I hear One Thousand? Nine Hundred? Eight? Hold it! What's happening here? This table is worth at least Twenty Five! Take another look at it! Look at the fine scratches and chips! No refinishing here! Look at the fine alligator varnish! This cannot be reproduced by man. Now, what do I hear? Somebody open it and we'll go from there."

"One Hundred dollars!"

"We have one. Do I hear two? One fifty? One twenty five?"

"One oh five!"

"I can't accept less than a twenty five bump. I don't want to be here a week, milking. C'mon folks, get with the program. Don't let that lady steal that table for a measly C-note."

Simon, the auctioneer looked at Carl, who shrugged his shoulders and said; "Let it go. Try the next piece."

The fine old grandfather clock was opened at two hundred and was not bumped.

"We are being brother-in-lawed!' Carl whispered to Simon.

"What do you want to do?"

"Declare a drink break!"

"Friends, due to technical difficulties we will have a short break. Take this opportunity to refresh yourselves at our free wet bar. We will continue shortly."

Simon and Carl retired to the butler's pantry to partake of some private stock.

"These sons of bitches have our balls in a vise. Whatta we gonna do? If we call it off, we'll lose our credibility and I'll never get rid of this shit!"

"I think I know the answer, Carl. I'm the only one here licensed to hold an auction. If I can't call, we will have to postpone it."

"Everybody here knows you are able to continue. How can you get out of it?"

"I can fake a heart attack. God knows I'm about to have one anyway."

"You think you can pull it off?"

"I know damn well I can. I am a part time actor in an amateur group down in Lauderdale."

"But how will that help us? We will still have to hold the auction when you 'recover'."

"We will have to bring in fresh meat."

"But who?"

"I know all the exiled Cuban aristocrats and professionals. They will welcome the chance to bid on some fine Americana."

"How long will it take you to contact them?"

"We will apply the modern miracle of telephone. Two days should do it."

"Can you recover from a heart attack in two days?"

"Modern medicine does wonders!"

"Give these vultures another ten minutes at the bar and then we will resume the activities."

"People, we seem to have corrected the difficulty. If all of you will reclaim your seats, we will try to sell something else. And please, show a little more interest in these fine objects."

The next item was a full size replica of Venus DI Milo, which had graced the entrance foyer. The spirits from the bar had mellowed the crowd somewhat and the statue opened at five hundred, but still nobody upped the bid. By this time Simon had loosened his tie and unbuttoned the three top buttons of his shirt. And he was getting short of breath and there was a purple hue to his complexion. A man in the front row noticed his distress and asked; "Simon, are you all right? You don't look too good."

"Carl, hand me that glass of water. I just got a little excited about that last piece going for such a ridiculous price."

When the next piece, a fine signed Tiffany hall lamp, opened for only two hundred, the proverbial straw broke the camel's back. Simon gripped each side of the podium with both hands that were turning white and started gasping for breath and groaning, "Ahhh, uhhhh, ahhhh, uhhhh." He then fell backward carrying the podium with him, it landing on his stomach. A finer exhibition has yet to be seen on Broadway.

Carl jumped to his aid, pumping on his chest and giving him mouth to mouth. Simon squirmed around trying to avoid Carl's slobbering mouth. He whispered, "Lay off Dammit, I don't need your garlic breath, just beat the hell out of my chest and yell for somebody to call an ambulance!"

Effie Lou was squealing for the phone. "Oh Lordy, Lordy, Simon's dying! Everybody back up. Give the pore bastard some breathing space. Hello, hello, he's dying, send someone quick!"

"Mama, you didn't tell them where to go. Call them back."

"Hello, this is Effie Lou Jones. I reside at Number Thirty Swordfish Alley over in Palm Beach and my auctioneer just keeled over with a heart attack. His name? It's Simon Legume, we are holding an auction of my fine furnishings because I've decided to move back to Atlanta, Georgia. What? Oh yes I do like it down here, but my husband has had some financial difficulties and I need to go back and help him in his business. What? I'll ask him. Hey Simon, the ambulance people wants to know if you have any insurance."

Simon wards off Carl's blows to his chest long enough to sit up and nod his head in the affirmative.

Carl says; "That's a hell of a thing to ask a dying man. Effie Lou come beat on Simon's chest and I'll tell that penny-pinching son of a bitch what I think of him."

"Now Carl, don't get him too angry, he might not come at all and then who's gonna call the auction of my fine pieces?"

"Don't worry, Effie Lou, everything's gonna work out fine. Hello, this is Carl Jones and if you don't send an ambulance out here right now, you will be hit with a lawsuit that will make the national debt look like peanuts. What? Oh, that was my wife. No. And yes, the victim does have insurance. What? Oh, it was going pretty good until Simon had that attack. No, there are no good used tires listed. Maybe you can charge the insurance company enough for this trip to buy a new set. Do you think the ones you have will make the trip out here? If you don't go over thirty five? I guess we will just have to wait. Simon, do you think you can hold on until they get here? It'll take about twenty minutes."

Simon now wards off Effie Lou's blows long enough to sit up and nod his head yes.

Carl announces; "The ambulance is on the way and there is nothing else anybody can do at the present time except Effie Lou who has the situation well under control. We might as well go have some more drinks."

When the crowd has gone into the other room, Simon pushes Effie Lou back and exclaims; "Get away from me! You have just about broken all my ribs! There's nothing wrong with me, so stop trying to revive me."

"But I don't understand. I saw you turn purple and fall down just like you was dying. What's wrong with you?"

"Not a damn thing. Carl and I are trying to get your ass out of a crack and save all your fine furnishings from being stolen."

"I thought something funny was going on, this is the first auction I've ever seen that everybody was not fighting over every item. The stuff I have here should cause a riot."

"And indeed it would have if someone had not organized the crowd. They all know each other and it was easy to do."

"And I bet I know who did it. It was that damned Gullie. He even looks like a sleaseball. What can we do?"

"Don't worry about a thing. We have it all figured out. I go to the hospital for a few days and we give rain checks."

"What good will that do? The same crowd will be back."

"We will invite some fine competition for your fine furnishings. And this competition has just about as much money as these bastards."

"I know it's not nice to ask, but where did they get theirs?"

"When they left Cuba, they carried out whatever Batista left behind."

"I just can't hardly wait. This will be real interesting."

In due time, the ambulance did come rolling, just to carry poor Simon away. And the circle was then broken until he did recover someday.

And a miraculous recovery he did make two days later. Effie Lou called all the original participants and announced the auction would resume the following afternoon, same ground rules. Same time, same place.

She explained that the Lord was indeed on her side for allowing Simon such a fast recovery. The only difference now would be that it would be held in the back yard where the cool breezes might ward off a similar attack. No, she had no reason to believe there should be any. Around dusk, there will be a nice easterly wind that will cool things and keep the mosquitoes away. The chairs were set up facing the back terrace where Simon had his podium. The original chairs were set up between the terrace and a low hedge, which divided the rear yard. A few noticed the bleachers behind this hedge to accommodate the new participants.

Gullie asks Carl; "What's the bleachers for? Are you expecting more people?"

"Well Gullie, I'll tell you what happened. You know Carmella, Effie Lou's maid. When she got off the other night she went down to the Little Cuba Bar and told everybody about Simon's heart attack. Of course they all wanted what was going on. She told them he got all worked up about the items not bringing much money and naturally they all wanted to get in on the action. One of the higher-ups, I think he was one of Batista's exiled colonels called me and more or less invited the whole colony. I told him about the up front charge, thinking it would scare them away. He said five hundred was front pocket money for most of them and they wanted to attend. I tried to get out of inviting them by saying we could not accommodate the whole colony. He is the one who suggested moving it to the rear yard and I was stuck."

"Oh shit! This is gonna ruin everything!"

"Ruin what, Gullie? I think it's a good idea."

"Er, er, what I mean is our crowd don't get along with those wetbacks and they might leave and there goes the auction."

"I disagree. If 'your people' leave the auction might be even better. I noticed they were mighty tight fisted the other day."

"Oh, they just had not got into the swing of things."

"Well, if they want any of Effie Lou's fine furnishings, they damn well better start swinging this afternoon. By God!"

"Maybe they will. I know of one piece that I've just to have."

"What's that, Gullie?"

"It's that large painting of that nude woman lying on a bunch of satin pillows eating a turkey leg with all those black eunuchs fanning her fine body. She looks like a sultan's concubine. I didn't know those Arabs ate turkey."

"Pig is what they don't eat. They also eat lamb and grape leaves."

"Ain't no wild turkeys in the desert. All I ever saw when I was over there was goats and lizards."

Carl inquires, "When were you over there?"

"My business used to take me there a lot to check on my poppy fields."

"You must have a chain of florist shops."

"Not exactly, Carl how's your health?"

"Fine. Why do you ask?"

"It seems you have some kind of mouth disease."

"I see Simon approaching the podium, Gullie, find your seat."

"I must speak to Abe first."

"There he is, sitting by the pool."

"Please excuse me then. I must speak to him privately."

"By all means, do."

Gullie huddles with Abe. "Hey Abe, do you know what that fool Carl has done?"

"I haven't the foggiest. I see all those bleachers but what does it mean?"

"He says it's all Carmella's fault, but I know damn well he's lying. She don't associate with those people down at the colony. She thinks that because she works over here, she's better than them."

"Gullie, what in the hell are you talking about? You're making no sense at all."

"He came up with some cock and bull story about her telling those Cuban misfits about the auction and they are going to screw up our scheme. Can you call the Chief of Police and put up a roadblock to prevent them from coming over here?"

"Ain't no way, Gullie! Your little ploy is getting out of hand. I'm in as deep as I'm going to be. Trying to steal that broad's junk just ain't worth it."

"But my neighbors are going to kill me. They don't usually pay five hundred dollars for a few drinks and prime rib."

"How about that last Republican fund raiser?"

"That was different. It was for a good cause."

"Anyway, it's too late to do anything about it now. They're starting to fill up the bleachers."

"Good God! Look at them! I bet there is at least a thousand! I wonder where they all parked?"

"Ha! I bet all our fine neighbors will have to replant their great lawns now. Their jalopies are parked everywhere."

"I wonder where the 'elite' are. The way Carl talked, they have more money than a show dog can jump over. Those cars sure don't represent wealth."

"They maintain a low profile. The law limited the amount of cash they could bring with them. Legally, that is."

"It's a shame the way some people have no respect for the law."

"I carry a sack of rocks around with me for those who wish to cast the first stone."

"Don't you get smart with me, you refugee from the garment district. You're the one who approached me about the auction the last time I was and did."

"Was what and did what?"

"Was host and did furnish food and drink."

"I didn't 'approach' you. We just announced it while we were enjoying your booze and horses' ovaries. If I remember correctly, it was you that 'approached' the rest of us with your hare-brained idea about stone walling the bids."

"Well, it would have worked if Simon hadn't have had that heart attack."

"I don't believe he had one. He recovered too quick. And it was too convenient for stopping the auction."

"Them fools don't have that much sense."

"They are a lot smarter than you give them credit for. Remember the 'technical difficulties' they claimed stopped the auction for a short while and how quick Simon had the 'attack' shortly after they started back? I saw Carl and Simon sneak off into the butler's pantry during the break. I bet they were plotting a way to foil our plan. Besides, I didn't see anybody taking care of the 'technical' problem."

"Forgive me, Lord, for I have misjudged two of my fellow men, the sons of bitches."

"Well, there's nothing we can do about it now. We have got to bite the bullet and pay what we have to if we want anything."

"Some of that free booze might make the bullet taste better. Let's go fill up before the auction starts."

"A capital suggestion!"

CHAPTER NINETEEN

"Ladies and gentlemen, if you will find a seat, we will start the auction shortly. I wish to thank all of those that showed concern for my problem. Luckily it was not as serious as it first seemed. The fine care with which I was blessed hastened my recovery. Of course my health insurance will soar astronomically, but what the hell, what's money for anyway?"

Abe exclaims, "Listen to that bastard! I bet he paid the ambulance driver to take him to a motel rather than the hospital."

"Gullie that would be easy enough to check. But who gives a damn now? The damage is done."

The first item offered was the painting of the nude woman lying on satin pillows eating a turkey leg and being fanned by black eunuchs. Simon tried to get an opener for one thou. No one jumped in. Simon then called for eight. No one snatched the hook. Then he started declining in one hundred dollar increments. When it got down to two hundred, Gullie jumped in. Simon called for three. A man in the bleachers gave him the half sign and then it was up to Gullie to bump to three. Which he did, reluctantly. The bleacher went to four. Gullie was looking like Simon before his 'attack'. He was not to be outdone. He felt a two hundred raise would scare off the intruder. It did not. It only added more fuel to the fray. It became a shouting match. Intruder; "eight!" Gullie; "Twelve!" Intruder; Fourteen!" Simon stepped back and took a swig of water, he was not needed now. The intruder came down out of the bleachers and started walking down the aisle toward Gullie, who was headed back toward the bleachers. They met halfway, nose-to-nose and toes to toes. Now they could shout at each other knowing with satisfaction they were spraying each other with saliva. When they finally had to retire and get two towels, the intruder was the proud possessor of the painting for a mere five thousand dollars. Simon instructed the winner to go over to Mary's table and give his name.

"My name is Geronimo Rodriguez and I own a villa down on Biscayne Bay and this painting will be the final touch to the extensive remodeling I have done since my purchase of this property."

"All I wanted was your name, not your life history. And oh yes, I need to see the letter of credit from your bank."

"What is this letter business you speak of? I no habla. I pay in gold."

"That will be more than satisfactory. And I do hope you will find more items to your liking."

"I am sure I weel."

Geronimo re-entered the fracas with vigor and dedication. Gullie had met his match and retreated to the wet bar for solace and consolation. Others of his ilk would test the waters only to find it too hot and too deep. And this went long into the night did this one-sided activity continue until all of the fine furnishings were now owned by the expatriates of Miami. The one item Effie Lou was adamant against selling was the Rolls. She said she needed it to retreat back to Atlanta in style. Carl was so elated over the results after Mary shared the good news with him, he easily agreed to her wishes.

But Butch also wanted to share in this windfall. He wanted to purchase the rented Chrysler.

"Absolutely not!"

"But Dad."

"Don't 'but dad' me, dammit. You don't need that car. You've got that fine Volkswagen and that's all you need."

"I don't want to fly back to Atlanta. In a plane, that is. And besides, if you go back with me, we can save the plane fare. And that might pay for the car."

"Why can't we all go back in the Rolls?"

"You and mom would probably kill each other before we got out of Florida."

"Who will accompany her then? That's a long way for one person to drive, especially a woman."

"Jonas, Phillip and Mary. Think of all the money we'll save."

"That might work. Phillip can be chaperon to keep Effie Lou and Jonas straight."

"Don't count too much on that, with him and Mary together in the back seat."

"Maybe she and Effie Lou can sit in the back and let Jonas and Phillip take turns driving. How much do you think we can get the car for, Butch?"

"Probably less than you owe me for helping you."

"What are you talking about? You wouldn't charge your old dad for all the fun you have had since we came down here."

"With all the auction brought in, you are going to owe Simon about fifty grand, and I think I think another fifty split between Mary, Jonas, Phillip and me would be fair."

"Simon has agreed on ten grand and you forget the rest is already on my payroll. I might give them a small bonus for their help down here."

"You are the epitome of greed personified."

"If you have any hope of getting that car, you had better watch your tongue."

"My opinion shall change with possession of that automobile, Dad, if I cut out my tongue, may I have it?"

"You won't have to do that. Just keep your mouth shut and don't tell your mama how you got it."

"She will want to know how I acquired it."

"Just tell her you were the millionth person renting a car and you won it."

"She's too far removed from the turnip truck to believe that."

"Then tell her I loaned you the money and you are going to pay me back ten dollars a week."

"That's even more ridiculous than your first suggestion."

"I don't think so, remember you will be getting a dividend from the antique shop."

"I forgot about that. Will I get enough to pay for the car?"

"Maybe. We'll have to wait and see."

"Let's call the rental agency and see what kind of deal we can make."

"Good morning, this is your friendly Economy Rent a Car. What can I do for you?"

"Lady, I think your company is mis-named. We rented a car from you people the other week and the Arabs will have to drill another well just to supply it with gasoline."

"Oh, you must have the Chrysler. It's a bitch ain't it? We have put three sets of rear tires and it doesn't even have five thousand miles on it yet. It's gonna break us."

"I think we might be able to help you. It's just what we need to put on our drag strip up in Atlanta."

"Are you saying you might be interested in a purchase?"

"If the price is right."

"Just a minute. Hey Charlie! Get your ass on the phone! We got a turkey that wants to buy that gas guzzling monster Mopar!"

"Hello, this is Charles Bonney. I'm the manager. Did I hear right? You want to buy that fine Chrysler? Why, that's the most favorite rental piece we have on the lot. We couldn't possibly entertain the idea of parting with it."

"Charlie, I did not call you people to listen to a bunch of bullshit. I know that hulk is a liability for your company and you would love to be rid of it. I am prepared to relieve you of this burden for a reasonable figure."

"What is your conception of reasonable?"

"We will pay all the rental fees up to now and give you ten cents a mile for it."

"How many miles does it show now?"

"A little over five thousand."

"Make it twenty cents and it's yours."

"I can't do that. It needs a new set of tires right now."

"That's hard to believe. We just put on a set right before you rented it."

"I think the rear end is out of line. I will be buying a pig in a poke. The best I can do is fifteen cents."

"Get your ass and your money down here right now!"

"Butch, if we want to get home without that car breaking me, we will have to change the rear end."

"Do you really think it's out of line?"

"Of course not, dummy. It's just geared too low. That's why it's wearing out the tires and using so much gas. We need to put something like a 2.76 in for the run home."

"Do you know how fast it will go then? I'd say about around one sixty."

"If we go up A-1-A, we won't have a chance to be tempted."

"That won't get us all the way to Atlanta."

"But it'll damn sure get us out of Florida. And we can take the back roads the rest of the way."

"There's some long straight roads in South Georgia. And they have very little traffic on them."

"We shall rise above ourselves and resist the temptation."

"I doubt if I can elevate myself that far."

"I'll help you."

"I shall drive and you watch for cows and possum."

"Don't forget the local constabulary."

"Dad, should we stop at some of the tourist attractions? We need to expand our horizons."

"We'll get all the expansion we need poking along on these narrow roads."

"Do I detect a note of impatience? We could take the better heavily traveled routes."

"No, I need some dawdling time. I've been in the rat race so long. I just want to turn off for a while."

"That doesn't sound like you are going to be good company."

"I've got a two track mind. I can talk while I'm dawdling. I am sure glad those wild Indians bought the house. I think I got enough out of it to recover all your mom pissed away while she was playing the high society bitch."

"Don't expect me to take sides in this feud you have going on. You probably have muddied the waters some yourself."

"I know I have, but I was the prime mover who made all the money she took for granted."

"Is that a fact? Are you forgetting Harold? You sang a different tune at the memorial service."

"Oh God, you're right. What was I thinking? Thank you for reminding me. I seem to be cut from the same cloth as your mother."

"We are all human and neither of you was raised in the lap of luxury."

"It wasn't too bad right after the Great War but it was really hell after the crash in '29. I was only eleven, but I still remember going to bed on an empty stomach many times."

"Don't spring that shit on me about walking five miles to school in all kinds of weather."

"I would probably have been better off if I had to. That would mean we lived on a farm in the country and most people out there at least had enough to eat. Unfortunately we lived in town only a block from the school and had to buy everything we ate."

"What's so bad about that? That's what we do now."

"Now most people have the money to buy food. At least some kind."

"Yeah, I heard about a family who was living off dog and cat food."

"That was probably to draw sympathy. Some people food is cheaper than pet food."

"It's the packaging that runs up the cost of food now."

"We used to buy bulk. It sat around in the stores in barrels."

"The health inspectors had a hand in stopping that."

"The stores had spittoons scattered for the snuff dippers and tobacco chewers."

"But how was their aim?"

"Great, they even had spitting contests for distance and accuracy."

"Well, I'll bet some of the store cats slept in the barrels."

"That was better than being infested with rats. Besides, the cat hairs would float off when the food was cooked."

"That was indeed the 'good old days'."

I remember back in '46 I bought a '36 Buick from a music professor for three hundred dollars. He had the original invoice showing he paid six hundred for it brand new. Besides the upkeep, he drove it ten years for three hundred dollars. That's only thirty dollars a year!"

"Did it have power steering?"

"No."

"Did it have air conditioning?"

"No."

"Did it have power brakes?"

"No"

"Did it have power windows?"

"No."

"Did it have power seats?"

"No."

"Did it have automatic transmission?"

"No."

"Did it have windshield washers?"

"No."

"Would it burn rubber in every gear."

"No."

"It seems this car was a better deal."

"You have never heard me say those were the good old days."

"I have heard some people say they don't build them like they used to."

"What they mean is they used to be able to repair them in their backyard with a few simple tools."

"I can understand how that would be missed. About all you can do now is check the vital signs and give transfusions when needed."

"Speaking of vital signs, how's the gas?"

"We've got plenty if the next station is in the next block."

"Down here there's always four at every intersection."

"Welcome to the great horsepower race."

"They are making a lot of economy cars now. I had a Nash Rambler that would go more than five hundred miles on one tank of gas."

"How many gallons did it hold?"

"Twenty six. Of course when you filled up, you'd better be going downhill for the first two hundred miles. I got so tired of it, I wouldn't put more than ten gallons in it at a time."

"It just shows you can't have the best of two worlds. But I know how I can."

"How?"

"Keep this car and the Volkswagen."

"You have now arrived."

"How's that?"

"You are a two car family."

"You might say that, if one person can be a family."

"You are getting old enough to start thinking about a family. How old are you now?"

"I was twenty six last month. I've been thinking about it. How old were you?"

"When I what?"

"Married Mom."

"Twenty. I was twenty two when you were born."

"I had better get started if I don't want to be an old man when he is twenty six."

"If you had one tomorrow, you will already be over the hump when he is."

"What hump and is what?"

"The half a hundred hump and when he is your age now."

"Have you anyone in mind?"

"In mind for what?"

"To wed."

"Not exactly. There are lots of candidates."

"I imagine you are considered quite an eligible stud."

"In some circles, possibly."

"What does that mean?"

"Mostly the party circuit, you know the singles bars, billiard parlors and the like. Not exactly the right candidates for the mother of your children. Shit, most of them don't even know how to cook nowadays."

"You might need to search elsewhere."

"Like where?"

"Small towns, old family farms, country churches."

"That's a joke. Everything within a fifty mile radius of Atlanta is contaminated."

"I know for a fact that South Georgia still is virgin territory."

"Probably in timber only."

"Oh no, there are still some old families that hold a tight rein on their children. But you have to get to them before they are sent off to college. They have a tendency to go astray then."

"I don't know anyone in that area."

"Tell you what, I know some people down there and we can stop and visit a while."

"I thought you were busting your ass to get back home."

"No I was busting my ass to get away from the Cuban invasion."

"I bet in ten years, the majority will speak Spanish only."

"It has already taken on a foreign atmosphere."

"Whereabouts are you talking about visiting?"

"I don't intend to visit anyone down in that Hell-hole."

"I'm talking about South Georgia."

"Oh, excuse me! It's a small obscure town between Valdosta and Thomasville on US 84. I got to know the sheriff and two school teachers pretty good back in '64 when Phillip and I were out scouting for antiques."

"Yeah, I remember now. When you got back was when you were talking crazy about some cats being abducted by aliens in a flying saucer. I didn't know you indulged in hallucinogenic substances."

"Son, I haven't touched a thing since back in the fifties when I experimented with some Peyote."

"What's Peyote?"

"It's a form of cactus in the Southwest the Indians in Mexico used in their religious ceremonies. They claimed they could see the Great Father and his domain."

"Did you see him?"

"No, but I saw Moses."

"How did you know he was Moses?"

"I don't know. I just did."

"Did you think you could fly?"

"I thought I could. I had enough sense not to try flying off a cliff, but I did try jumping off my roof."

"Did you fly?"

"Straight down. But I was lucky. I wasn't but ten feet off the ground and it was soft. It had been raining all week and all I did was sink up in the mud."

"How in the world did you find out about that stuff?"

"I had a friend that was pretty kooky and he read a book by Aldous Huxley about the sacred mushrooms of the Mexican Indians. It was titled something like 'The Gates or Doors of Perception' I believe. Anyway we decided to try some. I don't know how he found out about the Peyote, but he ordered a bunch from a woman in New Mexico. She must have had it growing in her back yard because we sent her twenty dollars and she sent us about a bushel with a note wishing us good luck. We followed her instructions and cut it into bite size pieces. It was the foulest tasting stuff I had ever tried to eat. I threw some trimmings out the back door for my goat and he turned his nose up and walked away. We decided if we were going to get serious with this, another method of consumption needed to be developed. We decided to reduce it to a concentrate and spike soft drinks to make it more palatable. It's a wonder it didn't kill us."

"Was it poisonous?"

"Not in its raw form. The stuff was an alkaloid and we cooked it in an aluminum pot and it reacted. I don't know what we wound up with, but we thought we were dying. We probably would have if we had not puked our guts out. I think we took an overdose. I had given some to another friend of mine and he did not get sick at all. But other things happened to him."

"What happened?"

"It was Saturday morning and he dropped by before he went down to the creek to fish some. And I gave him a little. I told him he might see God or at least some of His Angels. He said he had always wanted to see an Angel. When I saw him Monday morning and asked him how did he do, he said he almost drowned. He didn't see God, but he did see some of the most beautiful white horses cavorting on the opposite bank."

"What's so unusual about that?"

"The other side was a jungle. It was so overgrown with vines and bushes, a horse couldn't even walk over there much less cavort. He said all those horses were playing in a large meadow. And that's not all that happened to him."

"What else?"

"There was a small island in the middle of the stream separating the two banks. The stream between him and the island was about twenty-five wide, but he thought it was about three feet. One nice step would get him closer to the horses. He wanted to ride one of those horses. That one step cost him his entire fishing gear and tackle box. And nearly cost him his life. He managed to get back to his bank about two hundred feet downstream. When he got back to his car, he decided to take another route back to the road. He couldn't understand why he came the way he did when here was a good short cut right between these two beautiful oak trees. Because the trees were so far apart he threw caution to the wind hand headed right between them. Much to his surprise he found out too late only six feet separated them. The vehicular momentum propelled the car to a point where the venerable oaks were looking in the car's front windows. This had a somewhat sobering effect on my friend and he had the presence of mind to leap into the rear seat and extricate himself through a rear door. He walked the rest of the way out of the woods."

"What become of the car?"

"He called a friend with a wrecker and got him to pull it out the way it went in. The only damage was cosmetic. The doors weren't hurt. He had two crunched fenders to remind him of his near meeting with God."

"The doors of perception were slightly warped. Could this cat thing be a flashback?"

"No, there were too many witnesses. The only thing that hangs on is something that has no bearing on it. I can stare at a tile floor like in the bathroom and make my feet go through the floor."

"How can you do that?"

"I think I can show anybody how, if they follow my instructions."

"Instruct me."

"Stand with the tips of both shoes touching one tile joint running from the left to the right. This works best on a small black and white pattern. While staying perfectly still, focus on a black tile in front of your toes. Then start crossing your eyes, focusing on a point above your toes. As you bring your focus to a certain point, the two adjacent black tiles in the original line will merge and your eyes will lock on them. This will place the floor at a level somewhat higher than your feet and your feet and lower legs will go through the floor. If you have trouble focusing at a closer point, place a finger as low as you can and start bringing it up. Your eyes will follow rather than being focused on the surface of the floor. It takes a lot of practice, but it is enjoyable."

"A safe and economical trip."

"Right. And that's not all. When you have mastered this, try focusing on a point below the floor level. This takes more practice, but when you can you will find yourself floating way above the floor."

"This, I have got to try. Now tell me more about the school teachers."

"They are a lot of fun. And they are smart too."

"Can they cook and keep house?"

"I'm sure they can. When they were with us, we had other things on our minds."

"Oh shit, sounds like they are tainted."

"They are not! They are highly respected ladies that teach Sunday school and sing in the choir at The New Elim Primitive Baptist Church at The Hooterville Crossroads."

"How did these fine ladies get tangled up with you and Phillip?"

"Er, they like to party on weekends."

"They sound a mite loose to me.

"Not at all, they are just bored stiff. The only ones there is to date around there are Bubbas and Juniors that only talk about corn, soybeans, peanut crops and who's got the best coon dog. And it's hard to double date in a pickup truck. The only way they will go out is together."

"That might present a problem. I might feel uncomfortable double dating with my father, especially knowing you are cheating on mama."

"When you see these ladies, all your inhibitions will be stripped away."

"Which one do you like, Dad?"

"I like both, but I seem to wind up with Nellie."

"What's the other one's name?"

"Lilly."

"How old is she?"

"I think she's about your age. Maybe a year or two older."

"They're getting better all the time. Suppose I like Nellie the best?"

"I don't think you will, and you can't have both."

"Would they move to Atlanta?"

"I believe they keep their bags packed, just in case."

"What would mama say?"

"I have a feeling that when they get back, all our problems will be solved."

"Why do you say that?"

"It would take a blind idiot not to notice how she and Jonas look at each other."

"Yeah, I remember way back how they used to run Harold and me out of the office occasionally, but I was too young to know what was going down."

"Or too infatuated with Marybelle."

"I am the first to admit that. I don't think I will ever get over her. But I must get on with it. I don't want to wind up old and gray alone like I suspect Mary will."

"I bet some changes are in store for Mary, Butch. Have you noticed how she's changed since what happened to Marybelle and Harold?"

"Yes, she has a faraway look in her eyes now and she's not as intense as she was."

"She is bound to be plotting some great move in her life."

"Her one great interest, Harold and Marybelle do not need her anymore."

"And Joe and Dolly seem to be well fixed in the antique shop."

"She's a good woman and does not need to wither on the vine. I'm surprised you have not been sniffing around her, Dad."

"Butch, don't mess with the hired help."

"You could fire her."

"That would break her heart. She must leave by her own will if she so desires."

CHAPTER TWENTY

The father and son team cut across to Live Oak before they got too far north so they could spend the night and get an early start to Quitman the next morning which was a short distance from Hooterville and the ladies. Carl said he would call them from the motel room so they wouldn't make any plans for the next day, which was Saturday.

They found a fairly modern motel on US90. It was of 'attached' construction as opposed to 'detached'. The old detached types stood alone with a lean-to carport on one side. This one was constructed in a large semicircle fashion with a paved drive passing in front of every door, with room for parking in front. On the inside of the semi-circle stood majestic live oaks centuries old and festooned with Spanish moss. In a clearing between the oaks was a swimming pool, with a sign stating 'No Attendant. Swim At Your Own Risk'.

Butch commented; "I see how this town got its name."

"This area is full of these old trees. And also plenty of white sand."

"I hope there's none in the beds."

"There shouldn't be. These units are air-conditioned. I doubt if the windows will even open. I'll ask the desk if there are phones in the rooms."

"Also find if there is a good restaurant nearby. I'm getting hungry. I'll wait in the car."

"We're in luck. The rooms have phones and there's a sea food place right down the road."

"Good, let's clean up and go eat."

"We had better try calling the girls first before they start prowling around. This is Friday and I know them."

"I'll be washing up while you call them."

"This is the desk. How may I help you?"

"I want an outside line."

"Is this a local call?"

"No, I want the Hooterville Crossroads up in Georgia."

"You cannot dial long distance from your room. I will have to place the call for you. Whom do you wish to call?"

"A girl named Nellie. She's a school teacher up there."

"What's her last name?"

"Hell, I don't know. She's the only schoolteacher named Nellie in that town. The local operator should know her."

"I'll try. Hello, Hooterville operator?"

"Yes, go ahead, Live Oak."

"I got a man who just checked in my motel and he wants to talk to Nellie, the school teacher."

"Is this a business or personal call?"

"Hello, Nellie!"

"No, this is not Nellie. This is the desk. The Hooterville operator wants to know if this is a business or personal call."

"I'll be damned!"

"Well?"

"Well what, desk?"

"Is it which?"

"Which what?"

"You must be from that area, sir."

"No, why do you ask?"

"You talk like one that does."

"Does what?"

"Come from that area."

"No, I just spent a few days up there once."

"It don't take long."

"Just try to get Nellie on the line. It's personal."

"If it was business, you would be entitled to a discount."

"Please get me Nellie before the sun goes down."

"What's the sun go to do with it?"

"You don't understand, I've got to catch her before she goes out on the prowl."

"Sounds like Nellie is an alley cat."

"Lady, my patience is wearing thin. Please get me Nellie."

"I'll try again. Hello, Hooterville operator. This man says this is a personal call and he wants to talk to Nellie right now."

Hooterville operator, "I might catch her before she goes on the prowl."

"What's with you people up there? Don't you have homes to go to?"

"It's mighty boring up here. If I wasn't working, I'd be on the prowl too."

"What hours do you work?"

"I come on at four and get off at midnight. There's nothing going on when I get off."

"I don't ever get off. There's always some fool that wants to talk to somebody in Diddy-Wa-Diddy at three in the morning."

"You ought to shut down the switchboard around eleven."

"I tried that once and it nearly cost me my life."

"Mercy! What in the world happened, Live Oak?"

"One guest went out to get some air about two in the morning. He had some sweet young thing with him when he checked in and he probably needed some by then."

"Some what?"

"Fresh air. Anyway, he noticed my kitchen was on fire. He ran back into his room and tried to call me and I had turned the damned switchboard off. He finally went to my bedroom window and beat on it until I woke up. I haven't shut it down since. I even put a big bell in the bedroom in case something happens."

"I've heard about some new fangled systems that don't need an operator."

"I have too, but I hear they are expensive."

"It's been nice talking to you, Live Oak. I'll try to get Nellie now."

"Hello, Nellie!"

"Sir, this is the desk. Nellie will be on shortly. It seems all the lines were tied up."

"This is Nellie, who's calling?"

"Hello, Nellie! This is Carl. How are you?"

"Oh Carl, it's good to hear your voice. Where are you? Are you at the motel? I can come right over. Is anyone with you? I can bring Lilly with me."

"Slow down, sugar, we are in Live Oak and we will be up there in the morning. We need rest tonight. We just got in from Palm Beach and we're draggin' ass. I need to be in my best form when I see you."

"You got that right! I'm hornier than an over-sexed she-wolf in heat! It's been too long!"

"I've got my son with me. Tell Lilly we will be there in the morning."

"You've got your son with you? That doesn't sound so good. Does he know about the birds and the bees?"

"I certainly hope so. He's twenty six and if he doesn't, there's no hope for him."

"That's better. I might want him for myself. How does he look?"

"He is a bigger and better replica of me."

"Maybe I won't bring Lilly."

"Dahlin' you can't love but one and I hope it's me."

"I was just joshing. You know who I love."

"We'll pick y'all up at the apartment in the morning. Right now we're going out and get some seafood."

"Eat plenty of raw oysters, 'bye for now."

"Man, you sure can talk some trash!"

"All in a day's work, son."

Even though the cafe was just a good walk down the road, Butch insisted on driving. He said he was too tired to walk. It was a cinder block building painted Flamingo pink with glass building blocks set into each corner. A neon sign out by the road proclaimed SEAFOOD STEAKS AND CHOPS. The entrance was through a glass jalousie door. The floor was covered with black and white tile and the tables and chairs looked like refugees from a fifties dinette right off a small kitchen of a nine hundred square foot bungalow. Our heroes began to have some misgivings about their choice. They then discovered they had no choice. The other eating establishment had succumbed to a fire some years back. This message left them with the thought that it was safer in Live Oak to cook in the backyard. They chose a table in a corner close to the glass blocks. It was only after they had sat down they noticed the inside of the blocks were illuminated with neon. A real fifties look. The table surface was covered with a plastic laminate now generically known as "Formica" which is a trademark name such as "Frigidaire" so often misused by the uninformed. The table was made before the advent of plastic edging and was trimmed with anodized aluminum. This trim presented a barrier that trapped assorted foodstuffs to lie there and ferment. A lot of customers, while killing time waiting for the food to arrive would try to remove this collection with their fingernails and when their food did arrive, they would have to make a trip to the washroom in an attempt to remove the gleanings. Another activity performed by some of the younger set was to lift their feet off the floor and with a table knife in hand, touch one of the exposed connections on the neon tubes and wait for the waitress to come and lean and touch the metal trim with her belly.

The results were well worth the risk involved. Usually this happened when the poor victim was bringing glasses of water on a tray. No real harm would come to the victim, just a blood-curdling scream that could be heard for blocks. And the glasses of water went flying in all directions. This was the reason plastic tumblers were used.

Now comes our heroes' waitress. "Iffen you bastards want to be served here, that young one had better put down that knife. I don't intend to get my belly burnt again. That trick landed the last one in the hospital with a cracked head."

"I'm sorry, lady, I meant no harm. I just enjoy the tingle it gives me. It whets my appetite."

"I'll give you a few minutes to browse the bill of fare."

The menus were sandwiched between the sugar bowl and the napkin dispenser. They were protected in a yellowed plastic cover and written in pencil. This scene was repeated in three thousand like places throughout Florida and probably all of Dixie. There were no exotic dishes like Grizzly Bear Steaks, Fried Rattlesnake, Grilled Armadillo or none of the other delights offered by better restaurants.

There was offered one twenty-ounce T-bone for $1.95. The price made it suspect and it was passed over. A reasonable choice seemed to be the Captains Sampler for $4.25. It included fried scallops, two deviled crabs, fried clams, one large trout, and a piece of Grouper, French fries, slaw but no oysters. The waitress was called over and asked about the absence of oysters. They were told no self respecting restaurant would dare serve oysters during any month that did not have an "r" in its spelling. It is assumed that all of them take these summer months off to make love. They ordered the Captains Sampler anyway.

The corner they chose proved one better picked for a more temperate climate and they moved to a table, which was in the path of a violent windstorm produced, by a monster window unit type of air conditioning. The evaporator drain hole must have been clogged for it was putting out a frigid fog of wet cold air directed towards Carl and Butch. They had to move to a calmer climate over to one side of the windstorm.

They must have arrived early for before they had finished, the room was packed. Surely this had to be the only place to eat within fifty miles, because it was not the food that attracted the masses. Carl noticed most of the people were ordering the T-bones or hamburger steak. Having his curiosity aroused, he asked the two men seated next to their table exactly what was the attraction.

"It's like this, one of our own was hauling a load of cattle to the abattoir in his rig when a kid ran out in front of him. He jackknifed the trailer and it overturned killing his whole load. We all went down with our knives, axes and chain saws and dressed out the load. We froze all we had room for and the cafe put the rest on special. We all have got to eat it up before it spoils."

"Are you telling me there's nothing wrong with that meat?"

"That's right."

"Damn, Butch, we just wasted four dollars and sixty cents."

"Not really, dad. I was all puckered up for some seafood. I ate enough steak down in Palm Beach."

"You all from Palm Beach?"

"No, we're from Atlanta. We were down to close out some property."

"You in the real estate business?"

"No, I just had a white elephant I needed to dispose of."

"That's all there is in Palm Beach."

"What do you do?"

"I own a fish camp over on the St.Johns. I just left over there earlier today. Some rich people in a Rolls stopped in and inquired about buying my camp. They also said they just closed a deal in Palm Beach. This is a peculiar coincidence."

"Were there two men and two women?"

"Yes."

"Was one of the women rather hefty?"

"That was the kind thing to say, but rather understated. Do you know them?"

"Damn right I do! That was my wife and three employees of mine. And you say they were interested in buying your fish camp?"

"That was the impression given me."

"What was the outcome?"

"I am not at liberty to say. The rest of the conversation might be considered privileged information."

"You sound like an attorney."

"I have been known to dabble in the law."

"Have you had the fish camp long or is that also privileged information?"

"No. I took it in on a bill owed me by an accused murderer."

"Did you get him off?"

"Yes, that's why I ended up with the camp."

"Butch, I wonder what they are up to?"

"Beats me, it sounds like it was a mistake to let them ride back together."

"This might cost me a hell of a lot more than three plane tickets."

"It also might be a blessing in disguise."

"How do you figure that?"

"Palm Beach was a liability. This could be another asset."

"Sir, it seems I might be a principal involved in this transaction. Is this facility in the black?"

"Very far in the black."

"If I prove to be a principal, would I be privy to the transaction?"

"How could you be a principal?"

"I hold the purse strings."

"And they hold none?"

"I cannot speak for the other three, but my wife has no control. She don't own diddley squat."

"She was the one doing all the talking. It seemed she was negotiating for the group. All of them were interested in it. The other lady acted like one of substance. The men served as coaches."

"In what way?"

"They were proposing a working interest."

"Well, I'll be damned. Butch, you and I were just talking about Mary's far away look. Mary and Phillip! I'll just be damned! They shall all be missed."

"What does that mean, Dad?"

"It means we will be free to pursue our own love life and I'm glad Mary has finally came out of her shell. I am absolutely in favor of what I have heard so far!"

"Sir, let me introduce my son and me. I am Carl Jones; the president of Carl Jones Enterprises and this is my son Butch. I am prepared to pursue this business with you at your earliest convenience. Anytime after this weekend, that is. We have pressing business up in Hooterville Crossroads."

"Is that a fact! I have done some business up there myself. In fact, that's how I became owner of the fish camp."

"I don't understand. Who murdered whom?"

"Nobody was murdered. Just some disgruntled family members were causing the local sheriff some grief."

"You don't mean Joe Billy Buford the Third? Why, he's a good friend of mine. What was he charged with?"

"Putting a rattlesnake in some gangster's car and causing him to wreck, which killed him."

"When did all this happen?"

"It was back sometime last year."

"Man, this is news to me. What was the fellow's name?"

"Lucius Popejoy."

"Never heard of him."

"The world will be a better place without him. Even his family members didn't grieve. All they were trying to do was shake old Joe Billy down for some bucks. But it didn't work. They didn't get a dime."

"Yeah, but poor old Billy Joe lost his fish camp."

"He didn't give a damn. He has property scattered all over Florida."

"I can't believe this! You mean Joe Billy, that country redneck is a man of substance?"

"That might be considered an understatement. He is one shrewd cookie."

"How did he get his money?"

"That is privileged information."

"Of course it is, I had no business asking."

"Why don't you look him up if you have the time? He can tell you more than I, if he will."

"Oh, I'm sure he will."

"By the way, my name is Roscoe Appleberry and my offices are in Lake City, St.Petersburg, Orlando and Miami. I try to stay in Lake City, that's where I live. Anyway, call there and they can get up with me. Here is my card."

"And you might say you dabble in the law? Ha! Sounds like you might be more than just an attorney for Joe Billy."

"Come to think of it, just about everything I do is privileged information."

"I'll wager a tidy sum you are acquainted with Abe Moses and Guilano Generosio."

"No comment."

"The world seems a small place indeed."

"It's just a matter of the circles one travels."

"Amen."

"Mr. Jones, with all my other interests, I don't need that fish camp. It takes personal attention to stay in the black and I can't give it any of mine. I can make you a deal that with the proper supervision; it will pay for itself in four years. That's a twenty five percent return on your investment. Where else can you find a deal like that?"

"I know plenty."

"Are they legal?"

"No"

"This one is."

"I will definitely get back to you next week. Butch, finish licking your plate and let's go back to the motel. I want to be in Hooterville Crossroads by nine tomorrow."

"Isn't that a mite early to start partying?"

"We need to see Joe Billy and some other people. I want to ask him about the fish camp."

"Who are the other people?"

"A farmer named Zeke. He and Nellie are supposed to be writing a book about the cats and flying saucers. And we ought to go see Nellie's granny."

"What do they know about cats and saucers beside that's what they drink milk from?"

"It's a long story. It would be better to get the story first hand from them, if possible."

"What does that mean?"

"People in that part of the state have a propensity for dialog deviation."

"Worse than us?"

"Much, much worse."

"What helps?"

"Booze and barbecue in great quantities."

"Are these essentials available there?"

"Fortunately, yes."

"I anticipate this encounter with great expectations."

"Your patience shall be rewarded."

"Tell me more about Joe Billy now that Roscoe has left."

"Phillip and I met Joe Billy on our last trip down to that area. He's a fine fellow to have on your side. It's best to try to keep him there."

Upon entering the motel room Carl exclaims, "Good God! It's colder'n a well digger's ass in this room. What did you set that thermostat on?"

"You know it was awful hot when we first got here and I wanted it to get cool in a hurry."

"Butch, I'm ashamed of you! Here you are, a graduate of Georgia Institute of Technology. And you come up with some stupid shit like that. A thermostat cannot accelerate cooling. It can only limit it."

"What can I say? I must have hung around mama too long."

"Women have a natural excuse, you don't."

"What do you mean?"

"The part of your brain you use for logic is missing in females."

"Are you saying they have an empty cavity in their heads?"

"No, it's filled up with other stuff."

"Like what?"

"Cooking, washing dishes, cleaning house, shopping and making babies."

"You know you're right. I'm not worth a shit at any of those things."

"Open the damn door and let some this cold out."

"I don't want to fight mosquitoes all night. Put a coat on."

"I didn't bring one."

"Wrap your ass in a blanket then."

"I'll get under the cover. I'm ready for bed anyway."

"Goodnight."

"Oh, call the desk for a six thirty wake up call."

"Desk."

"Hey, we need a wake up call."

"For what? It sounds to me you are already awake."

"You must be a whiz at housework."

"I do pretty well. What brought that on?"

"Forget it. Just wake us up at six thirty A.M."

"When?"

"What do you mean, when. I just told you."

"I meant what day?"

"Saturday."

"Tomorrow?"

"Puleeze!"

"There's no need to get bent out of shape."

"I'm sorry."

"There's no need to apologize. This happens all the time."

"I bet. Good night."

At two A.M. the phone rings. Butch answers. "Is it six thirty already?"

"No, I forgot to ask you something."

"What?"

"We have coffee and Danish in the office every morning. Do you drink leaded or unleaded?"

"What in the hell are you talking about? We don't drink gasoline."

"Oh, that's just an expression I picked up down at the cafe. It means regular or de-caf."

"Hello is it six thirty?"

"No, it's only six, but I have to go to the bathroom and I might not be finished by then."

"You must have a problem. Are you constipated?"

"Not so you can tell. I am only on page forty of the Sears catalog and I try to get in ten pages every morning. I need to finish this one before the new one comes out."

"Is the coffee ready?"

"Yes, it's on the little TV tray beside the desk."

"Butch! Wake up. The coffee's ready."

"Bring me a cup."

"Hell no, get your ass outta bed and accompany me to the office."

Butch dresses and goes out and cranks the car.

"This is ridiculous, the office is only fifty feet from here. We're not driving."

They walked into the office. There was a hot plate a pot on a hot plate turned up to high. The coffee was boiling. It was thick. It must have been on for a half hour. Butch comments, "It's a wonder the whole town hasn't burned down." There was some Styrofoam cups and non-dairy creamer and a cup full of sugar with a stained spoon in it.

"I'm not putting this shit in my stomach! Let's go down to that cafe and see if we can get a decent cup of coffee. You can drive over there."

"Gee thanks, dad."

The same waitress was there. "You must work all the time."

"No, I take off after the breakfast rush. It helps to break the day. That way, I can get in a little shopping and housework."

"I bet you're good at that."

"What can I get you?"

"Just coffee."

"We don't serve 'just coffee' to touristers. You'll have to order breakfast."

"This is crazy. I've never heard of a place where you couldn't order just coffee."

"We can't keep our doors open on 'just coffee'."

"How about the regulars?"

"Your purchases subsidize their drinking."

"I see, stick it to the tourists."

"We are the only game in town."

"Well, bring us the minimum."

"The minimum what?"

"Butch, we're getting close to South Georgia."

"In that case, we had better order a big breakfast."

"I guess you're right. Bring me three eggs scrambled well and a thick slice of country ham. Oh, and grits and biscuits."

"Make mine the same."

"The same what?"

"You're right, Dad. Bring me the same as he ordered."

"We've got hamburgers on special. I can give you a real deal on that."

"We don't eat ground cow for breakfast."

"I'll bring your coffee right out."

"I guess it's a good thing she woke us up a half hour early. I didn't plan on eating breakfast."

"What were you planning, starving me to death?"

"I thought we would wait and eat with the girls."

"What's wrong with eating now and then again with the girls?"

"A twenty six year old man should have stopped growing years ago."

"I must have a high metabolic rate."

"Or a bottomless pit for a stomach."

"Whatever."

"Here comes our food. We need a refill."

"A refill of what?"

"Maybe you should have a big breakfast, too."

"Why do you say that?"

"On second thought, it probably won't. Just bring us some more coffee."

"Look at that section of bone in the ham."

"What about it?"

"Look how round it is."

"So?"

"They say there's only one part of the bone in a pig's leg that perfectly round."

"And what is the significance of that?"

"At least that response is much better than 'so?' If there is only one part that is perfectly round, it means that these two pieces of ham came from different pigs."

"Couldn't one have came from the left rear leg and the other one came from the right of the same pig?"

"No, if you look closely, you can see the side walls lean in the same directions. If one was a left and the other was a right, the walls would lean in the opposite directions."

"By gosh, you're right! How did you learn all this trivial nonsense?"

"By whom else but Harold?"

"I never noticed Harold involved in trivia."

CHAPTER TWENTY-ONE

"Do you know how to get to Hoots County from here?"

"You can't, Son, you have to go to Greenville first and then head north for Quitman."

"Shouldn't there be a hyphen in Quitman?"

"I imagine originally there was, but it was probably shortened to eliminate confusion."

"Yeah, I can visualize the conductor on a train calling out 'Quit, man!'. There's no telling what all the men on the train stopped doing."

"There's not too much to do on a crowded train."

"You're not too old to remember how to improvise."

"I never had the opportunity on a train. The back seats on a Greyhound bus are a different story."

"My short life has been a sheltered one."

"You have many years ahead of you."

"I don't believe I'll ever catch up with you."

"Rear wheels never catch front wheels."

"They damn well try on this vehicle. If they were larger, they might."

"If they ever do, I don't want to be in it."

"That might be what happens when an irresistible force meets an immovable object."

"Yeah, Butch, you damn well don't want to be caught between them."

"Just look what happens to all the bugs on our windshield. And that's no comparison of what would happen to you."

"The air pressure front that precedes the windshield cushions the insect's impact."

"Tell the bugs that. It will make them feel better, Dad."

"I've often wondered how it would feel to be smashed by some heavy falling object squashing me on a flat surface."

"You would become the ultimate thin man. You would be able to squeeze through small cracks."

Dad asks, "Why would I want to?"

"It might cross your mind."

"I wonder what was Harold's last conscious thought?"

"He had no preparation time. I think he is in oblivion now."

"What do you mean, no preparation time, Butch?"

"If a person has some notice of his demise, he is able to think about the hereafter, and he may be able to go to his conception of paradise."

"I see. Maybe the churches serve some useful purpose after all."

"I know you have heard the phrase 'prepare to meet your maker'."

"I cannot accept that Harold is no more, anywhere. Or Marybelle either for that matter."

"How do you figure that?"

"They were more than just what we knew. I mean, more than just some bones and flesh. They had great minds."

"Are you inferring intellect determines ultimate survival?"

"Some go through life as if they are unconscious. More like sheep than people."

"Why sheep?"

Butch asks, "Have you noticed how sheep accept their fate with a resignation unlike most humans that try to alter their course in life?"

"This would lead me to believe sheep and other animals know more about the great scheme of things and so knowing, they have little or no concern of what happens to them in their lifetime."

"I have never thought of this as you describe it, Dad. It seems you are saying it is not a matter of faith with them, as it is among humans."

"Something protects their psyche. An antelope will try to avoid a lion, but when it realizes the flight is futile a resignation descends and I feel they are protected from pain at this point."

"It is a pity humans have to rely on strong pain killers in the agony of a terminal illness."

"Butch, I once had a dog I loved more than one should and I had to have her put to sleep. In her final moments, she looked at me with forgiving eyes as if she understood that I was trying to prevent her from suffering in her final days. Just the thought of the look in her eyes brings tears to mine."

"I am glad I came with you on this trip. I have been exposed to sides of my father's nature I never knew."

"Don't get too wrapped up in this new found respect for me. I may suffer a great setback in your eyesight when we meet the girls."

"At times, we all revert back to our primitive instincts. I will try to forgive you."

"Thank you, my son."

"It looks like we are coming into Greenville, what do I do?"

"Take a right when you see a sign pointing to Quitman."

"What do I do when we get to Quitman?"

"Get out of there as fast as you can."

"Why?"

"Because we'll be so close to our destination, my legs will start twitching and I'll break out in a cold sweat just thinking about Nellie and Lilly. And you sure don't want your old dad going into convulsions that close to paradise."

"The more I hear about these school teachers, the more I want to learn. What grades do they teach?"

"Hell, I don't know, we never got that far talking before more pressing matters were at hand."

"Maybe I'll find time to ask a few questions."

"Don't count on it. If you ask 'how are you?' it will take three hours for them to answer."

"Now I understand why you don't even know their last names. You were afraid to ask."

"No, it was other 'pressing matters' that kept us sidetracked."

"Maybe I can avoid these other pressing matters."

"If you even try, I'll disown you. You will shame me. I have already told Nellie you know all about the birds and bees."

"What's mother nature got to do with this?"

"Everything, son, everything."

"Then I shall curtail my speech to engage in groping."

"Don't come on too strong too quick, remember these are fine ladies. Wait for an overture."

"How long will that take?"

"If you live up to my expectations, not too long."

"Minutes, hours, days?"

"Let me put it this way, we don't have days and the hours are precious."

"Where will we eat breakfast?"

"At the City Cafe. The pig joint won't open until lunch time."

"What will we do between breakfast and lunch?"

"That will be overture time."

"Who overtures whom?"

"That will be up to the girls. Turn left down a black top road right before the Quitman city limits sign. I know a short cut to their apartment."

"How far?"

"Not far, just keep going down that road until you see a duplex on the left with a Mustang and Volkswagen parked in front."

"Wow! You mean one has a new Mustang?"

"Yes. It belongs to Lilly. Nellie helps support her granny and can't afford a new car right now."

"I feel those circumstances might change in the near future."

"If you take up with Nellie, they won't."

"Why do you say that?"

"I doubt you can support her and her granny."

"Point well taken."

"Slow down. We are getting close."

"I see a Mustang, but no Volkswagen. I wonder where's Nellie?"

"Pull up beside the Mustang and blow the horn."

The horn sounded only once when the front door was slammed open and the two ladies tried to get through it at the same time. Both were squealing like stuck hogs.

"Carl! Carl! We thought you got lost. We have been waiting since the sun came up. Come in!"

"My Gawd! Nellie, just look what Carl has brung us! Wow! Carl, this is you made over and in a better package too. Butch, how much do you weigh and how tall are you?"

"Mam', I'm six-six and weigh two hundred and twenty pounds."

"And I don't see one ounce of fat anywhere. Let me feel those biceps. Ooo, Nellie, I wish you'd feel that arm. I bet he could throw us under each arm and carry us away to glory!"

"Now girls, he might carry one of you away, but not both. I need some companionship also. You must choose and Nellie, I think you should back off for reasons we shall discuss later."

"Nellie, please can I have him? You got Carl and he is all you need. I have more urgencies. Big Boy, do you have a mind to fit that gorgeous body?"

"I have known to carry on a fairly intelligent dialogue among my peers."

"I wish you would listen, Nellie. Most hunks I know can't do nothing but grunt, which I must admit, comes in handy at times."

"Lilly, stop talking trash. Pigs grunt. Us humans pant and groan."

"People do more than that. I had one in the saddle once and I swear to God, I thought he was dying. He kept hollering, 'Oh Jesus! I'm coming!' Of course later I found that was just a figure of speech, to express the ultimate."

"The ultimate what?"

"Butch, see what I was talking about?"

"Dad, I'm enjoying it."

"Enjoying what? We haven't did anything yet."

"Lilly, I am liking you more as every minute passes."

"Passes what?"

"Dad, this is great, but I believe we had better get some breakfast in these ladies."

"Nellie, where is the Volkswagen?"

"Oh Carl, that will take a while explaining. We can talk while we eat."

"We can go in my car. It has more room than the Mustang."

"Ooo Nellie, just look at this car! You could put my little Mustang in the trunk. Oh Butch, please let me drive it. I love it!"

"I don't know Lilly, this is no Mustang I don't know if you can handle it."

"Don't let that little Mustang fool you. Appearances are deceiving. When I ordered it, I had the dealer to install a Thunderbird engine and a four-speed transmission. It stands up well against the pickup trucks the Bubbas and Juniors that hang around The Dairy Queen in."

"Well, just be careful."

"Oh shit, I can't even reach the pedals."

"Try those buttons on the left of the seat."

"Whee! This is great. Electric seats! I can't see over the wheel."

"Pull that lever on the left side of the column under the turn signal lever and pull down on the wheel."

"Whee! This is great! I could just sit here and get aroused. The steering wheel is now down against my legs."

"You can move back up a little."

"Nellie, you tend to your business in the back and I'll tend to mine up front. Butch, slide over here and wiggle the wheel for me."

"When you get going, it will wiggle all you want."

"How come?"

"I think one of the front wheels is a mite bent."

When she pulled out of the drive, she turned left instead of heading back towards Quitman. Carl asks, "Which way are you going?"

"This road goes straight past the City Cafe and it's long and straight and level."

"Oh Lord, Butch, you keep a tight rein on that filly. We don't want to run into the ass end of one of those big tractors that the farmers drive down here like they own the damn roads."

"Don't worry, Carl, they're all in the fields this time of day."

"Then watch out for possums."

"They only come out at night."

"Then watch out for hound dogs."

"They're all asleep under the front porches."

"Then let her rip!"

By the time the transmission shifted into third, the speedometer was registering one forty. And Lilly backed off. If she had not, she would have overshot the City Cafe. As it was, she had to lock all four wheels and do a slide into the parking lot, which was not paved and an immense cloud of dust surrounded the entire premises.

A couple of her contemporaries were emerging from the front door, picking their teeth, and dirt was sprayed over their stomachs which was not covered by the short tee shirts they were wearing. This was the accepted dress code in these parts if worn with low-slung blue jeans that hung precariously on their low hips. Lilly recognized these two, which were naturally addressed as "Bubba and Junior".

"Hi, Bubba, hi Junior, how y'all like these wheels I'm driving?"

"Wow! That's some piece of work. What did you do, trade in the Mustang? Iffen I'da knowed you wuz gonna do that, I'da liked to have had a shot at buyin' it. I bet they didn't allow you much for it, knowin' how you rawhided it."

"No, no, Bubba. I didn't rid myself of that fine car; this here one belongs to my friends, I think. Hey, this is your car, isn't it, Carl?"

"No Lilly, it belongs to Butch."

"Butch, I knew I liked you, but now I think I love you."

"Golly Lilly, we hardly know each other, yet."

"We'll get better acquainted tonight."

"I look forward to it."

"Meanwhile, let's go in and fortify ourselves for the forthcoming events."

"That's a wonderful idea. It's been too long since I ate breakfast."

"You mean you have already eaten once this morning?"

"Being prepared is my motto. One never knows what events one might experience during the day of a young virile male."

"Do not exclude females. We also need vast amounts of energy."

"God bless the women."

"The City Cafe was the exact replica of the one in Live Oak. Butch comments, "These types of places must be a franchise."

Nellie doubts it.

"Then they must use the same architect."

Here the similarity ended. There were six fine corn fed waitresses clad in halter-tops and extremely short shorts. The atmosphere was definitely an improvement over the last one visited.

"Now I know why the Pig Joint manager and cook eats here. Tasty food is not a requirement here. I wonder if they serve coffee without ordering breakfast."

"Surely you want more than just coffee."

"Nellie, my requirements are unlike my son's"

"Well, at least get a ham biscuit. They're great and you need something in your mouth to talk like us when we're eating."

"That's a good suggestion. I never could understand what you were saying when I was just watching you eat."

"Good, I thought we could all go out to granny's after we eat."

"I'd like to see granny again. Maybe I can talk her into selling some of her fine antiques. And we need to drop in on Zeke too."

"Oh, haven't you heard about Zeke? Of course you haven't. How could you? Off way up in Atlanta and way down in Palm Beach tending to all your businesses."

"What happened to Zeke?"

"Well, I'm sure you remember about the cats."

"Definitely, how could I ever forget?"

"Some have short memories."

"Not I, go on."

"On where?"

"Take a sip of that coffee and gather yourself."

"Anyway, I was going out to see granny one day to see if she needed anything from Thomasville. I had to go over there the next day for some school supplies. The school was going to reimburse my trip expenses and I thought I would kill two birds with one rock."

"Nellie, I think the term is one 'stone'."

"What difference does it make, Lilly?"

"You know school teachers must get everything right. For the sake of the children."

Butch injects; "That's right, Lilly. Technology is advancing so fast that all the textbooks can be rendered obsolete overnight. It's important to keep up to date on new sayings."

"That saying is as old or older than 'a bird in hand is worth two in the bush'."

"If you had one in hand, you would neither use a stone or rock."

"That depends how you acquired the bird. You may have used a stone."

"I would never kill a bird, unless it was attacking me."

"That's silly. What kind of bird would attack you?"

"A bald eagle might."

"It's against the federal law to kill an eagle."

"What if it was attacking you?"

"They do not attack humans without provocation."

"What kind of provocation?"

"Like trying to steal young eaglets from the nest."

"That's impossible. They build their nests far above the reaches of man. It's even against the law to possess one single eagle feather."

"What would anyone want with only one eagle feather?"

"Maybe to adorn their headgear."

"I don't wear feathers in my hat."

"Yankee Doodle did."

"I would like to find out what happened to Zeke before the day is over."

"Keep your britches on, Carl. You shall know what I know."

"And what do you know?"

"Not very much. It is only hearsay. As I was saying before I was so rudely interrupted, I stopped at Zeke's on the way to granny's and the place looked deserted. I got out and walked around to find a sign of life. My first impression was correct."

"How so?"

"It was deserted. The tractor was still in the field. When I say deserted, I mean the human element. The entire farm was fenced and cross-fenced with hog wire and there were a lot of those miniature houses scattered about the place where the sows have the piglets. The odor was not pleasant to my delicate senses so I left."

"He must have turned it into a hog farm."

"I don't think so. Zeke wasn't very big on pig. I think he sold the place. I went on up the road to granny's and the first thing I saw when driving into the front yard was the big black mammy that used to work for Zeke. She was sweeping the front yard. You know how granny hates grass. She will pull up every sprig that tries to struggle up through that hard pan. That yard had been swept so much; all the surface roots on those big oak trees were exposed. Some of them are as big as my legs above the knees, and you know how big they are, Carl."

"Nellie, I love the size of your legs. Legs with no meat are like a song without music."

"Undoubtedly that doesn't apply to mama."

"Shut up, Butch. Go on, Nellie."

"I axed her what was she doing over here, and she said she was sweeping the yard. I said that couldn't be all she does. She said 'I washes clothes and cleans the house some too'. I said I mean what happened over to Mr. Zeke's?"

"That ain't what you axed me."

"It sure is funny how some people say 'axed' instead of 'asked'."

"Shut up, Butch. Go on Nellie."

"I said I'm 'axing' you now."

"I was out in the back bilin' some of Mr. Zeke's clothes in that big wash pot when a long black car drove up. Land sakes, I swear it was a block long. Out comes at lease eight honkies all dressed up in black suits and ties like they're gonna funeralize somebody. They axed me where Mr. Zeke be. Or sumpin lak that. I looked 'round the back of that block long car an I spied a tag that sed yew ess govmint, Washington, DC whutever that ment. I tole them he went to the back fotty and will be back shortsome."

Lilly exclaims, "Ooo, I bet that had something to do with the cats and saucer."

"Then I 'axed' her what happened next."

"Nellie, for the sake of brevity and our sanity, please forego the quaint dialogue and continue in your own words."

"As you wish, sir. I was only trying to re-enact it as close as I could so nothing would be missed in the translation."

"I believe we can follow and glean the high points of the happening satisfactorily if you stick to the English language."

"When Zeke showed up, the men went into the house with him and told mammy to continue her task of cleaning clothes. They stayed in the house for over an hour and then all of them got in the car and drove away after Zeke told mammy to put out the fire and go home, he wouldn't be needing her anymore. He also said he wouldn't be back and to turn the cows loose in the cornfield."

"Well, I'll be damned! What else did she say?"

"Nothing, that was it. Except when she found herself out of a job, she went over to granny's to see if she could use some cheap help."

"When did all this happen?"

"The best I could tell, it was about three months before I went out there."

"Were you two able to do any work on the book before this happened?"

"No, Zeke started acting funny and had that faraway look like he was pre-occupied with some problem. The last time I saw him out there, I looked on his desk and saw a lot of official looking letters from Washington, DC and Dayton, Ohio. He saw me casually looking at them and he hurriedly placed some other books over them."

"I think Harold was right. We'd best forget all about this."

"Did he really say that? I would like to meet him."

"You can't now, it's too late. He is not with us anymore."

"Did he move away?"

"In a manner of speaking. You remember me telling you about him and Marybelle getting married and organizing that church? Well, some hate group blew it and them off the face of the earth."

"Nellie, I told you something like this would happen!"

"Shut up, Lilly. Oh Carl, that's horrible. Did they find who did it?"

"No, they probably never will. It could have been just about anybody. Practically the whole city of Atlanta was against them."

"Lilly and I try to be tolerant of all races. It's a shame others can't."

"Nellie, don't get carried away with that thought."

"Oh, I mean within reason and taking into consideration the times we live in. You might say we are closet liberals."

"Just keep it in the closet."

"Lilly, if you ever get a craving for a dark skinned man, I'll smear my whole body with black walnut juice and stay out in the sun for six months."

"Butch, between the way you talk and that beautiful car you have, you're going to have one hell of a time getting rid of me."

"I, unlike Harold, now have no desires to co-mingle with diverse races for the sake of future generations, Lilly, and if you are of like mind, I see no reason why we shouldn't pursue this acquaintance to a more desirable conclusion."

"And what conclusion might that be?"

"If I might prevail upon you to shed this yoke that you carry in this God-forsaken place and accompany me back to Atlanta, I feel that some equitable arrangement might be made for us to cohabit in comfort with or without the benefit of matrimony."

Nellie says, "That's the closest thing to a proposal you'll ever get. Grab it and run!"

"I am overwhelmed! I have not known this fine man for more than one hour and I am expected to make a decision that will affect the remainder of my life. I must have more time. Give me until tomorrow morning."

"Nellie, if we have finished with Zeke, I'd like to know what happened to your Volkswagen."

"I haven't finished with Zeke yet."

"How long will this take?"

"Not long, that is, if I am not continually interrupted."

"Please everybody, control your inquisitiveness and try to keep interruptions to a minimum. Go ahead, Nellie."

"Well, first I went to Joe Billy, you met him. He's the sheriff of Hoots County. And I asked him what happened to Zeke. He told me he had a call from Zeke from Wright Patterson Air Base up in Ohio and he asked Joe Billy if he knew a good lawyer that could dispose of his farm. He told him who to get in touch with. It seems his name was Roscoe Appleberry."

"Damn! The world is surely shrinking."

"That was number one."

"What was number one?"

"Number one interruption. I'm keeping count. And that's number two"

"Whatever, go ahead."

"That's about all I could find out. The next thing was when I went by out there and saw all those pigs."

"Now I bet he has all the pigs and honey he needs."

"Who's that, Lilly?"

"The owner off the barbecue place. He is the only logical one around here that needs a lot of pigs."

"What's this about the honey?"

"Carl, Nellie and I once speculated on how he cooked all the farts out of his baked beans and we concluded he used a lot of apple cider vinegar and honey."

"Come to think of it, I remember the ease with which I digested all those beans we ate before we pulled the pig out towards granny's the last time I was down here."

"Dad, What in the hell are you talking about? Pulling a pig out to granny's? How do you pull a pig?"

"It wasn't a live pig. It had been barbecued. And we used a rope tied behind the station wagon."

"And to think, for all these years I have looked upon you as a sane and stable person. Have I misjudged you?"

"At the time it seemed the most normal and natural thing to do. In retrospect, I now consider it just a mite bit out of the ordinary, but no more than the other things that transpired on that trip. You see, the barbecue place was overrun by a bunch of wild cats hanging around the dumpster and we volunteered to entice the cats out to granny's with the pig. She could have used the cats to rid her barn of rats."

"Did any of you consider what would happen after the cats finished with all the rats?"

"That question did not enter into the spirit of the endeavor. At this point, our minds were not too clear in regards to the consequences of our actions."

"In other words, the entire group could be accused of overindulgence of the spirits."

"Changing the subject, tell us about the Volkswagen, Nellie."

"That is a fine idea. I choose not to be indicted by your son, who cannot possibly appreciate our actions because he was not there to witness or participate."

"Oh, I would have liked to have been."

"Number ten, or was it twenty? Oh hell, I'm not going to keep count anymore. Go ahead, Nellie."

"You don't know this man. His name is Jubal Wilkerson. He lives over in the next county and he drives a Volkswagen just like mine. I mean, it's identical. Same color and everything. It even has a dent in the right fender like mine. I bent mine in a close parking space at a super market over in Valdosta right after I got it. It broke my heart. But I got over it in time. I didn't get it fixed because I figured if I left it like it was, I wouldn't have to suffer through another experience like that. If I had it fixed, I was afraid I would do it again. Like it was, I didn't give a damn if I did it again."

"I know the feeling. I worry about my Mustang all the time. I made up mind that if I ever get another new car, I will have the dealer pre-ding it, then I won't have to worry about that first dent."

"Now this Jubal was a ladies' man, particularly married ladies. He took up with this lady, named Bertha, I was acquainted with and when the husband was at work, he would sneak over there for an afternoon of fun and games. What other people do is none of my business and I will not judge them, that is, until it affects me. The husband had a suspicion of what was going on and he would drive by his house at random times during the day. This confirmed his suspicions. And he dwelt on the problem at length. Finally he had an inspiration. By the way, he drove one of those ready mix cement trucks. You know those monsters that take up most of the highway with their mixer turning and churning up the cement mix. Unfortunately for me, I chose the wrong day to go visiting Bertha."

"How so?"

"It happened the very same day the husband elected to check up on his wife. He was delivering a seven-yard load to a construction site. The first thing he saw was what he thought to be Jubal Wilkerson's Volkswagen. Remember Jubal's was a twin of mine and he did what he considered an act to protect the purity of married women, especially his. Being this an unusually hot day, I had left my windows open. The husband stopped his truck alongside my auto and with the chute fully extended, did with malice aforethought; unload seven yards of concrete through the open window. This was around noontime and as women are prone to do, engaged in important conversation for the next seven hours. We were so engaged when the husband appeared on the scene. One can only guess what kind of marathon he thought was transpiring in his bedroom that would consume seven hours. When he opened the front door he observed us sitting on the sofa engaged in important conversation.

"He immediately inquired as to the whereabouts of this Jubal person. I replied that as we were the only two persons present, we had no idea where this Jubal person was, 'But his car is out front, where it has been for the past seven hours.'

"I told him that is not Jubal's car, it's mine.

"And he says, oh shit!"

"I ask, why is that expletive necessary?"

"And he says, 'that expletive will not hold a candle to those you will utter once you have examined your bug. It will never crawl again'

"Fearing the worst, I inquire, what has happened to my precious mode of transportation?

"It was a case of mistaken identity. Once I explain, I believe you will understand my actions." He replies.

He explains to me.

"I told him I have been a victim of his misguided wrath. What great wrong have you perpetrated against me and mine?"

"I have dumped seven yards of ready mix into your car."

"I scream, Eeek! Don't just stand there! Go wash it out!"

"Can't do it, it has had seven hours to set up. I'm afraid the case is terminal."

"My poor car cannot possibly be the receptacle of seven yards of ready mix! It would not hold it."

"The remainder of the load was deposited over the top and it now stands a monument to my misguided wrath."

"I squeal, 'Do not try to conceal the evidence. You will hear from my attorney. Do not attempt to remove it from the street."

"Nellie, nothing short of a D-8 could do that."

"I state, I believe Jubal should forfeit his right of possession of its mate. Any other day, that would be his car sitting out there. I shall also institute legal proceedings against him."

"Bertha cries, 'Oh Nellie, I'm so embarrassed. We need to try to keep this out of the courts and newspapers.'

"I tell her, nothing will satisfy my anger except maybe a new car."

"My husband already owes for seven yards of ready mix."

"That is no concern of mine. Your domestic problems are no concern of mine. What does concern me is that I depended on that car to carry me around. There is no public transportation in this town. I will not suffer from your indiscretions or transgressions."

"We can't afford to buy you a new car. I imagine you have insurance. Talk to your agent."

"What can I tell him, Bertha? That a giant dirt dauber decided to use it for a new home?"

"That won't work, their nests are not nearly as hard as concrete."

The husband offers; 'I'll try to make Jubal give you his car."

"Why would he do that? I ask."

"Do you think he would rather hear his voice change?"

"He squeaks a lot now. Or so I have been told."

"I tell him to do what he can. I called Lilly to come and get me."

About this time, Carl had finished his eggs and ham and had started on the hot cakes and maple syrup. "What was the outcome?"

"My carrier was notified and they are going to take action against the ready mix company."

"The company carries liability insurance on all the employees, while they are on the job."

"Well, he was certainly on the job, if it was pouring concrete."

"Meanwhile, they are trying to locate me a like means of transportation."

"An eight year old Volkswagen might prove hard to find."

"I don't know, Butch, have you noticed how many are on the road now? They must breed faster than rabbits."

"You better believe it, Nellie, since I bought mine, I have been noticing how many there are. It's funny how you don't notice a particular type until you get one yourself."

"Sugar, that might apply to a Volkswagen, but I bet it doesn't to your beautiful Chrysler."

"Come to think of it, Lilly, I haven't seen the first one since I got mine."

"Got your what?"

"Hey waitress, bring Lilly a plate full of hot cakes and another jar of that maple syrup!"

"Nellie, I don't need any."

"Oh, yes you do!"

"Do what?"

"Butch, your old dad normally wouldn't give you any unsolicited advice, but you might had better defer your decision past tomorrow morning."

"Not to worry, Dad, once she gets up to Atlanta and breathes some of that thin air, she'll come around."

"I guess you're right. It's probably the atmospheric pressure and high humidity down here."

"I'm sure it is, at least I hope so."

"Girls, what's this I hear about some charges brought against Joe Billy?"

"Where did you hear about that? It wasn't in any of the newspapers."

"We ran into his attorney while eating the Captain's Special Sampler In the City Cafe In Live Oak."

"You mean Roscoe Appleberry?"

"No one, but."

"I'll be damned!"

"I've already said that."

"I don't believe you have exclusive right on that phrase."

"It must be public domain. I must come up with an original phrase."

Lilly says; "How about, 'I'll be dipped in shit.'?"

"I don't think that would be appropriate to be used in all circumstances."

"Neither is the classic one. We have to modify it when we're teaching Sunday school."

"In that case, what is acceptable?"

"I use 'I do declare'."

"That is incomplete, declare what?"

"No more than damn what?"

Butch offers; "I believe the use of either shows a lack of command of the English language."

"Sugar, I know of no one that possesses a complete control."

"You're right, Lilly, we all suffer from a deficiency in that respect."

"I met a man once that had complete command and I couldn't understand a damn word he was saying when he was attempting to communicate with us lower forms. He wound up being a recluse because he could find no one to converse with."

Butch blesses the illiterate.

Lilly agrees, "They are the salt of the earth."

"I can't go so far to say that. Some have their own dialect and no normal person can understand them either."

"Like whom, Nellie?"

"Cajuns, those that speak Gullah, and those who inhabit Brooklyn, to name a few."

"What's this Gullah you speak of?"

"Gullah is a dialect spoken by the ex-slaves who inhabit the low country between Savannah and Charleston, especially on Daufuskie Island."

"Nellie, you are a wealth of information, even though most of it seems to be of a trivial nature."

"Most of which I am forced to teach is of a trivial nature."

"How about the square root of two?"

"The accuracy of modern framing squares renders the equation obsolete."

"It was necessary in the construction of the Pyramids."

"People nowadays don't go around building Pyramids."

"This will change."

"Why do you say that, Carl?"

"Harold told me that more would be built in the future."

"I assume he was privy to information not available to us lower forms."

"Nellie baby, I know for a fact that was true. And also Marybelle, even though it was of a different nature. You will have to take our word on that now, for the world has lost two that had knowledge that could benefit all mankind. Albeit was misdirected."

"I cannot grieve for what I have not experienced, Carl."

"Life must go on."

"I think you could come up with a more original phrase."

Lilly asks, "How about 'the wheels keep on turning'?"

"Honey, I've heard that before."

"Butch, I think it's impossible to utter anything that has not been voiced in the past."

"I have heard that enough monkeys pounding away on enough typewriters, given enough time, will put on paper everything that has ever been written and ever will be in the future."

"Awesome"

"Meanwhile, we don't have enough monkeys, or enough typewriters and we absolutely do not have enough time."

"That's right, Nellie, so we can suffer through trite clichés and make do the best we can."

"I'm willing. How about the rest of you?"

"I think I can speak for the rest of us if it will speed up the gathering of pertinent information, such as, what in the hell happened to Joe Billy?"

"I will rise above myself and try to continue without being diverted. But it will take a small amount of cooperation from the group."

"We all shall also try to rise above ourselves and restrict our questions to the matter at hand."

"Thank you. Carl. I will now attempt to continue. This Lucius Popejoy had two sons that he was grooming to take over his operation in the remote chance he was unable to avoid the long arm of the law. Since he was taken in his prime, and his sons were deprived of the wealth of information he had in his grasp when he was suddenly taken away, much to the relief of all law abiding citizens in this and all neighboring counties. Said sons decided to seek recompense through the judicial process. The aforementioned sons went to the prosecuting attorney and prevailed upon him to present their accusations to the grand jury for indictment."

"Did they?"

"Did they what?"

"Indict Joe Billy."

"It seemed some members of the grand jury had some illicit associations with the alleged victim and they prevailed upon the remainder to issue a true bill. They figured this would get them off the hook of a cover up. Assuming the local judge, who was a good friend of Joe Billy's, would throw the case out."

"Did he?"

"Did he what?"

"Throw the case out."

"Here was the problem. When the case came up on the calendar, the judge was in one of those drying out clinics down in Tallahassee due to his inordinate consumption of alcoholic spirits. A judge was called in from the next county to fill in and he had crossed hairs with Joe Billy on a number of occasions over jurisdiction problems and Joe Billy knew he was in trouble. That's when he called in the big guns, namely Roscoe Appleberry. He knew this would cost him his ass, but that was better than taking a chance of getting fried. This attorney was a criminal lawyer, which I consider a redundant statement, who was renown for his ability to get the most vilest of criminals off with not so much as a wrist slap."

"I hear it cost him his fish camp."

"That's right, but he didn't give a damn. He won that camp in a high stakes poker game that he frequented down on the Withlacoochee River southwest of Clayattville. It was also rumored that the fish camp had belonged to the hanging judge from the next county. Had it not been for the high priced lawyer, his fate was sealed. It was considered only fitting that he was to give up the camp."

"How did he get Joe Billy off?"

"The first thing he did was to load the jury with cronies that leaned in Joe Billy's favor for various reasons."

"Didn't the prosecutor strike any of them?"

"Of course not, he didn't want to prosecute Joe Billy in the first place. The trial was a sham. The press was excluded because the jury was not sequestered because that would work a hardship of them, so to the only way to keep it 'fair' was exclude the press. That's why it was not reported in any paper, the closest one with any clout was in Tallahassee and this puny trial did not concern them. It took only twenty minutes for the jury to render a not guilty verdict in direct contradiction to the judge's charge. Needless to say the judge was incensed and high tailed it back to his own county where he had more power."

"I must see Joe Billy after we finish breakfast about the fish camp."

"Are you interested in that fish camp, Carl?"

"Not directly, but it just might have some bearing on our relationship, Nellie."

"If you think you are going to stick my ass down there to run it for you, you're crazy."

"Honey, I wouldn't do that to you. In the first place, I couldn't stay down there with all the things I have going on up in Atlanta. And as that would put you even further away from me, I could not bear the thought. What I had in mind was to buy it for my wife as part of a divorce settlement."

"How do you know she will go along with your scheme?"

"It's not mine, it's hers. It's funny how problems have a way of solving their selves, without you laying a finger on them or spending too much time trying to solve them. This is what happened to me. As I said before, my wife doesn't understand me. She was coming back from Palm Beach with some of my help and how, I do not know, they happened upon this fish camp. They must have convinced each other this was a perfect place for all to spend the rest of their days, I guess. Anyway, you remember Phillip Morse. He was riding back with Effie Lou, Jonas Perkins and Mary Pitts. Mary was Harold's mother. I can't say what really happened, but I think Phillip and Mary got together. Now I'm not saying in a carnal way, Mary is a wonderful person, but since Harold and Marybelle is not around anymore, she seems to have diverted her attention to other avenues. This might also be the case with Jonas and Effie Lou. They were always sniffing around each other back when I first got started over twenty years ago. I hate to see Phillip, Mary and Jonas go, but it will be worth it if Effie Lou is in the package. That will leave the door open for me to welcome you in."

"Where is this door?"

"In Atlanta, naturally."

"What about my teaching job?"

"You will have a full time job teaching me how to enjoy the finer things that life has to offer the both of us."

"What about Lilly?"

"I believe Butch has some ideas concerning Lilly."

"What about granny?"

"Granny's a tough old biddy. You will be only a phone call away. We can hire someone permanent to help her, if she needs it, and if she can get along with whoever we find."

"She will never consent to someone moving in with her. She is too set in her ways."

"No one will have to move in with her. It can be a daytime job."

"A dependable car will be needed."

"That can be arranged easy enough, don't forget I own a used car lot."

"Suppose she gets sick or breaks her hip?"

"What will happen if any of that happens now?"

"I'd call in professionals."

"Over the telephone?"

"I get your point. I still will need to visit her occasionally."

"There are good roads and fast cars. Besides, we will need to come back down here when the need arises, to fill up on barbecue and beans."

"What kind of needs?"

"It will probably be necessary to keep our conversations understandable."

"You mean like I try to tell you what happened sometimes?"

"Something like that, you might run into a situation like a UFO or something."

"I went for a ride in one once."

"We might even talk about that in the distant future."

"I really need a man to confide in sometimes. Of course, I have my gynecologist but that's on an impersonal level and Lilly's a good listener, but she usually has the same problems I have."

"I don't know if I can get into menstrual cramps and P.M.S., but I have a good ear and I can try."

"What's wrong with your other ear?"

"I use it for an exit for irrelevant items that happen to drift into the other one. But do not confuse this with selective deafness."

"What's the difference?"

"Selective deafness blocks some information before it gets to the processing center."

"I think I would have been a fine interpreter for the UN if I only knew some foreign language."

"Why do you say that?"

"I think most women have the ability to talk and listen at the same time. That way, we can cut our conversation time in half."

"Why then, does it take women so long to talk over the phone?"

"There is much to discuss."

"Why do I hear a lot of one sided telephone conversations with a lot of pauses then?"

"There are many reasons for this. Sometimes the other woman might have a pot boiling over and the phone cord won't reach the stove. Or they might have to answer the door or nature's call."

"Nellie, you have cleared up a lot of questions about the working of the female mind, but I have many more."

"Like what?"

"Female logic, for one."

"That is beyond the scope and understanding of any male."

"We must all suffer in darkness."

"I'm afraid so, but do you love us any less because of this?"

"No, we love you because of this. It adds to your enigmatic charm."

"There are many things that must be left unexplained between the sexes."

Butch says; "I try to keep my relationship with the opposite sex on a level somewhat like the animals."

"I hope you don't have a rutting season."

"No Lilly, I am ready to rut at the drop of a hat."

"Praise be!"

"Carl, aren't there any good barbecue places up in Atlanta?"

"There are many, Nellie, but I know none that have fartless beans. And I believe that consuming great quantities of such is not conducive to great sheet activity."

"Yes, it does take the edge off."

"Nellie, I bet we could come up with a recipe using honey and apple cider vinegar that we could market up there which would be a great benefit to all lovers."

"I'll tell you what Lilly, I will help you develop one and you and Butch can market it. All I want is enough of it to keep Carl and I compatible."

"I have been aware of the needs of such a recipe. It seems the idea has merit."

"Butch, do you really think so? This could give my life new meaning. If I go to Atlanta with you, I will dedicate my waking moments to this cause."

"Lilly, don't get carried away. I have some other things in mind for us. First, we will have to be domesticated."

"How do you mean? I thought I was already."

"Not completely. You now share an apartment with Nellie and I can't visualize the four of us sharing a like place in Atlanta. We all need our own space. It's only the right thing to do when couples are starting down the road of life. Besides I might have a few habits that I would not like my father to witness."

"Son, that goes for me also."

Lilly asks, "I see your point, Butch. Nellie and I have some things we don't share either. What other things do you have in mind towards my 'domestication'?"

"Things that I am not suited for."

"Like what, Butch?"

"To name a few, cooking, cleaning house and washing dishes."

"I figured with all the fine restaurants in Atlanta, we wouldn't even need a kitchen."

"There will be time when we will want to spend a quiet evening at home. When I get home from a hard day's work, I might need to clean out the gutters or mow the lawn. There is always something that needs fixing when you have a home of your own. Dad knows only too well what happens when you set your wife up in a castle and she is waited on hand and foot. Idle hands are the devil's workshop."

"You know, you're right about that. When Nellie and I are sitting around with nothing to do, the first thing we think about is going out on the prowl."

"What do you think, Nellie? Do you believe we can be domesticated?"

"It will definitely be a new experience for us, Lilly, but I for one feel the need for a change. If it comes with the package, I can adapt."

"If you can, I can."

"Butch, will we have a small bungalow with a white picket fence around the front yard?"

"You have been watching too many old movies on television. What I have in mind is a three bedroom ranch house with two and a half baths, and a two car attached garage."

"Who in the world needs a half bath? You don't have any half assed friends that will be staying with us, do you?"

"Absolutely not! The term is a misnomer. That's what they call a room with only a john and lavatory in it. It is usually close to the kitchen and carport. To be used for quickies when you can't get all the way to the other end of the house. It comes in handy if you have the squirts or you have been drinking too much beer in the backyard."

"I know the feeling. There's been many a time I had to go behind the hedge in front of the apartment and Nellie was too slow in unlocking the door. This usually happens after a night of prowling and beer guzzling."

"If two people are living together, they need two bathrooms. If there are five, they need five bathrooms."

"The act of getting up and making the trip is highly suggestive and everybody wants to go at the same time."

"I knew an old man that had eight kids whom he enjoyed beating on all the time. He had to put in eight bathrooms because every time he hollered 'shit!', all his kids busted their asses getting to a bathroom. Every time his old lady dropped another young'un he would add another bathroom. When he ran out of money he had a vasectomy."

"His urologist should have castrated him earlier."

"Nellie, that's a bad thing to do to any man."

"How about a rapist or child molester?"

"I must give this more thought."

"Great minds through the centuries have given this problem much thought and there seems to be no solution."

"Give the victim a sharp knife."

"Ugh! I can't eat another piece of this link sausage. Let's go find Joe Billy."

"With Lilly driving, we won't have to look for him, he'll find us."

"Hee, hee, I'll bet he'll have one hell of a time catching us."

"Lilly, don't you go getting him pissed at us. I want to keep him on my side. He can tell me a lot about that fish camp."

"Oh, all right. I'll just cruise around by his hiding places and we'll probably run into him."

They found him behind the very same billboard that caused him to lose the fish camp. But this time there was no damaging evidence to be witnessed. He was fast asleep behind the wheel of the patrol car. Carl walked over to the car and slapped the top over the driver's side twice. When he drew back for the third slap, Joe Billy jumped up and hit his head on the sun visor and then pulled his gun and shot three holes through the roof. By this time he was wide awake and saw Carl running back to Butch's car. Joe Billy shot once over Carl's head and yelled. "Halt! Eat some dirt! And don't move till I get there!"

Carl yelled, "Don't shoot! It's me, Carl!"

"Carl! What in the hell were you trying to do? Get yourself killed? I've been sort of skitterish ever since that damn trial. Them Popejoy boys swore to get me."

"Lock their asses up for terroristic threats."

"I couldn't prove it. They only talk about it among their friends."

"Maybe talk is all it is."

"Mebbe so, but I ain't taking no chances. What brings you down here?"

"My son and I were on the way back from Palm Beach and thought we would stop by to see you."

"Hi Lilly. Hi Nellie. I haven't seen you two since that fool made a big rock outta your Volkswagen. I hope you got compensated for it."

"Thank you, Joe Billy, but I'm not worried about that anymore. I think Carl has a solution for my problems."

"What did he do, give you this fine car Lilly is driving?"

"No, this belongs to Carl's son Butch. Butch, this is our fine sheriff, Joe Billy Buford the Third."

"Nice meeting you, I hope."

"Just don't try testing me with that car. The one I drive is no slouch."

"I wouldn't dream of it. I intend to use this only for street transportation."

"Don't try to shit me. I know what happens when a man your age gets behind the wheel of a beast like that. The temptation is too great. I bet Lilly wasn't driving it like a little old school teacher."

"If you have something hot, it's a sin not to use it."

"You have demonstrated that fact around town many times."

"I only like to have a good time like any red blooded American woman. Anyway, you won't have to put up with us much longer. We're moving to the big 'A' town with these fine men."

"I figured Carl was lying when he came by here just to see me."

"No, that was the truth. I wanted to ask you about that fish camp of yours down on the St.Johns."

"How'd you find out about that? Anyway, it's not mine anymore."

"That's how I found out about it. We ran into Roscoe Appleberry over in Live Oak yesterday."

"What's that son of a bitch doing? Spreading privileged information all over Florida?"

"It wasn't like that at all. He told us some people coming up from Palm Beach were interested in his fish camp and that's how your name came up."

"What did he say about me?"

"He said you gave him the fish camp for getting you off a murder charge."

"I would have got rid of it in any case. For one to be successful, you have to live there to keep the help from stealing you blind."

"How did that other Judge manage that?'

"You seem to know a lot about my business."

"I know nothing that is not common knowledge in this town."

"If that's all you know, I've got nothing to worry about."

"I don't want to know about your business. It's none of mine. But I am interested in that fish camp. That group who wants to buy it is my wife, Phillip and two other employees of mine."

"Is that a fact? Sounds like a bunch of rats leaving a sinking ship."

"Not at all. They have my blessings. One of the principals involved has in the past inhibited my actions in the romance department."

"Surely that couldn't have been your wife."

"None other."

"What about the others?"

"Of course, I shall miss them, but I have never been one to influence another in major decisions."

"What about Nellie?"

"That's different. That's personal."

"I see. What do you think, Nellie?"

"Whither he goest, I will also. That is, within reason."

"I've been up there a few times and I couldn't wait to get back here to God's country."

"Why then, do you take so many trips to the Florida panhandle?"

"That's different. Those are business trips."

"Yeah, monkey business."

"Carl, hurry up and remove this woman from God's country. She has too much common knowledge."

"Before the sun sets three more times on God's country, we shall bother you no more."

"You shall be missed. But don't forget to visit."

"You did not tell me how that other Judge managed the camp."

"He also had a wife inhibiting his freedom. He moved her down there to manage it."

"Did she come back up here to God's country?"

"No, she took off with one of the fishing guides and the last anybody heard from them, they were seen heading down US17 towards Lake Okeechobee. They cleaned out the bank account and took the best boat and trailer behind their station wagon."

"Ah, another adventuresome couple. There must be something in the air in Florida."

"The only thing I ever felt in the air was bugs and mosquitoes. I wouldn't dare ride a motorcycle down there."

"Butch and I couldn't get out of there fast enough. Of course we were busting our asses to get up here to see Nellie and Lilly. And you too, Joe Billy."

"Yeah, you just couldn't wait to see my charming face."

"Don't get sarcastic, Joe Billy. You know I consider you one of my best friends."

"All right, just don't try to kiss me."

"We're going out to see granny. Do you want to come along?"

"Hell no! I drove out that way about a week ago to see how the work was coming on that bridge that washed out, and stopped at granny's to say hello. She came running out of the house blasting away.

"I was lucky that I had just turned off the road and it just sprinkled my car. Look at all those dimples on the hood and door. It's a damn good thing it was a scattergun. Lord help me if it had a full choke. I wouldn't be here to tell you about it."

"Have they got the bridge fixed?"

"Nellie, don't you care about what's happening to your granny? And no, I don't know about the bridge. I wasn't going down there to see and have to come back by her place again. So I high tailed it back to town and tried to find you. Where were you anyway?"

"Lilly and I took a week off and went down to Panama City. We needed to get away for a spell. That's why we were going out there today to see her."

"Well, all I got to say is you better go in a tank. The way she was acting ain't no telling what she will do."

"Did you see that old black mammy?"

"I shore didn't. Maybe you had better go see her first. She might shed some light on the situation."

"Do know where she lives?"

"There's a pig path running alongside the railroad opposite the springs. She lives about a quarter mile down it."

"You can't drive a car down that trail, it's filled with washouts and gullies."

"You will have to walk in."

"You have upset me about granny. I wonder what's got into her?"

"I heard her shout something about the Russians coming. I guess she thought I was one of the invaders."

"This is so strange, first Zeke ups and takes off and now this. Do you think it has anything to do with that UFO?"

"I don't know. It was a week ago and maybe she has settled down by now, but I wouldn't take no chances. I think you had better see Matilda first."

"Who is Matilda?"

"That's her name."

"Whose name?"

"The black mammy."

"Oh."

"The conversation has been reduced to a non productive blabber. I suggest we terminate this and head out for the pig path."

"Good thinking, Butch. Sheriff, we will try to see you again before we leave."

"That's good, Carl, let me know what you all find out about granny."

CHAPTER TWENTY- TWO

"This is as far as I can drive, Nellie. You are going to have to walk the rest of the way."

"Please come with me. I don't want to walk this way alone."

"Get Carl to go with you. I need to stay here and keep Lilly company."

"I'll go with you, honey."

"I'll go too, Dad, if Lilly comes."

"Oh all right, the walk might do all of us some good. We need to work off some of that big breakfast anyhow."

"All of you follow behind me. I'm pretty good at jumping gullies and such."

"Son, where did you learn to do that?"

"Harold and I got a lot of experience rounding up all those 'UFO' parts scattered all over Jonesboro."

"There weren't any gullies out there."

"No, but there were a lot of drainage ditches and some were very deep."

"I fell into a drainage ditch once."

"Later, Nellie, later."

"This is not bad walking at all. I bet your car could make the trip."

"We're not there yet."

"Ooo, look up ahead. I bet that washout is four feet deep and twelve feet wide."

"Somebody has dug out some steps on both sides."

"We shall use the stairs."

"Lilly, you don't see stairs out in the wilderness."

"Whatever, I'm going to use them. Follow me."

"Watch out for snakes in the Kudzu."

"That stuff is taking over the South. You even see it on the outskirts of Atlanta. Nobody can get rid of it."

"I know how, Carl."

"You do, Nellie? Tell me."

"Start a rumor it's good to smoke, that it will get you high like marijuana or some of those cow pasture mushrooms. Then the government will spend billions to eradicate it."

"Somebody told me it was good to eat if you know how to cook it."

"Did they tell you how to cook it"?

"You need one of those old hammer mills. You fill it up with a mess of it and pound it to a pulp. It's real tough and stringy. Then put in a big wash pot like the one we saw at granny's and boil the hell out of it. When it starts to boiling and foaming like it was going to run over and put out the fire, throw two big hams in. When the hams get done and float to the top, pull out the hams with some big tongs and then pour the rest out on the ground. But don't do it on your lawn. It will kill the grass."

"Suppose you pour it back on the Kudzu vines?"

"In that case, it will act as a high powdered fertilizer and the Kudzu will really go wild."

"Lilly, tell me more about those mushrooms."

"Son, don't take up any more bad habits."

"Don't worry, Dad. This information is for research purposes only."

"You don't see any around here, but up in Montgomery and Toombs County, there are those big cattle farms that raise Black Angus cattle. The mushrooms grow in cow pies. Aside from the onions, this is their number one crop. But they are not sold in stores. You have to sneak out in the pastures after dark and harvest them. I think it's illegal. And you probably have to wear boots in case you step into one of the pies."

"I stepped in a cow pie once."

"Not now, Nellie. I see Matilda on her front porch."

"Hello Matilda, remember me? I'm Nellie, granny's granddaughter. I saw you over there after Mr. Zeke left town."

"Yessum."

"Don't you help granny any more?"

"Nome."

"Why?"

"She randed me off."

"Why?"

"Sumpin got atta her."

"What?"

"Hants or sumpin."

"Can you tell us anything else?"

"Nome. I gotta go in now."

"Thank you Matilda, you have been a lot of help."

"Yessum."

"Is that all you are going to ask her?"

"Yep, let's go."

"Bye, Matilda."

"Bye."

Back in the car Carl wonders exactly what went on in that one sided conversation. "You should've pushed a little harder."

"You don't push these people. They don't trust white folks."

"What can we do now?"

"If we knew a black emissary, we could send him to question her further. I don't know one, do you?"

"Nope, then what else?"

"We can go on to granny's."

Is that a good idea?"

"We can stop out of shooting range and yell at her."

"Can you make her hear you?"

"I have good lungs."

"So I have noticed."

"No better than Lilly's."

"Thank you, sugar."

"Lilly, stop here at the edge of the fence. I don't think the shots will reach this far."

"I don't want my fine car to go back to Atlanta with a bad case of acne."

"Then let me out and back up another thousand feet."

Nellie walks up to the end of the fence and starts to yell for granny. Soon granny comes running out of the house wielding a long butcher knife.

It was so old and had been sharpened so much, the blade was no more than a half-inch wide where it had originally been over one inch, but it was still sharp enough to shave a grizzly bear.

"Granny! It's me, Nellie. Where's your rat killing shotgun?"

"I used up all the shells runnin' them damn Russians off."

"Granny, there are no Russians around here. What did they look like?"

"They come in a long black car. It was as long as my front fence and full of Russians. They musta been twenny in it. They wuz all dressed like a bunch of funeralizers goins to plant some big shot."

"What did they want?"

"I dint give them buzzards a chancet to say nothin'. I jest started blastin' away with my rat killin' shotgun. They hightailed it the same time I was down to one shell."

"And they haven't been back?"

"No"

"Granny, what happened to Matilda?"

"She was in league with them varmints. The fust thing they did after they got out of thet goldanged awtymobeel was go straight over to my wash pot where she wuz bilin' some of my clothes an' surrounded her on all fore sides and talkin' low to her. I couldn't hear a dadblamed thing they wuz sayin' and I got good ears. I heered you hollerin' like a stuck hog from way up the road while ago. That's when I started blastin' away."

"Did you hit any of them or Matilda?"

"I shot over their heads. I dint want to kill them, I jest wanted to run them off."

"What about Matilda?"

"They put her in the car with them. They had a hell of a time pushin' her through one of them doors."

"Nothing has happened since then?"

"That crazy sheriff come nosin' around last week and I used my last shell on him. Please go back in town an' get me some more shells."

"I'll bring you some the next time I come back out here."

"Whuttul I do till then?"

"Keep that butcher knife sharp. I came out here with Carl and Lilly."

"I see some other one in thet fine car. Who is he?"

"That's Carl's son. I think he and Lilly might get married. And I might be marrying Carl."

"Is he gonna be movin' down here?"

"No granny, I will have to move to Atlanta."

"Who's gonna take of me?"

"You do a damn good job taking care of yourself. Besides, we are going to find somebody local to drop in on you to take care of your needs, like groceries and shotgun shells."

"I'll never see you again."

"Oh yes you will, I'll visit you so much, you'll get tired of seeing me."

"Who do you think will come way out here to check on me?"

"Until I can find someone, maybe Joe Billy can drop by, if you promise not to shoot at him. Like you did the other day."

"I thunked he wuz one of them Russkies."

"Can I bring in the others? I want you to meet Butch."

"Who's Butch?"

"That Carl's son. That's his fancy car Lilly's driving."

Nellie waves to Lilly, motioning her to come on in the yard. Butch says; "Boy! Look at that old woman, she looks like a dried up prune. Lilly, you're not ever going to look like that, are you?"

"Butch, that old woman is pushing the century mark. Of course, if you don't take care of me and abuse me, I might wind up looking like that sooner. I now assume you are taken with me for the physical attraction only."

"I love your fine mind and your zest for living as well."

"You two stop talking trash and get out and greet granny. And keep your mouths shut about her appearance."

"Hey Carl, I heered you done swept my granchile offa her feet and gonna take her way up to thet big city."

"Those are my intentions. Granny, meet Butch, my son. Butch, this is granny."

"Pleased to meet you, granny. Nellie and my dad have said great things about you. You are all I expected."

"Flowery talk won't help. I jedge everbody by their doins' and not their talkin'. You ain't no Russkie is you?"

"No mam, I am a red bloodied American capitalist, seeking my fortune."

"Like I sed, fancy talk is cheap."

"What would you like me to do?"

"I gotta a big pile of firewood out back thet needs splittin'."

"It's not sweetgum is it?"

"There ain't no sweetgum on my propitty. I dug all of thet damn stuff up by the roots years ago."

"Do you have a log splitter?"

"I do now."

"What type of compensation do you have in mind?"

"I'll give you free rent on thet dirt yore car is sittin' on."

"Well, I just might back it out to the road then."

"You won't git fur on fore flat tires."

"My car doesn't have four flat tires."

"Mebbe not rat now, but I still got thet knife in my hand."

"Where's the woodpile? Dad, I think I like her, she has a way with words."

"I found that out on my last trip down."

"Yeh, thet's when you all cleaned out my larder."

"Granny, you know damn well you came out mighty fine on that deal, so stop complaining."

"I know, I got no right to speak hard about it. I still got some of thet money left. I been thinkin' 'bout doin' it ever weekend iffen I had some way gittin' people out here."

"You won't get anyone out here until you forget about shotguns and Russians."

"Iffen yew want to teach a old dog a new trick, give him a ham bone. I won't do a flip fer a bone, but I might fer ennuf cash."

"Trust me granny, you don't want to start feeding a bunch of folks out here. Just keep on doing what you want to, slopping hogs, tending your garden, sweeping the front yard and running off Russians. You need to spend the twilight of your years in peace."

"The sun ain't half down yet. I have many moons left."

"I know you have, but don't mess them up with new ideas. Leave that to us young folks."

"Humph!"

"Granny, I have split all the wood. Anything else you want me to do?"

"No, I swept the yard before you come. Sit a spell."

"That's a mighty fine ax you have. How old is it?"

"It wuz my grandaddy's. 'Course it hadda a lot of handles put in. I broke the last one tryin' to bust open a big rock. I got a idea it wuz hollow and sumpin wuz in it."

"What did you think was in it?"

"It looked lak a dinosewer aig. And I figgered iffen it wuz, maybe I could save it and nurse it back to growin."

"Why would you want a dinosaur?"

"I thought I could train it to pull a plow."

"They tell me they are dangerous."

"Not iffen you git 'em young an' love it some. It works on any animal"

"I don't think it would work. Their brain is no larger than a pea."

"This is acydemik anyway, Nellie, I don't aim to bust enny more ax handles."

"Do you need anything before we leave?"

"Well, the wood is split an' yew don't have enny shells, so git."

"Granny, it was nice seeing you again, we'll see you real soon when we come back down here."

"Thank you."

"If I'm back down here again, I'll split some more wood."

"Thank you."

"Bye granny, don't worry about a thing. I'll find somebody real nice to check in on you before we leave."

"Never mind. I wuz takin' care of myself long befoe you wuz borned."

"You were a lot younger then."

"Do whut you want to."

"Lilly, when you drive off, don't go scratching up her front yard. She's got it looking real pretty."

"I'll wait till I get back on the road."

"Wait till you get way down the road. I don't want a dust cloud messing up her house."

"I'll try to control myself. Where do you all want to go now?"

"Honey, I'd like to see those famous springs I've heard so much about."

"No problem. It's right down the road. It might be nice to stop a while and lay in the cool grass."

"How high is the grass?"

"Privacy high."

"I anticipate this with bated breath."

After stopping in the turn off, Lilly says, "Butch, I hate to rain on your parade, but it looks like all the grass is dead."

"I wonder what caused that?"

"I bet it was that U.F.O."

"Let's not go in there. I got a funny feeling it might affect us too."

"Drive on, Lilly, to more greener pastures."

"We can't do that. We might roll into some fresh cow pies."

"Just the thought of that has cooled my ardor."

"I just want to drive around and show you some of our beautiful scenery down here."

"We won't see much at the speed you like to drive. I'd like to at least count the telephone poles."

"Where I'm going to take you, there are no poles."

"Well then, I'd like to count the pine trees."

"You can't do that either. There's too damn many."

Lilly drove out US Highway 84 West for about ten miles and turned off to the left down a sandy dirt road, kicking up rooster tails of dust.

"Stop the car, Lilly. I want to drive."

"Aw, Butch, I was getting into this. Why can't I drive?"

"This is stark pristine beauty and I want to savor it. You cannot control your desire for thrills, which are diametrically opposed to mine at the moment. You shall have a better group of thrills later, as for now, let me enjoy what I cannot experience in the undulating terrain of the area in which I reside."

"I yield to the young man who has so eloquently voiced his passion, at the moment."

Butch turned into a sandy track leading off to the east just wide enough for the car to clear. He stopped just far enough into it to still be able to back out and not to be seen from the road. He cut the engine and told every body to listen.

"Listen to what?" All asked.

"The music of silence. All the world's riches would not buy this up in Atlanta. If you found something close it would be interrupted by the sound of jets leaving the airport."

After their ears adjusted to this new peace, the clicking of the cooling exhaust system was heard, as well as the occasional rewinding of the dash clock. When these distracting sounds had abated, the gentle breeze through the tall pines came to them as God's whisper. In the distance a hawk was heard crying for its mate. In less than five minutes, there were no dry eyes.

"This is a most holy experience. I have never appreciated such before. How did you find such joy in so small a thing?"

"Nellie, this is no small thing. Harold taught me how to hear God's voice."

"I wish I had known Harold."

"And I too, Nellie. I might never again have the urge to prowl."

"Sugar, if you will allow me, I shall share with you all the beauty Harold has shown me."

"Allow you! I beseech you! Lead me on to paradise!"

"I cannot take you there, but I will try to show the way as best I can."

"Carl, did you know your son was a disciple of Harold's?"

"Yes, and I was too, as long as I had the pleasure. But in a vastly different way. He and I dwelt in the world of material things, but I knew he knew things he did not share with me."

"Did his mother and father know this person?"

"He and his father never met. He died before Harold was born. Mary must have known more about him. She developed a serene countenance after he left us. Like maybe he is still with her. As well as her long dead husband."

"I wish I had that kind of faith, I am afraid of loving anyone with all my heart. I know the devastation I would feel if a loved one was taken."

"Lilly, you should not be afraid. If you love someone enough, death cannot separate the two of you. As I had loved Marybelle and Harold. There was nothing carnal about this relationship, once I got over my infatuation with Marybelle."

"My prejudices would not allow me to feel that way about someone of a different race, except in a carnal fashion."

"I will teach you tolerance you have never known."

"Will I shed the shackles of intolerance and prejudice?"

"If we live long enough."

"I intend to live a long time. Don't you?"

"As long as you live, I live."

"You drive back. I have found new motivation."

"Dad, why don't you and Nellie sit up front and you drive? Maybe Nellie wants to drive. Lilly and I can enjoy the back seat. Speed does not fill me at the moment."

"The only thing it filled me with was anxiety."

"We should get back to the apartment and start packing."

After moving Lilly's Mustang, they backed the car up to the front door.

"This car won't hold all this stuff, Nellie. You two just pack some suitcases which will fit in the trunk and I'll send a truck down for the rest."

"We can't do this. Lilly and I must give the school notice. And we need time to sort out the things we want to keep. I don't know what to do with everything else."

"We're real good at auctions."

"That's a good idea, Butch. I'll still send a truck down and we'll take all of this shit to the junk auction."

"I'll have you know our shit is not junk."

"Honey, that's just a figure of speech. This way, you can sort it out in Atlanta at your leisure."

"Good, now all we have to do is give notice."

"Can you do this over the phone?"

"If the principal is not off fishing, or prowling around."

"Does he do that?"

"I believe all persons involved with the teaching of other's brats are guilty. It's a occupational hazard."

"Call and find out."

"Hello, Mrs. Prince, this is Nellie. I'm fine. And you? Oh, I'm sorry to hear that. Is it serious? I'm glad. Is Ben home? Oh. Can he be reached? Oh. Where on Lake Blackshear? Oh. What kind of boat is he in? Oh. Yes, it's important. Lilly and I want to give our notice, we're moving to Atlanta. Yes I know, but we won't be teaching school up there. Yes, we both have pistols. Yes, we know how to use them. Joe Billy gave us instructions. What? Oh, 44 Magnums. I don't know about that. I think it would be better if we told Ben in person. We'll drop by Warwick and try to find him, but be sure to tell him the minute he gets home in case we don't."

"Butch, we can go with you and Carl if you can go by Warwick so we can tell Ben."

"Can we get there from here?"

"No, but we can from Albany."

"Any place to eat up there?"

"I think so. If there's not, we can stop in Cordele later."

"That sounds mighty iffy. We had better fill up on ribs and beans before we start. When does that rib place open?"

"It will be open by the time we finish packing."

"Shouldn't we try to see Joe Billy before we leave?"

"Carl, while we're packing, try to get him on the phone and tell him to meet us there."

"I'll try. Hello, is the sheriff in? No, I don't want to report a crime. Yes, it's personal. Yes, he knows me. What? Oh. Carl Jones. No, I'm from Atlanta. Yes, I'm from Atlanta and I do not want to report a crime. Yes, I know that's out of his jurisdiction. No, I don't want to call the state police. I want Joe Billy. Well, get him on the radio and tell him to meet me at the rib shack. Yes, I've eaten there before. Yes, they are good. No, they didn't give me the farts. You do? Wait a minute. Hey Nellie, this woman at the sheriff's office say she knows what they put in the beans. See if she will tell you."

"Hello, this is Nellie.What? Yes, I teach. Who? Mrs. Snodgrass! Well, I do declare! Of course I know your son. No, I don't hate him. He did? That's a barefaced lie! I did no such a thing. I do not use a bullwhip in class, only a paddle with a few holes in it. No, I didn't make him drop his pants in front of the class. I took him into the cloakroom. That's the only way you can monitor the severity of the punishment. What? By the color of the flesh naturally. I never go farther than a rosy pink. Oh, I'm sorry you feel that way. I can live without the recipe. I think I know what is anyway. What? Apple cider vinegar and honey. Be sure to radio Joe Billy Carl's message, it's real important. Bye."

"Well?"

"That old bitch wouldn't give me the recipe because I gave her son a small attitude adjustment the other day. Anyway, I was right about the recipe. She was in tears when she hung up. I sure busted her bubble."

"Do you think she will relay the message?"

"I'm sure she will. She could get into a lot of trouble if she didn't."

* * *

"Welcome, ladies and Mr. Jones. Who's this fine young fellow you have with you?"

"This is my son, Butch. We are on the way back from Florida and we just had to stop for some of those fine ribs and beans."

"I just got back from Florida myself the other day. Did some good fishing down on the St. Johns. Caught the limit in thirty minutes. Sure was some excellent eating. They cooked them up at the restaurant at the fish camp. I heard rumors about it changing hands."

"I heard that too."

"Are you familiar with this place? There's a lot of camps down there."

"Is this one out of Seville off 17?"

"How did you know?"

"And it's owned by Roscoe Appleberry?"

"Joe Billy had to tell you. That's not at all like him."

"It wasn't him. I'm involved in the purchase in an indirect way."

"The world shrinks daily. What can I get you?"

"Bring a pitcher of beer while we wait on Joe Billy. He's supposed to meet us here if he got the message."

"Don't count on it. I just saw him in his patrol car barrelling ass out the road towards the Lonesome Pines Motel out on US Highway 84 West."

"I bet that damned Ephriam is causing somebody some grief out there."

"Better them than us."

"Dad, what are you talking about?"

"That's where we met Joe Billy. It was a case of mistaken identity. Or a warped sense of morality on the part of this damned Ephriam."

"This can't be what's going down this time. We're here and that self appointed protector of the community's morals doesn't go on duty until tonight."

"Then he might show after all. He was probably chasing some speed demon."

Before the second pitcher was empty, Joe Billy come sliding into the parking lot, spraying gravel over the adjacent cars.

"Where were you going in such an all fired hurry a few minutes ago?"

"Shucks, when I get behind the wheel of that damned car, I get so wrapped up in the chase, I plumb forgot where I was going."

"Where were you going?"

"Here."

"You want a swig of this beer?"

"You ain't got no hard likker?"

"It's too early in the day for that, besides we have a long drive ahead of us."

"You going back today?"

"Yes, and we have to stop up at Warwick and try to find Ben Prince."

"What do you want him for?"

"Nellie and Lilly needs to give him notice of their intentions. His wife told Nellie he was up there fishing."

"I think he was lying. I saw him heading south towards Tallahassee early this morning."

"His wife must have been confused. Maybe I should call her and verify this."

"Don't, Nellie. I don't want to investigate another homicide. She's one mean bitch when she gets riled up."

"Well, I could call him tomorrow from Atlanta."

"I wouldn't count on that either. His back seat was piled high with suitcases and he was pulling a U-Haul."

"Ooo, I bet he was defecting too."

"I couldn't blame him. He shore was hen-pecked."

"And I bet there was a deficiency in the romance department too. He was always trying to play grab-ass with me when we would meet in the hallway."

"What was your reaction, Lilly?"

"I told him there was a time and place for everything and this wasn't it. He asked me 'when and where 'and I told him in the next century on the moon. I think he got the message."

"You must have been having a bad day. I have never known you to repulse amorous overtures."

"Nellie, that's unfair. You know I discriminate."

"Yes, I know. They must be breathing and male."

"And don't forget I must be in the mood, Nellie. But don't worry, Butch. I have, since I met you, dispensed with mood swings."

"I love stability."

"And stability you shall have. I promise."

"Call the manager back. I'm hungry."

"Does this mean, when we move into our dream home, I will spend my waking moments in the kitchen?"

"No Lilly, the kitchen will be used mostly for throwing together snacks to tide us over between the meals we shall consume in Atlanta's finest."

"Will these 'snacks' be store bought?"

"Mostly. At times we might have to fire up the oven. I like a slice of summer sausage and cheese warmed on one of those round butter flavored crackers."

"Sounds like we will also need a cooler full of beer."

"Definitely."

"I look forward with watering mouth."

"Are you ready to order, fine people?"

"By all means. We need the W.F.W. And more beer."

"Carl, what's the W.F.W.?"

"Nellie, that's the Whole Flaming Works."

"I think you cleaned that up a mite."

"I am always the gentleman."

"Won't that be somewhat hazardous for four people to be traveling together in the close confines of an air conditioned automobile, Dad?"

"The ribs, as well as the beans are prepared by the same secret recipe."

"Good, my saliva glands are now secreting voluminously."

"Speaking of close confines, Butch, I have often pondered a problem."

"Maybe I can clear it up for you, Lilly."

"Assuming the insurmountable odds against this happening, if an air tight room was filled to capacity with people and all inhaled simultaneously, would everyone's ears pop?"

"I must have more parameters before I can figure this.

1-Did anyone have their mouths open?

2-Did everyone inhale by expanding their chest cavity or did they use their stomach to operate the diaphragm?

3-If they expanded their chest cavity, did the expansion coefficient displace the air removed from the room and nullify the results?"

4-What was the room temperature?"

"Forget it."

"Great minds ponder when idling."

"Since I have met you, I have no desire to idle."

"Full speed ahead! Our life shall be like a roller coaster ride. We will be filled with mixed emotions. Thrills, panic, euphoria, fear, exuberance, satisfaction and finally peace. Some poor souls choose a merry go round."

"Nellie says; "I rode a roller coaster once."

"How did you find it?"

"I didn't. I had a date and he took me to Jacksonville Beach and he knew where it was, Carl."

"Have some more ribs."

"I'll eat one more. That's all I need."

"Need for what?"

"Dad, you had better eat a lot more yourself."

"Maybe a nice ride up the road will clear our heads."

* * *

This is not a western. This small loving group will not ride off into the sunset and live happily ever after. Instead they head north to Atlanta, all with new resolve to better their lives. Lilly dreams of her new home with great expectations. Butch is thinking of how to keep her happy and to suppress her tendency to prowl. Carl is wondering if the change in Nellie's environment will help him understand what goes on in her head. And Nellie, what can be said? She's just looking out the window.

The reverie is broken when Butch swerves to miss a wild hog crossing the road. The shoulder is soft and he almost loses control, but the car stops with the two right wheels mired in the rich black soil.

"I hit a wild hog once, Butch. You did the right thing. They can turn a car over."

"This is not a Volkswagen, Nellie. I doubt that one could turn this monster over."

"I wasn't in my Volkswagen, but I rode on two wheels for about one hundred feet. I was lucky no other cars were on the road."

"We need some luck right now. Let's all concentrate on willing some Samaritan to appear coming up behind us."

After twenty minutes of willing and concentrating. Help is not forthcoming. Not wanting to waste any more time waiting for a miracle or such, Butch decides to walk back down the road to where he saw a dirt driveway and seek help.

"Sugar, I'll walk with you. Let me get my walking shoes out of the trunk."

"Carl, are you willing to stay here with me for God knows how long instead of keeping them company?"

"Under the circumstances, we might keep them company. We need to walk off some of that big meal anyway."

"Are there any tissues in the car? I feel we might need some."

"You are not going to start crying, are you Nellie?"

"Those are not the type of secretions I might need to expel."

"Oh."

"How far was that driveway, Butch?"

"It can't be even a mile, I don't think. I don't really know."

"Damn! Butch, I believe your conception of distance could use some improving. My feet says we have already been walking two miles."

"I walked ten miles once."

"Not now, Nellie."

"I see it! I see it!"

"See what, Carl?"

"The dirt road, Nellie, the dirt road."

After walking up the dirt track about a quarter mile, Nellie breaks the silence.

"This looks just like the road we were on this morning communing with nature."

"Butch sugar, give me the box of tissues. I have some private communing to do myself."

"Don't go in the woods too far. There might be some more wild hogs in there."

"Don't worry. I see a nice clearing over there behind that big oak tree. That should do nicely."

She was back in less then five minutes. Looking relieved and mortified.

"You won't believe this, but I was using somebody's front yard for a bathroom. Or you might say, a rest stop."

"Nature's callings take precedent over modesty."

"When I get started, modesty takes a back seat until I finish."

"I heard of a man once that had his maid in the short rows when his wife caught him and started beating him with a broom. He told his wife to wait a few minutes and she could shoot him, he didn't give a damn."

"I know that's right. Even if a tornado was coming, it would have to wait for me."

"Men!"

"Tee, hee. Women too."

"Now, Nellie."

"How can somebody's front yard be deep in the woods?"

"They must consider all these woods from here to the highway to be their front yard. The house is facing that way."

"Big front yard."

"How do you get to the house"?

"This road curves a little up ahead and their driveway comes in from the side."

"Did you see any signs of life?"

"No. But I did see an old John Deere tractor in the front yard."

"We best approach from the front. They might be as trigger happy as granny."

"Butch, a wise suggestion."

"You all go ahead. I need take advantage of the facilities."

"Nellie! That is their front yard."

"That didn't stop you. Besides, I'll go in the road."

"It was too late when I saw the house. What if a car comes?"

"I'll move over to the side so it can pass."

"We'll wait for you beside the tractor."

When they got within five feet of the tractor six of the finest specimens of black and tan coon dogs came running out from under the front porch raising hell. Carl, Butch and Lilly all jumped up on the tractor to keep from getting eaten alive, or so they thought. About this time, 'Junior' came running out the front door onto the porch yelling at the dogs. He was wearing no shoes and had on a pair of faded overalls hanging on his shoulder by one strap. His face had a week's growth of stubble. And he was picking boogers from his nose with one hand and holding a can of beer with the other. The dogs stopped barking and started sniffing at the appendages within reach. And wagging their tails.

"Are y'all bastards tryin' to steal my J.D.?"

"No sir, we were trying to get away from your fine dogs. We must have spooked them."

"You damn shore did. They ain't used to people coming up from the front yard. Everybody 'round here uses the side driveway. What are y'all doing out here in God's country anyway? My dog's are not for sale. They are state champions. I been offered thousands for them from them rich people over in Thomasville. They have even hired people from Florida and Alabama to try to steal them."

"We have no interest in your dogs. But we would like to hire you and your tractor. We ran off the road trying to miss a wild hog and got stuck."

"I know just the place. I hit one up there and turned my pickup over in the middle of the road."

"I told you they could, Butch."

"I believe you, Nellie."

"Them damned hogs are a nuisance. They're always coming around, rooting up my yard and botherin' my dogs."

"Don't the dogs run them off?"

"Man, they are coon dogs. They don't give a hog the time of day. No self respecting coon dog will. They don't chase rabbits either."

"Do you have a chain and what will you charge me to pull us out?"

"How bad are you stuck?"

"Just the two right wheels. It ought to be easy."

"Five dollars will do it. Did y'all walk here?"

"Yes, and we need a ride back."

"You can all ride in the back of the pickup. My little brother can drive you. 'Course you'll have to share the room with the dogs. I can't leave them here if we both are gone. Them damned thieves might be watchin'."

"Can one of us ride up front?"

"No. That seat is reserved for my number one dog. He won't ride in the back with the others."

"Will the others ride with us?"

"The more the merrier."

"Little Bubba! Git yore ass out here and try cranking the pickup. We got a job to do."

"Aw, Junior, I was busy whitlin'."

"This is more important."

The battery was dead in the truck. And they had no jumper cables. Not that it would have done any good. The tractor had a magneto and a big flywheel that was spun by hand to crank it. Little Bubba set all the controls in the proper position and grabbed the flywheel and before it was turned two revolutions, it fired right up. Modern technology is wonderful. He then hooked the chain to the front bumper of the truck and all piled in. Dogs and all. The truck caught before it got to the highway and Junior got off and unhooked the chain. As soon as they got on the blacktop, Little Bubba goosed the truck and passed Junior, hooting and hollering. Our group held on for dear life. The five dogs took advantage of the fact, as both hands were busy holding on, and proceeded to wash everyone's faces. The odd dog, with no face to wash opted to wash Lilly's bare legs.

"Hey dog, stop at the knees. I'm not into kinky stuff."

"Lilly, you disappoint me."

"Butch, you are not of the canine persuasion."

The rear window in the pickup was missing and number one dog had his head sticking out the opening observing the tongue orgy and started howling. He was being left out, but he knew his place and dared not to venture into association with his inferiors. He did stick his head out far enough to get in a few good licks at Carl's ear.

By the time the tractor got to the car, all the tissues were used up and scattered along the highway.

As they climbed into the car, all the dogs tried to follow. They also wanted to go to Atlanta. Four grown humans and six dogs make a car full. Junior finally persuaded all to get back in the truck and everyone was finally on their way to their destinations."

"They even licked all the sauce I spilled on my blouse."

"I bet that didn't thrill you as much as my having a leg lick."

"Don't bet on it."

Carl and Butch thought dogs as house pets were not to be considered at this time. Maybe a cat. Certainly not purebred coon dogs. Anyway, they cost too much.

"Those were sweet dogs, maybe we should entertain the purchase of some."

"No, Lilly, that would be a disservice to them. The urge to hunt is inbred into their genes and they would live a frustrated life if they could not follow their instincts."

"My instincts do not make me a brood mare."

"Humans are different. We have many distractions to keep us from succumbing to our animal urges."

"That did not deter the slaves. They populated the South with their kind."

"That was their only enjoyment. And it pleased their masters. It was very profitable."

"I never owned a slave."

"We know, Nellie, we know."

"Butch, we need to outrun the sun."

"I can't do that headed north."

With the exception of stopping at intervals to replenish the fuel and use the facilities, the trip was uneventful albeit thrilling.

The sun won. This was a disappointment to Nellie and Lilly, both looking forward to entering the great city with vision unrestricted. There was some consolation in viewing the bright lights and traffic. The latter that was shocking.

"Good Lord! You can never get your car in high gear here. How do you vent your frustrations?"

"By constantly changing lanes and using your horn."

"How in the hell can you change lanes? All are full."

"Just pick a car smaller than yours and bluff the hell out of it."

"Freeway poker!"

"You got that shit right. Watch!"

Waiting for a about the length of the car, Butch swerves to the left and enters. The small car he cut off locked all four wheels and caused a chain reaction that reached rearward for a half mile. A steady squeal of tires was heard fading into the rear distance. By the time the driver of the small car recovered his senses, twenty cars behind Butch in his previous lane had cut in. The driver of the small car resolved to trade his car tomorrow for a tank suitable of surviving this maelstrom.

"Whee! I hope you will train me the rudiments of that maneuver. I shall need it to survive here."

"Lilly, in no time at all you will be a qualified driver. This is akin to stock car racing. All you need is a gap, which you consider of appropriate size. Like a jungle, this is no place for the weak of heart."

"Carl, forget about replacing my Volkswagen. I want something more substantial."

"Small cars also have their advantages. They are shorter and will fit into smaller gaps. And if you drive a beat up one, you will have one more advantage. Pick out a nice shiny one to cut off. They won't take a chance of ramming you."

"I still like pretty cars."

"They don't stay pretty long if you are aggressive."

"Maybe I will need two. One for sane driving on the road and one for this traffic."

"Most everybody here has two."

"I can see why."

"One for work and one for play."

"I don't understand the rationale of the urgency to pass the automobile immediately ahead."

"That urge is as American as apple pie."

"I think it is an exercise of futility. There will always be one ahead, regardless of the number passed."

"That is the mindset of the geriatric faction traveling among us."

"Apropos to the quote 'wisdom improves with age'."

"Nellie, you are wise beyond your years."

"When do we eat?"

"Butch, is that all that is on your mind?"

"Only when I'm hungry. Like right now."

"I'd like something fancy."

"Tell us what, Nellie. French? Italian? Mexican? Greek? Oriental?"

"I am not a sophisticated world traveler. I only want something not available in South Georgia."

"Escargot?"

"Say what?"

"Snails."

"Ugh! How do you eat them, with a straw?"

"No, they are rather firm when cooked."

"I think I will pass."

"I stepped on a bunch of snails once."

"Not now, Nellie."

"Let her go ahead, Dad, I'd like to know what happened."

"I was out at granny's moving a wide board from the garden. Granny always has a garden, to supplement the grocery buying. She grows squash, pole beans, collards, corn, beets and grits."

"Grits? You can't grow grits. They're too hard to pick off a grit bush. You have to have special equipment to harvest them. And the machines are very expensive."

"Maybe I was wrong about the grits, she probably buys them at the store, Butch."

"Now is not the time, sugar, but I'll tell you about grits later."

"What's to tell?"

"To you, a lot."

"Continue with the snails, Nellie."

"Well this wide old board blew off the side of the barn about a year before and it was too heavy for granny to move so she just worked around it. I took a rope and tied it around the cow's neck and the other end to the board. Her name was Elsie. She gave a lot of milk."

"She must have. I see it all the time in stores."

"That's not the same Elsie, Lilly. Granny's cow was named after the other one."

"In removing the board, it hit a rock and turned over, exposing the underside. That's where the snails were clinging. I stumbled on the rock and my feet hit on the board. My legs flew out from under me and I hit the ground like a turd from a tall cow's ass. They were indeed slick. They must taste good. The hogs had a feast that day. But you know hogs; they'll eat almost anything. I won't, I'm no hog."

"You sure acted like one at the pig joint."

"That was different. I was eating hog."

"Cannibal."

"Nellie, have you eaten lobster?"

"And if they are anything like crawfish, I don't want any. The only thing I'll suck on is the marrow in a pig bone."

"You won't have to suck on these. They're real large and you use crackers to get in them."

"They must be mighty tough crackers. All I have ever seen will even crumble if you hold them too tight."

"These crackers are not the eating kind. They look sort like a pair of pliers and you use them to crack open the claws."

"The English language is funny. Have you ever seen a plier? Or a scissor? Or a pant?"

"You don't see a pant. You hear them. I don't know about the other two. I heard a pant once."

"I know, Nellie, how well do I know."

"Dogs pant all the time, except when they're sleeping. And sometimes, then, when it's real hot under the front porch."

"That's because they have no sweat glands. They pant to cool themselves."

"It never helped me. I think it made matters worse."

"You are supposed to use a fan."

"There aren't any in the back seat on a hot summer night."

"I wonder what Joe Billy is doing right now."

"That was a weird thing to bring up now, Nellie. You might as well tell us what you know about you know what."

"Oh Carl, I was just running off at the mouth."

"I think you just put your foot in it."

"Speaking of foot-in-mouth, Carl, I think you are guilty also."

"Dad, what in the blazes are you two raving about?"

"Trust me Butch, you don't want to know. You might consider this privileged information. Nellie and I will thrash this out later. Young lady, we have much to discuss."

"I was just trying to get me some insurance against speeding tickets."

"You have been playing dangerous games. With some very heavy hitters."

Lilly now has caught the disease. "I bet I know who got the ones we couldn't find."

"Shut up Lilly."

"What did you do with the rest, Nellie?" Carl asks.

"I burned them."

"Dad, what kind of women have we got tangled up with?"

"Just two fun loving girls that needs some guidance. No harm has been caused."

"Ha! Just a murder and a fish camp lost."

"All has worked out for the best. Just everybody forget about this and let's find that restaurant. Case closed."

* * *

"Come over to this tank and pick out one you like."

"Butch, you didn't say anything about eating something alive. I don't think I can do it. They look dangerous."

"Lilly, the cook takes your choice to the kitchen and cooks it. This is how you are guaranteed it is fresh."

"I sure hope it tastes better than it looks. It's horrible."

"Once you overcome the initial trauma, you will be addicted."

"You mean they are habit forming?"

"Not in a detrimental fashion."

"I'll try one if you will, Nellie."

"I yield to the voice of experience."

"How do they kill them?"

"Drop them in boiling water."

"How gruesome! Do they accept their role in the food chain?"

"I have no idea. I have never communicated with one. The lines of communication among man and sea creatures are very limited.

Porpoises and Orcas, to name two, are an exception. They are mammals. We try not to eat them."

"We eat other mammals. Why not the ones you mentioned?"

"There are too many other fish in the sea which are good to eat. Even sharks."

"Eat them before they eat you."

"Something like that."

"How about eat or be eaten? Or kill or be killed?"

"The war of survival is nothing to take lightly."

"I'm sorry Mr. Lobster, but it's either me or you. I want that big ugly one that's attacking his brothers and sisters."

"He can't do much damage. If you notice his claw has a wooden peg in it, which renders him harmless."

"I like this pretty bib. It should keep my blouse clean. I sure needed one down at the pig joint."

"We all did."

"I am getting to like civilization up here."

"Don't get your hopes up too high. There is also a seamy side of life here as everywhere."

"I shall try to remain aloof. You will help, won't you, sugar?"

"We will not lead a cloistered life. I will teach you how to survive in these environs."

"I like a little cloister every once and a while."

"That's what a well secured bedroom is for."

"Cloister and secure me, baby."

"While we are on the subject, where are we going to crash, Carl?"

"I have in mind a fancy downtown hotel with all the amenities, Nellie. We will tell them we just flew in from the west coast and want the finest."

"Why not tell them the truth?"

"If we told them we just drove in from Hooterville Crossroads, we would be lucky to get a room in the basement. I went to Montreal once and wanted to stay in the Chateau Frontenac and told them I wanted a clean reasonable room. The bellhop led me down a dark long hall to a small room with a view. The view looked out on an airshaft surrounded on all sides by tall brick walls. It was clean and reasonable. And that was all."

"Can we get the penthouse?"

"We can try."

* * *

"Welcome sir, to the Excelsior Arms. May be of service?"

"We have just arrived from the west coast on our way to Rio and we would like your finest accommodations for the night."

"I was under the impression there was a direct connection to Rio from LA you went well out of your way to see our fair city. Surely you will want to stay over for a few days to enjoy the attractions. Is this your first trip to Atlanta?"

"Oh no, I was originally from here. I still hold many interests here."

"I thought you sounded like a true Southerner. Have you been away long?"

"Not as long as I have spent at your desk."

"I'm sorry, I like to greet all our visitors with small chit-chat."

"We would like the penthouse suite, if available."

"If it is for only one night. An Arab oil-producing potentate has it booked for one month beginning tomorrow night. I trust your group will not damage it. We have been working three days modifying it to his requirements. Do not scatter the sand around too much."

"Sand?"

"Oh yes. We removed all the furniture and carpets and brought in five yards of sand to spread evenly over the entire floor."

"Where will we sleep?"

"There is ample room in the tent for your group. It is large enough for the Emir and ten concubines, which travel with him."

"A tent?"

"Yes, the last time he visited our fine establishment, no special preparations were made and he got homesick and cut his visit to two nights. We were despondent. We were looking forward to a month's stay at one grand per night."

"It's a wonder you didn't get fired."

"What do you think I'm doing behind this desk? I owned the hotel and I was going to use the money on a called note."

"Who owns it now?"

"The Emir."

"Carl, I can't sleep on a pile of sand tonight. Maybe on the beach in Rio, but not in Atlanta."

"There are fine Persian hand made rugs in the tent."

"No camels or goats?"

"Only a few small potted palms."

"No eunuchs?"

"No, they stay home to guard his harem."

"He is not bringing his full harem?"

"They wouldn't fit in his plane. If he came on his ship, he could have brought all of them plus a few camels."

"How about the goats?"

"He never brings them. He picks some up locally at that trashy auction that Jones fellow runs out on the Southside."

"We'll take it."

"Your name?"

"Calvin Bristol."

"Of the Sacramento Bristols?"

"Distant relatives. I have lost touch with them. And this is my son, Butch Bristol and his fiancée, Lilly and this is Nellie."

"Again welcome, I trust you will find the arrangements adequate. How will you be paying, green or plastic?"

"Plastic."

Nellie inquires, "My plastic is green. Will that do?"

"Honey, this is on me."

"I'm glad. I fear the tariff would exceed my limit by astronomical proportions."

* * *

"We had better take off our shoes before we go in. No telling how deep the sand. I did that once on that beach off St. Simons and I never got all the sand out."

"Jeeze! Look at the size of that tent! We need the girls to do some belly dancing to set the mood."

"We don't have the proper attire."

"Call room service. Get some halters and veils and hip hugging long skirts. Oh, and two quarts of Vodka."

"We'll need a flute and a drum."

"Don't get any snakes."

"We want to see the girls wiggle, not snakes."

"I'll play the flute and you can beat the drum, Dad."

"If we are to perform, we will require some desert fruit."

"Like what?"

"Oh, some bananas, strawberries, grapes and dates."

"Nellie, how you carry on, we already have dates."

"Lilly, I'm talking about the kind you eat."

"Oh."

"And we need some kind of sticky stuff to hold a strawberry in our belly buttons. I doubt if you brought any real rubies with you."

* * *

Room service finally came after a lengthy wait. Accompanied by the manager.

"I'm sorry sir, we took so long. Some of the items you requested were not in stock and we had to send out. I trust you are not contemplating charging admission to this function. The hotel has strict rules regarding this sort of activity. If there is to be money made, the management must handle the arrangements. The government is real pushy about collecting entertainment taxes and we could be held responsible."

"This will be a private party solely for the benefit of my son and I."

"I am relieved. We got into a hell of a mess with a rock group a while back that told us they wanted to have a small jam session. They lied. Once they got set up, they called all over town and invited all of the drug culture to attend at ten dollars a head. The place was swamped. And the noise was horrendous. The other guests complained and called the police. Imagine! The illustrious Excelsior Arms raided! I still have nightmares of it."

"I assure you, you will have no trouble from us."

"Am I invited?"

"If you have a mate, and special consideration will be remembered at bill paying time, we might entertain the thought."

"I might be able to arrange a substantial discount on our regular rate."

"What is your definition of substantial?"

"Forty per cent."

"Come back in a half hour fully equipped."

"It won't take that long. I have a full time in house concubine on the premises. And the Emir also left a Hookah and some hashish in the storage room."

"Forget the hashish."

Lilly wants to know the difference between a hooker and a concubine.

"Sugar, not hooker, hookah. It's a Mid Eastern water pipe that is used to smoke tobacco and other ingredients."

"I assume this is not a plumbing water pipe. I can't imagine how you could smoke anything with plumbing."

Nellie says, "I used a water pipe to put out a fire once and it smoked."

"That was the fire smoking, not the pipe."

"Well, the pipe didn't smoke, but the hose I had attached did. It got too close to the fire. I had thrown a cigarette down on the front grass and the front yard caught fire. It was in the winter and the grass was real dry. It scared the shit out of me. I spit on them now before I throw them away."

"We won't have that trouble here, with all this sand."

"Don't put your butts in the sand. Remember, the Emir comes tomorrow. And don't burn the rugs. They are priceless. I shall bring some ash trays when I return shortly."

And shortly did he return. And by his side was a magnificent black woman of the Watusi tribe, or a descendant thereof. She was well over six feet tall and outfitted in dress similar to that of Nellie and Lilly. She strode in with the grace of an antelope. Her long arms were adorned with gold bracelets and three heavy gold chains around her long neck hung down between her impressive cleavage. Her ear lobes were stretched downward with the weight of more gold ornaments. Her skin shone as if it were well oiled. We suspect this was indeed the case as when she stepped in the sand it clung to her feet and ankles. The manager introduced her as Tabamarabutu. She also answered to Taba, which was more convenient for the group.

"If it pleases all, Taba will start by introducing some rare movements not seen before by western eyes. Perhaps Lilly and Nellie will be inspired to follow, and I guarantee we will be entertained as never before."

"It pleases the hell out of us. We have never done any belly dancing before and we need all the help we can get. The closest we ever came was some belly rubbing. I was wondering what we were going to do."

"Just watch Taba a few minutes and I think you will pick up on it. Calvin and Butch, start the music!"

"No, no this will never do!"

"What's the problem, Taba?"

"The music. It sounds of a dying goat kicking a washtub. I need the music of the soul. We must have more instruments and players."

"But where will I find them?"

"The orchestra in the ballroom is playing to an empty room as we speak. Conscript them!"

"This penthouse cannot possibly hold all of them."

"Open all the doors and let them play on the terrace."

"What will the neighbors think?"

"Fool! There are no neighbors. We are on the twenty- fifth floor. Maybe a few pigeons will be disturbed, but who cares?"

Carl thinks, and this was going to be a small private party. No wonder this fool lost this hotel. But what the hell, we all need some excitement and some good may come out of it.

"Bring on the band!"

"We will have to set up a service bar in the hall. Those musicians will not play without the proper inducement."

"Let it be done, manager!"

"Yes, Taba dear."

"Nellie, this woman weeds with a wide hoe."

"She sure does, I wonder what she has on that manager?"

"Those long legs and oily body ought to tell you something. I bet that is a sight to behold."

"We may see it yet. The night is young."

"I wish I had my Polaroid."

"It's in the car. I'll send Butch down for it after a while, when things starts to pick up."

"Dad, I feel a mite out of place in this conventional attire. Perhaps we should find more suitable garments which will be better suited with the theme."

"You have a point. Mr. Manager, do you have any suggestions that would put us in a more appropriate mood that will be more conducive to the festivities? We are most uncomfortable in our present threads."

"It is too late to return to the costume facility, but we have plenty of sheets and pillow cases in the linen room. I shall call housekeeping and ask their advice."

"Housekeeping. Joe speaking."

"Joe, this is Mac. I know, I told everyone I was off for the night. Where? Oh, I'm up in the penthouse and we need you to send up the floor maid with some sheets and cases. Oh, and yes, have her to bring some scissors and a bunch of safety pins. No, we do not have an elephant up here that needs diapering. No more questions, please. Just send what I requested. Charge them to the Emir."

Gertrude rode the elevator to the penthouse while mumbling about what that crazy manager was now up to. I hope he doesn't cost me my job like he did his. I need my job. What with my sorry assed husband who won't find a job and me with eight snotty nosed younguns to feed. Since the hotel got that new fangled garbage grinder, I haven't had much luck supplementing my measly salary with table scraps.

"Come on in Gertrude, I commend you on your promptness. With you trying to raise eight snotty nosed kids, you must have gained some expertise in tailoring. If you will be so kind as to take these two fine gentlemen into the adjoining bedroom and with your fertile imagination and sharp scissors, attempt to drape their bodies with your linen in a manner somewhat akin to the garments the Emir wears."

"This is not in my job description. Ample compensation will be required."

"That is no problem. Mr. Bristol is very generous."

"As you wish, sir. You two hunks follow me."

Carl and Butch obediently follow her and close the door.

"I don't think I like my man going in there with that strange woman with the door closed."

"Neither do I, Nellie. She might have been run hard and put up wet, but I suspect there's still some fire left in her. Butch, you open this door right now!"

Butch sheepishly cracks the door. Lilly slams it full open.

"Ah ha! You two have yet to be in here five minutes and both of you are already down to your drawers!"

"Lilly, how else can we be fitted in our new duds? They won't fit over our street clothes. There will be many times I will have to strip before professionals. I grant you most will be of the medical persuasion, but there may be others."

"This woman is no professional! If she is, more the reason I will not tolerate this!"

"Madam, I take exception to that remark. I'll have you know that being a floor maid is an honorable position and I always conduct myself in a ladylike manner. That is, until I get home amidst eight howling brats and a drunken husband. Then I have been known to lose my cool. Anybody would."

"If an apology is in order, we will give one. However we insist to be present during this fitting."

"Apology accepted. Now sit down and shut up and let me continue with my task. First I will cut the corners out of the cases for leg holes and cut holes around the perimeter of the opening to insert a drawstring to prevent them from falling and creating an embarrassing problem."

"What's the problem? They will have their shorts under the casing."

"Oh no, Emirs never wear shorts. What with having such an enormous harem and the necessity of being ready at all times."

"Ready for what?"

"Please Nellie, use your imagination."

"OK. Just don't use a hard knot in that drawstring."

"I don't think I will have to cut up the sheets. They are for twin beds and they will drape satisfactorily."

"Good. We might need them later for cover."

"Why? It's not too cool in here."

"For modesty's sake."

"Oh. That's right. We may have to consummate our engagements."

"Girls, girls. Don't get too far ahead. We have a party to attend. First."

* * *

The party was a smashing success. Following Taba's lead, the girls picked up on the intricacies of the dance and were soon outperforming their teacher. They fared much better than Taba. Because of her well-oiled body, she was soon covered with sand while rolling in it. Part of the dance, of course. It stuck as opposed to the girl's shedding of it when they got up and started to wiggle and shake. The costumes had a tendency to shed also that met with the approval of the viewers. Luckily this was only a token shed, which provoked lustful thoughts to be quelled later.

The band quit at two a.m. This was at the request of the participants as the fine music had deteriorated to a cacophony of discordant sounds due to the massive consumption of spirits by the players. By four a.m. the remainder was scattered across the sand in slumber. No consummation had taken place. The sheets had long been doffed and cast aside. As no privacy was needed in their present state.

This scene remained as in a still life rendering by a famous artist until eight a.m., which was disturbed by the premature entrance of one Emir and his entourage.

CHAPTER TWENTY THREE

"Oh Mother of Muhammad! By all of the Camel Driving Saints! Oh, Allah! Whom hast thou allowed to trespass into my hallowed domain? Who are these infidels that hast defiled my honored tent?"

With drawn scimitar he approaches the one infidel that he presumes to be the perpetrator of this foul invasion. With the upturned toe of his sandal, he nudges the ribs of Carl.

"Nellie, stop tickling me. You know how this arouses my libido."

"Foul swine! Camel dung! I shall cut out your libido, if you will pray tell me where it resides. If not, I will find an appendage, which I am quite familiar with and relieve you of it! I will eunuchize you and commit you to my harem as a guard!"

"Oh my God! Who is this maniac! Mac! Mac! Wake up! I am being attacked by some foreign devil! My manhood is being threatened!"

"What? What? Oh my God! It is the Emir! We are in deep camel caca now.

"Oh Illustrious one, what bring you here at this early hour? We were not expecting your honored presence until much later."

"The winds of Allah blew strongly upon the hindquarters of my jet assisted carpet and we descended into your fair town slightly prematurely, never to expect such foul desecration of my sanctum. You have much explaining in order to save your unworthy behind. You may be thrown from the parapets of this castle for the vultures to feast upon! Prostrate your unworthy self before me and plead your case."

"Oh eminent one, let me introduce myself. I am Calvin Bristol and these other unworthy ones are in my pilgrimage to the hot sands south of here for meditation. We in our journey needed some respite from our hazardous journey from the far west on the shores of the great blue water. Your kind keeper of this magnificent establishment found kindness in his great heart to allow our humble party to rest our weary unworthy bones here. He allowed us only one night, knowing your illustrious presence would need this place today. And as no other rooms were available at the inn, I prevailed upon his conscience to allow us to rest in your rooms, not knowing the evils of the unspoken one would descend upon us and convert your tent into a receptacle of orgy. It is all of my doing and please do not find your manager in violation of your honored trust."

"But I find him here in the midst of you infidels sharing your evil ways. I see evidence of pork ribs and distilled spirits, strictly forbidden in the Koran, the blessed words given to our great disciple of Allah."

"Please realize we are not of the Moslem persuasion and found no wrong in our revelry. Granted, we may have been guilty of transgressing far to the side of material enjoyment, but we are only lowly beings with the urge implanted in our genes by the great Creator of all things, Heaven and earth and all else."

"Cease with all this camel dung. I too am cursed with these urges. I abstain from the eating of foul scavengers and the drinking of spirits, but Allah has commanded for all to be fruitful and multiply. Pork gives me turmoil in my lower regions and the spirits force me to ignore the commands of Allah."

"I rest my case. We kneel before you in judgment. Please consider we are all cut from the same cloth of the great tailor above."

"If I were an agnostic, I would question the sharpness of His scissors. However, since I am on a sabbatical and find mercy in my heart, I do not condemn you. This will be done by a higher authority in time."

"Your mercy is gentle as the rain that falls on the earth in spring."

"From your tongue flows the words of a true follower, with the exception of the name you claim is yours. I feel this has been stolen. I have seen you before. Your countenance brings recollections of goats and junk chariots. I am confused."

"I admit I am guilty of this small error, but since our need of rest depended open it, I feel it was justified."

"Out of your mouth now flows garbage. How could this be justified?"

"I felt if my true identity had been known, we would be denied a room here."

"Ah! So you are truly the dealer of goats and junk chariots among other unmentionables."

"A good shepherd has a duty to his flock to insure them of bountiful sustenance, and all are not blessed with underground wealth."

"Ah, this is true. I am truly blessed and I kneel to Allah and praise His Name every waking day for my good fortune. And I realize that some must sweep carpets and pick up camel droppings."

"Cannot these unfortunate ones also have pride in their work?"

"Yes, I do not condemn them for their work, but for the fact they choose not to rise above their lowly station in life in an endeavor to better their plight, blaming it on the Will of Allah.

"I was once one of those unfortunate ones."

"Indeed? And how did you come to your present somewhat questionable lofty station?"

"By perseverance and with the help of a messenger from above."

"Allah is not concerned with the doings of a goat and junk merchant."

"Be that as it may, I was inspired and guided by a being not completely of this world."

"Mayhap he was from the netherworld and cast an evil spell upon you."

"If you had known him, your judgment not would be as biased as it seems to be."

"I would like to meet this wondrous person."

"Alas, this is not possible. He departed from this plane of existence years ago."

"By his own choosing?"

"Not entirely. He did practice actions that hastened his exit. Not of his own choosing, but he did place his faith in the goodness of man. And unfortunately lost. I am sure his soul survived, as did his sweet wife's. They were carried away in a chariot of flame and thunder."

"An honorable way to go, as do many of my subjects. It is a direct road to paradise."

"Oh, he did not drive a explosive laden vehicle into the enemy's camp, as do some of your people. Or so I've heard."

"All lies!"

"I would choose to go as they did, entwined in loving embrace with my lover." Says Nellie.

"Who is this wench who dares to enter into our conversation?"

"She is my intended, as soon as I shed the shackles of a prior commitment."

"Why shed? Simply retire her to your harem."

"That is not our custom."

"Your ways are impractical. It involves litigation, which is expensive not to mention alimony and child support. Become a follower of Allah or his prophet Mohammed or Joseph Smith."

"Pastor Smith's survivors abolished that practice ages ago."

"A foolish action."

"I feel it was for political purposes."

"You live in a strange land with strange customs. The masses should follow, not lead."

"Any system must face the test of time. Ours is only as a newborn babe in the history of civilization. Check back in one thousand years."

"If only we could. We then would have the wisdom of Allah."

"It is indeed a tragedy that each generation does not learn the lessons of their forefathers."

"It will ever be thus."

"All this philosophical mouthing will gain us naught as far as resolving the matter at hand."

"And what is the matter at hand?"

"How can we gain your favor after all the inconvenience we have caused your illustrious person"?

"Inconvenience? Nay! I have enjoyed our discussion. Intelligent dialog can solve all the world's ills if it is diligently pursued."

"Spoken as a true statesman!"

"You four are welcome to share my tent, but Mac and his concubine must leave us. I will deal with him later."

"Be merciful towards him, as I was the instigator. He was only trying to fatten your coffers."

"I shall take that into consideration."

Mac and Taba backed out the door bowing deeply. Nellie and Lilly thought it best to remain silent until directly spoken to. The Emir's customs have great merit. By lunch time the three men had solved all the problems that plague our world. If only they could convince the remainder of the world's population to abide by their program. A task that was easily forgotten after a feast was ordered up from room service. The Emir promised to visit them at the auction the following week. He said he had a weakness for local culture and bargains.

"Of course your illustrious presence shall be welcome. However I have some misgivings of you arriving in your present magnificent attire. I fear it would have an intimidating effect on the ambiance generated by our participants."

"How can you say that? We would have a lot in common. I was raised among goats and camels; they were raised among pigs and mules. I walked among date palms on hot sand; they walked among pines and oaks on red clay. We had no sandals, they had no shoes. Where we had sand between our toes, they had red mud. We are brothers. We hunted jackals and they, possum. But my present station may have some disturbing effect on them and I shall take this into consideration. If you could furnish me with some appropriate garments, I will appear in as you say 'incognito'. You must arrange for some discreet area for me to alight my chariot and change. Then I shall mingle with the masses and enter your fine establishment. You do allow persons of color, do you not?"

"But of course! We are not bigots. Besides it is now the law of the land not to discriminate. Anyway, we have some of our finest southern boys that show more tan than you, with the exception of the back of their neck which is colored a dark shade of red. About the same shade as the color on their rebel flag which they display with pride on their pickup trucks."

"How interesting. And how tolerant are they?"

"Some need improving, but they behave in public. Most of the time."

"And other times?"

"We allow no alcoholic beverages at the auction."

"Then I have nothing to fear, right?"

"Let us have faith."

"Is that not what your departed friend had?"

"His was not applied in the correct manner."

"The adder dealt a fatal blow to Cleopatra. Her faith was not strong either."

"I believe she was trying to end her life."

"I have heard of some religious cults here which practice the handling of poisonous reptiles. Are they trying to end their life?"

"I don't think so. I don't know. I avoid those places with great effort."

"So you have small faith."

"When it comes to rattlesnakes, you can bet your ass I have none."

"I have no asses. I use camels for the heavy loads."

"A wise choice. I hear they get over one hundred miles to the gallon."

"Some even more, dependent on the load, of course. If only they would consume oil rather than water. Water is at a premium in my land."

"And I would like an automobile which consumes water."

"Strange lands have strange customs."

"Enough of this prattle. I have enjoyed your company, but all good things must end. I have a busy day ahead of me and your group must excuse me. I trust I shall see all of you next week. Do not forget my disguise."

"It has indeed been a pleasure and we look forward to seeing you at the auction."

CHAPTER TWENTY FOUR

"Butch, go get the car and I will check out with the girls."

Mac was at the desk, looking haggard and worried. "Oh God, Calvin, what have I let you get me into? I fear for my job now more than ever. Where shall I go? I will lose my suite of rooms and the company of Taba. No more eating a turkey leg in the kitchen. No more visits to the wine cellar. Oh, woe is I."

"Calm down, Mac. It is not as bad as it seems. The Emir is a good person and you do well handling his establishment. I have interceded on your behalf. He can be very reasonable if approached in the proper manner, which I have done. We are great friends now. He promised to visit my auction next week."

"What do you mean, your auction? Here in town? You led me to believe you were only passing through. Have you deceived me? Who are you anyway? I felt there was not a ring of truth to your story."

"I am sorry to have misrepresented my group. I felt it was the only way to obtain a room here. I am Carl Jones and this is Nellie and Lilly, formerly of Hooterville Crossroads employed as teachers of our young South Georgia heathens. And this is truly my son, Butch."

"Then you are the Jones of the infamous southside auction. What is this world coming to? To think I allowed you people to defile the Emir's great tent! Have you no morals?"

"Now back off, Mac. If I remember correctly, you had one hell of a time yourself last night."

"Be that as it may, I am appalled! I was under the impression I was accommodating some relatives of the California Bristols. Whom, I understand are fine people."

"And we are not? Watch yourself. I may persuade the Emir to sell me this hotel and then you would really be out in the streets."

"You could really do that? Where would you get the funds?"

"Out of my petty cash."

"I have misjudged you. You are truly a man of substance, and I have great respect for anyone with great clout. And class. You are a man which will go far."

"I have been far, that is why all I want to do now is check out and get back to my digs, which I have neglected too long."

"Possibly much too long. There was a news item the other day about a small riot out there."

"So what else is new? We have them occasionally."

"Oh, I know that. This one seemed to be exceptional."

"In what way?"

"They say it started with some kind of a take-over fight."

"Oh my God! Effie Lou must have beaten us back! Figure my tab. I must be away to protect my interests. I will talk to you later, Mac."

"Butch, we must make haste. Your mother has arrived before us and is making trouble at the auction."

"Aw Dad, it can't be all this urgent. She has led me to believe she has corrected the error of her ways. Besides I'm hungry enough to chew the ass end off a Billy goat."

"Me too!" Nellie and Lilly proclaimed as one.

"Well, I could use something myself, although I will not express my feelings as graphically as you just have. There's a small diner on the way where we can get a small bite."

"A small bite won't wash."

"Won't wash what, honey?"

"Wash away the hunger pangs which are gnawing away at my innards, Lilly."

"Then a small diner won't wash either. I don't want to sit at a counter amidst strangers."

"There are some booths."

"I need elbow room. A real sit down breakfast like at granny's, Carl."

"Ah, that would be nice. Butch, do a flip flop and turn right back at the last intersection."

"In all this traffic with masses of commuters dashing to the caverns of commerce in downtown Atlanta?"

"Rise above yourself. We will hold on tightly."

"Maybe I can find a gap when that light up ahead changes."

"If not, make a gap."

Butch waited until he spied a timid soul following the car ahead a full car length instead of the normal three feet. He jerked the wheel to the left and floored the accelerator. His trusty steed responded instantly. Rubber burned. The timid soul locked his brakes and turned crosswise blocking both lanes of oncoming traffic. Butch had found his gap.

"Butch, you should start braking unless perhaps you desire to negotiate the upcoming corner on two wheels."

"Right, Dad."

"That's right. I said a right turn."

"I was on a road once that made a right angle turn to the left."

"That was a ninety degree angle, Nellie."

"Oh, I thought it was a right angle."

"It was, but calling it that sounds a mite ambiguous."

"I have much to learn about your local customs and dialect."

"I shall teach you, darling. Slow down Butch, the driveway is directly ahead on the right. And dodge that big oak that has to be driven around."

"Wow, look at all the scars on it at bumper level."

"I wonder the age of this monster. I bet Sherman's troops sat in the shade of it."

"It couldn't have been this large then."

"Of course not. That would mean it stopped growing when he came through."

"The conflict may have shocked it."

"No, Nellie. It is shown in the painting at the Cyclorama in Grant Park and it is not this large. That's why it was not removed when this restaurant was planned. The local garden club pitched a bitch when they discovered it was scheduled for destruction. Hence the circuitous route of the drive. See that small bronze marker at its base? It praises the efforts of the club of its perseverance and determination to save the monster. They have been sued many times because large limbs are always falling on parked cars."

"I shall park well away from it."

"You may have trouble finding a space. Everyone has the same idea. Except tourists. Look at the tags on the ones close under it."

"Wow! Nebraska, Maine, Ontario. California and look one is from Rabun County."

"Those are hillbillies. They don't care, it looks like many limbs have damaged it in the past."

"That's the advantage of driving a pre-dinged vehicle."

"It does have its merits. You can find easy parking spaces."

The entourage found an ample table in a corner and ordered fare not necessarily of the quality of Granny's but certainly of the quantity.

"Well, I'll be damned! Butch, look who's sitting all by himself over there."

"I don't believe it. Isn't that Roscoe Appleberry?"

"In the flesh. I'll see if he wants to join us. They haven't brought his food yet."

"Well, Roscoe you are indeed a sophisticated southern traveler."

"I can say the same of you. When did you get back?"

"Only yesterday. What brings you way up here? Or is that privileged information? Come join us."

"I can do that, join you, that is. The other, well you know how that is. But only half, the other half concerns you. I am following up on your proposal concerning the fish camp. I intend to see you after I see the Emir at his penthouse at the Excelsior Arms"

"A manifestation of our shrinking world. I just left the Emir."

"Are you it is the same Emir?"

"How many Emirs own hotels in Atlanta?"

"Many"

"How many own the Excelsior Arms?"

"Are you a friend of his?"

"I am now. We spent the night in his tent."

"How is that possible? You could not have flown in from the middle east this quick."

"We didn't. He has a tent set up in the penthouse."

"I suspected he was a strange character."

"Possibly, but he is a very likeable fellow."

"With his loot, he can afford to be."

"You got that shit right. Still it is strange, most are paranoid."

"Undoubtedly you have not visited him at home. He lives in a desert fortress with an army to protect him."

"I would too, what with millions of jealous knife wielding subjects wanting a piece of the pie."

"Thank goodness it's not like that over here."

"I can't believe you said that. You must live a cloistered life."

"Not really, I just don't frequent or mingle with that element."

"How about at the auction?"

"I have adequate protection there. And we screen the undesirables."

"I see what you mean. It is good to have friends like Joe Billy."

"Salt of the earth."

"Indeed. But I hope you have no intentions of handling Effie Lou in that manner?"

"Only as a last resort."

"Take my advice. A settlement is the most economical way. Good attorneys are expensive."

"So I've heard."

"The fish camp is a fine way out."

"I trust we can resolve this matter quickly. Effie Lou is back in town and is starting trouble at the auction, I think."

"Do you want to retain me as your counsel? You know I am a criminal lawyer."

"I hope I won't need a criminal lawyer."

"You might if you are not represented in your confrontation with her."

"My son will act as a moderator. He has good rapport with his mother."

"Then let him moderate and you try to keep your mouth shut."

"That's sound advice, Dad."

"I yield to more stable minds."

"Good, call me at the Excelsior Arms after the moderator moderates. I should be finished with the Emir by tonight."

"Not if you two try to solve the world's ills."

"We did that the last time we met. It took all night."

"Did you accomplish anything?"

"In our minds only. None others will listen."

"Great minds are always crying in the wilderness, with no one to hear their logic."

"And thus it will ever be."

"Grasshoppers all."

"And ants suffer the efforts of eradication."

CHAPTER TWENTY-FIVE

After a hearty breakfast, the trip to the auction site was relatively mild. By Atlanta's standards. The incoming lanes were jammed and a few rear end smashes were seen, but as our group was headed in the opposite direction, all was calm.

At the long barn, a few early consignors were forming a line to get the prime spots that are the best. After registering, they would go into the diner to fill up on coffee and discuss their finds. One person said he would precede the garbage truck collecting in an affluent section and glean choice pieces before the truck crew grabbed them for their personal collection. A pickup truck was used to receive the artifacts. It was driven by one of the crew's son. After this truck was filled, another son and another truck would take his place. When the collectors followed our hero's trucks, pickings were slim. Dead animals, broken whiskey bottles and cigarette butts were passed over by all.

Another person commented that he knew now why he was having such bad luck at the dump. He must take up the former's practice. As these good routes were considered the private possession of the initial instigator, prudence had to be used not to violate another's rights. Serious consequences may result. These types do not resort to legal remedies. All unclaimed routes must be acquired on a first come, first basis. It was decided that anyone desirous of staking a claim must spray paint all the garbage cans on his chosen route. Colors were designated for participants. This was democracy in action. God bless America.

Carl strode into his office to find Effie Lou seated behind his desk. Jonas was sitting on the desk.

"I see it hasn't taken very long for you to establish yourself as queen of the realm. Did not your experience in Palm Beach teach you anything? You should know that assuming command requires experience, tolerance and wisdom, traits you have not exhibited in the past. Jonas, I felt you to be a guiding influence for my wife, instead it seems you are misguided by her questionable charms. I want a full accounting of your rumored actions."

"We thought we had found a way to resolve our dilemma, but in facing reality it is not easy to solve major problems."

"When one is involved in a quagmire, the sensible thing to do is seek help. I, too, want to extricate myself from this mess I find I am in. We mutually want to relieve ourselves. It will take cooperation. We both must give a lot and take a little. Please explain what you have tried to do."

"Mama, please listen to Dad. I think he has found a way out."

"Oh Butch, I thought I had found a way too. On the way back, we stopped at a fish camp that was for sale and it appealed to the four of us. We felt we could work together for a common good. Mary reminded us we have little in the way of finances. Well, compared to what it would take to swing the deal. Mary could hold up her end and Jonas and Phillip agreed on a working interest. But poor me! I was made aware by Mary you hold all the purse strings, and I was at your mercy. So I came back here to claim what I feel I deserve for being a good wife through all the lean years."

"I, too, recognize your early contribution to my success and think you deserve some compensation, but do not try to usurp my authority by illegal means."

"Carl, I tried to convince her this was not the way. I have always found you to be a reasonable man, but she undoubtedly has her own opinions of you. Only you can straighten this out. You have the required resources."

"Jonas, I know you to be a level headed man and I commend you for your efforts on my behalf. Are you sure this fish camp is a good workable solution and are you willing to give up what you have here and move to Florida?"

"What have I here? Only a good job and in love with the bosses wife. A lonely life I lead here. I think a change will be for the better for all."

"What about Mary and Phillip? I had no idea they were so enamored with each other."

"That happened on the way back. They were sitting in the back seat discussing their likes and dislikes and found something in common. Phillip had lost his family years ago in a catastrophic automobile accident and you know Mary's circumstance. She only has her parents who are self-sufficient and do not depend on her and everyone needs to be needed and wanted. She thinks she has found that in Phillip."

"I will miss you all."

"Does that mean you will help us with the fish camp?"

"I do not want all of you to start a new life with a tremendous debt over your heads. It will cause dissension and bickering if there are any hard times in the future."

"What are you saying?"

"That I will purchase the camp as a settlement to Effie Lou for her contribution to my success. It will be up to her to arrange an equitable financial agreement between the four of you."

"Do you mean this is all I get?"

"Mama, shut up while you are ahead."

"I was only testing the temperament of the negotiations."

"They have now been tested. Please resume Dad."

"Roscoe Appleberry will be out here tonight and we should all meet with him to finalize the arrangement. With Mary and Phillip attending. Now I must get busy and find another auctioneer and bookkeeper. I only hope I can find someone half as good as the ones I am losing."

"I hear you have already found a replacement for me twice as good."

"Only time will tell, Effie Lou, I am sorry it didn't work out with us. We will always have the memories of our early years together. We did have some good times didn't we?"

"Sometimes I wonder if Harold might have wrong in trying to help us."

"Don't say that, Mama. He was only trying to help me and I think he did a damn good job. God bless him and may he rest in peace."

"If I know Harold, he is not resting in peace wherever he is. He is probably trying to reorganize Heaven, if there is where he wound up."

"His heaven may not be ours."

"He has probably started his own with Marybelle at his side."

"If he has, there is where I want to go when it is time."

"Don't rush it, Butch."

"Never fear, Dad. I intend to spend a long and happy life with Lilly."

"May we all find the elusive happiness we all have been searching for."

"Amen."

CHAPTER TWENTY SIX

"Where are we, Harold?"

"I don't know, Marybelle. The last thing I remember is going to sleep in your arms."

"Do you think we are having a common dream?"

"This does not feel like a dream. Besides common dreams are rare."

"Could it not be? Harold, our souls are so bonded."

Calmly, Harold says, "I think we are dead."

"I am not dead! Death is blank, nothingness, no feeling. I feel! I am aware! I love you!"

"I'm sorry, dear, dead was a figure of speech. I think we are dead to the world we were in. I wonder what happened?"

"It probably has something to do with that crazy effort we were attempting."

Harold laughs, "Yes, I believe so also. Stupid, wasn't it?"

"We did not think so at the time. Why do we feel different about it now? It seems so less important now."

"See I was right. We are dead. Only death could deter us from our mission."

"I guess you are right. I feel no urgency now. About anything."

"Peaceful, isn't it?"

"How long do you think this will last?"

"Probably until we get bored, Marybelle."

"Do you think we will ever want to go back"?

"Not me. I am enjoying the weightlessness and the absence of all the encumbrances visited on the physical vehicle."

"I feel somewhat like I did when I was a ten year old girl and had boundless energy. I used to think I could jump over the moon."

"Speaking of the moon, I don't see it. Or stars either. In fact, I don't see anything I recognize."

"What do you see?"

"I don't know. I wonder why?"

"Do you think we are blind?"

"If we are. I'm sure it is only until we adjust."

"We are not blind. We are in a fog. But not a white fog."

"But there is no color, Mary Belle, we must be existing on a sub-atomic level below the wavelength of visible light."

"Then I want to move up. I need to see something."

"A spark of initiative. We must be starting from scratch. This might be where all entities originate."

"Then why are we here? We have been originated previously."

"Possibly because we did not conform. We were immune to the contemporary concepts and dogma."

"Then much is to be said for formal indoctrination."

"More than I thought."

"But then we would have not met."

"Then this is worth whatever is has cost us."

"And we have only our minds and free will. We must get to work."

"How do you propose to do this 'work'?"

"Work with our minds. It is all we have at the present."

"If we are successful, we can create an environment of our choosing."

"Honey, help me to call up an atom."

"Why?"

"We might be able to shrink it and we can exist where there is visible light."

"You can't shrink atoms. We can only enlarge ourselves."

"What's the difference?"

"Someone once told me that a student at Princeton was walking back to his room late one night and saw Einstein out on his front lawn in his pajamas pushing an acorn with his big toe. Inquiring of the purpose, the student was informed he wouldn't understand."

"I use that retort whenever I am asked a question that I have no answer for."

"I doubt that was his reason. He was probably rearranging a universe."

"Stop deviating. Help me get that atom."

"On the count of three, start. One, two, three go!"

"Here it comes!"

"What kind is it?"

"Mm, it looks like carbon. We are still in the right neighborhood."

"I'm glad. At least we are in our own domain."

"Thankfully, it could have been silicon. Now that we have gained expertise, we must hurry or we shall be caught in some chemical compound and we might find that detrimental."

"I see a light! We are getting upstairs."

"I see more. They are beckoning to us."

"Decisions, decisions, to which shall we be attracted?"

"We must halt here and consider the options. Other enticements must surely follow."

"You mean like a sales pitch or a travel brochure."

"I think not. We are dealing with free will here. Most likely the color of a light that closely matches our aura."

"That makes sense. Look, there are more of varying hues. Our message was received."

"Choose one."

"That iridescent fuchsia is close, but not quite right. Maybe a lighter shade. More subtle."

"Honey, we are not picking out drapery material for our bedroom."

"I know, darling, but it needs to feel just right. This is a great decision. Our future might depend on it. That was what was wrong with our last world. Too many conflicting auras."

"It was not a perfect world."

"I know, I wonder how it got so messed up."

"Bad planning, with no past experience to base it on. Pure experimentation."

"Maybe, but would we like to exist among our clones?"

"It might prove to be excessively dull."

"You're right. Maybe it was not the conflicting auras. But what else could it possibly be?"

"I think some evil force had crept in."

"This is getting us nowhere. Let's go for broke and choose that closest one."

Once the choice was made, all other lights disappeared and they were drawn to the remaining one. The light receded, beckoning them toward it. Beautiful rays extended from the source and surrounded them in the form of a tunnel. At intervals similar to a logarithmic nature were formed in concentric circles appearing closer together as the circles receded towards the source. The speed of their approach increased exponentially as they were drawn to the light. Time lost all meaning. As their speed increased they merged into one. And then they changed into a small sphere of pure energy soon to be merged with the source light. Nirvana was close.

"Hannibal, you have chosen a very unorthodox method of coming home."

"I do not understand. Home? Hannibal? This is not my home. I am not Hannibal. Where's Marybelle? Who are you?"

"I am Peter, The Gatekeeper. I see you need debriefing again. Please follow me."

They enter the Great Gates and proceed to a place of indescribable beauty in which J.C. was waiting.

"We have a problem with Hannibal. He has appeared here in a manner with which I am not familiar. In his transit it seems he has suffered from a case of amnesia. And he asks of a soul he identifies as 'Marybelle'. This appellation signifies one of the female gender. Much must be discussed."

"Hello Hannibal, you have done well. I remember our discussion of other mansions and you have chosen a divergent path. This is why you don't identify with Hannibal. You have evolved extensively since your last visit. You have our undying gratitude for your work in the nether regions, which we have yet to find a viable solution. But this is our problem, not yours. We made the bed and must lie on it. If you insist on retaining this other soul as an individual entity, it can be arranged, but not in my backyard. We can arrange transit to the place you desire. I understand you want to try your hand in creating a perfect world. I wish you luck. You will need it. Especially if you insist on opposite sexes. That was what caused all our problems at the onset. The terms 'perfect world' and 'opposite sexes' are incompatible. Listen to the voice of experience."

"Is it not my prerogative to attempt it?"

"Of course it is, but as I saith 'not in my Domain'. Peter will make the arrangements for your transit. Farewell."

As they were walking to the newly formed ejection system which was put into use after Lucifer's ill advised attempt of ridding this place of undesirable ones. Other worlds were contacted by the new link and souls not desirous to dwell here were hastened on their way to more suitable surroundings. Peter's job was now a snap.

"I'm sorry about this, Hannibal. J.C. can be pretty hard nosed sometimes. Things have been going much more smoothly since the new system was installed and He doesn't like to see potential boat rockers. Excuse me from continually addressing you as Hannibal. What do you desire to answer to?"

"I am Harold and my mate is Marybelle. Wherever she is. I hope I shall meet her again."

"Never fear. She was merged for entrance here. She will re-emerge in transit."

"Thank goodness. I cannot exist without her."

"We are finding that more the case with diverse religions proliferating below."

"Goodbye Harold. You are indeed a unique soul."

CHAPTER TWENTY- SEVEN

Carl got his wishes. Effie Lou got hers. Lilly got hers. Nellie got hers. Mary and Phillip got theirs. As did Jonas, but he had his work cut out for him. Besides his work at the fish camp, he spent his every spare moment adjusting his wife's attitude and eating habits. The workload given her helped immensely. She had no time for soaps and chocolate covered cherries. Jonas truly loved her in spite of her shortcomings and it greatly affected her attitude. She now discovered Carl had stopped loving her years ago. He had never given her the attention she craved and she took up her bad habits to replace the loving she had lost. She was also frustrated in her mind about Jonas while she was trying to be a good wife. This time it was going to work. With no Butch or Harold underfoot trying to keep her straight with his or her misguided efforts. She missed Marybelle more than anyone, probably because of the load she had taken with the housework. She must look around for someone to help down here. But she would not be a raving beauty to distract the minds of Jonas or Phillip. She remembered the tragic results of the last case of miscegenation she was exposed to. The poor fools. Maybe one hundred years from now but not any sooner. She believed it was all right to serve other races in a business, but don't ever mix business and pleasure.

Mary worked in the office, keeping the books, receiving the money, making the bank deposits, paying the bills and doing everything else that came under her job description.

Because of his experience with things mechanical, Jonas kept the boats and motors in tip top shape. He missed his former position as shop manager, but he enjoyed getting his hands dirty again and wearing old clothes. He did not miss wearing a tie. He had thoughts of expanding if business improved and hiring some help. But this can wait.

With his comic personality, Phillip was a natural to greet the customers and handle the advertising and publicity. If Harold and Butch were still around, he dreamed of them constructing a giant fish to be seen by gullible anglers. That would really get this place off the ground. He decided it might be best to offer a friendly spot that offered much fun. They would apply for a license to serve alcohol in the restaurant. He would take this up with Effie Lou, she being in charge of the eatery. At the present time, she was the only one with help. She leaned toward the refugees from the south across the channel, fondly remembering Carmela. She had picked up the rudiments of the language in communicating with her former house worker. She was not fluent with it but she had no trouble getting the message across to the cook, dishwasher and busboy. None understood English worth a damn and the customers had a ball listening to her with her southern drawl attempting to speak Spanish. The tower of Babel on the St. Johns. But the food was good. Cuban soul food.

Both couples got married to their respective intended in Palatka by a justice of peace. They took up residence in the two nicest cabins. Primitive but air-conditioned. Only the budget ones reserved for the frugal was not. They had swamp coolers. An item Phillip stated he would replace when he got around to it. Along with a small increase in the rent. We shall have no truck with purse chokers. Our clientele must be upgraded, slowly but with determination.

Not the case with Carl back at the auction. He felt his clientele were the salt of the earth. Doing their part in the new recycling rage that was sweeping the country. Conservation is the keyword.

Among this group he spied a promising individual with a great gift of gab. He approached him with a proposition. He would clean him up, buy him some decent clothes and get his teeth replaced. Only the promise that he would never again be a dumpster diver and ample compensation persuaded this derelict to discard the accouterments of his former profession.

After the Herculean task of renovating the former diver, Carl introduced him to the Saturday afternoon assembly.

"Ladies and gentlemen, it is my honor and privilege to introduce to this fine group our new auctioneer. As you all know, Phillip had moved on to greener pastures and a new life. I know all of you, as well as I wish him Godspeed in his new venture.

"Before me is an auctioneer extraordinary, coming to us from a rewarding previous occupation. I take pride in introducing you to Gabriel Johnson-Jones. Let's all give him a hearty welcome and wish him well in his association with this fine place."

Applause and cheers resounded throughout the hall. After the tumult waned, one former associate made a comment; "There is shore something strange about that feller. He looks a lot like old Gabby. But it couldn't be. This dude has class. Look at the way he carries hisself. He struts like one of them Britisher Field Marshals I seen back in the Great War."

"You're crazy man, ain't no way that's old Gabby unless he been recycled like we are doing our merchandise."

"Mebbe Carl ran him through one of them new car washes."

"They ain't enough water or soap in Atlanta to make old Gabby look like that."

"Y'all shut up and let's listen to what he says. If it's Gabby his tongue will give him away."

"Honored friends, I speak presumptuously calling you friends but as time goes by and we get to know each other, I trust these words will be true. I intend to uphold the tradition my predecessor strove to maintain. I run a tight ship. I will try to be fair when any disagreement arises. But bear in mind my word is final with no appeal. Mr. Jones has seen fit to place his confidence in me and I am honored by his choice. Under my guidance, I will attempt to make this a showplace of Atlanta. No, I take that back. The whole South! I thank you in advance for your cooperation. Now let's have a lively and fine auction."

"Well, I'll be damned! It sounds like Gabby, but I ain't never heard him talk them kind of words."

"If it looks like a duck, walks like a duck and quacks like a duck, it's gotta be a duck."

"I'm gonna corner him after the festivities and find out if it is him. I know some things that only him and me know. I'll get the truth outta him."

"This first item of lot number one is a fine replica of an original walnut Chippendale dining table. If you examine it closely, you will see one leg has suffered a compound fracture caused by the former owner, incidentally weighing in at three hundred and eighty pounds, tripping over his son's skateboard he carelessly left in the dining room. In his ensuing flight he landed in a perfect two point landing upon the corner supported by the now damaged leg. If you care to examine it more closely, you can it has been restored by the application of adhesive tape. A touch of walnut stain has been applied to the tape in order to restore it back to its original beauty. Now who will open the bid at two hundred dollars for this fine piece? Don't be timid. Speak out!"

Carl was pleased with Gabby's baptism in the arena of the fine art of merchandising. In time, he will exceed Phillip's expertise. And the crowd loved him.

"Gabby, this is you, ain't it? What in the hell happened to you?"

"By the Grace of God and with Mr. Jones' help, I have been restored to my former self and profession from which I inadvertently fell due to Dame Misfortune."

"By God, I knew it was you! You did great and I'm all for you. Just don't forget your old buddies."

"I would never do that, we have had many a good time together gleaning. Maybe your luck will turn someday. What did you do in the past?"

"I was a political appointee as an errand boy for the late Senator McCarthy."

"May the Lord have mercy upon your soul."

"I am now resigned and content with my plight."

"I was too, but you never know what's around the next corner."

"Good luck in your new venture. By the way, what will happen to your route?"

"It's up for grabs. Do you want it?"

"You can bet your sweet ass I do! It is the crème de la crème of all Atlanta."

"We can retire to my digs and negotiate over a bottle of Muscatel and cigars."

"Some things never change, do they?"

"I had to make a lot of sacrifices to assume this glorious position, but giving up my Muscatel would be what I consider the most supreme one."

"What have you given up?"

"Well, for one thing, I now totally immerse my body daily. I fear I shall shrivel away. And I now have to subject my head to a bi-weekly trim at the local tonsorial parlor. The indignities of it all! I do hope all this is worth it. However I have given my word to Mr. Jones and I must persevere. At least as long as I can tolerate it. But give up my Muscatel? Never!"

"You might have to start imbibing in a more sophisticated manner to ease the tension."

"Like what?"

"On my present route, I see a great quantity of empty bottles that once contained Single Malt Scotch, Sour Mash, Bourbon and various Canadian blends."

"I have been told that some of these are detrimental to your liver."

"That's all I used to drink when I was up in Washington, DC."

"And look at you now."

"There's nothing wrong with my liver. Of course I admit that I too had to wash daily."

"What's that got to do with what you drink?"

"If you drink fancy liquor, you are expected to wash more often."

"I wonder why?"

"I think drinking fancy liquor, heightens your sense of smell."

"That's why I love Muscatel, it dulls mine."

"Mine too, now I'm not an alcoholic, but I drink it in self defense of the company I keep."

"Yes, there is a delicate aroma associated with our profession."

"Wouldn't it be nice if all households separated the good artifacts from the kitchen scraps? There's nothing I hate worse than a discarded purse filled with rancid hog lard."

"Hog lard? Mercy! What section of town does your route take you? On my route only the finest vegetable oil is used for cooking."

"Why do you think I'm busting my ass to get yours? No hog lard!"

"You seem to be of a caliber suited to assume the duties of my previous occupation. What are some of your other qualifications?"

"Well, for one thing, after sorting the chaff from the desirable merchandise, I always restore the containers back to their original condition and placement."

"Yes, that is important to maintain the integrity of the route. No evidence of pilfering must manifest itself for the primary collectors to suspect any foul play. They must assume these clients of theirs are of a frugal nature and discard only non-usable items."

"Of course, I, at random times, do leave a choice piece for the collectors so they will not be discouraged with their occupation."

"That is wise indeed. There is nothing worse than a disgruntled collector. They will dent the containers and leave them in complete disarray. Not to mention the tidbits of items scattered on the lawns."

"That is important. We do not want the clients upset and report the performance of collectors to their superiors.

"Also, I keep up to date on all the important holidays and forego my gleaning on these days. The keepers of the households are sometimes not aware of the preempted collections and place the containers at curbside one day early. You must not appear on these days, as your work may be discovered."

"You are indeed well versed in the rudiments necessary to protect your interests. I believe you are well suited to assume the responsibilities associated with this awesome endeavor. Refill your cup with Muscatel."

"Thank you. Of course, I am not prepared to compensate you in excess of my means. I can only offer a token amount, nothing near its worth. But bear in mind I shall strive to maintain your high standards in this work. I believe no other of our group should be considered as they have only the lesser lucrative routes and do not have the training as you and I."

"I am not a greedy man, but in principle, I cannot hand this jewel over to you gratis. That is not good business practice. A token must be given."

"Anything within my means."

"How about a case of Muscatel?"

"Done! Let's shake on that."

At the next auction date, Gabriel showed with new resolve and brighter spirits. Carl was pleased with his selection of a replacement of Phillip. Now all he had to do was to indoctrinate Nellie in the duties left void with Mary's departure.

"Honey, I need your help."

"Anything within my power. You have been my salvation and deliverer from the cruelties of my former profession and I shall be forever grateful."

"If it is not asking too much, I would like for you to fill Mary's shoes, temporarily of course. Only until I can find a suitable replacement as I have done with Gabriel replacing Phillip."

"Carl baby, you know how big my feet are and Mary might have had small feet."

"That was only a figure of speech."

"Oh. I must familiarize myself with this local dialect."

"This is not concerning foot or shoe size. It pertains to the duties she performed for me in her capacity as an employee. This will give you purpose and it carries with it ample compensation."

"I was under the impression you had freed me from servitude."

"As I said, this will be temporary. I will need just a short time to find a permanent replacement."

"That is a familiar statement. I knew a man who took a temporary job and retired at it after forty years."

"I assure you that will not happen here. I don't intend to spend the rest of my life in this business."

"I hope you intend to spend it with me. Doing the business of enjoying each other."

"And as I do now. This job is for a widow woman who enjoys the distractions which this position offers."

"This time get a big fat one that is not tempted to run off with the hired help."

"That didn't keep Effie Lou in harness."

"She wasn't big and fat when Jonas starting sniffing around, so you said."

"That's right, she was one good looking broad."

"There seems to be a bit of nostalgia in your voice."

"After all, she was the mother of my son. And she didn't get pregnant by us just sitting around talking about how we were going to pay the grocery bill."

"You must have thought you could live off of love."

"We tried that at first, but we got hungry before the first night was over. Wedding nights use up a lot of calories."

"You should have had air conditioning. You don't sweat as much."

"That's what happened to Effie Lou after she moved into that big house over on West Paces road. She left the thermostats turned down to sixty five and never changed them until winter came."

"I remember you telling me she didn't even go to the store."

"No, she had everything delivered."

"Now that's what I call the lap of luxury!"

"It might be, but it plays hell with your figure."

"That won't happen to me. I like to get up early every morning and run about a mile."

"Well don't wake me. I get enough exercise in the bed with you."

"You could get up and fix a big breakfast while I'm running."

"I'd rather take you to a diner."

"I'll be all hot and sweaty."

"We can shower together."

"That won't work. We would have to take two. One before and one after."

"After what?"

"Carl, you know how all that soap and rubbing arouses me."

"O.K. We'll shower separately. Then go to a diner."

"And also a big breakfast makes me horny."

"I don't know if I can handle two showers every morning."

"Maybe if we turn the thermostat down real low, we won't have to take the second shower."

"Dream on! You know we now have to change the sheets every day."

"We might have to forego our morning ritual."

"That's the best time for it."

"Let's table this matter and get back to your pleading."

"I was not exactly pleading. I was only asking for a favor."

"Please excuse my poor choice of words. Remember, I am only a simple school teacher that dealt with young brats and they plead all the time."

"I thought they whined."

"Also that, but they plead when they need to go to the rest room."

"I do too."

"Do what?"

"Plead."

"When?"

"When I need to go."

"Go where?"

"To the rest room."

"You went five minutes ago. You don't have prostate trouble like Zeke did?"

"I don't need to go now! But I might start pleading any moment now."

"For what?"

"For you to gather yourself together and pay attention."

"I am all together. Just look at my fine body."

"I know, how well do I know! I was referring to other regions."

"I have no other regions."

"I was referring to the cerebral department."

"Oh."

"I still love you."

"Sounds to me like it is a physical attraction."

"That too, but there is more to you than just that."

"What? Like my ability to keep books? Well, I don't know how."

"That's no problem. Mary can tell you all you need to know."

"She's gone to Florida."

"We have telephones."

* * *

"Hello, Mary? This is Nellie. Nellie Clyatt. You remember. I came up from Hooterville with Carl, Butch and Lilly.

"Yes my name is still Clyatt right now, but I hope that will change soon. Carl wants me to fill in for you until he finds a permanent replacement.

"Oh, I'm sure he means it. What? Make him marry me first? Why?

"I see. I'll see what I can do. In the meantime can you help me? I know nothing about keeping books. You will? Good. I'll be calling you from time to time when I need some help. Thank you, Mary, and how are things going down there? That's great! I'm glad you all are doing so well. Bye and thanks again."

* * *

"Carl, I talked to Mary and she will be glad to help me. I will consider helping you if."

"If what?"

"If you marry me first."

"That sounds like Mary has told you something."

"Just female talk."

"Honey, don't you trust me?"

"You are a man."

"What does that signify?"

"It signifies that I'll trust you more if vows are spoken. As it stands, I am only a live-in."

"The state recognizes common law marriages."

"Only after seven years."

"You do have a point. Let's talk to Lilly and Butch and maybe have a double wedding."

"I don't want to marry Lilly and Butch, only you."

"The state also does not recognize polygamy. I will be marrying only you."

"What then does Butch and have to do with this?"

"I thought it would be nice and it won't cost as much. We can get discount for multiple ceremonies."

"It would be nice, but if they balk, we can go ahead with a single."

"Lilly, Carl has proposed. Well, I guess it was a proposal. There was no soft candlelight or music, but he did plead, in his own way naturally. He thinks it will be nice if we have a double wedding."

"The only double wedding I ever saw was that Hicks boy knocked up Sally Jeffries and her daddy used a double barrel shotgun to persuade the perpetrator of the foul act."

"That's not what he meant. He would like for you and Butch to join us in a double ceremony."

"I'm enjoying everything like it is, but I'll feel Butch out on this idea. One more feel won't hurt him. He does have a lot of bruises though. This is the first time he has encountered a healthy South Georgia woman. But he's getting the hang of it."

"Let me know real soon. Carl wants me to help him at the auction and I won't unless he marries me."

"Don't you trust him?"
"I'll trust him more after the nuptials. After all, he is a man."
"I love 'em."
"I do too, but this is different. It is just good business."

* * *

"Butch, let's get married."
"Aren't you satisfied with our arrangement?"
"Of course I am, sugar, but Carl and Nellie are getting married and Carl thought it would be nice to have a double ceremony."
"Ha! I bet he was thinking about the money he could save that way."
"He didn't get where he is by pissing money away."
"I can't figure him out. He squeezes a penny until Lincoln shits and the next day spends a fortune on some crazy scheme."
"That's the mark of a successful man."
"I guess so. Do you really want to get married?"
"I'm happy like I am, but we should humor Carl. After all, he is your dad. And from him, all blessings come. Well, some anyway."
"That's a hell of a reason to get married. He didn't ask me when he married mama."
"You weren't around to ask."
"You're right, I forgot. If you really want to, it's all right with me."
"I'll call Nellie and tell her."

* * *

"Nellie, we'll do it."
"Do what?"
"Get married."
"I can't marry you."
"I don't want to marry you. Anyway, it's against the law. I'm talking about Butch and I."
"Are you sure?"
"Sure, I'm sure. And we both love Carl and this is what he wants."

"What do you want?"

"I want to spend every conscious moment with Butch."

"I think you're doing that now."

"But this will make it permanent."

"I'll tell Carl."

CHAPTER TWENTY- EIGHT

Being not exactly heathens, but embracing no particular faith, Carl and Butch opted, with the girl's questionable agreement, to hold the ceremony at the only location they could feel completely at ease.

"Honey, I know you and Lilly went to the Hooterville Primitive Baptist Church at the Hooterville Crossroads, and I know you taught Sunday school there, but you know how Butch and I feel about organized religions. We feel that it would be grossly hypocritical for us appear in one of these houses of worship with cynical thoughts. This would be starting our union off with a lie. And we feel we should be honest with you girls when embarking on such a momentous journey."

"I don't want to be married among a bunch of goats and pigs. I fear one would eat my corsage. And the odor would not be conducive to the atmosphere which should be present at such a ceremony."

"I feel the presence of livestock has been heavily exaggerated. True, a token amount filters through occasionally, but not to the extent to defile the premises. We can hold it on a Monday. That will give the clean-up crew all day Sunday to fumigate and decorate the place properly."

"We'll have it on Tuesday. Forget about them decorating the place. Lilly and I will take care of that."

"I was planning to invite all my friends to the function, and most of them are out gleaning on Tuesday getting ready for the Wednesday action."

"Surely you were not planning to invite all *those people* were you?"

"They are the salt of the earth and my friends."

"Do they have any decent clothes?"

"You have witnessed the miraculous transformation I made possible on Gabriel. I shall rise above myself and again do miracle work."

"The next thing I might expect from you is to walk on water."

"Only if I know where the submerged stumps are located."

"Well, after the Saturday night auction, they will have all day Sunday for you to perform your miracle work on them."

"If we start real early Sunday morning and work all through the night, I think I can do it."

"Lilly and I will need two weeks to plan everything and I want to invite a few friends from Hooterville."

"Surely you don't intend to invite any of *those people* do you?"

"Touché."

"Exactly whom did you have in mind?"

"Maybe Granny, Joe Billy and that nice manager of the Pig Joint, to name a few."

"Joe Billy might come. There's no way you can get Granny up here, she thinks this place is infested with Blue Bellies and Russians."

"I know, but she would enjoy an invite anyway."

"Yeah, it probably would give her a chance to rant and rave some."

"That's just as important to her as cooking and eating or shooting her old shotgun."

"Butch will want to invite some of his old college buddies."

"I assume they are also 'the salt of the earth'."

"They were, but they have been corrupted by a formal education."

"It is that bad?"

"No, but it gives them a different perspective of life. Most have a tendency to forget their roots."

"I imagine they are capable of reevertin'."

"In certain instances."

"The only cases I have been exposed to are when they are subjected to great emotional stress or overindulgence of alcohol. I trust none of these elements will manifest at our wedding."

"Possibly only a mild punch."

"Well, if anyone gets out of line I will dispense some well placed punches of my own."

"I was under the impression that a woman changes her personality only after the tie has been made. Aren't you being a mite premature?"

"There is no logical explanation of a woman's prerogative. Spending over twenty five years with Effie Lou should have taught you that."

"Traumatic experiences are well to be forgotten."

"Do you have a minister in mind?"

"I thought of Gabriel. He is very eloquent."

"Is he ordained?"

"I doubt it, but I can get him a mail order ordaining by the time of the wedding."

"Just as long as he doesn't try to auction us to the highest bidder."

"I shall caution him to use restraint."

* * *

"Gabby, have you ever entertained the thought of becoming an ordained minister?"

"In what religion?"

"I had in mind The International Inter-Denomination Universal Church of Dis-Organized Religion."

"Is that legal?"

"The State of Georgia says so."

"It might come in handy at times. Why?"

"I thought it would be nice to have someone of the cloth to hold an invocation before the auction."

"Yes, to bless all the combatants before the fray. Is this your sole purpose?"

"Not exactly, there is one more small thing."

"I don't do funerals or weddings."

"Make one small exception. Butch and I want to marry and we need a preacher to make it legal."

"To reiterate, I don't do weddings. Especially when two males want to marry."

"No, no, I don't want to marry my son, perish the thought! We want a double wedding and marry Nellie and Lilly."

"That's different, especially with you being my boss."

"I usually won't ask any of my employees to do anything I won't do, but this is different. I can't do my own wedding."

"Some Arabs do."

"I thought they only had the power to divorce any of their many wives."

"What's the difference, getting in or getting out?"

"Here, it's easy to get in but hell getting out. How well I know."

"And still, you want to get burned again?"

"This time is different."

"Famous last words."

"Don't be impertinent. Will you or won't you?"

"As I said, you're the boss."

"Good, I'll call the diploma mill."

"This will require a small consideration."

"The awarding you with a diploma or whatever should suffice."

"Only if I take advantage of it. I must think of ways to exploit this new windfall."

"As long as it doesn't interfere with your duties here."

"This job is a snap. I have plenty of spare time."

"Phillip used to go on scouting trips with me."

"You will probably have to give up that practice now."

"Why do you say that?"

"Your new acquisition might put a damper on your wanderings. I saw her looking around the 'merchandise' for a ball and chain."

"It might be wise for you to modify the standard vows exchanged."

"I'll work on it."

* * *

"Nellie, we must talk."

"We do talk."

"I mean more."

"About what?"

"About my business."

"Mary said she will help me with the books."

"I'm not worried about the books. I'm worried about how you feel about my going out of town on business trips. Sometimes I might be gone for a week at a time."

"How well do I remember. Every time you came down to see me, it was one of your 'business trips' that brought you."

"Now things will be different. I will have someone waiting for me to hurry back. And I shall."

"What will I do while you're gone?"

"Go shopping with Lilly."

"We used to prowl a lot."

"Those days are no more."

"This will take some adjusting."
"Butch can help while I'm away."
"Won't he be going with you?"
"No he has other interests. I had Gabriel in mind."
"Is he married also?"
"I don't believe so."
"He will be a corrupting influence."
"Ridiculous. He will be an ordained minister."
"Has he been neutered?"
"No."
"See to it."
"Nellie, you are being unreasonable."
"I am only trying to protect my interests. I am only interested in you. And your welfare."
"We might be on welfare if I can't tend to business. Besides, this will be temporary until I find a permanent bookkeeper. Then you can go with me."
"Goody, then we can mix business with pleasure as you used to do."
"I promise you this will be only for a short time."

* * *

"Butch, Nellie told me she was going to help Carl with the books at the auction."
"I wondered how he was going to replace Mary, so he conned Nellie into it, eh?"
"It is only temporary until a permanent replacement is found."
"Then what?"
"He has promised to take her on the business trips."
"Things will never be the same."
"As they shouldn't be. After all, they will be husband and wife."
"The only time I went off with Dad, we had one hell of a good time."
"I was there, remember?"
"You and I might have to go off on some 'business trips' some too."
"What will we be doing?"

"Looking for some new ideas for investing and making money, on the surface anyway."

"Can we afford it?"

"We can't afford not to. The world does not stand still for anybody. If you don't go forward, you go backward."

"That's why I didn't like my job. I was stagnating. Well, not like a swamp does, but you know what I mean."

"Broaden your horizons, not your butt."

"You got that shit right!"

"The sooner we get married, the sooner we can start the new program."

"Nellie and I have got that all under control. Everything is going according to plan."

* * *

Gabriel is standing before a full-length mirror in his pad. The mirror was an ornate one with a small crack in the left hand lower corner. It was in a place that did not obstruct any normal reflection, but was inappropriate to no longer grace the great hall where it had hung for generations. The accident was of a freak nature. It was being lowered from its resting place for a periodic re-papering if the wall when it slipped from the grasp of the remover. The ensuing impact with the terrazzo tile floor caused the minute chip. His insurance carrier amply rewarded the owner and the victim was deposited at the curb on collection day. Gabriel collected it right before the regulars came. Now it adorned a wall in his bedroom proudly. He was clad in his drawers only with a few sheets of hand written paper in one hand and a bottle of Muscatel in the other.

After polishing the rough spots and when he was satisfied with his recital, he showered and donned his best suit and proceeded to the auction barn where a great crowd was assembled. Even Granny showed up with Joe Billy.

"Oh Granny! I'm so glad you came up. Who's looking out for your place?"

"Joe Billy deputized two of his friends to go out there for a spell. I told them if everything was not the way I left it, they would feel the wrath of my trusty butcher knife."

"You are looking fine and you are talking like us now. What happened?"

"I felt I could stand a little grooming, sos I hired a tooter. Being I was coming way up here in Yankee land"

"Granny, this is not Yankee land, you are still in the Deep South."

"This is as far north I have ever been and it is sure different up here."

"This town is in the fast lane."

"I've been in the fast lane ever since I got in Joe Billy's squad car. That man drives like a maniac. He kept his siren squalling all the way up here."

"Where is Joe Billy? I want to see him."

"The last I saw of him, he was over yonder talking to Carl and Butch."

"Joe Billy! I am sure glad to see you."

"When I got Nellie's invite, I hightailed it out to Granny's to see if she wanted to ride up here with me. She sure surprised me. I thought somebody had snuck in her old body. She has gained a new command of the language. She musta got her invite before me and had made up her mind she was coming somehow. When I suggested she come with me, she jumped at the chance."

"How would she have come if you had not invited her?"

"I think she was thinkin' about ridin' a bus, not knowing how far it was."

"It is just as far in your car."

"It don't seem as far when you have the law on yore side."

"That does make a difference. Where are y'all staying?"

"We can't stay. I just took off for the day and she has to get back so my deputies can go back to their regular jobs."

"What do they do?"

"They make the finest bootleg in Hoots County, with my blessing of course."

"But you are the sheriff."

"That's a part time job."

"I see a new side of you every time we meet."

"I'm just a good old boy at heart."

"A rich good old boy."

"Don't get nosy."

"Never! Come join the assembly. I must take my station."

"Ladies and gentlemen, brothers and sisters, friends and acquaintances, and others, whomever, we are gathered in this familiar place because, due to the unusual mix of diverse personalities and beliefs those attending and with the intent of not offending the various faiths, we have determined that no one house of worship would be accepted by all. Besides we found not one that would allow this ceremony to take place on their premises. Bigots all!

"The reason for this gathering is to join two loving couples with the bonds (or shackles) associated with such a union for the sole purpose of these four souls to be able to cohabit legally. The approval of their respective Gods have long before approved of this union. This is for the purpose of legitimizing it in the eyes of the law, all four being law abiding citizens. Also they do not desire for any offspring, purposely or accidental, to be branded by our society as bastards, an affliction such unfortunate ones carry to their graves. This is a grave injustice to lie upon the heads of the yet unborn. To this end, we now enter in the more formal aspect of the ceremony, with a few alterations, agreed upon by all participants.

"Let it be understood by all I am joining Carl to Nellie and Butch to Lilly to eliminate any further confusion about who is marrying whom. For the sake of brevity, no further mention of names will be uttered. You might say this is a blanket set of vows without the benefit of a blanket.

"You four come a little closer to the podium. The men on one side and the women on the other, and face your intended. I will ask the questions and you will answer in the affirmative when you agree. If you don't, keep silent. Just shake your heads. Grinning is allowed. Snickering is not.

"The women are allowed to shed tears at the proper time. The men will not. They can grimace. Grunts and groans are permissible with certain questions.

"Do you men realize the legal ramifications this union will place over your respective heads?"

"Yes" In unison.

"Do you women accept these men as your keeper and provider of all things material and vow to act accordingly?"

"Yes" With grimaces.

"Do you men accept the fact the women control the bedroom activity, and your wants may be nullified by things physical or mental?"

"Do you women realize that the excuse of headaches can only be used when you are really pissed off and cannot be used as a perennial excuse? The consequences can only lead to an unhappy home and the supplicants may seek solace in the arms of another?"

Grins supplant the serious countenances on the women's' faces along with a giggling "YES!"

"Ignore that last stupid question."

More giggles.

"Do you men accept the fact that you cannot use selective deafness in the dialog with your mate until at least twenty five years of cohabitation has elapsed?"

Scowls emanate from the males. A questionable look appears on their faces and Carl calls 'time out' for a huddle with Butch.

"Where did Gabby come up with that shit? At times this will be our only defense when they get on a rambling mouthing."

"I object, Your Honor!"

"Carl, you are not in a court of law. State your objection."

"It seems you have been deprived of female companionship for too long and do not realize the burden this vow will place upon us."

"How so?"

"Due to the peculiar nature of these two women, at times this practice must be employed by us to maintain our sanity."

"Are you suggesting these two are exceptional in this respect"?

"Due to my limited experience with the opposite sex, I cannot speak for women in general, but I have found in my travels, this seems quite commonplace."

"I need to get out more. What do you women have to say about this?"

"About what?"

"I see what you mean, Carl. Let's strike that question."

"Thank you, Your Honor."

"I notice it is nearing lunchtime. I call a thirty-minute recess for all to retire to the lunch counter. Do not discuss any part of these proceedings with each other."

"Gabby, that was a good move to recess. We're selling hot dogs and hamburgers like there was a recent famine."

"I grasp every opportunity possible."

"You have mustard on the tip of your nose. Wipe it off before you resume. This is supposed to be a dignified happening. And come over here for a minute, there's someone I want you to meet."

"Gabby, this is a good friend of mine, Joe Billy Buford the Third. Joe Billy, this is Gabriel Johnson-Jones, my new auctioneer, who has replaced Phillip."

"Pleased to meetcha. You sure you ain't a judge? You shore talk like one."

"Thank you, sir. I have not enjoyed the honor of that profession, sadly."

"Why sadly?"

"I feel I could make some sweeping changes in our justice system."

"Like what?"

"Swift punishment for the guilty, freedom for the innocent."

"It ain't that easy, people tend to lie when their ass is in a crack."

"You speak as if you are acquainted with the system."

"You can bet your ass I am. I'm the high sheriff of Hoots County down in South Georgia."

"I would like to discuss this further, however now I have a duty to perform."

"Get with it. That's what I drove all the way up here for."

Rap, rap, went the gavel.

"Friends, if you all will gather around, we will continue with the nuptials."

"Where's Butch?"

"He had to relieve himself."

"Cold feet?"

"No, I think it was a real urgency."

"I had one once."

"We know, Nellie."

"Nellie, pay attention."

"I will, Lilly. Just as soon as everybody has returned."

"It's sweet of you to want to wait on Butch."

"Three quarters of the group won't get us married."

Butch comes running zipping up with a wet streak down one pants leg."

"That was a real urgency, Butch. Is everything all right?"

"Whew! It is now."

"Look at your pants."

"Oh shit! I need to go change."

"Like hell you do! You're marrying me right now. Just keep your legs together so no one will notice."

"Yes, Lilly, dear."

Gabby says, "This is starting to sound like a regular marriage."

"I thought it was."

"Do you mean you have never been to a normal one?"

"I went to a shotgun wedding once, but it didn't seem normal. The victim was kicking and screaming and had to be tied down."

"I've been one a lot like that, but it wasn't a shotgun wedding."

"What was it, Butch?"

"Let's just say there was a reluctant groom."

"Why?"

"Well, the bride's father had blown a large wad on the wedding, and the groom got the jitters at the last moment and the father in law to be, you might say coerced the would be groom with threats of bodily harm."

"All that one needed was a shotgun."

"That crowd didn't use shotguns, but there were plenty of fully automatic weapons around."

"Goodness, why?"

"The bride's father was a don in the organization."

"I hope he's not here."

"He's not, Lilly. He got rubbed out in a barber shop in New York City."

"Interesting. Now let's get on with our abnormal wedding."

"In lieu of nose rings, the four appearing before me has chosen to use finger types. At least this part is conventional. If the ladies will extend the finger they desire to be decorated, the men shall place upon the respective fingers their token and utter a few choice words befitting the occasion. Carl, you go first."

"Gabby, I wasn't informed that I would be required to speak, but here goes.

"Nellie, if I can get your attention for a few moments, I would like to say to you, While this ring only embraces your finger, my arms and everlasting love shall embrace your body and soul as long as we shall both live or love each other, whichever last longest."

"Say what?"

"Nellie, just say the same goes for me, and give me my ring."

"Now Butch, it is your turn."

"Thank you, Gabriel. Due to my limited experience and not as eloquent as my father, I will attempt a few words of my own.

"Lilly, I came to you in the prime of my life, young, somewhat innocent and naive. I have in the past been sure of things encountered by me and have been able to rise to the occasion to cope with some expertise, the events that have confronted me. Until now. Wow! This is quite different. I am at a loss for words. I can only say with all my heart I shall try to be the man you expect me to be and will never find solace or love elsewhere. Now stick out your chosen finger."

"Will this one do?"

"I don't think it will fit on your thumb. Try another one."

"Try this one."

"I don't think you should use your little one."

"You're right, it will inhibit my nose picking. Let's use the one next to it. Now stick out your chosen one."

Nellie reaches deep into her cleavage and withdraws a modest ring and places it on Carl's finger and states, "With this ring, I now take you for my spouse, protector and keeper of my body in a manner to which I have grown accustomed. As long as I can endure."

"Now what's that supposed to mean?"

"A wise woman leaves her options open. I trust I will have no reason to exercise them."

"I can only try to keep you happy."

"That's good enough for the present."

"I believe that these unions have been previously consummated. On that note, I pronounce these proceedings ended. Now let's all get on with the reception. For my many friends present, I have stashed behind the counter a case of the finest Muscatel which you all love and are welcome to help me enjoy."

"Carl, that was the most moving ceremony I have witnessed since I saw that serial killer get electrocuted down in Reidsville. Gabby really has a unique command of the language."

"It must have been, Joe Billy, it even affected your use of the English language"

"Eloquence is contagious. Granny and I will use our time together on the trip back to improve more."

"Hoots County will never the same."

CHAPTER TWENTY-NINE

"Jonas, Mary told me that Nellie told her she and Carl got married the other day."

"Effie Lou, didn't you expect that?"

"I guess so, but it's so soon."

"You really don't know how long they have known each other, do you?"

"No, but I don't think he met her on the way back from Palm Beach."

"Phillip could have told you that, Effie Lou."

"What would he know about them?"

"He has been on a few trips with Carl."

"But Carl told me they were business trips."

"On the surface, supposedly."

"Do you mean some weren't?"

"Not altogether."

"Does Mary know?"

"I'm sure she does, Phillip tells her everything."

"And to think, she still married that rascal."

"Effie Lou, when a couple embarks on a new life, it is best to leave the past behind."

"Jonas, you are right, look at us. Of course, you know my past, and I know some of yours. And that did not deter us. And Butch married Lilly at the same time."

"I wish them well. Anyway, we don't have time to dwell on the past. The present is upon us and the future is coming on strong."

"Right, there is a lot of activity going on down at the Cape and we need to think of some way to reap some of the benefits."

"Phillip and I were talking about just that the other night. We talked about some publicity stunts, but ruled them out. We need to establish a good credibility base, and scams will not do that."

"It didn't hurt the antique shop."

"This is not an antique shop or a tourist trap. We have to appeal to the family types."

"That will not fit into your plans to get a liquor license."

"It will if we have some type of entertainment for the kids. Something which can keep them out of mama and papa's hair while they are trying to let it down."

"I'm against the kid part. Family types have limited funds as a rule. And it will play hell with our liability insurance premiums. They are high enough now without all the crazy kids renting running around getting into Heaven knows what."

"Forget about the kid part. We seem to be doing all right the way we're going."

"Damn right. We are in the black and have money in the bank. I'm happy, Mary's happy, you and Phillip just stick to what you are doing and leave the management to us."

"I *would* like to get away once in a while. I'd like to see some of Florida before I die."

"It would be nice. Maybe one of my kitchen help can learn how to keep the boats running and I have got the kitchen under control. We could alternate with Mary and Phillip to run the place and we all could take off some. Separately, of course."

"I'm sure they will go along with that."

"If they will, Jonas, just promise me one thing."

"What's that, Effie Lou?"

"You won't want to go fishing."

"Don't worry. I had in mind a little betting at the dog tracks."

"I didn't know you were into dogs."

"Someone told me you could stay ahead if you watch the dogs go to the starting line. Always pick one that stops and takes a shit. He will run better."

"I run better to the rest room if I have the squirts. I usually saunter back afterwards."

"That's different. These dogs are on a strict diet and don't get the squirts. You wouldn't either if you ate right. You eat like a Mexican. They have cast iron stomachs. And all that Tequila they drink helps."

"If I get that license, maybe I can change that. Good whiskey and spring water never hurt anybody."

"I won't eat the worm."

"Fish do."

"I'm not a fish."

"You drink beer like one."

* * *

While engaged in this important conversation, Effie Lou and Jonas were sitting in the swing on the front porch of the restaurant. Effie Lou noticed a beat up 55 Chevy station wagon with Pennsylvania license plates drive up to the cabin office. It had a terminal case of skin cancer, probably due to lack of any TLC and the hazards of driving the salted down streets of western Pennsylvania, famous for constantly being inundated with record snowfalls in the harsh winters experienced there.

Mary was tending store at this time.

"Good afternoon, sir. How may I help you?"

"I have recently retired from over forty years working my ass off in the steel mill in Pittsburgh and this is the first decent vacation I have had the pleasure of enjoying. My wife died twenty years ago and I lost my only son in the Great War and have been living alone ever since. And now I would like to catch up on my fishing I have neglected for so many years. If I like it, I might move down here. I understand the winters are fairly mild, or so my affluent friends inform me. By the way my name is Adolphus Julian Pitts." Extending his hand.

Mary turned white as a newly laundered sheet. And started trembling.

"Mamn, what's the trouble? You look as pale as a ghost. Is it something I said"?

"It most certainly is! My name is Mary Maloney McDonald Pitts Morse. The Morse being added only recently. In the spring of 1944 I married a young soldier in Aiken, South Carolina who was from Pittsburgh. I believe this man was your son. His name was Patrick Alfred Pitts."

"Oh my God! He was my son! And you are the Mary he wrote us about. Why didn't you ever get in touch with us?"

"We were together only a short time and he didn't have time to tell me your address be before he had to go overseas. I have often wondered about his parents. When I received the telegram, I was devastated and was unable to think straight. And afterward I had his son and that occupied my every waking moment. Our son was also taken from me before his prime and I retreated down here to start a new life. Please forgive me for my negligence."

"I also have been negligent. We, too, were also devastated about Patrick and did not know how to get in touch with you. So, I had a grandson! Well, I'll be damned! Was he a good boy"?

"The best. I never felt he was totally mine. He was a strange child, with knowledge that could not be gained here."

"What do you mean, here in Florida?"

"No, he never came to Florida, he departed this earth years ago. We lived in Atlanta at the time. That's where he was born. And I stayed on there with my parents until early this year. He and his wife died in an explosion of a church he had founded."

"What a terrible way to go."

"Not really. The suffering is placed upon the ones left behind."

"I know what you mean. It would have been better had I left with my wife, but we have no control over such things."

"There must be a reason things happen as they do, though I'll never understand them."

"If things had been as our choosing, we would have never met. There might be a message here."

"I feel at times Harold is still with me."

"Who's Harold?"

"Oh, he was my son. I originally named him Patrick Junior, but he exhibited such strangeness so unlike Patrick, I had to have him re-christened 'Harold Gilmore'."

"Bad genes?"

"Nothing like that, it was more like he came from some alien place beyond our understanding. Shortly after he gained the power of speech, he began speaking a language that had been dead thousands of years."

"It wasn't just gibberish?"

"No, I found out through a friend it was ancient Sumerian."

"Never heard of it."

"Only teachers of ancient language have."

"You have re-opened a lot of old wounds I thought healed. I must hear more, but for now, I need a place to crash. My bones and my car need a long rest. What have you to offer? I don't need anything fancy like those high priced motels all along the coast. It doesn't even have to be cooled."

"We have some reasonable cabins with swamp coolers that we have not installed air conditioners in yet. And they have small kitchens where you can cook your catch if you're lucky and so desire or you can bring them to the kitchen at the restaurant and they will cook them for you for a small fee."

"This sounds great. I should have come down here twenty years ago when my wife died."

"We did not have this place then and you would have never met me."

"Things must work out for the best, after all."

"We shall see."

* * *

After Mary had installed Mr. Pitts in cabin number seven, Effie Lou and Jonas were sitting in her office when she returned.

"Mary, when did we start renting to destitute transients?"

"This gentleman is special, Effie Lou"

"How so? Perhaps an eccentric millionaire?"

"No, this is hard to believe. That man is Harold's grandfather."

"The hell you say! Did you invite him down? I didn't think you knew how to get in touch with him."

"I didn't. This is pure coincidence. He just happened to come here. I still can't believe it. Of all the places here in Florida, he chooses this one."

Effie Lou asks cynically, "How do you know he is Harold's grandfather?"

"He had all the right answers. He has just recently retired from the steel mill in Pittsburgh and is considering moving somewhere down here."

"Sounds like Harold's work."

"What do you mean, Jonas?"

"Like you say, this is too much of a coincidence. It's either Harold's or Fate's hand involved and I put small stock in Fate."

"Do you really believe that?"

"I do, Mary. Let's keep our eyes on him and see what happens."

* * *

The next day they saw Mr. Pitts up at dawn and eating breakfast at the restaurant. When he was finished, he cleaned the table and took all the plates to the kitchen. Then he would go back to cabin seven and straighten it up and make the bed. He then swept off the small porch and raked the yard. When he finished that, he went to the shed and found a sling blade and cut all the tall grass at the river's edge.

On the third day, Mary approached him. "Mr. Pitts, it is not necessary for you to do what you are doing. We have help hired to do this work."

"I'm sorry Mary, if I have offended you. It's just that I have worked all my life and time weighs heavily on my idle hands. If I cannot help here, perhaps I should move on. I was not doing this in hopes of a job. I have an adequate pension to pay my own way."

"Forgive me, Mr. Pitts. I must have a suspicious nature. I have been a widow for so many years and I fear someone might take advantage of me. We appreciate what you have done, but we cannot allow you to work for nothing. It is against our nature."

"I do not consider this work. I consider it a privilege. Please do not think this as an imposition. I must keep busy to keep my mind from dwelling on things past. I feel my sanity is at stake."

"I too, have this problem. That is how I wound up down here. Perhaps this will be our refuge. But I insist on giving some compensation."

"If you let me stay, I guarantee I can carry my load. I notice your cabins could use some repair and I will gladly do it. I also like flowers. I can make this a showplace."

"Let me talk this over with my partners."

"I thought this was your place."

"No, my husband and another couple share equally here. All decisions are made by the four of us."

"I have met Effie Lou and Phillip. They seem to be good people. I hope they think I am too."

"I'll let you know, Mr. Pitts."

"Please call me Adolph."

* * *

That night the four of them gathered in Jonas and Mary's cabin after dinner to discuss Adolph. This was the former manager's cabin and was the roomiest and had the best air conditioning. It was here all business meetings were held. And naturally after the place had shut down for the night. Fishermen retire early and rise early. If this place had sidewalks, they would be pulled up at this time. The no vacancy sign would always be lit now at this time if it were true or not. They enjoyed their peace.

"We must discuss Adolph. I feel uncomfortable with the present arrangement. It is not right for him to labor so without compensation."

"I don't like to look into a gift horse's mouth."

"Effie Lou, it seems I still have a lot of work to do concerning your attitude."

"What's wrong with my attitude, Jonas?"

"Righting old wrongs require attitude adjustments. Greed is evil, just as much as overeating. Taking advantage of others can corrupt the soul."

"Not if they are taking advantage of you."

"Does Adolph fit in that category?"

"I don't know."

"Then I vote we give him the benefit of the doubt."

"He might be an alcoholic, Mary."

"Phillip, an alcoholic can't drink just one beer, as he does each night before supper."

"Hell, it even takes two or three to unwind my spring every afternoon."

"Jonas, you are entitled. What with working with those outboards everyday."

"Thank you, Mary."

"Then do we all agree to pay him a small wage and give him room rent or pay him more and still charge him rent?"

"If we pay him the larger amount, we will have to withhold tax and also pay sales tax on the room rent."

"Effie Lou, is that old monster, greed creeping back in?"

"I am only thinking of that most greediest monster of all, namely our government." "Yes, the more you feed it, the larger the appetite grows. We must not contribute to further its decadence. What they do not know might hurt them, but it will certainly help us."

The vote was unanimous for the smaller amount.

* * *

"Adolph, we have decided that in lieu of rent, you can do odd jobs and on top of that we can also pay you minimum wage for any extra work you choose to do."

"Mary, this is not necessary, but if you insist I will accept. I have no need for the money. Maybe I'll find a good use for it."

"We have no insurance plan. You'd best save it for any emergencies."

"I hadn't thought of that. I have enjoyed good health all my life and I guess I thought I would always."

"You never know what will happen. You might even be attacked by an alligator."

"I've noticed a few around, but they pay no attention to me. It might be because I take a bath every day and don't smell like a dog or a goat."

"You're probably right. Dogs or goats do not last long around here. We caution all our patrons to wash before taking a boat out. And use plenty of deodorant."

"I got on that habit after putting eight hours in the steel mill. On my way home, even the street animals gave me wide berth. I never got bitten on my way home."

"How about on the way to work?"

"I was allowed to ride the bus to work. They wouldn't even let me ride in the back on the way home. We tried to get the bus company to get one of those double decker English buses and let us ride on the open-air second level. They said it was not in their budget. It was probably for the best, there would most certainly have been fights for the front seats."

"It must have been a terrible job."

"It made a man of me and the pay was good. I have no regrets. I could even stoke the fires of Hell."

"I don't believe in Hell, Adolph. The threats of eternal damnation might keep the good people in line, but they are not the people who are in jeopardy."

"Mary, where do you think Patrick and Harold are now?"

"We won't know until we get there ourselves."

"Well, my curiosity is not going to get the best of me and force me to go find out."

"Nor I, it will happen soon enough without our help."

"All I want to do is get through life in one piece and alive."

"I want to hang around to see what happens next."

"Everybody in the ground wanted the same thing."

CHAPTER THIRTY

"Butch, when have you talked to your mother?"

"Nellie called Mary the other day and I got a chance to talk to mom a bit. She told me that Harold's granddad showed up down there a while back right out of the blue. Can you believe that?"

"I would believe anything even remotely connected to Harold."

"But this is unreal, Dad. What are the chances of this happening by accident?"

"Astronomical, what do they think of it?"

"They think Harold had a hand in it."

"Whether its true or not, believing that might give them some measure of comfort. I wish I could believe, but I'm too much an agnostic."

"Have you forgotten how Harold helped you back in the early days?"

"I have a compulsion to forget things I can't understand."

* * *

Wherever they went, and this is not within our understanding, Marybelle and Harold had set up a very high tech monitoring station equaling the one to which J.C. had access. They only used it to keep tabs on their loved ones left behind. And occasionally to interfere in matters which they felt would be beneficial to ones they had loved. To this end, Harold implanted a subliminal thought in his grandfather's mind to seek a milder climate to spend his old age. The net result of this was an urge for the old man to head south.

I don't know where I'm going, but I have a bellyful of this town and its winters. My old bones can use a lot of sunshine and new scenery. Nothing here interests me anymore. My old friends are either dead or have retired to St. Pete. I don't want to go there. I understand it is filled up with old farts that sit around and play checkers, bingo or shuffleboard. And I never liked any of these. I want to be around younger people. Not kids, but people with some sense. I like to fish. I never caught a really big one. There ought to be a place where you can go out in a small boat and fish and think. It can't be deep-sea fishing; I have a fear of getting seasick. I even puked my guts out from riding one of those crazy rides at a carnival once. God, that was a long time ago. Patrick was only ten years old. That was before the depression and we thought everything was great. I was young and strong and had a good job in the mill. Maybe that was why we survived the dark years. I miss both of them. If this old car will make it, I'm going to find some nice place on a river down there and plant new roots.

"Adolph, what prompted you to seek this place out? I cannot believe it was pure coincidence. Did you feel guided or inspired?"

"Mary, when you get my age, you don't question things beyond your understanding. Let's just say I had an itch."

"When did you first get this 'itch'?"

"I think it was sometime in the fall of 1965. My old wagon was ten years old and I was thinking of trading it in on a newer one. The dealer really ticked me off. He said he would allow me two hundred dollars for it. I figured I would take my chances on it lasting another thousand miles. It didn't, but I had it patched up for a hell of a lot less than a new one would cost."

"But it looks so rough. Didn't people laugh at you?"

"When people laugh at you, Mary, you are spreading joy."

"I never thought of it that way."

"Performance is what you need in a car, not how it looks. Besides, who would take advantage of an old man driving a wreck?"

"I wouldn't. That is the year we lost Harold and Marybelle."

"That's weird, it was about that time I felt a new sense of loss, and developed the 'itch'."

"I wish there was some way we could communicate with them."

"Don't go to any séances. My wife went to a charlatan right after Patrick was killed and it was heartbreaking."

"Don't worry, I believe if Harold wants to communicate with us, he will find a way."

"Maybe he has."

"Do you think your car can make it into town and back? Everybody's busy and we need a few supplies."

"I wouldn't hesitate to take off for California in it. Of course, I don't know how I would get back. Besides, my 'itch' has subsided."

"I had something much closer in mind."

"I need to know how much closer before I commit."

"Crescent City or possibly Palatka if you can't find everything there."

"Shucks, I could walk that far."

"Not with what I want you to bring back. Besides, there are lot of wild animals in the jungle between here and 17."

"It won't overload my old wagon, will it?"

"Not if you clean out all the junk you have in it. We only need some paint and nails and such."

"I'll have you know 'all that junk' represents the remainder of my earthly possessions salvaged from the liquidation of my 'estate' in Pittsburgh."

"Store it in your cabin until we get that shed behind it cleaned out."

"Who will determine what is to be thrown away?"

"I think you are capable of making those decisions."

"I don't know, Mary. I have examined the 'merchandise' and found value in every piece."

"I grant you that would be the case if we were at Carl's auction in Atlanta, but we are down here in the boondocks and there is no market around here for it."

"I'll ask around to see if anyone is interested in hauling it away."

"Try to be back before dark. I don't want you to wreck dodging armadillos out on 17."

* * *

Adolph left the next morning right after breakfast when the sun was just clearing the trees in the east towards US 17. Lake George was obliquely illuminated as well as the many small boats anchored quietly over favorite fishing holes. A few miles south of Crescent City, he observed a house he considered as a likely candidate to receive the contents of the shed. Well, he didn't see the house, only the tin roof gleaming in the morning sun. The remainder of the view of the house was obscured by mountains of assorted 'merchandise' suitable for gleaning by the more unfortunate of the area's population. At this early hour, there were already about a dozen cars and trucks parked on the shoulder of the road with the occupants cruising the valleys between the mountains. Some were carrying their purchases back to trucks, obviously to haul the loads to more lucrative markets farther to the east. Beside the driveway to the house was a shed with an open front with an old geezer sitting in an old rocking chair drinking a cup of coffee with a change apron tied around his pot belly. Everyone passing out with treasures was required to stop at this point and haggle the price. It was the proprietor's policy to not allow a customer to leave without his purchase, regardless of how ridiculous the price. Even at this early hour his change apron was approaching an overload. Adolph was quick to appreciate the potential of this enterprise and approached the proprietor about the possibility of purchasing the business. He was greeted with a stare that assumed he was insane. And a hilarious guffaw of laughter. He then realized his error. This was a cash business. There were no books kept. There was no sales tax collected. There was no payroll. Only a damn fool would want to part with such a gold mine. He apologized for his stupidity and then asked him if he was interested in cleaning out the shed. He replied he would consider it for a small fee.

"Do you mean to tell me you do not pay for all this stuff?"

"Hell no. Everything you see here are castaways. Most of all this was delivered to me by desperate people needing room for their new purchases. Some of which by the way, was purchased here.

"If their material has potential, I will let them dump it free. If it is slow moving stuff, they pay me."

"What does the county have to say about this?"

"My brother is the chairman of the county commissioners. And his son is the sheriff."

"And to think I wasted forty years of my life working my ass off in a steel mill."

"I myself toiled for naught in my early years. I tried truck farming here before I started putting my worn out and broken down equipment in my front yard to sell. Soon I was going out and buying old tractors and such to sell. The rest is history. To hell with farming!"

"It seems that your family are well established in this area."

"My original ancestors came to this country from England with Oglethorpe when he established a colony up on the Georgia coast.

The third generation migrated down here trying to escape those damn stinging flies that infest that part of the coast. Or so they tell me."

"I understand that colony was made up of convicts."

"Most were the victims of debtor's prison. Coming to this country was their only hope. They had to stay in prison until the debts were paid and they couldn't pay as long as they were in jail."

"Catch 22."

"Say what?"

"Damned if you do, damned if you don't."

"Well, Oglethorpe rounded up enough of them to start a colony. All welcomed the change of scenery."

"Just think, if your ancestors had not been dead beats, you would not be enjoying this Florida sunshine."

"Of course, this is a lonely life. I have to keep constant vigilance to protect my wares."

"Get some junkyard dogs."

"Unsolicited advice is unwelcome."

"I meant no offense."

"None taken. I tried some a few times, but they would take up with some of my customers and go home with them. I guess you have to feed them regularly."

"Well, I have to get on up the road. When I get back, I will bring a load for your appraisal."

"No garbage, mind you."

"That's probably why the dogs left."

"I hadn't thought of that. Maybe I'll get some more and accept selected garbage."

"If you do, also get some cats. They can eat the rats that the garbage attracts."

* * *

Now there was a man I truly respect. Earthly trappings seem to mean very little to him. I wonder if he was ever married. Probably not. He carried himself like a real free spirit, not encumbered by domesticity brought on by married bliss. Not that I regret for a moment the time spent with my lovely wife and child, but there was always the doubt about what other paths I could have taken if circumstances had been different. But for the infatuation of a hot bloodied teenager there might be I. Ah, for freedom from nightly baths and shaves. Of course I would have to prepare my own meals, but I think I could have learned if hungry enough. And clean the house and do the laundry, which I believe my wife carried these chores to the extreme. If you lived alone and things got too bad, you could always move and let the next tenant clean up the mess. But nowadays one must put up a deposit, forfeited if one leaves prematurely. It might be worth the forfeit, depending on the condition at abandonment. I must quit myself of these thoughts, now that I am a respectable retiree living in the land of sunshine. My ingrained discipline will see me through, I trust. If not, I must not allow anyone to inspect my living quarters .I have landed on a soft pillow. I like these people. Mary is an ideal daughter in law, if belatedly. And what is Phillip? My stepson in law? Effie Lou and Jonas are great people. They do not talk of their past. They must be trying to start a new life. I must not be too curious.

The sun was hidden in the trees in the west as he turned off 17 towards the camp. He marveled at the lush vegetation of the area. If one had an urgent call by nature to the roadside, it would indeed be by the roadside for it would be impossible to penetrate any deeper to gain privacy. Such thoughts were highly suggestive and should not be dwelt upon lest urgency forces itself upon the human waste disposal system. This process of thought prompted Adolph to unconsciously increase the speed of his vehicle. His acceleration was maintained until a deep dip across the road suddenly brought his thoughts back to the issue at hand; to wit; get the auto back in control. He suffered no ill effects from the incident, but a fifty-pound box of nails in its descent from being airborne, landed on the side of a gallon can of paint that had overturned. The impact forced the lid off the can and the pressure of the impact spewed green paint forward to decorate the interior, seats and the back of Adolph's head. Some reached the windshield, but not enough to impair the driver's vision. He saw no reason at this point to stop. There was really nothing he could do to rectify the problem without a good water supply and a high-pressure hose that was only available at the camp. So on he drove, with paint running down his neck only to stop when it reached his tightly drawn belt. He drove straight to the area designated for cleaning the boats and removed his shirt and spraying his head and back. The car could wait. He did not relish the idea of the paint setting up on his person. He had no one to peel hardened paint from his person, a fairly intimate chore.

Effie Lou was taking a break on the back steps of the kitchen when she saw Adolph's what seemed to her, strange antics.

"Jonas, come look what that old fool Adolph is doing. He just took off his shirt and is now hosing down his upper torso."

"He must've got into a hornet's nest. There's a lot of them back on the road."

"Either that, or some eagle has shit all over him. Look at all that green stuff."

"If it was an eagle, it was a mighty sick eagle."

"Maybe it was a buzzard."

"Buzzards don't get sick. Think of their diet."

"Enough of this speculation, I'm going to ask him what happened."

"Adolph, what in the hell happened to you? You look a mess."

"Effie Lou, a can of green paint exploded in my wagon and a little of it got on me."

"It's a pretty shade of green."

"I would have preferred a light blue."

"Come to think of it, blue would look better on you."

"I found everything Mary wanted, except we are short one gallon of green paint."

"Maybe the man will give you another one. That one must have been sour to explode like that."

"I doubt it. I'll go back tomorrow after I get my car cleaned up."

"You better clean it up tonight before it sets up."

"I wish it was on the outside of the car. It would've improved the looks."

"I think it improved the interior."

"Possibly, but I do need to get it off the windshield and the dash."

"It looks good on the seats."

"I might leave that."

* * *

"Eagle or buzzard, Effie Lou?"

"Neither Jonas, green paint."

"Why would he pour green paint down his neck?"

"Didn't, can exploded."

"High powered paint."

"The back end of his wagon is loaded with gallons and gallons of it."

"Maybe we should declare an emergency and evacuate."

"We could push the wagon off the end of the dock."

"It might kill the fish."

"Get him to park it behind his cabin. It needs painting anyway."

* * *

"Adolph, we are concerned about the paint. It might explode and take out the entire fish camp."

"Jonas, your fears are groundless. Your wife did inquire about what precipitated the explosion. It was a one-time event. It cannot happen again."

"How can you be sure?"

"I now know where lies the bump in the road."

"I see."

CHAPTER THIRTY-ONE

Carl, Nellie, Butch and Lilly were sitting at a table at their favorite watering hole. It was unusual to see all four there at the same time, but this was a special occasion. They were all celebrating their tenth wedding anniversary.

"Here's to us and may we have this many more."

"That's a hell of a thing to say, Carl. Why do you limit it to only ten more?"

"Nellie, it's like this. When you're ahead, don't push your luck. Of course I'd like at least fifty more, but I have become a realist. I will take what's left for me on the installment plan. And live every day as if it was my last."

"That makes sense."

"Damn right! And if we meet to celebrate our twentieth, I will say a toast to twenty more."

"Dad, that's pushing your luck. You should stick with ten at a time. You're not a spring chicken any more."

"Do you know something I'm not aware of? Have you been in touch with Harold?"

"Harold has not chosen to communicate with me, if he has the capability. I am only trying to be a 'realist'."

"Butch, you and Carl get off this morbid shit. We are here to have a good time."

"You're right, Lilly. You and Nellie tell us how the arrangements for our cruise is progressing."

"Well, we talked to a travel agent and she tried to set us up with a package."

"You mean like with a group that will have to stay together so some will not get lost?"

"Well, she didn't say that in so many words, but I suspect that might be the case."

"I object! I will not be herded around and rushed like a pack of sheep! And the progress of the group is determined by the slowest, which might be a fortunate couple celebrating their seventy fifth anniversary."

"Carl, you're being unreasonable. She knows all the right places to go and the right things to see."

"If Dad is unreasonable, so am I."

"Then just exactly what do you two propose?"

"Fly south, Nellie, get on a boat, party across, dock and rent a car."

"They have taxis, Carl."

"You have to tell the driver where you want to go and we don't know where we want to go."

"The driver can take us on a tour."

"Yes, to every tourist trap and clip joint on the island. It will end up costing us many times what a rental will cost."

"How about the hospital bills? You know they drive on the wrong side of the road."

"All you have to do is keep you mind on what you're doing."

"If you get all of us killed, Carl, I'll hate you the rest of my life."

"Nellie, I can do it. I know I can. Don't you remember when I went down a exit ramp by mistake and survived to the next interchange on I-285?"

"That was at three o'clock in the morning. And you drove on the shoulder all the way."

"I could have done better if you hadn't been screaming bloody murder. It was quite distracting."

"And all the cars were blowing their horns and calling you a stupid Yankee from Michigan."

"Yeah, and they gave me many a finger. It wasn't dangerous, but it was embarrassing."

"It wasn't as embarrassing as when our maid found my drawers in the dirty clothes the next morning."

"You need to get a handle on your emotions."

"What I need is a handle on your head."

"O ye of little faith! What happened to your confidence in your hero?"

"It was shattered way back when you let the Emir talk you into importing camels to our farm down in Henry county."

"That would have been a great idea had it not been for all the gullies and ravines on the land. Who could possibly know the wild dogs and coyotes would spook them and run headlong into the gullies and break their legs? And have to be shot?"

"And then you tried to market the camel steaks. Ostriches may have been better. I hear they have a low fat content."

"Yeah, and they can outrun coyotes. The world is not ready yet for my advanced ideas."

"God, but they're ugly."

"No uglier than camels."

"Thank goodness the Emir had no big birds."

"Oh yes, he indeed does."

"Does he eat them?"

"No, he keeps them for his many children to ride."

"He told you this?"

"Yes when I asked him how he kept his many children occupied. And other things they do."

"Like what?"

"Like building sand castles."

"From what I hear, there's plenty of raw material over there."

"Oil and sand. That's all he has."

"Poor bastard."

"We are digressing. We need to resolve the problem of the cruise."

"It has been resolved. Plane, boat and rental auto."

"How about hotel accommodations?"

"We sleep on the boat. And park on the dock. This way, we can see all the local color."

"There will be plenty of that. I understand that ninety five percent of the population has much color."

"That is not correct. There are white British there also. They fled the Colonies during the Revolution. George Washington got so pissed, he wanted to invade the islands and wipe them out."

"Why didn't he?"

"He had his hands full trying to keep the thirteen states from invading each other."

"It took them another eighty five or so years before they got around to that."

"Yeah, and some of them are still pissed."

Butch asks, "Its no wonder Congress has so much difficulty resolving important issues. We are only four and they are many."

"Yes, and in the great scheme of things, our problems are insignificant." Adds Lilly.

Butch says, "Lets put it to a vote."

Nellie: "Taxi."

Lilly: "I yield to Butch."

Butch: "I yield to Dad."

Carl: "The ayes have it. We rent a car."

Nellie: "Then I wont go."

Carl: "Nellie, have another drink."

It had taken ten more Martinis for Nellie to yield. The next day she denied acquiescing. She claimed she was taken advantage of. "Carl, you know how I get when I have overindulged. I will agree to anything."

"Anything?"

"Well, anything within reason and morally correct."

"What you agreed on fits within these guidelines."

"In whose opinion?"

"Mine by God, now don't let this be our first disagreement in ten years. I can't understand your reluctance. Give me fourteen good reasons why we shouldn't rent a car."

"Now you are being unreasonable. There are not that many good reasons why anybody on earth shouldn't do anything."

"How about a couple that already has ten kids?"

"They are already about eight kids too late for any help."

"God bless welfare."

"Or the Pope."

"One of these days somebody will change the rules."

"Do you really think so?'

"They had better. Otherwise, there will be standing room only."

"Didn't Harold have some thoughts on this? I remember Butch talking about it."

"Harold was a dreamer. He did not have a firm grasp on reality. It cost Marybelle and him their lives."

'I hope you don't go off on some wild crusade and get your ass blown up."

"You don't have to worry about that. I've seen too many crazies in the world who are content with things as they are."

"I think that includes you also."

"To a certain extent, Nellie, I hope I have the wisdom to recognize the things I can't possibly change. I only try to enhance my position in a world gone insane."

"Have I been an enhancement?"

"Beyond my wildest dreams."

"And you, beyond mine."

"This trip will be another exercise in enhancement"

"I'm sorry, I didn't look at it that way. It might be fun after all."

"After all what?"

"After all my doubts."

"No one wears the mantle of paranoia gracefully."

"I'll have you know I have not one paranoid bone in my body. I'm just what you might define as cautious."

"Divided by a fine line."

"What's divided?"

"Caution and paranoia."

"Wise ones are cautious, neurotics are paranoid."

"Past experiences make you cautious, traumas contribute to paranoia. Have you ever had an unpleasant experience on a boat?"

"I got seasick on a boat once, but it was a small one. This won't be a small one, will it?"

"You can't get seven hundred people on a small boat."

"I hope there will be no undesirables on board."

"Undesirables can't afford the trip."

"No commuters? They can be."

"Be what?"

"Now you're doing it."

"Doing what?"

"Forget it."

"Ten years has taken its toll"

* * *

"Lilly, you're over packing. We are only going to be gone a week."

"But Butch, it might get cold."

"We're not going to the South Pole."

"Knowing you and Carl, there's no telling where we will wind up."

"Not this time. We have to get back to our businesses."

"That's no excuse. Everything runs like clockwork."

"Yeah, for about ten days. Then the spring winds down."

"Wind it tighter."

"Trust me, we will be gone only one week."

"That's on the boat. We have to get there and back. There are no cruise ships running the Chattahoochee."

"I wish there were. I'm tired of tubing."

"Not to mention the pitfalls brought on by stupidity. Remember when we left one car at the take out point and drove the other car up to the put in and changed into our bathing suits and you left the take out car's keys in your jeans locked up in the put in car?"

"How can I forget that? The taxi ride back and forth cost me a small fortune."

"Don't forget the locksmiths bill for breaking and entering the put in car."

"The lesson I learned was to put all the keys around your neck on a tight chain."

"And put your cigarettes in a wide mouth plastic gallon jug."

"Soggy ones don't smoke too well."

"Do they sell them on the boat?"

"What? Jugs?"

"No, stupid. Cigarettes."

"Yes and they are duty free, but they still cost twice as much."

"Can't we smuggle our own on board?"

"Sure, and booze. But don't get caught. They will confiscate it."

"If they sell booze on the boat, we won't need to take any."

"The duty free shops won't open until they clear territorial waters. We might dry up before then"

"Well, I for one do not consider myself an alcoholic."

"Nor me, but I might need one or two to ease the tension."

"We should leave our tensions at the dock."

"Perhaps, but I worry about taking all our earthly possessions in suitcases on a boat."

"I wasn't planning on taking everything."

"You have enough containers scattered around for the job."

"You're being a smart ass. I have only packed my necessities."

"Your needs seem to surpass mine one hundred fold."

"You forget I'm a woman."

"Never! Come here."

"Wait. I must prepare myself. Let's see, in what suitcase does those necessities reside?"

"The act of love is not an act of Congress."

"Not for me. You carry your protection in your billfold."

"That's for emergencies only. You forget I was a Boy Scout."

"Yeah, and I was a Campfire Girl. They told me all about boys like you."

"We have done exceptionally well. Ten years and not a hint of over populating the world."

"Don't you ever want any kids?"

"Do you?"

"I have thought about at times, but I abhor the efforts of pregnancy and the rigors of childbirth."

"Me too."

"What do you mean? All you have to do is sweat a small amount of abstinence."

"I have the genes of a Billy goat."

"You could always take a trip out to our sheep ranch."

"Naaaaaa. That would be infidelity."

"I wonder if that's why the Moslems call us Infidels?"

"No way. They have many wives. Not to speak of their thousands of goats. It's because we do not accept Mohammed as our prophet."

"I accept Mohammed. I accept Buddha. I accept Jesus. I accept Krishna."

"You can't accept all."

"Let me qualify that. I accept all as prophets and Saviors of those who truly believe in them."

"An unusual stand for a female."

"I had a good teacher. You have taught me tolerance and have altered my preconceived notions born out of prejudice and ignorance."

"I also had a good teacher."

"Let's not get into Harold now."

"I'm not obsessed. Although I'll always remember him and Marybelle, may they rest in peace."

"Do I detect something more when you speak of her?"

"To know her was to love her."

"In a carnal way?"

"Well, maybe at first. I now consider it in adolescent infatuation."

"I had a teen age crush on my basketball coach in high school. He completely ignored me. I was freckled faced and flat of chest."

"You couldn't have been. Look at you now."

"I was a late bloomer."

"Marybelle wasn't. I bet she was born with tits."

"Wasn't she black?"

"Hell no! She was a wonderful tan with skin as soft as a baby's behind."

"All over?"

"Sadly, I never found out."

"Maybe if I spend a week on some tropical island's beach, I will meet your qualifications."

"Baby, you qualify, as is."

"Like in, 'as is, no return'?"

"You got that shit right. Anyway, I don't like Bikini tans."

"That's the only way you could get it. I'm not parading around in nature's underwear. In front of a bunch of rubber-neckers."

"I have a rubber neck when it comes to you."

"That's different. I have known you. And in the biblical sense."

"Viva le bible!"

* * *

"Dad, I was thinking."

"I hope that is not unusual, Butch."

"This is not the time for frivolity. I am serious."

"About what?"

"Driving down."

"In what? It will take a two ton truck just for the baggage."

"You should have better control over Nellie. I convinced Lilly to carry only the minimum."

"And what is the minimum?"

"One case for me and eight for Lilly."

"I'll try again on Nellie. Why should we drive?"

"I thought we might drop in on Mama and the rest."

"I would like to see Harold's grandfather."

"Then it's settled?"

"Not completely. We will try it out on the girls and make other arrangements about staying gone for more than ten days."

"No problem with the girls. Go is their middle name. And we can put a bigger spring on the business."

"What about the luggage?"

"Ship it down. What we will need will go in the trunk."

"We will have to take the stretch limo."

"That goes without saying."

CHAPTER THIRTY-TWO

"Butch, do you know how to get to the fish camp?"

"Get on 17 somewhere in Jacksonville, head south and turn right in Seville, stop at the first big lake."

"Do they know we are coming?"

"I talked to Mama and she is reserving two of their best cabins for us. She was all over herself about our coming."

"Is there mosquito netting over the beds?"

"Of course not, Lilly, these are fine air conditioned accommodations."

"Son, they must have made great improvements in the last ten years. Did your mother apprise you of their progress?"

"Well Dad, she mentioned they were doing well, but did not dwell on it."

"She must have indeed changed. She used to put great stock in rising above her station."

"The last few times I talked to her, she seemed more tranquil and not up tight at all. She said she now weighs only one thirty and feels great."

"Are you sure that was her and not Mary?"

"Of course. I know my own mama's voice. You know that never changes."

"A young boy's does. I saw a lot of that when I taught the third grade."

"Nellie, boys in the third grade are not old enough for their voice to change."

"You never went to school in Hooterville. Most of the desks were large enough to accommodate sixteen year olds. I used to carry a cattle prod to ward off amorous overtures."

"Horny little bastards, weren't they?"

"You better believe it. They wouldn't mess with the girls in the class because they were too young. They were afraid of being charged with child molestation."

"They weren't as old as the boys?"

"No, they were the right age for the class. You know, girls are more intelligent than boys."

"That's a bunch of shit. Most of the girls I knew were airheads."

"As I have stated, Butch, you didn't go to school in Hooterville."

"Now that you mention it, I knew very few boys at Ga. Tech from South Georgia. And none at all from Hooterville."

"The lucky ones that did go to college went to Athens."

"Why was that?"

"Football scholarships."

"We had a football team also."

"What do nerds know about football?"

"All of us weren't nerds."

"Did you play?"

"Some."

"Your physical attributes qualified you, but did your mental?"

"I kept my intelligence under wraps the first year, then I considered a good education should take priority."

"A wise decision."

"Considering the path I chose, you are right. I had no desire to involve myself in politics."

"Didn't you know how to lie?"

"I wasn't too good at it. I never developed the quality of lying while eyeball to eyeball."

"What would you do, look at your feet and your ears turn red?"

"Something like that."

"You would have never made it. You need to get a shit-eating grin on your face and roll your eyeballs to one side. And answer difficult questions with, 'we're working on that. I'll get back to you later'."

"I couldn't do that. I would stutter and utter a lot of ers."

"I always felt my son was too honest to be a good politician. And they have to be lawyers and everybody knows all good lawyers went to the University of Georgia."

"And play football."

"I can't believe Effie Lou has lost so much weight, son, they must not have soaps down there, or chocolate covered cherries."

"She said everybody carries their portion of the load."

"What kind of load has she?"

"She runs a fine restaurant."

"Most cooks sample their cooking and get fat."

"She doesn't cook. She does the buying and carries a big stick to keep the help from stealing."

"I used to carry a cattle prod."

"We know, Nellie."

"You do? How in the world could you know that?"

"You just told us about ten miles up the road."

"That must have been when we saw that big lake on the left."

"That was the St. Johns river."

"Were we in Jacksonville?"

"No Nellie. We went through there way back up the road"

"Couldn't have. I didn't see the roller coaster."

"That was out at the beach and it isn't there anymore."

"That's a shame, I wanted to ride it again."

"The old wood ones get rickety and are condemned."

"Like the one at Lakewood Park?"

"Yes, most all the old ones are gone now."

"That's a shame. Stop as soon as you can, Butch. Nature is calling."

"That's a good idea, I need to stretch my legs."

"Aren't they long enough now?"

"That was a figure of speech, Nellie."

"Figure this speech, I got to go!"

"I saw a sign about a flea market right ahead. We'll stop there."

"We don't need any fleas."

"They don't sell fleas, they just call it that."

"What do they sell?"

"Assorted merchandise."

"Like Carl sells at the auction?"

"Some, but not all of it. Sometimes they have fine bargains on new stuff and they sell it much cheaper than the stores."

"How can they do that?"

"Sometimes a retailer goes belly up and closes his store with a big auction.

The people that buy everything store it maybe in a spare bedroom and brings some of it to the flea markets. They have very little overhead."

"Dad, explain to Nellie."

"What do you think I have been doing for the last ten years?"

"Carl, there must be something you neglected to explain to me. I'm still confused."

"I love you, Nellie."

* * *

"Nellie, do you think it's safe to use these facilities?"

"Lilly, give me that disinfectant spray you carry in your bag. I'll stand on the seat."

"Don't slip. I'd have to call a plumber to extricate you from that john."

"Where would you find a plumber?"

"I saw a man in a booth coming in that had a lot of bathroom fixtures and he might could do it."

"I'll be extra careful. I do not wish to expose myself to a perfect stranger."

"He didn't look too perfect to me."

"That was another figure of speech, Lilly."

"Hurry up. Watching you has given me the urge."

"Now where in the hell have our men got off to?"

"I see them over in aisle four. I wonder what they're doing?"

"It looks like they are arguing with the salesperson."

"You can't call him a salesperson. Look at those overalls and that straw hat."

"What would you call him?"

"Possibly a Florida redneck."

"Do they have those down here?"

"I think they are everywhere. Let's go over and see what is so important."

"What's up, Honey?"

"Dad and I found something we are interested in and the booth manager thinks we are some stupid Yankees."

"Nellie, see what they are called."

"I thought a manager had to wear a coat and tie."

"Undoubtedly not at a Florida flea market."

"Sir, you look like a man with above the average intelligence, who might recognize the same qualities in me. And in doing so, do you actually believe I would pay the price you are asking for these items?"

"Forgive me for misjudging you. I presumed you came from Pennsylvania and acquired some of the local dialect for the sole purpose of deceiving me. In our bargaining, I have discovered a true Southern gentleman."

"Now that we understand each other, let's resume our haggling."

"I do not consider this haggling. You are in the process of trying to chisel me and I am involved in protecting my interests."

"I do not fault one for doing what he is impelled to do, but save your spiel for some legitimate tourists and give me the bottom line for all these items."

"I must get all I can to supplement my meager social security allotment, which places me and mine below the poverty level."

"Do you report this supplement?"

"Of course! Do I look like one who cheats his beloved government?"

"No more than I."

"We are all brothers under the skin. I do not like to give in to intimidation, but I recognize the needs of brothers and I will give you a colossal discount if you take all the said items."

"What is your interpretation of 'colossal'?"

"Fifty percent."

"Sold! Butch, bring the car around and let's load."

"Dad, there's at least ten cases here. Where will we put them?"

"Possibly this fine gentleman has some rope so we can tie the boxes on the roof."

"Yes sir, I happen to have this new roll of parachute shroud lines which I am prepared to sell at a bargain."

"I won't need the whole roll. How about just selling me what we will need?"

"I can't break the roll. If I did, I wouldn't know how much is left, and I would have to measure every purchase."

"What do you want for the roll?"

"Well, there's five hundred feet on that roll and I normally get ten cents a foot for it. If you take it all I'll let you have it for five cents a foot."

"Butch, how much do you think it will take to secure our merchandise?"

"Dad, buy the whole damn roll and let's get out of here. Maybe mama can use the rest as fishing line."

"Young man, what does your mama fish for, whales? If she does she might want some of these fine used harpoons I happen to have at a bargain."

"No thank you. The lake she lives on has no whales, she probably will us the rope to tie up alligators."

"Alligators are protected down here. I can't understand why. They will eat your dogs and I've heard they can carry off small children."

"That's horrible. I hope they don't get Junior's pretty coon dogs."

"Nellie, we saw those dogs over ten years ago and I didn't see any alligators around there."

"Lilly, were you looking for any?"

"No. I was too busy looking for snakes."

"I wonder what happened to Junior and Bubba and all those dogs? They were sweet."

"Who, Junior and Bubba?"

"Lawd no! I was talking about the dogs."

"Don't tell me you all know Junior and Bubba. Why, they have a booth over on aisle ten."

"Oh Carl, let's go see them."

"Nellie, it's probably not the same ones."

"I guess you are right. But it won't hurt to find out."

"Well, all right. It won't take but a minute."

"Sir, is this aisle ten?"

"Yes it is, can I interest you in some of these fine pipe wrenches? They are practically new and I need to move them today. My rent's due and I haven't sold doodley shit today."

"I'm sorry, but I have no need for them. Can you direct us to Bubba and Junior's table?"

"Sir, if you are going to see them, you'll need at least one of these wrenches to protect yourself. They're two mean sons of bitches. Just last week they sent a man to the hospital when they caught him shoplifting. They had to take ten stitches in his head and he been walking wobbly ever since."

"We don't shoplift. We just want to speak to them. We haven't seen them in over ten years. And we don't know if they're the same ones."

"Could be. There's not too many around here."

"Too many what?"

"Mamn, I believe we were talking about Bubbas and Juniors."

"Oh."

"Nellie, I swear I believe it's really them. Junior looks fatter and the other one, that I presume is Bubba looks a lot older now."

"Lilly, remember it's been over ten years since we saw them. Most teenagers do get older."

"Some of the wild and crazy ones don't."

"You're right. I know some forty year old teenagers."

"I didn't mean that. I was referring to the ones that get killed in automobiles."

"I saw one get killed once. He passed me on a hill and ran head on into a peanut picker."

"Did it kill the peanut picker?"

"It was a machine,"

"Oh. Did it hurt the driver?"

"You don't drive peanut pickers. You operate them."

"Whatever. Did it hurt the operator / picker?"

"No, he landed in the peanuts."

"Did you know him?"

"Oh, no. I think he was imported."

"What do you mean? Was he a wetback?"

"I don't know about that. I thought he was a greenback. There was green stain all over his back."

"Probably from lying in wet grass, bareback."

"I always thought that was the woman's position."

"I doubt that. He would have picked a nice shady spot under a tree."

"Perhaps there was an urgent need at the time."

"If there was, then he was a lazy bastard. The idea! Letting a woman do all the work."

"Lilly, must you always involve the sex thing in all dialog?"

"I have been known to converse on other matters."

"Name one instance."

"I'll have to take some time to remember."

"Sugar, you do seem to have a preoccupation on that subject."

"Butch, would you like it any other way?"

"When we have been married fifty years, we will have to discuss this again."

"Do you think we will last that long?"

"Not the way we go at it."

"Go at what?"

"Nellie, I think it is time to see if that is really Junior and Bubba."

"You're right Carl, we do seem to stray frequently."

"Constantly rather than frequently. Hello, sirs, I am told you two answer to the names of Junior and Bubba."

"And if we do?"

"We had a mild exposure about ten years ago in South Georgia to two fine souls known as you are called. We were curious as to whether you might be the same."

"As a matter of fact, we did reside up in God's country back then and so it is a possibility we are they. Under what circumstances might have we met?"

"Our station wagon got stuck on the shoulder north of Hooterville dodging a wild hog and we enlisted the aid of two gentlemen with a John Deere tractor to extricate said vehicle. These two lived about a quarter mile off the road and had the finest lot of black and tan coon dogs I have ever seen."

"By God! That was us. Did you all get to Atlanta in one piece? We never heard any more of you. We were concerned of your welfare, seeing the lovely distractions accompanying you."

"Indeed we did. As a matter of fact we wed these two fine distractions forthwith and now are celebrating our tenth."

"Tenth what?"

"Wedding anniversary. You must have recently moved down here and not been able to partake in South Georgia's great barbecue."

"Unfortunately that is not the case. Old habits are hard to break. Lord knows we try. After we lost the old home place, Bubba and I enlisted at ABAC in Tifton to improve our lot. But this was to no avail. Our ways were too ingrained. Even though I must admit our speech improved somewhat."

"You say you lost that fine home we saw you at? What in the world happened?"

"After mammy and pappy died in a shootout one Saturday night at the festivities closing the week of the annual coon hunt contest, which by the way they took first place, thanks to our fine brace of dogs. There were some innuendoes that our parents might have cheated. Of course pappy was forced to defend his honor and in the ensuing altercations, our dear parents succumbed in a fusillade of buckshot. Sheriff Buford investigated and it determined it was an unfortunate accident."

"Really?"

"Yes, the carnage he viewed, he stated was the worst he had ever been exposed to. No one escaped without wounds of various degrees. What was worst, a lot of fine coon dogs died that night, trying to defend their masters. Such a tragedy. Such a waste."

"What a shame!"

"Yes, we lost all our dogs. We buried mammy and pappy on the back side of our property where we felt the wild hogs would not molest their remains and tried to go on with life."

"And?"

"With pappy gone our income was gone. You see, he had a still and made the finest moonshine in the area. He had his own secret recipe that he had not the foresight to pass on to us. One day Bubba was trying to run off a batch and let the boiler get too hot and it blew, causing a great conflagration, which without control wiped our fine stand of virgin timber and the old home place. The ground was covered with pine straw a foot deep. Pappy always said when it got two feet deep; he would call in the trucks and sell it for a fortune. Alas, this was not to be. We sold the scorched land at an auction and got enough money to go to Tifton and enroll in the college. We tried to work after school to keep going but it was not to be. About all we knew to do were bus tables and that didn't bring in enough money. Then we set up a stall in a local flea market and things got better. In fact, things got so good we said to hell with college and started full time at our new endeavor. The market was only open on weekends and that gave the rest of the week to glean. We were the ones that introduced the fine art of dumpster diving to Tifton."

"Why did you leave?"

"Tifton is a small town and as soon as word got out about what we were doing, everybody started diving. The competition was so great, we had to seek greener pastures, and so we moved down here near Jacksonville with its unlimited resources. Especially with so many boats bringing all that shit made in Taiwan and Japan. A lot of merchandise has a way of getting lost on the way to the great warehouses."

"Ah, a golden opportunity."

"Yes, but it is hard work."

"I can imagine. And the fear of getting caught."

"No, not that. It's the moving and storing heavy crates. You see, we cannot display our wares as if we had an unlimited supply. That would demoralize the market and prices would tumble. We must bring out a few pieces at a time."

"You are not approaching this problem right. If there is indeed an unlimited supply, then you should wholesale it to other dealers."

"That would create a lot of unwanted exposure, which might be considered hazardous to our health and freedom."

"Surely other avenues can be found. How about all the bankruptcies that can be exploited?"

"We have considered that, but it would take someone with a lot of clout."

"That, I am proud to say I have."

"Really?"

"I now do not have the time to involve myself at the present, but when we get back from our cruise I will be back to talk to you again."

"We shall look forward to your return. And all of you have a nice cruise. When does your ship leave?"

"Oh not for another week or so. We intend some time with my ex wife and her husband. They have a fish camp out of Seville."

"I know the place well. They serve fine food at the restaurant, even though it has a Latin flavor. It seems unusual a former husband and wife still get along."

"There were extenuating circumstances involved. She had a thing for my service manager."

"This is no concern of mine as long as is does not affect our future relationship."

"Trust me, it shall not."

CHAPTER THIRTY-THREE

"Carl, you're not going to involve us in an illicit activity, are you?"

"Of course not, honey, but I have a few ideas on how to clean up his operation."

"But why bother? We certainly don't need more money. Our grandchildren will be hard put to piss it away even in their lifetime."

"Grandchildren? Nellie, I can't believe my ears. You have yet to drop any kids yourself, and you have never gave me reason to believe you were so inclined."

"Well, maybe step-grandchildren."

"Lilly, what in the hell is she referring to? You and Butch aren't making babies are you?"

"Up to now we have been only making fun, but one's mind does wander to a more productive endeavor."

"Well, I'll be damned! What happened to the fun and frolic bit?"

"There is a time for all things and that time is drawing to a close. I think about growing old with Butch, not that I'll mind that part but we might need something different to keep us occupied."

"You have made a good point, I'm getting too old to start a new family and you and Butch could make Nellie and I proud grandparents."

"I was thinking more along the lines of a bunch of champion black and tan coon hounds."

"Butch, damn you! Here we are talking serious shit and you talk about dogs."

"Lilly, I'll make a deal with you. You can have all the babies you want and I'll love and care for them, but I still want a few dogs. I have never forgot that soulful look those of Bubba's gave me when we were riding in the back of that old pickup truck. They needed a lot of tender love."

"All I remember about them were their long tongues and wiggly tails."

"They were men dogs and only had rapport with the same gender. Let's defer this matter to more appropriate moments. I believe we were discussing Dad's latest hair brained scheme."

"It is not so wild. I'm no good at making babies, but I damn well know how to make money. And I think this is a wonderful opportunity to join up with two hard working souls who are now down on their luck. You might consider it just a favor returned."

"Dad, I must admit you are successful in most everything you stick your finger into."

"Most everything? Ha! Name one that did not turn out as planned."

All three in unison, "Camels!"

"Name two!"

Silence.

"I have made my point."

"Sugar, why do you keep looking out the rear view mirror? You're not speeding are you?"

"No Lilly, I'm just checking on Dad's merchandise. It's piled real high on the top of the car and I am afraid if I speed, some may blow off."

"You did secure it properly, Son?'

"To the best of my ability with the meager length of cord at my disposal."

"Meager length? My God, you had five hundred feet!"

"You know I'm not too adept at securing things, so I wove a net around the whole caboodle."

"Maybe Effie Lou can use it for a fish net."

"I doubt it. It will have to be cut off at each intersection."

"That sounds like a wild police chase or a posse trying to catch some bank robbers."

"Who robbed a bank?"

"Nellie, I love you."

"I know, but why?"

"I guess it's your way with words."

"Are we there yet? I'm getting hungry. I got to pee."

"Who needs kids? No dear, we have still a long way to go."

"We'll stop in Palatka and eat."

"That's where they got married."

"Who, Butch?"

"No Nellie, we got married in Atlanta. Don't you remember? It was the same time you and Carl did."

"Did what?"

"Get married."

"Oh, then who got married in Palatka?"

"Effie Lou and Jonas and Mary and Phillip."

"Oh. How far is this Palatka place?"

"About thirty miles."

"I can't wait. Stop the car."

"I think there's something up ahead. Just cross your legs and squirm."

* * *

"I wish you would just look at this place. I know I have never been here before, but it looks mighty familiar. It's weird."

"There are places like this all over South Georgia and Northern Florida."

"It must be a chain."

"I don't think so. The builders were cost conscious."

"I'm not really hungry. It was a subterfuge to get immediate relief."

"We should get at least a token amount for using the facilities."

Because this was not the noon rush hour and all the help was off for a while, the owner waddles over and greets them. "Hello folks, what will you have?"

"Just bring us a token."

"Beg your pardon, Mamn?"

"That's what my husband said we should order."

"Sir, could you be more explicit?"

"Just bring me an order of fries and a T-bone on the side."

"Make mine the same."

"And what would you ladies desire?"

"Nellie, I think I want some catfish. Are they de-boned?"

"We have some filet."

"I thought that was a small steak."

"Would you prefer that?"

"What?"

"A prime Filet de Migon broiled to perfection, bacon wrapped and served with a delicate mushroom sauce."

"If you can do that to a catfish, I'll take it."

"Me too."

"Ladies, this request is somewhat unusual, but we can try."

"You mean you want a catfish filet bacon wrapped with mushroom sauce?"

"If that's possible, Carl."

"Lady, for enough money, I'll put a propeller on that filet and make it fly."

"That won't be necessary. I don't feel like chasing a flying fish."

"If you so desire, we can furnish a butterfly net."

"Just do what you have to do. All this conversation is making me hungry."

"Thank you. Now if that will be all, I'll place the order with the cook with the special instructions."

A few minutes later a huge black man with a tall white cook's cap came over to their table and asked who ordered the special fish filet.

"My female friend and I, why, is there a problem?"

"Not really, I always like to meet those rare customers with unusual requests. Where before have you experienced such a delight?"

"We haven't, it just sounded delicious."

"Well this is a first for me too, and under these circumstances, we cannot guarantee the outcome and it can't be sent back."

"Sent back where?"

"To the kitchen."

"Oh, I thought maybe you meant back to the farm. We ordered it and we will eat it if at all possible."

"Let us know how you like it. We might add it to our regular bill of fare."

"What's that?"

"Just a sophisticated term for the menu."

"That won't be hard to do. Just scratch through the phone number and add it there. It doesn't need the phone number anyway."

"Why do you say that?"

"Well, if someone is sitting here and reading the menu, they wouldn't need to call over the phone. I see a pay phone over there and it would be more economical to just holler."

"That would do for the menus placed on the tables, but a lot of our clientele likes to take one home so they can call up and order in advance. And sometimes they want us to deliver."

"Really? You do deliver?"

"In some cases. We have a three wheeled motor scooter for that purpose."

"Cushman, no doubt."

"Yes, it was originally one used by the local post office. The post person wrecked it one day after stopping at house where a pre-Christmas party was going on and he was invited in for a sip of eggnog. Unfortunately he overindulged and ran off into that frog pond up the road. The postmaster considered it totaled and sold it to us. A lot of wet mail was delivered the next day. By, I might add, a new carrier."

"What happened to the old one?"

"Well, that wasn't only a frog pond. It seems a few alligators had also taken up residence in said pond and the man was never seen since."

"That's horrible."

"Yes in a way, but the mail service has really improved since then."

Carl says, "This is very interesting, but shouldn't you check on the order?"

"I don't need to check on it. It's not going anywhere till I get back."

"Well get back, we are starving."

"Yes sir!"

"Next time you girls order straight off the menu. No deviations."

"Carl, don't be an asshole. You know we like to try new things."

"In the future confine your inquisitiveness to things other than wild suggestions to inexperienced cooks in the boondocks."

"To me, he impressed as being very well versed in the art of exquisite culinary preparation. That's a fifty cent way of saying that son of a bitch wields a mean frying pan."

"Nellie, are you trying to say that concoction you dreamed is fit to eat?"

"Sugar, these morsels are probably the best tasting fish I ever popped a lip on."

"Let me try some."

"Oh Hell no! If you want some order it."

"I'm full up to my tonsils on T-bone and fries. Maybe I'll ask the chef, not cook mind you, for the recipe. I might persuade Effie Lou to prepare some later."

"Would you really, Carl? I would like to have some more later myself."

"Asking is cheap. Answers might be expensive."

"Cost is no object. I must have that recipe."

"I'll see what I can do."

Carl goes to the kitchen and sees the cook (chef) sitting at the prep table stuffing his gut on the very same type dish Nellie and Lilly had just consumed.

"By God, this is some pretty good shit. I had some left over and since I am not a wasteful person and hated to put in the can for pig slop, I felt it was my duty to try it. Thank goodness I did. Those pigs would never swill slop again."

"Is it that good?"

"Try this piece I had not eaten yet."

"But it has flies all over it."

"Shoo them off. They didn't eat much."

"But they carry germs."

"Sir, you are inferring that I am disease laden. I'll have you know I have been eating in this environment for the last fifteen years and have not been sick a day since I started work here."

"Perhaps you should catch and bottle these flies and sell them as a cure-all."

"I cannot attribute my well being exclusively to the flies."

"To what then?"

"Well, as you can see, this kitchen is not air conditioned and I sweat profusely and consume approximately a quart of gin daily. Sweat is a good way of ridding the system of poisons."

"What about the gin."

"It helps restore the fluids expelled."

"I don't do much sweating anymore and I drink Scotch exclusively."

"Single malt?"

"But of course."

"That's good, but you need to sweat more. I bet all your pores are clogged. And refrain from all these newfangled deodorants. They inhibit the natural processes."

"So I can tell."

"And they can cause sebaceous cysts in your armpits."

"Occasionally I am plagued with those. But that is a small price to pay to be socially acceptable."

"That's where the gin comes in. It dulls the senses."

"Of you or your peers?"

"Both. It is better not to deviate from your station."

"But how can you expand your horizons?"

"An occasional joint seems to suffice."

"This only takes you into a fantasy world which has no relation with what's really out there."

"Look sir, I am a poorly educated person and realized my limitations years ago. I am resigned to my lot in life and am quite comfortable with it. I need no one to come along at this late date and try to confuse me. Just shut up and try the fish."

"You are indeed truly blessed. And the fish is delicious. Flies not withstanding. My trip to your kitchen is to persuade you to part with the recipe and preparation of this dish. For my wife, of course. She loves it."

"Just tell her to stop by often and enjoy it."

"You don't understand. We are just passing through and probably never come this way again. I can make it very worth while to you to impart with this information."

"What is your conception of 'worth while'?"

"A weeks supply of your favorite gin."

"One year."

"Six months."

"Nine months."

"Done. You will need my mailing address."

"Why?"

"I am not fool enough to accept a nine months supply at one time. It would lead to my ruin. It must be sent to me weekly. You seem to be an honorable man and I trust you."

"I am. But what if should I die before?"

"Add a codicil to your will."

"Good business."

* * *

"Did you get it?"

"Of course."

"Goody. Where is it?"

"On this wrapping paper. I hope we can read it. It was done with a marking pen and took up about a yard of paper. I rolled it up and put a rubber band around it."

"It took you long enough to get it."

"I had him print it to be more legible."

"I could rewrite the entire constitution quicker than that."

"Some dialogue deviation was necessary to set the mood."

"We must set a lot of moods. We all are very proficient in that respect."

"Either a curse or blessing, I know not which."

"It is better than discussing what happened on yesterday's soaps."

"Mind expansion."

"I don't mind."

"I love you. Nellie."

"I meant I don't care."

"Oh."

CHAPTER THIRTY-FOUR

After such a vast consumption of epicurean delights, all but Butch were fast asleep. Great willpower was required for Butch not to pull off the highway and join them. But they were already far behind schedule and he was anxious to se his mama.

By the time they arrived, every one was wide-awake and were ready to greet the group that departed years ago to seek their own fortune and a new life.

"Butch, is that really your mama coming out to greet us? I wish you would look at her! She is as trim as the day we were married!"

"That's her alright Dad. I would recognize that smile anywhere. The years have been kind to her. And look at Jonas. He doesn't look a day older. They must have truly discovered the Fountain of Youth. I wonder where Mary and Phillip are. If they look as good, I will be tempted to give up the rat race in Atlanta and move down here"

Nellie comments; "I bet they keep in shape fighting off these damned mosquitoes. I have never seen so many and just look at the size of them! Why, there are some that could carry off a small child."

"Nellie, those big ones are love bugs. They look so large because they are mating."

"Lilly, what do know about love bugs? Are you an etymologist?"

"No, but I had a butterfly collection when I was a child."

"What's that got to do with love bugs?"

"In pursuit of my hobby I went far afield seeking new specimens and happened upon a community of such bugs. It was my first exposure to the sexual habits of insects. Of course I was well aware of what went on in the barnyard."

"And behind the barn too, I'll wager."

"Oh no, this was in my pre-puberty days."

"Ha! From what you told me you got it on with little Jimmy Snodgrass when you was just ten."

"Oh, we were just curious and only fooling around. We were not too sophisticated and didn't know what the Hell to do. Anyway, my pappy caught us and I got a good hide tanning on my backside. That deferred my curiosity for a few years. Of course I had to take a lot of cold showers back then."

"Things change, don't they?"

"And for the better, I must add."

"You girls stop all that prattle and greet our friends. Hello, Effie Lou, Jonas. Long time no see. I must say you both look great. Jonas, you had the vision to see what I could not. It does my heart good to see the two of you so happy."

"Carl, eat your heart out!"

"Effie Lou, that's no way to greet the father of your only child."

"I'm sorry Jonas, but I had to let it out."

"That's perfectly understandable, Effie Lou. We did have a lot if good years between us and I am perfectly content with Nellie now. One never knows what the future holds for any of us. Let's not dwell on what might have been and get on to a greater life for all"

"My, Carl, you have certainly mellowed."

"Aging and mellowing goes hand in hand."

"You got that shit right!"

"Mamma, speak to your only begotten son!"

"Butch honey! Is that really you? Of course it is! My, you have turned into a handsome hunk! Genes do have a way of working right."

"Don't forget that half are mine."

"Carl, you were just the stud. Beauty lies on the maternal side."

"Studs give strength and character."

"Mamn, I can personally testify to the truth of that statement. He is all you both say he is and I am prepared to stay with him for the rest of my days."

"That's sweet, Lilly and I wish the best for you both."

"Thank you."

"And that goes for you too, Nellie. And of course, Carl."

"Thanks, even though it was an afterthought."

"I'm sorry, Carl. I am all flustered seeing all of you again after such a long time."

"Where are Mary, Phillip and what's his name?"

"His name is Adolph and they had to run up to Palatka this morning. They should be arriving back any time now. Let's all go into the restaurant and have something cool and get away from all these bugs."

"That would be beneficial. Lead the way!"

"We have lemonade, tea and any kind of soft drinks you would like."

"Mamma, you seem to have a well equipped bar so I assume you have something a mite harder than the list you have just recited and my throat is exceedingly dry at this moment."

"What's your pleasure, Honey?"

"I could use a cold beer."

"Anybody else?"

"I think we all could."

"Any particular type?"

"Bar brand is fine."

"That will be draught. And it's not from horses."

"I hope not."

"Jose! Draw four."

"Si, Si."

"And bring me a lemonade."

"Si, Si."

"Where did you get him?"

"Oh, he's a second generation Cuban expatriate."

"This far north?"

"Miami will not hold them all now. They multiply like rabbits."

"You habla Espanola?"

"Enough to get by. And I use a lot of sign language."

"No trouble?"

"They are hard workers and are very grateful to be living in the Promised Land."

"No trouble?"

"Well, they keep me busy helping them with their automobiles."

"Break down a lot, Jonas?"

"Weekly."

"Old?"

"Antiques. All of them seem to be on a nostalgia kick."

"Antiques are one thing, derelicts are another."

"Theirs are both. But Jonas doesn't mind. In fact, he enjoys it."

"Still likes to get his hands dirty, huh?"

"Its in his genes. But he cleans up before bed."

"Same old Jonas."

"Carl, there's a lot of satisfaction and challenge in these old cars. They can be repaired without a lot of special tools and knowledge, not at all like the new ones. They lost me when they did away with carburetors and went to computers. I can't even fix Effie Lou's new Cadillac. Have to bite he bullet and take it back to the dealer. It embarrasses the shit out of me every time I take it in and some young smart ass hooks up the analyzer and it tells him what part to replace. Thank Heaven it's still in the warranty. If one of our Cuban boys ever buys one, I'll fire him on the spot. I don't know what's going to happen when these monsters go out of warranty."

"They still sell at our auction."

"How can that be?"

"We enjoy an uninformed clientele and sell as is."

"Caveat Emptor."

"You got that shit right! And a lot of these new 'mechanics' moonlight in their garage for their friends. In fact I employ some to help get my cars running good enough to move through the auction."

"I guess I'm just an old dog that can't learn new tricks."

"I can't believe that. It's probably because you don't want to. Why should you?"

"I guess you're right. I don't have to. It might be different if I still worked for you. I think I enjoy what I'm doing down here, but I might be fooling myself. I still have a latent itch."

"Jonas, you never told me that."

"Honey, this has nothing to do with our relationship. You have made me perfectly happy and I don't regret a minute of it. Besides, I had my hands full getting you back in shape."

"Jonas, I must say you did a wonderful job."

"Carl, I must admit it was a great challenge and I am proud of my accomplishment."

"You assholes are talking like I was an old car that Jonas has restored"

"Well, you look like you just come off the assembly line. Don't you feel better now?"

"Carl, you are right. Jonas was my restorer. It's no telling where I would have wound up if not for him. And I am grateful. I'm sorry I spoke so harshly."

"Mom, you have nothing to apologize for. I am glad to see you in such fine shape and so happy. Of course I miss you, but seeing you now I feel it was the right thing to do."

"Enough of this syrupy drivel. Let's get on with the present and immediate future. Like what are you people going to want for dinner?"

"I had a wonderful new dish for lunch up the road and I think you will like it, Effie Lou."

"Is it easy to fix?"

"I think so. I have the recipe in my purse."

Nellie hands it to Effie Lou and when she starts to read it, she first starts to read it, she grimaced and the starts grinning. "Is this for real? Who in the hell came up with this? Who fixed it? Who wrote this? Why?"

"In the proper order, yes, the cook, he did, and I wanted to try it. Any more questions?"

"You say it was good?"

"Delicious."

"Well, I'll be damned! Sounds worse than catfish stew."

"I like catfish stew too."

"I didn't say it wasn't good, Lilly. I like the taste, but it looks yucky."

"So does pizza, but ain't it good?"

"Without anchovies."

Lilly says, "I like anchovies."

"It takes all kinds, Nellie."

"To do what?"

"Eat every thing that's cooked. I hear tell some even eat possum."

"Not me, they look like overgrown rats."

"They are marsupials."

"Mar what, Nellie?"

"Marsupials. Mom, they carry their young in a pouch like kangaroos."

"I have never eaten those either."

"You won't have a chance unless you go to Australia."

"That's something else I don't intend to do."

"What?"

"Go to Australia."

"I wouldn't mind, could we go Carl?"

"Not in the near future. We haven't even got to the Bahamas yet. And the way this conversation is going, even that seems a long way off."

"Never fear sugar, we'll make it."

"I'm getting to like it here, now that we are inside where the bugs can't get to us"

Jonas jumps in, "Carl, they are not too bad. You should have been with me way back once when I went down to Louisiana to help a friend build a fishing shack down in the bayou. Man, they were eating us alive. There was one of those big syrup kettles in the yard. I guess they call them kettles; it looked like a cross between a wash pot and a World War One helmet. Anyway this whatever it was, was out in the yard-"

"You already said that."

"Said what?"

"Out in the yard."

"Excuse me, sometimes I get carried away."

"To where?"

"That was one of those figures of speech, Nellie."

"Oh, go on, Jonas."

"Where was I?"

"You were talking about whatever it was."

"Oh yes, anyway we spied it before the mosquitoes ate us up and we crawled under it. It was big enough to hold four people. I was leaning against one side when I felt a prick in my arm. I jumped back and ran my finger across the wall and felt something like a needle. I say to my buddy 'buddy run your finger across this'."

"Buddy says, my Gawd one of those attackers has stuck his stinger through the wall."

"He had brought his claw hammer with him, it was in that little strap on the side of his overalls. He took said hammer and proceeded to brad the beak. Before he finished, another popped through the wall, and then another, but he kept on. The sound was deafening. Suddenly we saw light around the bottom of whatever it was. It was being lifted! When it rose high enough, we reached around the edge and grabbed the two handles that were located on the outside of whatever it was. We were swinging in mid air and holding on for dear life. I asked my buddy what was happening. He said they were taking us back to their camp for the big ones. Before it got too high, we turned loose and dropped in the water next to the shack. The last we saw of them they were heading south."

"Did the fall hurt?"

"Not as much as those alligators that kept nipping at our asses."

"Needless to say you survived."

"Yes, and I have yet to return to Louisiana."

"I am glad you have not lost your touch."

"In what way, Carl?"

"In your flair of digging yourself out of quagmires you create with your vivid imagination."

"Thank you. You're no questioning my veracity, are you?"

"Absolutely not."

"Honey, you never told me about this."

"Love, this was way before I had the pleasure of meeting you. Many things had happened in my young life. Too many for me to remember until some like subject is discussed."

"I think I hear Adolph turning off the highway now."

"Mama, how can you, considering the distance from here?"

"Its like this, you see his muffler fell off his rattletrap about five years ago and he refuses to buy a new one."

"New what?"

"Muffler or automobile, Nellie."

"I wonder why?"

"He says his horn doesn't work and if he were to install a new muffler, he would have to buy a new horn also so people would get out of his way."

"And another car?"

"He says it has sentimental value. And long as it runs as good as it does, he sees no need."

"How can he tell if the motor is knocking?"

"That's the beauty of it. If he can't hear it, he doesn't have to worry about it."

"Does he have no self-esteem?"

"He says material things do not count."

"He sounds like Harold."

"In a lot of ways they are alike. Let me tell you what he did a few years back. I don't remember exactly when, but it wasn't too long after he appeared down here. One day he disappeared and was gone for three days. When he returned, there was happiness and peace written all over his old wrinkled face."

"Where had he gone and what did he do?"

"He told me he just walked off into the woods to commune with nature and he came across a clearing where nothing but Saint Augustine grass grew. No palmettos saw grass, vines or bushes."

"How strange."

"That's not all. In the center of this clearing was, made of small stones and cemented together with tabby, a tall obelisk maybe twenty-five feet high, surrounded by a circle of like stones with a radius of approximately thirty-feet."

"Unbelievable."

"And when he stepped into the circle, he thought he was struck stone deaf. It was like when you come back down from a high altitude and the pressure increases on your eardrums before they pop. When he stepped back with alarm, he then heard the natural sounds of the wilderness. Birds singing, wind blowing and a high altitude jet passing overhead. And his ears did not pop. He then re-entered the circle and it happened again. He spoke out loud just to determine if he could really hear. He could, and his voice sounded like beautiful music. Then he tried singing, which he could not normally do and he sounded like one that had been voice trained since childhood. He had a small transistor radio in his pocket that he turned on and it sounded like a great symphony orchestra performing in Carnegie Hall. And there he sat, enraptured for three days."

"Why did he come back?"

"He got hungry. And he ate enough to last him three more days. He goes back now about once a month. We don't mind, he is a better person because of it."

"Maybe we should go."

"I'd like to, Carl, and we have been thinking about it, but we feel we should all go together, and we can't get off at the same time."

"Mamma, I have a suggestion. Get Adolph to take you four and we will stay here and watch the store. But don't stay three days."

"Don't worry about that. I can't go one day without food."

"Could Adolph before he first went?"

"Come to think of it, no. He couldn't go six hours."

"There may be nutrients in that strange atmosphere. If there are, we must find a way to insure your return."

"I'll take a large ball of twine and pay it out along the way. If we don't return in a reasonable length of time, send either Butch or Carl to get us."

"What if we don't return?"

"The rest of you come on in and to hell with everything else! Sounds like nothing else is important anyway."

"I've often wondered just what is important and what is not."

"It's all relative."

"To what?"

"Your environment. And everyone's is different."

"Yes we are all either victims or products."

"I thought free will was involved."

"Once it may have been, but I fear no more. There are too many thing that are not under our control."

"You mean that this may be our escape hatch?"

"It could be, but it might also be some kind of a trap. Remember the cats."

"I would rather believe it is that Golden Stairway to Heaven."

"That would be nice, but I think you have to work for that."

"Who knows for certain?"

"Only the ones that have gone on before us. And we would rather use an alternative route."

In unison: "Amen!"

"I see the enraptured one and his passengers have returned. He may shed some new light on this."

"Well, look who has arrived. Hello Carl, Nellie, Butch and Lilly. Its so nice to see all of you after such a long time."

"Hi Mary and Phillip, and I presume this is Adolph?"

"I guess you are Carl whom I have heard so much about."

"All good, I hope."

"We are not prone to discuss the shortcomings of others, since we have so many ourselves."

"And the ones that have no virtue?"

"None exists. And you must be Butch, Harold's good friend."

"I am a better person by having known him, God rest his soul."

"And I feel a great loss by never knowing him. But I feel I will join him soon."

"How can you say that? You are the picture of health."

"That is precisely why I feel as I do."

"I don't understand."

"You have not been to 'my place'."

"Your place?"

"I say 'my place' because I feel it was placed there for me to discover."

"And if I go?"

"You may feel differently. Everyone else even may. I have been prepared by a long life."

"You sound like you have given up."

"Oh no, it's just I feel that I have no more horizons to seek here."

"Let me ask you a few questions concerning it."

"If it is in my power to answer."

'I think you can. For instance, does this place feel like an enclosure or another dimension?"

"Both, that may be hard to explain. While I was first there I had some of the same thoughts and did some investigating."

"And?"

"First I walked in and out of the perimeter around the stones and discovered this quality was confined to the area embraced by the circle of stones. Then I asked myself if it was a finite enclosure or an infinite open ended cylinder."

"Did you determine which?"

"Yes."

"How?"

"First I climbed to the very top of the stone structure, which was easy because of its crude construction with plenty of foot and hand holds to gain purchase. Once at the top, with my head above the apex, I heard the natural sounds again. I first assumed it was a cylinder, but after some thought, I felt this geometrical does not appear in nature."

"How did you resolve this question?"

"The next time I went, I took my 'ear extension'."

"What in the world was that?"

"I'm glad you asked. I was very proud of my ingenuity. I went to Radio Shack and bought one of those inexpensive high output crystal lapel microphones and some shielded cable and connected it to my radio's volume control. Then I took one of our longest bamboo fishing poles and attached the microphone to the small end. Viola! My 'ear extension'!"

"Ingenious!"

"Thank you. Then with pole in hand, I proceeded once more to climb the structure. In this way, I could determine the shape."

"Which was?"

"A perfect hemisphere."

"Hold it! These also do not appear in nature."

"I know. And I am at a loss to explain it."

"This I have got to see."

"You can't see it, only feel."

"Then I want to feel. And I'm sure the rest of does too."

"I think it unwise for all of you to go together, maybe one at a time. This is a personal uplifting experience that is between you and your creator and must be done alone."

"Why do you say that?"

"A person's personality changes to accommodate others around them. It is like going under the knife on the operating table. No one can go with you. Regardless of how much you love them or they love you."

"Have you ever been operated on?"

"No"

"Then you have not ever thought of it."

Carl says; "I know exactly what you are talking about. When I was younger, I had a hernia repair and I'm here to tell you it is damned personal."

"I had a root canal done once."

"Nellie, I don't think that qualifies you. You probably had a local."

"No, it was done down in Tallahassee."

"Nellie, I love you."

"When can we go?"

"It will have to be on a Monday. That's our most slack time."

"Effie Lou, Adolph has said it would be best if we did not go at the same time.

"We could stand outside the dome and watch."

"You can't watch in an operating room and you can't watch this. Butch seems the most anxious and I will take him alone first. I assure you he will be all right. And then he can determine whether the rest of you should go en masse."

"You probably know best, since you seem to be the expert on this."

"No, Effie Lou, I'm not an expert. But I feel closer to Butch in the short time I have known him, maybe because he was so close to Harold."

"Yes, he was close to Harold, much closer than I and I was his mother or rather I gave birth to him. I don't know what I mean by that, but that's the way I feel."

"Mary, some people belong to no one and everyone at the same time."

"They belong to the ages."

"Phillip, what did you and Mary discuss with Adolph on your short trip?"

"Nothing."

"Why?"

"As you know, his wagon is not air-conditioned and what with the windows down and no muffler, we did not have a chance."

"You couldn't outrun the noise?"

"He won't drive fast enough."

"I'm trying for a half-million miles and I think I will make it."

"No way, at the speed you drive you won't live long enough."

"Be that as it may. I want it to last as long as I."

"If you decide to go into the dome and stay, what should we do with your car?"

"Give it to some of the hired help."

"From the comments I've heard from them, there is small chance of that/."

"Then dump into the lake as a fish habitat."

"There are laws against pollution."

"Call the crusher."

CHAPTER THIRTY-FIVE

It was hard for Butch to enjoy the food, drink and camaraderie of Saturday night with the dome on his mind waiting for Monday. They had designated it 'the dome' for want of a better description because they did not know what it was or what purpose it would serve. Adolph had no more curiosity about it. Just like he used to enjoy sex, he did not question the motive; he just enjoyed the pleasure it gave.

Later that night Butch and Adolph were strolling alone among the oaks and enjoying the chirps of the crickets and the hooting of the owls.

"Adolph, tell me more."

"About what, Butch?"

"The dome, what else?"

"What else, indeed! I thought you might have other things on your mind."

"How could I? Your experience has fascinated me."

"I have had other experiences. A person doesn't live to my ripe old age without many fascinating things happening."

"This is true, Adolph, and I have many myself. But all pales into insignificance compared to yours with the dome."

"I understand your curiosity. You are still young with a questioning mind. But I have learned to accept things I do not understand without wondering about the what for. Unless a person learns how to use the dormant cells of the brain, it will always be thus. Just be happy and thankful and enjoy."

"You're right, I enjoy certain types of music without understanding or try to analyze the rapture. Also sex."

"I don't remember the latter, but I still enjoy music. So I am not in a position to comment."

"We are straying."

"As we all are prone to do, Butch, especially your group."

"It is difficult to maintain a sensible dialog with minds so diverse."

"We are not in your 'group' at the present time, so act accordingly."

"I shall try."

"What was the main topic? I have forgotten."

"The dome."

"Ah yes, I feel it is not of this world, at least when I'm inside it. Well, maybe a small amount outside the large perimeter also."

"Is it different from where we stand now?"

"By all means. There are no insects in the grass or the air. And it is at least twenty degrees cooler than the forest surrounding it. And since I have been visiting, the grass has not grown to a point where is needs cutting."

"That sounds like a perfect place to build a home."

"That would be a violation of the sanctity which makes it so unique."

"I understand."

"You may think you do, but you have to experience the feeling before you completely will."

"Do you believe there is any danger of the possibility of me not wanting to return back to my group?"

"I think that would be better answered by you. Have you done and seen all you want to?"

"Hell no."

"Then you will return. If only to take your wife with you."

"Do you mean we might both stay?"

"I cannot answer that. I only know that if my wife and I happened upon it years ago after my son was killed, we would have never came back to the misery we suffered."

"Heavy."

"Yes, when I am 'in' I have no regrets about what has happened to me or my family. I feel a peace I have never known before."

"Like being 'born again'?"

"Possibly, I have no experience with that. But I have been exposed to some who claim they have, and unless they continuously practice their religion, they have a tendency to 'backslide' as the Baptists call it."

"Do you think that will happen to you?"

"The temptations of the flesh have long since abandoned me."

"And your ego?"

"The dome has erased that."

"I don't think I am ready for that yet."

"Then don't go."

"I think you are right. Maybe if I find I have an incurable illness, I might reconsider."

"That might be a calculated risk. Then it might be too late."

"Be that as it may, I'm not ready yet."

"What will you tell the rest of your people?"

"I will attempt to dissuade them as you have me."

"You are wise beyond your years."

"Whatever you decide to do, it has been a pleasure to know you and I wish you all the luck in the world."

"And others too, I hope."

* * *

"Dad, I have decided to not go into the dome with Adolph."

"Why, son?"

"I believe it is dangerous for people like us."

"And how did you arrive at this conclusion?"

"It's a place to depart when you are ready. And I don't think any of us fit in that category, yet."

"The only place I want to go in the immediate future is the dining room and fill up on breakfast and then go to that damned boat."

"I'm with you, heaven can wait."

The rest of the group had already started eating when they came dragging in.

"What kept you two? You knew we were to meet here at seven so we can discuss the trip to the dome."

"That's exactly what Dad and I were doing."

"Doing what?'

"Discussing the dome, Nellie."

"What about the so called dome, Butch?"

"We have decided not to expose our loved ones to such a temptation in fear the experience will alter your wonderful personalities."

"Any alteration may be an improvement."

"Are you not satisfied with your present state of mind, Nellie?"

"Of course I am, but I might appreciate some help in the confusion department."

"Nellie, I love you and your confusion."

"Thanks, Carl, but you might love me more with less confusion."

"I don't want to take the chance, you might become a dreamy eyed air head."

"I believed that was your conception of me now."

"Nellie, you have a wonderful mind and body and I want no changes."

"O.K., but I reserve the right to come back when we are old and wrinkled and our feelings for each may have changed."

"That's a reasonable thought."

"What about you, Lilly?'

"I go where Butch goes and do what he does."

Mary asks "And the rest of us?"

"You all have made a new life here and it is not in my province to advise you. However, I would like to think that there would always be a place here for us to visit in the future."

"I think some of us will be here for a long time. Especially Effie Lou and Jonas. If anything happens to Phillip, I'll probably be the first to try it."

"Honey, nothing's going to happen to me."

"You never know, how about that postman we heard about up the road?"

"I don't drink eggnog and ride around on a Cushman."

"Do you mean that really happened? I thought that man was just pulling our leg."

"How did you hear of it? It didn't make the national news."

"We stopped at a restaurant up the road and they had a three wheeler they made deliveries on."

"I never heard of a place that delivered food on a scooter."

"It was way up the road."

"That was where I got that recipe."

"I'm glad you stopped. I wonder if they would sell that scooter?"

"Adolph, what in the world would you want with it?"

"Mary, as you all think my mode of transportation has a terminal illness, maybe I should be looking around for something more economical."

"Do you have a death wish?"

"No, and there's no alligator ponds around here."

"Well. I'm against it. We love having you around. If you are dead set on doing something crazy, climb into your dome. It might be more productive."

"Mary, I don't 'climb' in it, I just walk in."

"That was only a figure of speech."

"Anyway, I only use it to 'refresh' myself.'

"I just go to the ladies room."

"Nellie, I did not use it in the same context."

"I am glad. No one should defile such a place."

"Mary, since you are Adolph's closest kin, by marriage that is, please keep us informed as to what transpires between him and the dome. I have developed a distinct affinity with him."

"Butch, you speak as if I have already moved in or out whichever the case may be. As I told you, I only use it to rejuvenate my psyche."

"Adolph, I think you will be moving out. You are presently here so I can't see how you can move in."

"Nellie, I think Adolph meant he might move in the dome."

"Move in there, move out of here, what's the difference?"

"I love you Nellie."

"And I you, Carl."

"Jesus! When did you say you were getting on the boat?"

"Monday morning, Effie Lou."

"Then let us make the most of the time remaining, and move on to less confusing subjects."

"For instance?"

"Let's talk about what has happened to all of us in the past ten years."

"We won't get through by Monday week."

"Well we can't just sit here staring at each other."

"I'm good at that, at times. Let me qualify that. Mostly it's at Carl."

"Nellie, is that what you have been doing while we are in bed and I am supposed to be asleep?"

"So you weren't really asleep. And you let me lay there staring."

"I just lay there trying to figure what's going on in your head."

"If you find out, please let me know. At those times, I have no earthly idea what's going on up there."

"Trust me, you will be the first to know."
"Carl, that's wrong. You will be the first to know."
"All right, you'll be the second to know."
"Sometimes I worry about you."
"In bed?"
"Heavens no! I have no worries when you are beside me."
"Are you all sure there is no earlier boat?"
"No, Effie Lou, I guess we're stuck here until Monday morning."
"Maybe we all ought to go to church tomorrow morning."
"Why on earth would we want to do that?"
"We used to when we were just one big happy family."
"A lot of water has been over the dam since then."
"Ha! The dam broke."
"Yes, we were all swept away in the torrents of time."
"Well, we all survived."
"Some of us."
"By the way, how are Joe and Dolly?"
"Happy as two dead pigs in the sunshine. They open the shop on weekends only now. They are involved in soap operas during the week."
"Well, it seems like everything worked out for everybody, except for poor Marybelle and Gilmore or Harold."
"Or Hannibal."
"Adolph, who in the world is Hannibal,"
"I'm sorry Effie Lou, that was a slip of the tongue."
"Slip of the tongue, my ass! You know something. What is it?"
"When I was in the dome meditating I felt that my grandson was once known as Hannibal."

Mary says, "I always felt there was more to that boy than we could possibly understand. He was forever going off to some place and leaving Gilmore behind to catch up. If that makes any sense."
"I think he has something to do with the dome."
"What, Adolph?"
"Like why wasn't it there before I came down here? At least I don't think it was. If it was why wasn't it discovered by someone else?"
"Maybe you were the first one that had a desire to wander in the boondocks."

“Nellie says, “He’s not. I used to get a craving to wander in the wild. Of course that was before I met Carl and wasn’t up to go on the prowl with Lilly.”

“Nellie, I can’t remember a time you weren’t ready to prowl.”

“It was a monthly thing.”

“That is an exception, but on mine, I did not go out and commune with nature.”

“It affects all females differently.”

“If it was not an indication of aging, I think I will welcome menopause.”

“And don’t forget the mid-life crises.”

“Only men have them. It’s only a manifestation of a feeling they haven’t sampled enough forbidden fruit. The fools! They should know there are too many apple trees in the world.”

“Now you women hold up for a second. That’s not it at all. We feel that like there was something we could have done a little better.”

“Like what, Carl?”

“Well, like not seeing everything there is to see, not being the success we aspired for when we were young and had the whole world at our feet, not doing enough to help mankind and losing our virility”

“You sound like you have some regrets.”

“No, Adolph, I passed the crisis with no great consequences and am now happy I survived.”

“Sugar, stay around until I reach mine. I may need some help.”

“Nellie, I hope I will always be there for you”

“Hurry up boat!”

“Effie Lou, don’t be unkind.”

“I try not to be Mary, but these two lovebirds are getting too syrupy.”

“They are not talking any different than when you and Jonas were coming back from Palm Beach.”

“I remember you and Phillip were carrying on also.”

“We were more conservative. Our relationship was in its infancy.”

“Yeah, you were always the quiet one.”

“I only succumbed to Phillip’s charm.”

“No regrets, Honey?”

“Never.”

"Carl, call the boat people and see if they have room for two more."

"Effie Lou, that would be great! I didn't know you liked cruises."

"Not for me, Nellie. For Mary and Phillip."

"Oh."

"Carl, don't pay any attention to Effie Lou, she gets this way sometimes when Phillip and I get syrupy."

"Mary, I don't mind what you two do, just don't get that sticky stuff all over me."

"I'm sorry, I guess we will have to confine our feelings to a more suitable time and place."

"That's what bedrooms are for."

"Well, do you and Phillip want to go?"

"No, Carl, we are perfectly happy here, for the moment."

Phillip asks, "What does 'for the moment' mean?"

"Only that we might want to go somewhere together later."

"That's right, we might have to escape from Effie Lou's tongue sometimes."

"What's wrong with my tongue?"

"It gets real sharp at times."

"I have to have one with all that kitchen help."

"We don't work in the kitchen."

"Thank goodness, syrup doesn't go good on tacos."

"Let's all go to bed."

CHAPTER THIRTY-SIX

No one really knows true reality, only his or her perception from a minuscule viewpoint. Therefore these diverse opinions of what is real cause much controversy. Once a consciousness is removed from this plane of existence, the question becomes more complex. If any survival does occur, as most believe, the personal aspect takes on new meaning. Worldly indoctrination may affect personal survival. If this be the case, many destinations must exist to accommodate various beliefs. Loved ones desire to be united with their mate. This might be true in cases where love struck youths are both taken away suddenly. As the years of cohabitation increase, individuals become more aware of their different conceptions of reality and realize no common meeting place awaits them. One becomes more callous due to the myriad of problems that they must face. There is a time when companionship is little help and a new inspiration must surface from within for one to maintain some bit of sanity.

Our friends have not reached this point with the possible exception of Adolph. He seems to have his shit together. We can only hope we can face the future with the tranquility he seems to have. Mary might be waiting to be reunited with her first love. Lets hope this will happen, but what is to become of Phillip? Are trilogies allowed in their heaven? I have doubts this has even crossed their minds. Effie Lou and Jonas are enjoying the now without any thoughts of whatever the future will bring. And Lilly and Butch, they are too young with too much ahead of them to give much thought to what seems like an eternity in the future when it will be necessary to regroup their thoughts. And Nellie, wow! What can we say? She lives in a world apart. God bless her. She is probably the sanest one we know. Carl, he has the tolerance of a saint. Without a doubt he loves Nellie. How else could this match survive? In his younger days he was a simple mechanic and now enjoys the fruits of his labors (with extra help). He feels he was blessed by knowing Harold and now expresses his gratitude by being a most tolerant person.

Harold and Marybelle have merged into a greater consciousness and have lost their individual identity. There is no conception of time there, as time is a function of earthly perception. There is no beginning or no end. How can there be? What was before the beginning? What will come after the end? These questions cannot be answered by one locked into a specific time frame. Without time to measure progress, progress cannot exist. The concept of reality without time involved must dwell in beings more advanced than anyone living. Everything that has happened and will happen must be happening as we speak. To unlock this mystery one must exit this plane. But the most of us are not ready yet. The 'final solution' is for all existence to end simultaneously. Some say this will be the *real* millennium.

ABOUT THE AUTHOR

Robert Wesley Dean 's writings can be described in many ways. Boring is not one of them! The man is complicated, intelligent and humorous with a southern gentleman's quality that will entertain and enlighten you. Wesley Dean is a world-renowned authority on the restoration and repair of coin operated amusement machines. His first book, *The Jukebox and Me* chronicles his real life experience in a combination of wit and humorous philosophy that is as southern as corn bread and collard greens. *Some of God's Children* is a hodgepodge of experiences of the many characters he met along his life's journey of seventy plus years. The heroes are sprinkled with philosophical teachings, wit and local humor. Join these lovable people, who for the most part are "Rednecks" within the truest southern tradition, as they journey through life with all of the unusual situations confronting them. You'll cry and laugh but most of all you'll think. Perhaps you will recognize someone you know…or maybe even yourself.

Printed in the United States
816800002B